A KING'S RADIANCE

L. R. SCHULZ

ZAPOUR
The Weeping
Zhanbu
WISHA
Darkwater
Isle
CRAW
Cree
The Sea of Sapphires
TROST
The Golden Forest
Illidor

Hirane
CRATA
KOGON
Veka
The
Abyss
Lumindal
Greyshire
Mountains
ZUTON
Lesken
Twin Lakes
Nanta
White Peak
N

Prologue

A light shone from above, seeping through the crystal-clear clerestory windows and bathing him in warmth. Raiz squirmed in his seat at the high table. Still a boy, he was unaccustomed to the deliberations of men and women at court. Even at breakfast, his brother and father always seemed to be in argument with one baron or another, fighting over small matters. It bored him, and he found himself constantly staring at the ceiling, as if drawn to the sun god's heat.

His forearm began to itch, and it took him longer than it should to notice something was wrong. Raiz shook his hand as though there was something within that needed to come out. His breaths came short and sharp. He shifted in his seat again, eyes darting to and from each guest at the table. People were beginning to notice, though their faces were a blur. He almost jumped out of his seat as a sweaty hand gripped his wrist in a tight embrace. He narrowed his eyes, focusing his vision. It was his brother, Dazen.

Dazen stared at him, open-mouthed, as if he knew exactly

what was happening. "Raiz, you must leave, now!" he hissed.

"What's happening to me? I don't —"

Raiz's hand vibrated, glowing white, radiating heat more intense than any flame.

"Come with me. Quickly," Dazen said.

But it was too late, Raiz had to release it. There was no choice. Two dozen faces stared at him as he fumbled in his chair, a bony forearm that was glowing white pointed in their direction. He could see his father, veins of worry popping from his brow.

His resolve reached its peak. Dazen twisted his arm as Raiz screamed. A torrent of white-light with a tinge of red poured from his palm with intense velocity. It beamed through the air, burning a hole the size of his head into the ceiling, sending shards of glass and splinters of wood raining down upon the high table. Time no longer had meaning as the heat continued to pour forth. He could hear his brother grunting beside him, refusing to let go of his wrist despite the pain he must be feeling.

His arm shifted, the sheer power too much to keep in one place. It drew a red line across the ceiling, threatening to bring it down on top of them.

And then suddenly, it was over. He looked down at his blackening hand and shuddered. The room stilled. Half of the royalty in Illidor were staring at him, horror wrought on their still blurry faces. Raiz, more horrified than any, took the only action that made sense. He ran.

Raiz climbed high into the night. Each step creaked louder than the last as he wound his way around the Moon-spire. He needed to get away from everyone, to recoup and gather his thoughts.

Age was wearing the centuries-old tower. Several times Raiz nearly skewered his foot on rusty nails that stuck out through the fading blue paint of the staircase. Still, to him, nothing was more magnificent. He poked his head through the ornate window far enough to admire the tower's white stone blocks glistening in the moon's light.

He was nearly at the top. Sticking his arm out, he welcomed the cool breeze as it stung his burnt arm, which had turned to a blackish charcoal colour. He withdrew his head like a turtle into its shell, listening as a light patter of footsteps rose from below. Raiz rolled his eyes, giving an annoyed sigh before continuing the climb, now two steps at a time.

It was Isha, he was sure of it. He thought he had lost her in the palace grounds, but his sister was always outsmarting him.

His legs shook as he reached the top. Opening the wide hatch, he climbed a small ladder and pulled himself into the attic. Relics older than the tower itself littered the floor. He ran a finger over an ancient plate of armour, drawing a line in the dust across its breast before clicking his fingers to rid himself of it. He walked past a blunted silver longsword, past its best years. Glancing at his charred arm, he wondered if he would ever be able to wield one now. An array of dusty gold and silver chalices lined the outskirts of the attic, the dim glow of their embedded gemstones shining in the light the moon cast through the window. He wondered how much of a fortune was kept here, rotting away to nothing. How much could he sell if he were to run away?

As intriguing as that prospect was, he had no desire for such treasure. What he wanted was much grander.

He undid the window-latch at the end of the room with a rough flick of his unwounded hand and forced it open, wood scraping against wood. He poked his head out of the window, this time allowing his body to follow.

Raiz sucked in a deep breath of fresh air, pulling his navy cloak further over his body so that it covered his neck. This was his treasure.

The city sparkled with a thousand dazzling lights, paralleling their counterparts high above in the sky. There was only one place in the city with a view this complete, and it was right here at the tip of the Moon-spire.

The city of Illidor stretched for miles. Raiz watched as thousands of people readied themselves for the day's end, oblivious to what had just happened in the palace. From the distant fields where farmers returned to their homes after a hard day's work, to the inner walls of Illidor where torches and hearths were being lit as parents readied their children for bed.

"Father's worried about you," came a voice from behind, causing him to jump.

He relaxed his muscles, eyeing his sister without even turning his head. Then he looked back to his hand, charred from a power he was too young to comprehend. "Father's always worried about something."

"And that something is usually you," Isha said, forcing her slight body through the window before making herself comfortable next to him.

A long silence followed, neither of the pair feeling the need to disturb the other. Raiz suspected she was just being patient and waiting for him to calm down. She always knew how to temper him so.

Eventually he gave in and turned towards his sister, her violet eyes glowing like a beacon in the dark of the night. She must be the only person in Illidor to have been born with violet eyes. His father and brother always seemed to think that made her special, but to Raiz she didn't need strangely-coloured eyes to be special. "Did Father send you here?" he asked.

"He didn't have to," she said, her voice soft. "You're my younger brother, and it's my job to make sure you're okay."

He gave a weak smile before moving in closer to his sister, draping his cloak to cover them both.

"Does it hurt?" she asked.

Raiz leaned his head against her shoulder, clenching and unclenching his fist. "It's fine now, I think. I... I don't know what happened. I don't understand."

Isha took his arm in her hands and kissed it. "It's not your fault, Raiz. Father should have warned you."

"Warned me? What do you mean? Did he know this would happen?"

"Well, not exactly. It's…complicated."

Raiz scrunched his face. "No one ever tells me anything."

"I actually have something for you," Isha said. "A present of sorts."

Raiz's eyes shifted towards his sister. He did like presents.

Isha reached into her pocket and withdrew something in her cupped hands. She removed her top hand to unveil the present within.

Raiz let out a light gasp, watching with a keen eye as a lizard-like creature crawled across her palm and onto her fingers.

"It's a Pricket," Isha said.

"A Pricket? It just looks like a lizard to me."

His sister stifled a laugh, watching as the Pricket made its way up her arm. It had a long, scaled body and clawed hands. Its tail wound around her forearm and formed into an overly large barb at its end, which seemed disproportionate to the rest of its body. "Here, take him," she said as she picked up the Pricket and placed him on Raiz's blackened arm.

Raiz flinched as tiny claw-like hands bit at his skin. To his surprise, the Pricket licked at his scorched skin with a long blue tongue. "What's it doing?" he said.

Isha stifled another laugh. "He likes you. Prickets feed on white-light. He'll help you the next time you build up too much Shine."

"White-light? Shine? You mean I'm like Dazen and Father now?"

"It would appear so. They really should have prepared you for this. But I suppose the white-light doesn't usually manifest in someone so young."

Raiz looked away. "Are they mad?"

"I don't think so. Just surprised is all, and a little shaken. Your outburst wasn't exactly subtle. Though Father did mumble something about your Shine being a touch red. No idea what that means but it seemed important to him.

"Now, what are you going to call him?" Isha continued, motioning towards the Pricket.

Raiz scratched his head, watching as the Pricket's barbed tail vibrated while he continued to lick Raiz's wound. "I'm going to call him Spike."

"A fitting name for a wonderful creature. Now, about returning to Father?" she said.

Raiz grunted, petting Spike on his back as his yellow eyes opened and shut. "Father can wait another hour, can't he?"

The three Glaive children stood straight-backed on the dais in front of their father. His presence was overbearing. It was hard to believe Raiz's skinny frame and bony elbows were wrought from the same physique.

Kron Glaive stood tall, with tense, broad shoulders. His angular cheekbones clenched tightly over a thick black beard as he cast a gloomy scowl over his three children. Raiz was the youngest of the three and, of course, the smallest. His sister Isha was two years his senior, twelve in total. She stood perfectly still, her innocent violet eyes blinking pleadingly at Father.

Dazen was the oldest. At fifteen he was already taller than most boys his age, his muscular body more resembling that of a grown man. Raiz wondered if his body would change like that when he was older, but he doubted it.

Raiz was nothing like his brother, or his sister for that matter. He was more… adventurous, is how he liked to put it, though his father often called it wild.

"Ahem," his father said, his cold stare bearing down on him and snapping him back to attention. "I have called you here to discuss a serious matter."

Isha shifted her feet. "Excuse me Father, I'm rather famished. Do I really need to be here while you educate Raiz on what he should have been told years ago?"

Raiz squinted at his sister, again wondering what she was talking about. What were they not telling him? He didn't ask for this power, and he certainly didn't know how to control it.

"Enough!" Kron bellowed.

The three siblings stiffened at this. It was rare for him to raise his voice so, especially at Isha.

"Raiz's manifestation of the white-light will be discussed at another time," Kron said. "Tomorrow is a day of great importance for the Kingdom of Trost. And also one of great strain. An Eagle is coming to Illidor."

To his right, his brother gasped.

"Are you sure Father? Why here? Why now?" Dazen asked.

Raiz's heart pounded with excitement. He had heard tale of Lumindal's famous Eagles. They were divinities, untouchable. Said to be immortal, their very presence breathing life into our existence. Hand-picked by the God of Light himself to represent His will on the physical plain.

Kron looked towards Isha and Raiz. "I will not have the two of you present when he arrives."

Raiz jerked his head straight. "That's not fair Father! I want to meet him!"

"No!" his father boomed, his voice cutting the air. He took a steadying breath and stepped forwards. "An Eagle's presence is unpredictable. Their tempers are short. To hinder him could lead to the end of Illidor."

All three siblings' eyes grew wide. "Surely one man does not have such power," Isha said.

Kron fixed her with another fierce stare. "Need I remind you of the city of Hirane? Of the False Kings War?"

She looked at him with a blank expression.

"The city is now a barren wasteland where nothing but the ghosts of a hundred thousand dead linger." He paused for a long while, letting his words sink in before continuing. "Do not inconvenience them. Do not speak to them. Do not even look at them. Dazen, you will be by my side. You are old enough to see them for what they are."

Raiz went to protest, hating Dazen for his special preference, but stopped himself. He was already in trouble for his earlier outburst. Best he not get himself into more.

"You two will remain in the palace, am I clear?"

No response.

"Am I clear!"

"Yes, Father," Isha and Raiz called in unison as they stared at their father's feet.

Kron waved a dismissive hand, issuing them away so he could have a more private word with Dazen.

"**I** can't see anything from here," Raiz said, angling his neck in an attempt to view the spectacle below.

"This is as good as you're going to get, so stop whining," Isha responded. She sat cross-legged along the white stone tiling of the Moon-spire.

Raiz's safe haven had turned into a temporary prison as his father and brother accompanied their esteemed guest in the oversized courtyard.

From his bird's-eye view, he could only just make out a few figures. Kron and Dazen sat side-by-side atop the central platform. The courtyard was at capacity. Hundreds of Trost's nobility had flocked to the capital to catch a glimpse of one of the supposed divinities.

"What do you think they're talking about?" he asked his sister.

"I haven't the faintest clue Raiz. Though I don't think I've seen Father so nervous before. He even yelled at me!"

Raiz hummed to himself, frustration overwhelming his senses. "Why does Dazen get to meet him? Why is he so important?"

"Because he is older. And because Father says so."

Raiz grumbled, "I wonder what he looks like. Does he glow? Is he a giant? Are his ears pointy?" He leaned in closer, slipping on a tile before bracing himself on the windowsill.

Beside him, Isha laughed. "Why would their ears be pointy?"

Raiz shrugged. "Read it in a book somewhere."

"In all of your ten years I have never once seen you with a book in your hands."

"You're not with me all the time! Maybe I read at night, when you're in bed."

"Huh, not likely."

Raiz ignored her and continued to spy on the proceedings. "When I grow up, I want to become one of them. I want to be an Eagle," he said.

His sister sighed. "You can't just become one of them Raiz, it's not that easy. They're not what you think they are."

"Then how? How do I become one of them? Maybe then people won't lie to me. Maybe then I'll know everything and can help people."

"Do you think I'm some sort of book on life or something? I don't have the answer to everything, you know."

Raiz shrugged. "Well, I'm going to get a better look."

Isha reached out to grab his arm but fell a finger length short. "Raiz wait! You can't leave the palace; you'll get us into trouble again."

"Don't follow me then," he said, squishing through the window. "I won't get in the way, I promise. Just want to get a good look."

Isha called out something else, but her voice became muffled as he flung the hatch open and began the descent. She would follow, he was sure of it.

His chest heaved as he reached the bottom, a sharp pain in his side making him feel as though he had been stabbed. Taking a couple of deep breaths, he began searching for an exit, freezing to a halt a mere breath away from a palace guard.

Zur's Light take me, he cursed inwardly.

He leaned against the wall and slowly crept to safety. He thought it over for a minute, deciding on the best course of action. He had grown up here and knew the palace's secrets better than anyone. He moved for a side door to the east. Another guard stood impossibly still at the foot of the door, his beady eyes ever vigilant.

Raiz looked from the guard towards a richly decorated clay

pot resting atop a table in the corner opposite him. He reached into his deep pockets, Spike biting him playfully on the hand, before he emerged with an oval-shaped rock he kept just for such occasions. Taking careful aim, he threw the rock at a sharp angle, shattering the pot into pieces.

"Sorry Father," he mouthed under his breath.

Just as planned, the guard shot to life, the white glint of his armour shifting towards the disturbance. Raiz wasted no time, bolting for the exit. He was out before his footsteps had the chance to whisper.

A sly smile creased his lips as he made his way around the winding passage leading to the courtyard. A sudden creak from behind made him fear the guard had seen him and pursued.

He huffed a sigh of relief when he saw Isha following his path like a cat stalking its prey.

Before she could catch up, he ran into a wall of people. He bounced on the balls of his feet, trying to find an opening somewhere, anywhere. But it was no use. He was too small.

He pushed and shoved to no avail, then forced himself back out of the crowd, pinpointing a spot that looked thinner than most.

"Watch it boy," cried a distressed onlooker as Raiz rudely trod on his foot. Several similar cries erupted from the crowd as he squeezed past, but he paid them no mind.

Eventually he reached the crowd's edge. It seemed as though the day's events were drawing to an end. People were dispersing, and what he assumed to be the embassy from Lumindal was heading his way, away from his father.

Raiz gawked in awe. The 'Eagle' was flanked by dozens of knights clad in black plate armour. Each bore the golden crest of an eagle's talon upon their breast: Four arching claws, sharp as a knife's edge.

He had heard of these knights before. The Knights of the Golden Talon, prized bodyguards of the Eagles and peacekeepers of the realm. Maybe Raiz could be one of them when he was older? They looked strong. Their matte black armour shimmered in the daylight. Each carried a long whitewood halberd with a short sword at their hip.

They marched towards him in practiced unison. Raiz shifted a step, making sure they had enough room to get past. As they drew closer, he snuck a peek at what was within. What he saw was not what he had expected.

The 'Eagle' was nothing more than a man. A rather plain and unattractive looking man at that. To Raiz's dismay he did not glow, did not have pointed ears, nor was he tall as a giant. He was adorned in hundreds of rich jewels and ornaments from head to toe. He carried a tall, decorated sceptre in his left hand, and over his fair skin he wore an elaborate bone-white robe that covered his feet.

What was truly disturbing, however, was what was before him. In front of him walked two abnormal-looking people shackled around the neck with a thick metal collar. One was a man, the other a woman. At least he thought she was a woman. Two goat-like horns shot upwards like stalks from her temples. She walked in an awkward motion, as if her back had been bent and set at a different angle. Her long black hair bunched at her shoulders in a matted tangle. Raiz looked on, stomach knotting, breathing doubling.

The other was just as abnormal, only more human looking. His distinguishing feature was his skin. Half was white and half black. It separated reasonably evenly down the centre of his near-naked body.

In his right hand, the Eagle held a long, black whip, and

Raiz's mouth hung agape as it rose and snapped through the air, placing a nasty gash upon the black and white man's back, red blood trickling down his side.

He winced as if the pain were his own. Suddenly he realised why his father had not wanted him to see this.

Having seen enough, he turned to leave and felt a thud as he crashed into something. It was Isha, she had found him. The impact sent her reeling sideways. He went to catch her just a moment too late. Her momentum propelled her forward. Forward, out into the open.

She landed headfirst into the foot of a knight, disrupting their march.

Before Raiz could bring her back the crowd grew still, a high-pitched voice cutting through the air.

"Hold!"

The entire band of knights stopped instantly.

"Who would dare disturb me so!" came a cry from within. "Show yourself."

Four knights parted to make way for the Eagle. His pale face turned a light shade of red as he peered down at Isha. "Argon, silence this filthy wretch."

Argon, one of the Eagles' personal guards — likely a captain —unsheathed his silver short sword and made for Isha. Panic flared inside of Raiz. What was happening?

Isha rose to her feet and looked the Eagle dead in the eye.

"Oh my," cried the Eagle. "Oh my oh my oh my. Argon, stop."

The black-clad guard stopped in his tracks as the Eagle himself moved for Isha, who was near frozen with fear.

"Your eyes, show them to me," the Eagle demanded.

Isha took a wary step backward but did not dare disobey looking up at the Eagle.

"A Mystic! I must have her Argon. I must have her for my collection. She has violet eyes! Chain her at once. Chain her at once!"

Two more guards ran towards Isha bearing a thick metal chain and collar. Isha screamed in protest. "Stop, don't touch me, please. Raiz, don't let them do this."

His fear conquered, Raiz leaped into action. Feeding on the sun's warm light, his blackened hand frothed with an intense light of its own. Though it burned his already injured hand, he paid the pain no mind, sprinting for Isha. He could not let them do this. This was barbaric.

"Isha!' he cried. Before he could reach her, a sword slashed through the air, cutting a deep gash into his right eye and sending him plummeting to the cobblestone floor. He cried out in pain, one hand reaching for the wound and coming away wet.

"Stay down, kid. Count yourself lucky the Eagle did not see what you just attempted."

Raiz looked through his one good eye to see Argon standing before him, his sword stained deep crimson.

Isha still wailed in the background, struggling against her captors.

What's going on? Raiz thought, looking into the crowd. *Why is no one helping her?* The dazed citizens stood motionless as statues, none daring to make a move against Lumindal's emissary.

Raiz looked for his father, blood mixing with tears as he howled for him. Surely his father would do something. He wouldn't let Isha be taken like this.

Kron Glaive stood on the platform, holding a crazed Dazen back, but he was unmoving.

"Father!" Raiz shouted again. But it was no use. Raiz didn't understand, could Kron not see? Was his vision hampered?

Isha continued to scream, fighting with everything she could, but it was too late. Raiz tried to get up, tried to come to her aid, but his wound was deep. He was losing too much blood. His vision blackened. Slowly he faded into a state of nothingness, his sister's screams calling to him, but he could not answer.

Nobody answered.

PART 1

Chapter 1
Raiz

To Raiz, only one thing was worse than the high-pitched sob of a crying mother: a dozen crying mothers. Some were widowed, their husbands lost to the brutal reality that was war. Others were married, though conscription to the armies of Lumindal had long ago quashed any notion of a happily ever after. Now, they were being forced to watch as their children were taken from them for no better reason than being born with the 'gift' of Shine.

The 'Shine' — one's ability to harness the power of Zur, the bright star in the sky that rose and fell each passing day — usually manifested during adolescence. Today was the day the people of Lesken paid their sacrifice to the ones who called themselves gods, the Eagles.

Raiz spat on the dry soil, watching as it sizzled in the face of Zur, who was making his descent, casting an orange hue across the city.

Spike — now four feet tall and twice as long — sat by his side, licking his hand as Raiz dripped excess Light from his fingertips. His scaly companion had been through everything with him these past eight years. Ever since the two of them had run away from home, the pricket had grown to be larger even than the biggest breeds of dog. His powerful jaw was sharpened with a knife-like row of teeth capable of severing limbs with one crunch. Though, Spike was not like that by nature. He was more of a cuddly puppy than he was inclined to show unwarranted violence. His huge, spiked tail vibrated and curled as he fed on Raiz's Shine.

"Preparations are complete. The Eagle will arrive before sunset," came a muffled voice to his right.

Raiz turned to face his companion. "Good work Draz, he will pay for this," he said, gesturing towards the crying mothers.

Draz nodded, his thick metal helmet glinting in the light. In the six years Raiz had known Draz, not once had he revealed his face. Even on the warmest days, the short and stocky ex-mercenary refused to remove his helm, reserving whatever lay beneath for himself alone.

Draz filtered back in line behind Raiz as they combed the streets of Lesken. Spike's skin turned a murky brown colour, camouflaging himself and mixing in with the dry landscape; a trick that had come in handy more times than one. They rounded the area for one last scout, refusing to leave anything to chance this day.

To his left clambered the hulking form of Aroha. Her monstrous, nearly seven-foot presence was hard to ignore in such a public setting. Though her size was indeed significant, it did nothing to diminish her beauty. Her bright hazel eyes, sharp cheekbones and long, braided brown locks were enough to draw the attention of even the most discerning of men. Combined with her bulging arm muscles and tendency to growl at any man who so much as ventured too close, she was hardly one to walk around unnoticed. She paid onlookers no mind, however. Today was not a day for fraternising. Today was a day for revenge. A day for death.

Rounding out their little band was Veil. In stark contrast to Aroha, Veil was as frail as they come; small, skinny, and extremely nimble, though she was perhaps the most dangerous of them all. She covered herself in an arrangement of dark cloth, more from necessity than fashion sense. Zur was out in full strength today and Veil was a danger to herself when she took in too much sunlight.

Raiz rubbed a finger across his scarred right eye, as he always did when a fight was near. It served as a reminder of his past, of what he was fighting for. Veil smiled brazenly at him, lips curling upward as she stared at him with those bright blue eyes. "Are you ever going to tell me who gave you that scar?" she teased.

Raiz gave a rough chuckle, returning her warmth with a grin of his own.

Aroha stepped in before he could speak. "Oh honey, if he hasn't told you by now, he never will. You can stop dreaming."

Veil looked from Aroha back towards him.

"I'll tell you who did it if Draz removes his helm and dances a jingle," Raiz said.

The three of them looked towards Draz with hopeful expressions, but the mysterious man remained impassive, his stare as cold as the steel upon his head.

The sombre proceedings soon overshadowed their moment of banter. The entire city had flocked to the streets to offer condolences. All around him stood shadowed faces full of hard lines and dark expressions. They knew the burden of loss. They had all paid their price. The King-Radiant and his followers — the Eagles — called it a great honour to be taken, but those who had any sense of perception knew the truth.

A well of anger surged through him like a bull let out of its cage, and not just anger towards the Eagles. The people of this town also angered him. How could they just let this happen? They were taking children, for Zur's sake!

He clenched his fists into tight balls. This reminded him too much of his father on that fateful day eight years ago...

He shook his head. Now was not the time to dwell on painful memories. He was here for a reason. If these people couldn't find the courage to fight, then he would do it for them.

A light touch on his shoulder caused Raiz to jolt to the side, hand clasped on the hilt of the dagger hidden deep under his coat.

"Calm yourself, Raiz," Veil said, showing no sign of fear. "You'll get your chance, but for now you must remain clear of mind."

Raiz tucked his dagger comfortably back into its hiding place. "Usually, it's me who does the calming," he said.

"My curse will not consume me today. I'll play my part. If my will threatens to become overwhelmed by 'it', I'll remove myself."

Raiz moved for her hand and clasped it within his own. He could feel the untamed power rushing through her veins even now. "We'll find a cure for this one day, I promise."

She huffed a dismissive sigh and pulled her hand away as quickly as he had taken it. "Let's focus on one problem at a time, shall we?"

Raiz nodded, accepting her choice for distance.

"Do you think it will be the one you're searching for? Do you think your sister will be here?" she continued.

Now it was Raiz's time to shy away. It was rare for an Eagle to venture this far outside Lumindal. This was the opportunity he had been waiting for. What he had trained for. Even if it killed him, he would see his sister free. Would hunt every last one of them for what they did to her.

Veil grabbed his arm and twisted him in a different direction. "Come, we must find a vantage point. They'll be here soon."

The four of them walked with their heads down over to a patch of ground overlooking the town square. They wanted no trouble with the city watch leading up to their plight. They were not here to spill innocent blood, but they would if they had to.

The city watch would not put up much of a fight. Not against Raiz and his crew. The city watch in Lesken was more of a skeleton guard, put in place to make it seem safe. He risked a glance at a couple of them as he passed. They were pale faced and scared, just like the rest of them, obviously wanting no part in the proceedings. But like everyone else in this forsaken world, they lacked the strength and courage to stand up to the unfathomable might of the King-Radiant and his legions.

"Isn't it enough they take our coin and crops to fill their already bursting treasury? Why must they take our children too?" he heard a skinnier looking watchman with a pockmarked face whisper to another.

He received a slap to the back of his head for his trouble. "Quiet! You mustn't speak on such things openly boy," said an older looking watchman before returning to the straight-backed posture more befitting a man in power.

Raiz continued on, pretending he hadn't overheard. But he had. This town wanted to push back. They wanted to fight, they just lacked the proper leadership and opportunity to discharge their latent anger. But Raiz had both, and he planned to make gifts of them.

As time passed the streets grew silent. Gone were the tears and whispers, overtaken by an overshadowing sense of dread. The populace of the small city that was Lesken had gathered together around the city square, an open space in the middle of dozens of tightly packed buildings. A large bell tower loomed overhead, its shadow casting a gloomy darkness over the crowd of anxious citizens. Only one passage stretched large enough for a mass body of troops to enter, so everyone's attention drifted towards the north.

An eerie aura crept across the landscape as the faint sound of footsteps echoed from beyond. The footsteps gradually grew louder, more synchronised. Raiz felt his anticipation growing, arching his head higher as if it might increase his visual prowess. It did not.

He needed to know if she was there. It was a fool's hope, but it was hope nonetheless. His eyes flickered towards Draz. The man was a genius, unopposed in the art of trap making. He was fingering the explosive resin in his satchel pocket, itching for the chance to use it, but he waited upon Raiz's signal.

The footsteps grew ever louder as the synchronised march of the Golden Talon company came into view. Raiz had learned that only a select few were actually labelled a Knight of the Golden Talon. These were usually much taller and hardier, their black armour lined with golden paint. Most were able to wield Zur's Shine. The rest were Blackwings, common foot soldiers, but even then their presence was far from un-intimidating. A wall of armour blacked out the horizon. They would have sent even the bravest of men scurrying from their path, but the streets were empty. All were gathered in the square.

Raiz found himself short on breath. The hairs on his arms stood on end, and his knee bobbed up and down as rapidly as

Veil could shoot her bow.

The wall of black came to a halt mere feet from the main body of onlookers. Fourteen children, none yet past their fourteenth year, stood before them, some clutching at their mothers' dress, others openly weeping.

The fact that this was done so publicly itched at him. As if they needed another spectacle to prove their strength, to assert their dominance over the population.

They had grown overconfident. So comfortable were they in their position and reputation that they didn't take even the simplest of precautions, and this would be their downfall.

The guard parted to make way for their leader. He stepped forth with open arms, clearly pleased with the distressed citizens' open display of obedience and submission. But no slaves accompanied him. There was no whip in his hand, and no sign of his sister.

Raiz twitched with anger, unleashing his fury with a hard punch into the stone parapet that left a nasty gash on his knuckles.

Veil placed a supportive hand upon his shoulder and he resisted the urge to shrug it off.

"To your positions, now!" he said. "Draz, take as many of them as you can."

Draz leapt into action without hesitation, moving with light feet despite the heavy metal upon his head. Veil too vanished from sight, heading to a rooftop with more of an angle from which to loose her deadly arrows.

Aroha stayed by his side. They would have a part to play, but first they had to wait.

The Blackwings below were ripping children from their mothers' arms, flanked by a half-dozen Knights of the Golden Talon. Raiz looked towards Aroha, her anger visible. Veins as big as his fingers bulged from her forearms as she gripped the hilt of her longsword.

"Not yet," he said. "We wait for Draz."

He knew she had heard him, but she did little to acknowledge the fact other than tightening her grip.

Raiz looked back towards the square. Almost all the children were rounded up, though one still hid behind his mother — a boy no older than Isha was when she had been taken. The boy's mother looked on edge, her tears replaced by a fury only a grieving mother could conjure.

The city dwellers sensed it. They saw defiance in her eyes, and would not let one woman be the downfall of their livelihood.

Raiz smiled. He liked this woman, wished more would be like her and fight. Just not right now. She was going to ruin his plan. He needed the company to remain at ease, at least until Draz was in position.

He let out a heavy sigh as an elderly man with a long grey beard placed a reassuring hand upon what Raiz could only assume was his daughter. The mother's fury did not dissipate, but it was enough for a knight to whisk her son away.

The boy did not go easy. He kicked the man in his face before pushing free and landing hard on the rough dirt below. The knight retaliated, slapping the child with a backhand strike.

His mother's anger reached its zenith. No longer could they stop her, her concern only for her son. She reached into her high laced boots and pulled out a short knife. She darted forward, arm raised for a downward strike, but she was too slow. The soldier caught her arm mid-arc.

Just as his fist reared to strike her, the ground trembled.

Raiz steadied himself, knowing what was coming. The high

stone bell tower rocked, slanting to the side as if the columns holding it had been smashed to pieces, which they had. Draz was nearly done, one more push should do it.

The company of Blackwings looked around in a daze, bracing themselves. The helmeted hero was good at what he did. He had planned for this, working in secret for days at the base of the tower. He had left just enough support beams standing so that when the time came, it wouldn't take much for it to crumble.

Raiz rushed down the side of the building, sliding down a drainpipe. Aroha merely jumped the distance, her strong legs supporting her landing.

The tower dropped.

The ground trembled again, and rubble ricocheted everywhere, spilling out into the open square. The wall of black was decimated as great mounds of stone crushed both plate and bone. A wall of swirling dust replaced it, choking the square. Draz had hit his mark.

Onlookers screamed; the entire populace was in a state of panic. The bell tower had killed most of those at the rear end of line, though a handful of Blackwings and most of the Golden Talon regiment remained standing, including the Eagle. Raiz locked eyes with the man. His mouth hung agape, arms flailing in the air in an attempt to rally his remaining guards to his side.

For a moment the whole square froze as if the dirt at their feet were ice. Raiz would not let them flee. They would bear witness to justice. They would find their courage. Even if he had to force it down their throats.

Pockets of people soon began to disperse, wanting no part of the events playing out. This was Draz's next task. In the corner of his eye Raiz spotted him, running from corner to corner, setting the ground itself ablaze. Not a dangerous fire.

He didn't want to burn down Lesken. But enough to dissuade anyone from fleeing.

This next part was the hardest, but also the most fun, for Raiz got to kill.

The remaining guard had rallied into a tight formation. With the path behind them blocked by the tower, they had but one way out, forward. They raised a line of shields, and a second line formed behind, pointing their halberds over the first.

Raiz felt a moment of pity for the poor townspeople trapped before him, readying themselves to defend their lives, a ring of fire on one side and certain death on the other. But Raiz had no intention of letting them die.

He felt Zur's breath upon his skin, feeding him his strength. His Shine was strong, stronger than any he had met save for perhaps Veil, though her power was still a mystery.

He clenched his blackened left hand tight. He was not a reckless kid anymore. He had spent years learning to control his Shine. The white-light was now his friend, not his enemy. He focused both his mind and body, willing it to come to life. A jet of Light streamed out of his hand. It burned the ground below him, a black mark trailing in its wake.

He tightened his grip, clasping the stream of Light as if it were a sword. Slowly the wave of heat began to bend. He shaped it with his mind and hand, crafting it into a weapon. Eventually, the stream lost its ferocity, the light solidifying into a rod of white-light, its core stained with red. His Shine always had a tinge of red, though he was unsure why.

Spike issued a high-pitched screech by his side, excited with so much white-light out in the open.

He waved the solid Light around like a spear, its tip curving and flattening, turning it into a large glaive. Only it had no weight, and its edge did not cut, it burned.

Raiz stepped forward, now fully aware that the entire audience was staring at him. The tightly packed knights did not falter, however. Arrogant and sheltered as they were, they were well trained soldiers, and would not go down easily.

Raiz curled his lip up into a sinister smile, his glaive vibrating beside him. Before he could make his move, an arrow rained from above. A knight in the front line dropped like a pin, his shield hitting the ground before his body. The shaft of an arrow protruded from his neck, staining his gold-trimmed armour red. More arrows harrassed their ranks, and more Blackwings fell to their power.

So, Veil had made her presence known at last. The front line adjusted to this new threat, Blackwings raising their curved shields high to cover the Knights of the Golden Talon and the Eagle within.

This was his chance. Raiz strutted forward with little grace. A spearman in the back thrust at him hard with his steel tipped halberd, but Raiz stepped aside with ease, severing its tip with a simple wave of his heated glaive.

In and out he danced, slicing limb after limb. The guard's steel armour was not enough defence against his Shine. Four Blackwings surrounded him, working in unison, forming a solitary defence while turning it into offence. Raiz cursed under his breath. Had he become like them? Too cocky and headstrong about his own abilities? He looked for a way out, to backtrack, but his path became blocked by another wall of black. He closed his eyes, ready to unleash the full power of his might, whatever the risk to his body.

Thankfully, he found it was not needed.

Aroha came crashing in, catching a man between the neck and shoulder, splitting him nearly in two before turning towards her next victim. Spike too, joined in the fray, biting through plate with a sickening crunch as bone shattered beneath, his thick hide too strong for their weapons to penetrate.

The three of them dispatched the four before him, arrows still raining from above, more hitting their mark than not.

A stream of Light whistled past Raiz's ear. He reared to see the three remaining knights band together, their hands glowing with Shine. Together they released a torrent of pure energy. It sped towards Raiz, but Spike was there. The pricket stood before the barrage, absorbing the blow, his hide unaffected by the searing heat. The stunned knights took a backward step as Raiz pushed forward and sliced through armour and flesh.

Within minutes, their ranks were eliminated. Raiz surveyed the area, searching for the one person he had come for, the one death that he truly desired.

The Eagle crawled on hands and knees, alone and unprotected. Raiz held back a laugh.

"Y-y-you are done for," the pathetic figure squawked. "This is high-treason. You will die for this, everyone here will die for this!" He screamed the last part, sure to make his words carry towards the crowd. His bone-white robe was stained a light shade of brown as he continued to crawl into the rubble. A silver torc coiled around his neck, the metal-pointed end of an eagle's wing drawing a line of red as it choked him in his struggle to flee.

Raiz pointed an outstretched arm towards him. "How does it feel? To be powerless? To have something taken from you? Your protection, your authority, and soon your life." He spoke loud enough for everyone to hear. They gathered around, eager to see whatever was happening through to the end.

"K-kill this man! I-I will spare your lives, I swear it. Just kill this man. Y-you can have your children, t-take them! Just see me safely to the capital and I shall see you rewarded," the Eagle said.

The crowd remained apprehensive, a mixture of murmurings the only audible sound.

Raiz turned from the Eagle and raised his hand to the crowd. "This man takes your money, *steals* your children! And you would have him walk away? You would have him continue to take? Because there will be more, he will not stop. There will be more deaths by his hand, more families broken with but the barest quiver of his rotten tongue."

He paused, letting his words have time to sink in.

"The Eagles are a lie. They are not divine. They are no messengers of Zur. They are human. A story plucked from history that they use to consolidate their rule! Maybe once they were great, but does this look like greatness to you?" He gestured towards the quivering old man.

"So, what say you?"

The air grew still, the silence was like an echo. Veil came down from her perch to stand by his side. She must have cut herself in her descent, for her protective clothing was ripped at the shoulder. A sliver of light shone through a gap in the buildings, exposing her skin to direct sunlight. Draz and Aroha worked to cover her, using whatever material they could find.

"Cut out his tongue!" cried an onlooker who Raiz noticed to be the angry mother.

A heavy cheer sounded from the crowd.

"Send him to the gallows!" called another.

Raiz shared a pleased look with his crew.

"N-nobody move!" came a shout from behind. "Or I slit his throat."

Raiz jolted his head around, his eyes wide with anger and

disgust. The Eagle had managed to get hold of a child that had been caught up in the wreckage of battle. He held a finger to the boy's throat, its tip glowing bright with Shine.

Raiz grunted in frustration. How had he not seen the boy? He had been too busy shooting off his mouth. He took a wary step forward.

"Not one more move from you!" the Eagle protested. "Or the boy dies." He stepped from side to side, not willing to give anyone a clean shot. "Make a path for me to depart, do it now!" he demanded, gesturing with his head to the ruined tower.

Raiz played along. He let his glaive dissipate to show he was no longer a threat.

No one dared to move, so Raiz made for a space where the rubble was least obtrusive.

The Eagle made his way towards where Raiz was clearing rubble, careful to take soft and meaningful steps. The boy remained impassive, likely too frozen with fear to retaliate.

"Raiz," came a voice. "Raiz!"

It was Veil. What was she playing at? "Not now, Veil, just let me handle this."

"Raiz!"

He turned away from the broken tower to face her.

"It's happening again, I-I don't think I can stop it this time." Shit.

Raiz sprinted, not towards the Eagle, but towards Veil.

"What are you doing?" cried the Eagle. "Do not test me! I will boil this boy alive if you so much as move another step in any direction but the one I say."

But Raiz paid him no mind. "Calm Veil, calm. Hold it in. Deep breaths in. That's it, there you go."

He was trying to temper her heart rate, but the tension and adrenaline from the battle and now the boy being taken were too much. Her hands were shaking near uncontrollably, her breaths heavy and contorted. Her arm twitched violently. Raiz went to touch her hand, to comfort her as she had him. But it was no use, her hand was boiling. It radiated heat as though she were the vessel of Zur himself.

"The sun! You need to get out of the sun!" he cried.

"I can't stop it Raiz, it needs to come out!" She gasped in pain as if she were about to implode. Raiz saw no other option. There was no calming her, no stopping it this time.

"Aim it upwards!" he shouted. "Channel everything you have, all of your power, and throw it into the sky! If you don't, we're all dead."

She had reached her limit, it was now or never. With a shrill scream, Veil lifted her arms high into the sky, palms open. She tilted her head back and let it loose.

A column of Light shot forth, first from her palms, and then her entire body. So intense was its velocity that the ground beneath her began to shake. The Light travelled up into the air, reaching higher than Raiz's one good eye could see.

The townspeople stood dumbfounded. Some watched in horror, others collapsed to the ground. Veil continued to scream. Raiz wanted to comfort her, wanted to share in her pain, but to do so would mean his certain death. He could do nothing but sit and watch the blinding light show.

That's it, he realized. He could take advantage of this situation. He twisted his body, pointing a finger with trained precision and speed. He channeled his Shine so that it reached the exit point of his fingertip. He was right, Veil's Light was so intense that the Eagle had been blinded. He had exposed himself just enough for Raiz to take the shot.

His finger burned with the buildup of so much energy in one place, until he finally released it, shooting an arrow of white-light forward.

After a moment, everything grew still. Veil's screams curtailed and the stream of light and heat dissipated into nothing. Veil collapsed into Raiz's arms, weak and disoriented, but alive.

The child who had been held hostage found his courage and sprinted towards his weeping mother. He left in his wake the agonising screams of the Eagle. Raiz's Light arrow had penetrated straight through his collarbone, leaving a gaping, cauterised hole.

Raiz rose to his feet, Veil's head lolling to the side as she relaxed into his arms. "He's all yours," he said to no one in particular, but so that everyone could hear.

Without another word he walked away, Draz and Aroha in tow. He had done what he had come here to do. There was only one Eagle he needed to kill with his own hands.

The people of Lesken found their courage.

Chapter 2
Isha

Vulnerability was a trick of the mind. The fear of being harmed, of being embarrassed. Vulnerability was the emotion of a coward, and Isha was no coward. Cowards ended up dead.

She stood with a straight back. Well, as straight as she could with a heavy metal collar around her neck. With a swift hand she adjusted the collar, moving it so that the cool metal no longer stuck to the left side of her olive skin. With a welcome relief it now stuck to her right side. Such simple comforts had become her only novelty during her tenure as a slave.

She let her hands rest at her sides before clutching the silken yellow dress they had forced her to don. It took all of her effort not to tear it open at the seam. She could present it to her 'master' as a gift, along with her teeth marks into his neck. Oh, how she hated the colour yellow. She would rather be paraded around the Great Hall naked than wear this for another minute. That was probably untrue, but yellow was the traditional colour of Zur, the sun this world labelled a deity for no other reason than it fed them magic. Zur had done nothing for her, had only ever brought her unhappiness, so why should she not hate him?

For now, she would leave it be, play her part. She would survive. Her taste in colour did not make her vulnerable, it simply made her feel alive. If she could still hate such a simple thing as the colour yellow, then she could still regain some semblance of her self-worth once she was eventually free of this place.

The same could not be said, however, for the recent addition to her 'master's' band of collectables. It brought bile to her mouth every time she thought of herself as a collectable. She was no object to place on a pedestal and be gawked at. But that is how 'they' saw her.

The frail looking young woman to her left continued to struggle, pulling at the chain attached to her collar in an attempt to either break the metal, or rip it free from the wall.

"It won't work, trust me, I've tried," she whispered, just loud enough for the girl to hear. In a way, Isha admired her tenacity. She remembered the days after they had taken her, before the fire in her heart had simmered. It hadn't burnt out, not completely anyway. She still yearned for escape. She had just become more calculating about it, locking the rebellious teenager away to be used at the appropriate time.

The girl paid her no mind, continuing to thrash and groan, choking herself in the process.

Isha let out a low growl. "Stop it now, you fool, you'll get yourself killed."

No response.

She wasn't Isha's responsibility. Why not just let her be killed and be done with it? Back to the peace and quiet of her own mind. Back to hating the colour yellow.

No, she couldn't sit idle while a girl died when she could do something to stop it, even if the girl was a fool. She still had some figment of a conscience left in her broken soul, otherwise she would have to admit she was just like *them*.

She leaned to her left and without looking stamped her foot down hard upon the young woman's toe. Isha raised a hand to her mouth, muffling any sound she might have made. She eyed the surrounding area to see if anyone was looking. They weren't, too pre-occupied with their own revelry.

"Quiet," she whispered, now that she had her attention. "What is your name?" Isha removed her hand from her mouth before wiping spit onto her dress.

"M-my name?" the girl asked, lip quivering.

Isha took a deep breath, focusing all of her energy upon not rolling her eyes. "Yes, your name, what is it?" she said as calmly as possible.

"M-Maitreya."

There, now they were getting somewhere. "Okay Maitreya, listen good if you want to survive. Are you willing to listen? Nod if you understand."

Maitreya gave a series of quick half-nods. At least she was no longer choking herself to death.

"I am going to assume you're new, and that Averardus acquired you on his trip east."

Maitreya spat on the ground. "I am no-one's property! I am no-one's slave to be 'acquired'."

Isha looked her up and down before raising her brow in a high arc. "I'm not going to argue a moot point with you, I'm going to save your life."

Maitreya seemed to settle at that, leaning against the stone wall in a relaxed pose.

"Today is a Sun Day. All the Eagles in Lumindal gather here to feast and pay homage to Zur. I'll tell you exactly what will happen. First, they will get the politicking out of the way. The King-Radiant will show himself, some foreign lord will probably come grovelling for a favour or two before leaving with his tail between his legs, and then the celebrations start. You're new. I don't know what's so special about you but more than likely Averardus will want to show you off. If you want to survive until morning, you won't struggle. You'll let them watch you, let them mock you. Even let them touch you. Don't waste your life on a petty act of defiance, not here. That will lead to a quick death."

"You want me to act like a doll to be played with? I'd rather die."

Isha issued another deep growl. "A submissive doll today will still be a doll tomorrow. Tomorrow is a new day. And a new day brings fresh opportunities."

Maitreya turned to face her. "And how many of these 'opportunities' have you sought? How many days have you lived like this? Why have you not escaped? Are you afraid?"

Isha's face went blank, not expecting such line of questioning from a girl who a minute ago was acting like a trapped rat. She decided to leave her to her fate, she had done her bit.

"Just don't die," she found herself saying.

Instead, she cast her gaze out into the Great Hall where the evening's feast was picking up pace. She hated it, she loathed everything about this place. High vaulted ceilings loomed over her like a giant cage. Velvet drapes dangled over ornamented windows, casting a gloomy shadow over the smooth, glossy marble floor. It was a fancy cage at least.

She hated the people even more, the self-titled gods among

men. They were nothing more than regular men and women. No, they were less, except that each of them had enough authority to dethrone even one of the six Kings of Zapour if they wished. But that hadn't been done in two decades, not since the False Kings War between the King-Radiant and the now dead King of Crata.

She forced herself to pay attention, though. Memorising every detail, listening to every conversation. One day, all of her gathered information would have its use.

"I think it best you leave her be for now," a deep voice sounded to her right. "You have done all you can. Only she can decide if she has the will to live, or if she will accept her fate as a death sentence."

It was Obeyun. Out of all the slaves in Lumindal, he was her favourite. He was her rock, her support system. A pillar to lean upon whenever she had an inkling of self-doubt.

He stood stone still, hands crossed and tucked neatly into his rib cage. Obeyun had been Averardus' favourite for as long as she knew. Some of the Eagles seemed to think it a competition — who could collect the rarest and most distinguishable humans in Zapour. They collected without pity, and without remorse. They used every Sun Day feast to show off their latest acquisitions and gloat among their peers. Fortunately for Isha's 'master', he had her. She was unrivalled in rarity. Some called her a 'Mystic', but she didn't really know what that meant. She couldn't do anything special, could she?

Unlike Isha, Obeyun's 'condition' was much more visible. He was not dressed in fancy silk and tailored clothing. Instead, he wore a simple loincloth. His barrel-like chest was on display, highlighting his mulitcoloured flesh like he was a painting hanging on a wall. Even as he spoke, he remained still, eager to see this day done.

Even Isha had to admit he was a marvel to behold. He was tall, his skin split down the middle as if he were two people stitched into one. From his bald head all the way down to his arms and legs. One side was black as charcoal, his native colour and the colour all children of Wisha were born with. His other half was white as snow.

"I'm just trying to help her, as you did for me when I was first sentenced to a life in chains," she said.

Obeyun's left cheek blushed as his lip curled into a smile. "You have a gentle soul. We will see it free of chain soon enough."

Before Isha had time to blush herself, Averardus came storming down the aisle.

"What was that?" he demanded, hands on hips, staring up at Obeyun. "Do it again."

Obeyun stared at Averardus with a questioning look.

"Well, smile! Do it. Do it now."

Obeyun forced his lip to curl, but it came out as a distorted smirk, unsightly and unnatural.

"Bah," Averardus continued. "Disgusting, do it properly. As you did before. And stand up straight, will you! That harpy of a woman will be here any moment. I refuse to have her thinking one of my prized jewels is losing even a hint of its sparkle."

Obeyun opened his mouth wide in the fakest smile Isha had ever seen, his rotting teeth more of an insult to his master than any words.

Averardus scowled. "Be careful to remember your place, swine. I may need your face on display today, but do not think that I will not paint your back red with the crack of my whip tomorrow."

The two locked eyes in a battle of will, neither backing down. For a moment Isha thought it was all over. Her friend's life finished. Dead because of a smile.

"Ah, Averardus! How good of you to show your face. And with such fine stock on display."

Averardus' anger disappeared in an instant, replaced by a grin of surprised annoyance at the arrival of his long-time rival. "Adela, how nice of you to grace us with your presence. I trust you will be bowing out of our little arrangement this year? You really should not leave knives around such valuable slaves. Who knows, maybe it will be your neck they target next instead of their own."

It took all of Isha's will to remain vigilant. She had been through this before. She was caught in a never-ending squabble between two of the most notorious people in Zapour, and she didn't care for it. They were supposed to be divine, a symbol of peace and prosperity. All the stories she had ever read growing up told of the heroic deeds of Eagles past. From vanquishing the destructive threat of the Skae, to the forging of the Seven Kingdoms. But now she could see them first-hand, and all they did was bicker like spoiled children.

She forced herself to pay attention as Adela blinked, giving Averardus the most sinister smile she could muster. Her lips were full, her hair long, and her makeup thick. Never had Isha seen anyone try to hide her age quite like Adela. Her flaws were carefully hidden by a vast arrangement of jewels and decorative clothing. Though even the richest of Eagles could do nothing against a battle with age. And her age showed, if not through the product plastered on her face, then through the little areas. The wrinkles around her wrists, the sunspots covering her bare shoulder.

So much for being immortal.

"Oh, quite the contrary, my dear," Adela said, "it is true that my previous stock had a minor accident, but they say good things always come after tragedy, yes?"

Averardus gave her a quizzical look through thin eyes. "I do not follow."

"Why, of course not dear. Let me relieve you of your curiosity. Have you ever heard of the Isidoku clan in Northern Wisha?"

Averardus stood there bemused, but Obeyun's eyes widened with piqued interest.

"I see your slave here has. Maybe he could enlighten you to the Isidoku clan's gift of height. One might even call them giants."

"Speak plainly. Save me the indignity of having my slave speak," Averardus said.

"Very well, as you wish. On my recent venture north, I acquired a giant from the Isidoku clan. He will be here soon, I am sure you will not miss him. He is eight feet tall after all," she said with a wink.

"Impossible, no man is that large."

"If you say so dear. I do like that you stuck with your usual two centrepieces again this Sun Day. I do very much admire their beauty, but would it kill you to change things up now and then? For variety's sake."

Averardus's face contorted, a vein popping from his brow. "I have a new acquisition as well, so you can save your pity for another."

"Oh, pray tell. Though surely it is not that mess of a whore you have tucked away over there." She motioned towards Maitreya. "She is as plain as the sun is hot."

Averardus smirked. "Her beauty lies not upon the outside."

Adela raised a brow. "I am afraid now it is I who does not follow."

"Argon, un-sheath your sword and hand it to me!"

Averardus said.

Argon, a captain of the Golden Talon and Averardus's personal bodyguard, had remained impassive throughout the entire conversation. He towered over the frail looking Eagle, his broad shoulders thick with muscle. He moved with practiced efficiency as he un-sheathed the sword from his hip and held it out for Averardus.

The Eagle took the blade in one hand, nearly dropping to one knee at the sudden unexpected weight. Isha had to suppress a laugh, instead forcing herself to stare deeply into Argon's hazel eyes. The two didn't speak, but that was always the case between them, foregoing words for subtle exchanges of eye contact. His glare wasn't like the other guards Averardus kept in his retinue. There was no malice behind it, no lustful desire. Just a simple innocence that she found rather refreshing.

"Watch, and you shall see," said Averardus, gripping the one-handed short sword with both hands. He held it behind his back and moved towards Maitreya.

Isha gasped. Was he going to kill her? Already? She had only just learned her name.

He thrust the sword forward towards her open stomach. Isha tried to close her eyes but found them unable to shut, as horror turned to wonder. Instead of unleashing the blood and gore that would usually follow a slash to the abdomen, the blade bounced off, as if struck by some invisible barrier.

Averardus stumbled backward, laughing as he did. "Hah! How is that for special," he said.

Adela's jaw hung open, but she quickly shut it, returning to her usual upright pose, feigning disinterest as she looked away. "That is a clever trick, care to explain?"

Averardus laughed again. "That is just it. I cannot. I found her in the east. One of my men tried to slit her throat, but the knife just kept bouncing off! I thought it might run in the family, so I tried it on them too. I was mistaken, turned out bloodier than I expected. I do so hate the sight of blood. But here she is. A beauty, is she not?"

Isha looked towards Maitreya to see a single tear running down her right cheek. All her earlier fight was gone.

"Well, colour me impressed," Adela said. "Though I must be getting to my seat. I trust you will come visit my recent addition later this evening." She curtsied and left without waiting for a response.

Isha was quiet the rest of the evening, choosing to live inside of her own mind rather than appease the animals making up the court of Lumindal. Oh, she would let them think she was interested, opening her eyes wide so onlookers could gawk and mutter to themselves in awe. All the while she cursed her mother for gifting her with violet eyes. Though she supposed she would be dead right now if Averardus had not kept her for them. Would death have been a better end?

Instead of lingering on possibilities that could have been, she enjoyed the smaller things. She listened with intent as the minstrel strummed his lute to an upbeat tune, the jongleur's soft voice suppressing her anxiety as she closed her eyes to the music, if only for a moment. If there was one thing she missed about life back in Illidor, it was the music. The Sun Day's festivities gave her the rare chance to reminisce over her past self.

Her revelry was short-lived, however, as the King-Radiant finally made his presence known.

Within seconds, the Minstrel ceased playing, his voice fading into nothing. The Eagles wasted no time reading the social cue. Those dancing stopped at once, and those preferring to socialise quickly gathered their wits and scurried back to their tables, seated and ready for the more formal part of the evening.

The chamber grew still, as Evanon Lightfire, the forty-second King-Radiant, son of the deceased Urion Lightfire, and ruler of Zapour and its Six Kingdoms, rose. Throughout the long history of Zapour, not once had the patriarch's bloodline been broken. And yet Evanon bore no son. No heir to carry on his name.

Said to be the mightiest of all the Eagles, the first touched by Zur's shining light, the King-Radiant stood above all else.

Despite her unfathomable hatred towards the Eagles and a deep disbelief in everything they preached, there was something real about the King-Radiant. She couldn't part her eyes from the scene as his indomitable stare bore down on those below. Unlike his Eagles, he did not dress as though his social standing or position depended on it. He was adorned in a thick fur coat, buttoned to the top. He leaned across his throne — made up of fifty spear-like columns of solidified white-light, reminiscent of the Fifty Spears of Lumindal in which they now held residence — and placed two powerful arms upon the table.

Joining him was the Queen-Mother, Lady Sephare. A woman who carried the equivalent reputation of a serpent. Her glare was an arrow, her smile a sword. Though it was not a person's body her blades yearned to bleed, it was their soul. Isha made a point to always avoid her sinister stare, especially with the interest Sephare has always taken in her.

"Herald!" the King-Radiant bellowed. "On with it. I grow impatient, keep your queries short and to the point."

As if out of thin air, a scrawny, awkward man appeared. His head was the shape of an egg, and his hook-like nose was long and pointy. "Yes, your Radiance, I will begin at once," he said, his voice calm and well-practiced. "I have with me representatives from Craw and Kogon. I present to you Prince Ancel Saelmere of Craw, and Prince Valter Balsto of Kogon." He gave a short bow, motioning the two forward as he made his way into the shadow of the crowd.

Isha grimaced. In her previous life she had been all but promised to Prince Ancel. With Trost bordering Craw, her father had wished to unite the Glaive and Saelmere families to broaden his influence and share in the Saelmere's wealth of fertile land. Her father might have been blind to it, but Isha had seen Ancel for what he truly was. Even at a young age, he had been a monster, beating his servants at the slightest inconvenience. She wondered what would have become of her had she married him. Maybe her life now was not so bad in comparison.

"Your Radiance," Ancel said, bowing so deeply his hands nearly touched his toes. "I bring with me a gift. I hope it is to your satisfaction."

A servant rushed forwards to present the gift. Isha had to squint, but it looked as though it were some kind of chalice. Its gold shimmered in the dim light shining through the paned windows above. Its rim was studded with oval shaped rubies, sapphires and even diamonds by the look of it.

"I have plenty of cups that fill my belly with wine well enough," the King-Radiant said, taking a large swig of wine from his own plain cup. "Speak your truth and begone."

"Yes, of course your Radiance," said the prince. "As you know, my family has always been and will always be your most loyal subjects. My father has provided you with —"

"I am well aware of my standing with the Saelmeres and your father! Do not patronise me, boy. Speak your *truth* and *begone.*"

Ancel stood up straight. His hand wavered, but otherwise he remained calm. "Very well, I come here along with my cousin from Kogon to seek your aid. The Cratans are out of control. They pillage our villages and threaten war upon our borders. With their capital...with Hirane no longer there, they are lawless and have turned savage. My people fear venturing too far into their terrain for fear of the sickness. With half of our Light-wielders in Lumindal, Craw does not have enough to defend our border. We are stretched too thin. I ask aid from the Golden Talon Company so that we may strengthen our borders and rout the traitorous scum."

Evanon did not respond immediately, choosing to clasp his hands together to form one fist. "And you are of the same mind?" he said at last, nodding towards Prince Valter.

"I am my liege," he said, thrusting a fist towards his chest.

The King-Radiant leaned forward. "Please enlighten me. I have here with me the joined might of two of the most prestigious names in all of Zapour, and yet still it is not enough to fight off a couple of...'savages' did you call them?"

Ancel's feet shifted uncomfortably. "They use hit-and-run tactics, and know their land well," he said. "My father has other conflicts to the south, he cannot spare the resources to "

Evanon waved a hand, cutting the prince off. "So, you would have me send my own? Bah! The Golden Talon Company protect and serve the city of Lumindal and the Eagles. They do not busy themselves with petty squabbles and border disputes. Tell your father he must offer more than a dusty chalice to gain the services of my men. Now begone, I grow impatient this evening."

Without another word, the two princes retreated, bitter in their defeat.

"Herald!" the King-Radiant bellowed again. "What is next?"

Again, the Herald appeared. "I have here a letter from the west, from across the Sea of Sapphires."

"Summarise it for me. I have not the time and would rather not listen to the drone of your voice."

"Yes, sire. It seems the Empire of Yagos has been usurped."

Mumblings and murmurings followed around the chamber as the crowd greeted the news with a mixture of shock and curiosity.

"Usurped?" the King-Radiant said. "So, that old bastard Percival finally found a sword in his back. Who was bold enough to pull it off?"

The Herald scrambled through a bunch of weathered parchment, looking for an answer. "Uhh, I'm afraid there's no name given, Highness. It says here the man calls himself the Sun Prince. I have a letter from him addressed to yourself, shall I read it?"

Evanon motioned for him to continue. "Make it quick."

The Herald scanned the letter, hesitating a moment before continuing with the request.

"What do you not understand about quickly, you fool?"

"My apologies, your Radiance, but the contents are..."

"I do not cull the messenger of bad news, only the cause of such. So read."

"Of course, ahem," the Herald cleared his throat.

"To the King-Radiant of Zapour, Evanon Lightfire.

"You need not know my name, for it is not my name that is important. If you must address me, you may call me the Sun Prince, for I take it upon myself to protect and defend our world's most beloved star. I have claimed Yagos as my own. The Emperor Percival has paid the ultimate price for his crimes. I turn my attention now

towards Zapour, not because I seek to conquer, but because your overuse of the Shine is destroying our world. I ask you now to peacefully cease your use of magic as a source of weaponry and destruction. If you continue upon your path, you will give me no choice but to stop you with force. This is not a declaration of war, but a warning. If you wish to understand my philosophy, you may seek me out. I aspire only to educate, but I trust my actions and my accomplishments speak for themselves as to my ability to dominate those who are less inclined to see sense in my words. I hope to hear from you soon.

The Sun Prince."

The Herald lowered his hands, awaiting a response. The entire chamber went silent, none daring to make jest or even whisper before the King-Radiant himself had the chance to speak.

Evanon issued a bellow of laughter, deep and genuine. It echoed across the high ceilings. Soon the entire Great Hall was full of laughter, all following Evanon's lead. Only Isha and the slaves didn't join.

Eventually the laughter ended as Evanon rose from his throne. "What nonsense is this?" he said. "Let me make it clear. This 'pretender' from across the sea wishes only to sow doubt in our minds. We are Zur's chosen." He spread his arms wide, holding his head high as if basking in his own glory. "We are the keepers of the Light. It is through our existence the world yet stands today."

Evanon's hand shook, and Isha could detect a faint trace of Light building in the palm of his hand. Before she even had the chance to blink, the King-Radiant shot a beam of red Light at his Herald.

The Herald froze. He slowly looked down to see the

parchment ablaze. With a burst of panic, he dropped it to the marble floor and stepped away.

"I bow to no foreigner. I bow to no one," Evanon said. He turned towards his mother and whispered something in her ear, likely asking her to see if the man's claim to Yagos bore any fruit.

Isha spotted a man hastily making his way up the aisle towards the dais before stopping to whisper in the Herald's ear. Isha could not part her eyes from the two. Knowledge was power. Watch everything, listen to everyone. Someday it would lead to her freedom.

"Y-your Radiance, apologies," the Herald said. "I am afraid I have just received dire news."

Evanon took a deep and steadying breath, before planting a fist onto the table. "Speak."

"It is Lord Saerus sire, h-h-he has been murdered."

The room went into uproar. Loud gasps, discordant chatter and panic washed through the chamber like a tidal wave. Isha could only smile.

"Who would dare kill one of my own?" Evanon shouted.

"I do not know your Radiance. But Lord Saerus was last known to be in Lesken, gathering Shine-sensitive children."

Evanon's anger was like a thundercloud. An aura of red Light surrounded his body as he rose from his throne in a fury. Isha had seen such a show of Light before, in her father sometimes when he became angered, but not like this. She could barely look, so intense was the heat. Even from across the room she felt his power. "Ancel, Valter. Step forward," he said.

The two confused princes scuttled forwards once more.

"Listen carefully and listen well. If you want so much as a single soldier of mine for your petty little war with the Cratans, you will see the ones responsible for the death of Saerus put to the sword. Do not cheat me on this, and do not return to me unless you have them in chains, or their heads upon a spike. Am I clear?"

"Yes, your Radiance," both Ancel and Valter said in unison.

Isha's smile broadened. There was someone out there fighting against these monsters. Someone with both the courage and the will to seek change, to seek justice. She just hoped they were prepared. One day Isha would join them in their fight. One day she would seek revenge for what they had done to her, to everyone. Today was not that day. But tomorrow was another day, and each new day brought fresh opportunities.

Chapter 3
Dazen

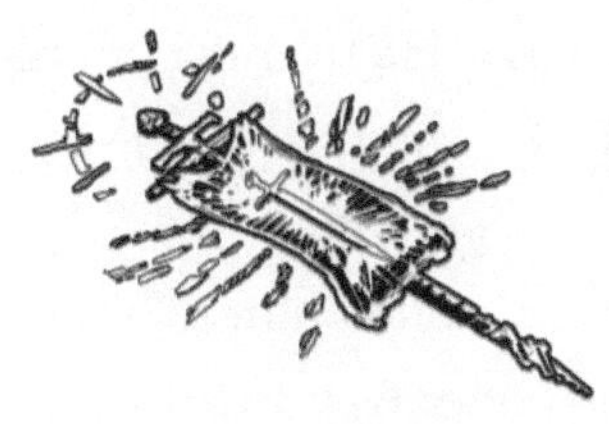

The early morning sunshine peeked over the battlements, shining brightly against the blunted metal of Dazen's long steel. For years his father had awaited the day the Kingdoms of Trost and Zuton made peace. Contrary to popular belief, Kron was not war hungry. He did not desire conflict, was no despot. He wanted only for Trost to persevere.

Seventy years had elapsed since Berolt Glaive — Dazen's great grandfather — had passed on the opportunity to become an Eagle, only to usurp the silver crown and claim the throne of Illidor as his own. Ever since then, the Glaives of Trost and the Levic family of Zuton had engaged in bitter dispute after bitter dispute. Now, an opportunity has arisen to start anew, to make peace.

"Are you sure you're ready for this?" he asked his opponent, who looked as though he had barely grown into his own armour.

The young prince of Zuton lowered his visor in a brave show of defiance before taking his stance upon the open field.

It was the wrong stance, but at least it was something.

Dazen liked the youngest Levic. Echo was too young to have seen an actual battle. He had spirit though, a raw tenacity flavoured with a composure usually birthed through years of experience.

Dazen charged, eager to show any would be onlookers what it meant to be a Glaive. He swung both his long and short steel with vicious ferocity, careful to pull each cut. He wanted to teach, not cripple the poor boy.

His father had instructed him to befriend the Levic siblings. Dazen knew of no better way to form a bond than through the clash of steel.

Echo retaliated, charging him. Dazen batted away his sloppy offence, slapping his sword to the ground. Dust flew into the air as Echo shook a gauntleted hand.

"Your blade needs a firm grip. Never let it waver, never let it fall," Dazen said.

He backed off, allowing the boy to pick up his lost weapon. Echo hugged the hilt with a vice-like grip and turned to face him.

"Fix your stance," Dazen said, waving a sword at the prince's feet. "Hips towards your opponent. Allows you to back-step and counterattack much easier."

Echo obliged, though before he could fully correct himself Dazen rushed in, deft cuts falling in a flurry of hand movements. Echo stumbled, backing into the corner before finding the courage to deflect and throw in a strike or two himself. The boy was young, but he was not without skill.

Unfortunately for Echo, he was no match for a Glaive's finesse with a blade. Dazen moved a touch to his left, watching as the light shone into Echo's visor. Taking advantage, he thrust a firm boot into his mid-section, following up with a blunt strike to the calf.

Echo tumbled, surfacing to find the blunted tip of Dazen's sword at his throat. Dazen held an outstretched arm and pulled when Echo grabbed ahold, using his other hand to remove his helm in the same motion.

"Well met," Echo said. If he was put off at all by Dazen's tactics, he didn't show it.

Dazen rubbed at the stubble on his chin. "I admit you are not what I expected. There is rumour the sons of Rayner Levic are not so welcoming."

Echo studied him before huffing a dismissive sigh. "There are also rumours in my country, about the Wolf of Illidor. They say his cunning is unmatched. They say to face him in battle is to stare death in the face. I am glad there is at least a little exaggeration to each."

Dazen curled his lip. "Indeed."

The two headed for the benches, splashing fresh water across their faces, which were already dripping with sweat.

"Those rumours are not all false though," Echo said. "Wait until you meet my brothers."

Dazen grunted. "Thanks for the heads up."

"May I ask you something?" Echo said, moving to change the subject.

"Of course. Though if it is about my victory, there is no such thing as a clean fight in war."

"No, it is not that," he said, scratching at his head before taking a seat. "Why do you never use your Shine in battle? I know you are able. You are the son of Kron. But in all the reports I have read, none mention you using the white-light."

Dazen squinted, studying the boy with renewed curiosity. "Would you like a hole in your chest along with a sprained wrist?" he asked.

Echo brushed the comment aside with a dry laugh. "I am not talking about the sparring pits. I speak of battle. I have heard the stories about you. About your clash with the Saelmeres in the north and of the battle of Black Rock."

Dazen took a steadying breath. "Just because I have a deadly weapon at my disposal, does not mean I have to use it," he settled on saying.

"But why not? You just said yourself, there is no such thing as a clean fight."

"Those who rely on Shine neglect other, more useful skills. Skills that when Light no longer shines will save your life."

Dazen clenched and unclenched his fists, feeling the surge of power flow towards his palms. "More importantly, some fail to comprehend the cost of using such magic. I have known more than one man to recklessly throw Light at his opponents only to come home with a dead hand, useless and blackened — unable to grip the hilt of a sword."

"So, you use it only in emergencies?" Echo said.

"Something like that," Dazen said, patting him on the back. "There is also more than one way to wield the Light. Would you like me to teach you?"

Echo bowed his head. "Zur's Light does not shine within me as it does my brothers."

Dazen sighed. "Self-worth is greater than the ability to wield the white-light Echo. Not being able to use it does not define you."

"Hah! You have not met my brothers!"

Dazen motioned for him to return to the sparring pit. "Come, we were just getting started."

The sparring pits were tucked into a pocket within the inner walls of Illidor. Stone encircled the miniature arena, casting a half shadow across the sand and dirt covering the floor. A burst of cool air drifted in from the east, bringing with it the pungent smell of perfume. Dazen's nostrils flared as it mixed with the sweat dripping from his nose. He forced a sneeze, looking up to the battlements to find two shadows hovering over him like a storm cloud.

"Pathetic, is he not?" said one of the shadows.

Dazen turned to see two grown men glaring down at him from the railing, their faces concealed in the sunlight. He squinted, lifting a hand over his eyes. The two figures stalked down the stone steps. He now recognised them for who they were. Echo's elder twin brothers, Huet and Petros Levic. The pair had briefly introduced themselves on arrival, though Dazen hadn't the opportunity to gain their measure.

"If you think you will fare better you are more than welcome to join me on the field," Dazen said, fixing them both with the stern expression usually reserved for those whose necks were soon to be parted from their head.

The two huffed, standing tall with their arms crossed, but Dazen could see through their charade.

"We have better things to do than poke each other with blunted sticks," said Huet. At least he thought it was Huet who spoke. The pair were so similar it was like comparing two shades of black. Huet ran a hand through his smooth silken hair. *Pompous asshole.* Dazen made a mental note that Huet's hair parted to the right, while Petros' parted to the left.

"You are probably better off giving him a wooden stick than a sword anyway. The poor bastard would more than likely stab himself in the foot rather than the flesh of an enemy," Petros chimed in.

Dazen's eyes narrowed into slits. "Echo is your brother, you shame yourselves sullying him so."

Huet shook his head to the side. "He is no brother of mine.

He holds our name and that is all."

Dazen could see Echo's arm tensing, his fingers curling into angry claws.

"I have Levic blood in my veins, just as you," Echo spat. Dazen looked down. The boy had all but drawn blood from pressing his nails hard into his now open palms.

"Blood stolen from our mother!" Petros cried, standing in front of Huet.

Echo's shoulders slumped. He shrank into his own body as if hit in the stomach. "I —"

"You know we speak the truth," Petros continued. "If you had not been born, mother would still be alive."

Tears welled at the base of Echo's eyes. Dazen could see the pain within. He hated bullies. Nothing in the world irked him more than a person abusing their power. But this was not his fight. He watched as Echo threw down his blade and stormed off towards the palace without another word.

Dazen tried to call after him, but it was no use. Turning back now would only lead to further embarrassment. Dazen eyed the twins with burning hatred. Even blunted, if he poked hard enough, he could stick them with a sword. Or maybe he would just snap their necks.

He took a steadying breath. If he struck now, it could mean war between their two nations. No, it *would* mean war. All his father had worked for...

He held his hand, forcing himself to stay still and hoping the two would leave before his patience ran thin.

Fortunately, the twins turned. "Told you he was pathetic," Huet said. "Your father wants to see you by the way, in his chamber. Sounded urgent." Huet let out a sinister chuckle.

Without thinking Dazen drew his short steel, turned, and flung the blade as hard as he could. It landed dead straight, embedding itself into the wall of the training pit, head height. "Show disrespect around me again and next time it will be your head," he said plainly.

Petros' eyes grew wide. He looked from the embedded sword back to Dazen. "Is that a threat?"

"Consider it a warning."

The twins took a half-turn back, narrowing their eyes at Dazen before shuffling off into the distance.

Dazen shook his head, disappointed with himself for losing his cool. Their quarrel reminded him too much of his own brother, now lost to him.

Kron Glaive lay in a dazed state as Dazen entered his bedchamber. Surrounding him were all the comforts a dying king required. An orderly arrangement of barely touched fresh fruit sat atop recently cleaned, plain white silken sheets. His chamber pot was at the ready. Dazen took note to cautiously avoid it as he stepped closer. He had at least half a dozen servants tending to his every need, each fluttering around, pretending their work was important.

Upon recognizing his son, Kron issued an inhuman groan and struggled to sit upright. With an aggressive wave of his hands, the servants left in a flurry of quiet footsteps. Once they were alone, he spoke, his voice croaking as if he were a crow who had lost its food. "Come closer, son, so I might see your face."

Dazen obliged, moving over to the bedside, though he had to half-hold his breath lest he catch his father's sickness simply from his stench alone.

"You asked for me, Father?"

"Yes yes," Kron said, pausing to cough three times into his handkerchief. "We have much to speak of."

"Are you alright? Has the sickness spread —"

"I am fine!" Kron croaked, sitting up straighter in his bed and fixing Dazen with an icy stare, reminding Dazen where he got it from. "I will beat this sickness, do not cast your doubt upon me boy."

"Of course, Father. I did not mean to —"

Kron waved his hand again. "It is not important. We have a matter to settle."

"Very well, what is it you wish to discuss?"

"There will be no discussion. I have arranged for you to marry the Levic daughter. Sumaya is her name, I believe. Yes, that sounds right."

Dazen stumbled backward, his breath catching in his throat. "You cannot be serious. I barely know her. She is but a child."

"She has passed her seventeenth year and has already bled. She is ready to bear child. More importantly, she is the princess of Zuton! You are my only son. Trost needs alliances if we are to stand against Craw. Glaive and Levic are to be united in blood. With the Zuton princess taking our name we can place this senseless conflict behind us." Kron leaned over and fell into another coughing fit, this one more violent than the last.

Dazen moved to comfort him, but a surprisingly strong push forced him backwards. "I am fine! I do not need my son to pat my back for me. You will be the King of Trost when I am gone. You need to start doing what is best for our kingdom, even if it means personal sacrifice."

Dazen let out a distressed gasp. "There are some sacrifices that are not worth the pain! Or have you forgotten, Father!"

A long pause followed. Both knew the conversation was no longer about the betrothal. The silence hung in the air like a fog that would never clear.

"Do not dare lecture me on sacrifice!" Kron roared. "Great

men must make great sacrifices. This family and I have given up everything to ensure Trost remains one of The Six Kingdoms, of which there are now only five!"

Dazen looked down at his feet. He despised the world for the way it was, hated how the image of his sister being taken still burned in his mind like it was branded with molten iron. He hated even more that he had done nothing about it. Still did nothing about it.

"You will marry the Levic girl. Am I clear?"

He looked deep into his father's fading brown eyes. "Yes, Father."

"Now leave me, I must rest if I am to announce the engagement at the feast tomorrow."

Dazen moved for the door, turning once to see his father settling back into his comforts. "Oh, and Father. Next time, do not send the Levic twins if you wish to speak to me. Not unless you want their heads upon a spike to be the centrepiece at my wedding."

"Bah!" Kron gasped in a mixture of laughter and a cough. "Best get used to them. They are your family now too."

Each step felt as though his pockets were full of stones as Dazen wandered the halls of the palace in a mindless daze. Betrothed? Him?

He supposed he should have seen it coming, he was a prince. And Prince of Trost at that. He could hardly be expected to choose his own suitor, to marry for love instead of political power and status.

But the feeling still itched at him. Why should he be denied the power of love? Denied even a choice?

Great men must often make great sacrifices. His father's words echoed in his mind even now. By all reports, Lady Sumaya was beautiful beyond measure, a rare prize sought after by hundreds of would-be suitors. Why then did he waver? His father had married for love, hadn't he? Celia and Kron's love for each other had burned brighter than any star in the sky. Dazen had seen it with his own eyes before his mother passed so suddenly from this world. Or was that love also a lie? Had his whole world just been one constant unending lie?

He forced such thoughts from his mind, instead focusing on the positive. Maybe the Princess wasn't such a terrible fit? She was young, true, but her beauty could not be denied. Was her character akin to that of her sinister elder brothers? Or was her soul as warm and gentle as her younger sibling, Echo? Perhaps she favoured neither, but Dazen was not one to let curiosity control his thoughts for long.

He shifted his step and made for Echo's chamber. He had been meaning to check on the boy after his ordeal earlier anyway.

After making his way through the winding passages of Illidor's unending palace, he came to a halt outside his newfound friend's door. He went to knock but found it already open. He placed a careful hand on the frame and pushed. The room was empty, the door to the balcony wide open, causing the chill from the morning wind to creep up his bare arms.

"Echo?" Dazen called. "Are you in? I wish to speak with you."

No response.

He walked towards the balcony, nearly giving up the search when he heard a flutter. With a curious eye he rounded the bend. His eyes grew wide as he noticed Echo standing tall on the balcony rail. He stared down at the courtyard below, his arms wide as if ready to embrace death.

"Echo no!" he shouted. "Do not do it!"

The youngest Levic staggered to the side, flinching further to the edge of the railing. With a yelp, his foot faltered, and he went tumbling over the side.

Dazen rushed forward. He leaned over the rail to find Echo's hand clutching at the stone. His legs flailed dangerously below as he hung there in a panicked state.

"Grab my hand!" Dazen called, leaning over the rail and thrusting an arm downward.

With renewed effort, Echo clasped his forearm in a tight embrace. Dazen pulled with the might of ten boars as he lifted the young prince level with him and threw him over to the safety of the balcony.

The two of them lay side-by-side on the floor, the sound of heavy breathing rising over the wind. Dazen clutched at his chest, and found his heart racing.

"What were you thinking?" Dazen snapped, before realising that this matter needed to be handled in a sensitive manner, not an aggressive one.

"I — I wasn't going to do it, I swear!" Echo said.

Dazen eyed the boy, who was already up on his feet. "Help me up, will you."

Echo took his hand and repaid the favour. "I am sorry, I did not mean to... You just startled me is all."

Dazen relaxed, though he didn't believe for a second the thought had not crossed his mind. "What were you doing up there?"

"I..." Echo's shoulders slumped, his face sinking into his body. "What purpose do I serve?"

"Pardon?" Dazen asked.

"What purpose do I serve in life? I am no warrior, no prince. I cannot wield the Light. My brothers do not let a day pass without taunting me. I could not even be born without taking my country's Queen from them. My own mother. So, what purpose does a failure like me serve among the living?"

Dazen paused, studying the boy. He gulped a heavy lump down his throat, took a deep breath and stared out into the cloudless sky. "I have no simple answer for you, Echo. Often, I find my own thoughts mirroring your own. For a long time, I too was lost. Perhaps I still am.

"But there is more to life than misery. Sometimes we just have to work hard to find it. If you want to change yourself, you must fight. Take the first step, fight for what you believe in and make it a reality."

Echo looked at him with a puzzled expression before issuing a sigh, following Dazen's gaze out into the blue sky.

For a long moment they stood in quiet contemplation. Dazen thought back on his own life. He thought on Raiz and Isha, as he always did. Were they safe? Were they even still alive?

He shook his head and clenched his fists. One day he would find them. They could be a family once more.

Echo stretched out a hand for Dazen to clasp. "Your words have moved me. You have my thanks. I will do my best to be the man I know I can be. I promise."

Dazen relaxed into a smile, taking his hand. "We will make a prince of you yet." He ruffled a calloused hand into Echo's sandy brown hair.

"There must be something I can do to thank you properly," Echo said. "For saving my life."

Dazen opened his mouth to speak, quickly shutting it again before finally deciding to simply ask what he wanted to know. "What is your sister like?"

Chapter 4
Raiz

Raiz watched as four silhouettes, each as tall as a tower, followed their every step, the shadows shrinking as they drew closer to the mouth of the cave which hung in a wide arch overhead. Raiz took one last glance at the open plains of Zuton before venturing into the darkness. Lesken was now a dot on the horizon, surrounded by a barren wasteland devoid of life. Nothing but a few dried-up trees and slithering serpents separated the city from where he now stood on the mountain peak. But he was no longer needed there, their fate was out of his hands.

Spike had ventured off on his own. As bonded as the two of them were, he was his own creature and came and went as he pleased.

Red and orange firelight flickered violently against the black stone as a wall of lanterns illuminated the inner sanctum of the cavern. Raiz couldn't help but stare in awe as great stalactite mounds protruded from the ceiling, pointing like a sea of spears as they rained down from above to obscure their path. He walked carefully past each of them, placing a hand upon one's tip. It was cool to the touch, and a small river of water rushed through his fingers, giving him a much-needed reprieve.

"You're late," came a voice from the darkness.

Raiz turned. Within the shadows came forth a man. Flimsy grey bandages covered his arms, stretching all the way to his shoulders as the dead limbs dangled uselessly by his side.

"The job is done," Raiz said. "The Eagle is dead."

The man took another step forward, revealing the clear outline of his mentor. He had taken him in when his own family had failed him, trained him in the art of white-light and honed his Shine to a deadly edge, no matter the consequences. Celik Thorne.

Raiz forced himself to look him in the eye, for Celik hated when people avoided his gaze. Imprinted on his ageing face was a black mark in the form of a hand. It stretched the entire right side of his face, with fingermarks of charred skin curling into his left cheek and forehead. The rest retained its normal pinkish tone.

"Did you get his name?" Celik asked, his voice harsh and rough.

Raiz was about to shake his head when Veil stepped forward. "I heard one of the locals name him 'Saerus'."

Celik spat on the wet stone. "Useless bastard, was Saerus. The world will be better without him. So how did he go? Cut him down yourself? What was he like? Did shit trickle down his leg as your Light stuck him?"

"Well, actually —" Veil began, before Celik moved to within a breath's distance, examining her like she were an animal ready for dissection.

"You're pale, and you slump. What happened? Did you have another episode?"

Veil went slack.

"I see, I shall have to keep a closer check on you. Were there any casualties this time?"

Raiz could practically feel Veil's self-consciousness as his own. He hated seeing her this way, couldn't imagine her suffering. Most people born with Zur's Light could dispel excess Light safely, but Veil had forever been unable to, forced to hold her Shine until she could hold no more.

"There were no casualties. We were able to direct the Light this time," Raiz said.

"I see. You must tell me all about it. Being able to control such power could prove quite the asset."

"My condition is not an asset!" Veil snapped. "You promised to find a cure."

Celik issued a low grunt. "In time my dear, in time. But you do not see as I see. Where you see an ailment in need of a cure, I see a weapon in need of direction. Do you not wish to take vengeance on those who have wronged you?"

"Of course I do. I will see Lumindal razed to the ground for what they did to my family."

"Then you must prioritise your desire. You cannot find peace without first sating your hatred."

Veil looked at her feet, her lips tightening into a thin line.

"So, is that how he passed then? Burned to a crisp? Turned to ash?" Celik prompted.

"No," said Aroha, stepping in front of Raiz. "We decided on a different route. A different course of action."

Celik tilted his head towards Aroha, his dead arms dangling loosely at his hips. "Did you now?"

Raiz eyed Aroha, biting his lip and wishing she weren't

always so damn honest.

"After we dropped the tower on their heads, we forced the people of Lesken to defend themselves, to find their courage," Aroha continued.

"Bah! Fools. I assume this was Raiz's idea, hmm?" Celik said.

Aroha bit her tongue.

Celik's eyes narrowed into slits as he stopped just short of where Raiz stood. "You are a fool, Raiz, did your father ever tell you that?"

"Many times," Raiz said.

"So, what was your plan eh? Give some king's speech inspiring a rebellion, in that shit of a city? Oh, what an idiot you are. If I had the use of my arms, your face would be red raw."

"But you don't," Raiz said. "And my face remains unmarred."

Celik grumbled a series of incoherent words as he paced the width of the cave and back. "We are not heroes here, Raiz, you should know that well. We do not inspire, do not seek a higher purpose. We simply kill, and then we leave. Am I understood?"

"Maybe killing isn't enough for me. You didn't see their faces as I spoke to them. The pain in their eyes, the defiance in their voices. The people of this world are ready to fight. They just need to be shown how."

"You don't know this world as you think you do!" snapped Celik. "And it's clear to me you don't understand the consequences of your actions."

"What I know, is that there is one less Eagle alive in this world. And an entire city has now found their voice."

"And they will sing a mighty song indeed, I am sure. They will sing until their lungs give out so that the world might know their triumph. But know that this shall be their last song. Their brief moment of salvation will be forever marred when the white-light rains down from the sky. Every seed you may have planted. Every thought of action, of deliverance, will be burned along with Lesken."

Raiz stood in quiet contemplation. Was he really doing the right thing? Should he have just killed the Eagle himself?

"What if we take them in? Teach them to fight. They still have many strong men. We could do it!"

Celik nearly burst into laughter. "You are insane, Raiz. We number five!"

"Then what is your plan? Because as it stands, we have taken out but one feather in a wing full of them. When will I be given the chance to kill the man who took my sister from me? When will we make our move on the King-Radiant?"

"Patience, Raiz! Patience. Your powers grow by the day, but you are not yet ready for that task. Your Shine is still young, soon it shall be ready. Soon the real battle will begin, the real enemy revealed. But you must rid yourself of these false convictions. They will end you quicker than any enemy ever could."

"And who is this real enemy? You expect us to follow you, to go along with your schemes, but you tell us nothing. I wouldn't expect you to understand anyway, you're a monster who thinks only of yourself."

Celik's mouth twitched, his beady eyes glowing with hatred. "Zapour is not ready to know what is coming. There are pieces that need to be removed before I reveal what is to come. In the meantime, I suggest you learn to hold your tongue. Talk it over with Veil. She understands what one with good intentions must sacrifice. She alone understands the true power behind Lumindal and the King-Radiant."

"Master!" Veil protested. "You promised you would not speak of it!"

Celik huffed. "That was before you allowed his mind to be clouded. You had best set him straight, or it will be us who suffer for it."

Raiz's face contorted, his jaw tightening. "So, all of your rules were for nothing then? Don't get too close to one another. Don't ask about our past lives. Friendships only lead to unwarranted emotion, hinder our decision making. That's what you said, remember?"

"This is different, Raiz. My rules are effective. But you have lost perspective. You need a reminder of what it is we hope to achieve here. And what is beyond us."

Raiz puffed an angry breath, turned, and stormed out of the cave. "Follow me and you die."

Raiz slumped against the hard stone of the mountain, its rocky edge stabbing at his back as his legs dangled over the cliff. He paid the pain no mind. It was almost refreshing to know he was still alive. To know if he moved an inch or two to his right, the pain would vanish. He wondered if the pain inside of him would go away as easily, but he doubted it.

He stared out into the black of night, picking out constellations as he had with his sister when he was a boy. His eyes followed the stars making up the spine of a sea serpent. That had always been his sister's favourite. An array of bright white dots in the sky stretching in a semicircle with a beautiful red oval-shaped orb at its end making up the eye. For a moment he was a child again, staring out the top of the Moon-spire. But there was no palace below, no guards keeping him in, no sister to keep him in check.

Sometimes he regretted his choice to run away from Illidor. Maybe he could have accomplished more if he were still a prince. But those thoughts always vanished as soon as they came. He couldn't have stayed there, not after watching his father let them take her away. No, he had to forge his own path, had to choose his own destiny. One day he'd return to confront his father, but that day was far away.

A shuffle of footsteps and the sound of a loose stone breaking away from the cliff caused Raiz to flinch. His hand caught alight instinctively as he turned, ready to blast whoever dared disturb him off the edge and to certain death.

"If you plan to kill me, we both know a sword is best. Unless you want me to have another episode. Might even take the mountain down with me, kill Celik and the others. That's what you want, yes?"

It was Veil. Though this was the real Veil. Only with the night could she be her true self. Even as the icy winds wound around mountain peaks and bit into her exposed skin, she refused to cover up like she was forced to during the day, when Zur's light was out in full strength. She wore a short blouse with the sleeves cut off, exposing her belly and arms to the night. Raiz relaxed his hand, pretending she was a ghost.

"May I sit?" she asked.

Again, Raiz ignored her, focusing on the constellations.

"I'm just going to sit," she said, arranging her petite body so that it rested on the stone a hair's width away from his own. She brushed a hand through short black hair, tucking a piece of her fringe behind her ear before hugging herself with crossed arms. "Is it just me or are the summer nights growing colder each year?"

Raiz flinched away. He wanted nothing more than to be close to her, to comfort her as she was attempting to comfort him. But it was as if his body and mind were two separate entities. Instead, he opted for conversation. "Ever thought of a coat?" he said, his tone laced with sarcasm. He quickly withdrew his gaze as she stared at him with dagger-like eyes.

"It's not just you," he continued. "The change is subtle, but every year Zur's Light fades a little further. I can feel it. Every day he offers me less strength than the last."

"He's not my god," Veil said, "and He never will be. I didn't ask for his Light, nor do I want it. So, he can fade out of existence for all I care. Maybe then I'll be normal again."

Raiz lowered his head. He hated himself for his own selfishness sometimes. "We'll find a way to free you from your pain one day soon. I promise it, Veil."

"We've tried everything, Raiz. Nothing drains it. One day soon it will end me. I can't keep this up for much longer. I'm a danger to you all."

"You are not a danger. You can control it; I saw you do it. There will be someone who knows how to fix you, I'm sure of it. We just have to keep searching."

She smiled at him and moved an inch closer. "If only Celik shared your compassion."

"All that old geezer cares about is himself. We need him, but his rules be damned. I'm sick of not talking to you, to Draz, to Aroha."

"Then don't listen to him. As you said, he's old. Old people tend to be hard of hearing," Veil said, a cheeky grin stretching the length of her face, highlighting her dimples.

"Did he send you here?" Raiz asked.

"No, but I think it's safe to assume he knew I'd come."

Raiz shrugged. "Are we wrong to have done what we did?"

Veil succumbed to the cold, wrapping a navy cloak over their bare knees so they would be safe from the chill. "There are a dozen definitions for 'wrong' in this world. We just have to decide which of them is the right one."

Raiz gave her a quizzical look, his eyes meeting hers for the first time this evening. "Do you think we were wrong?"

"I think that monster deserves to die a thousand more times for what he has done. If I had things my way, I would burn them all and drown their ash in the mother sea."

"So, we're of the same mind?" Raiz said, perking up.

"On that we're of the same mind. But our thirst for Eagle's blood is not the moral in question. Inspiring others towards a noble cause is a task worthy of the one you call god. But recklessly doing so leads towards chaos and confusion. This I know. It was my family and my people who suffered the consequences of failed rebellion."

Again, Raiz looked up at her. For the first time he could see behind the sparkle of her ocean blue eyes to the sadness within. She was broken, just as he. He wondered what a life would be like with her away from their troubled pasts. A life without a lust for revenge and free of consequence. Would two broken souls equal to one whole one?

"You're Cratan, aren't you?" he asked, his voice soft. He found himself wondering why he had never asked before. All of these years on the run, learning to fight by her side, and not once had he asked about her past. Maybe he had taken Celik's rules too seriously, or perhaps he felt if he pried too deeply into hers, she might then do the same to him, and he wasn't ready yet to share his pain.

She nodded, taking a deep breath. "I lived with my parents on the outskirts of Hirane. They were simple farmers, not a fighting breath in them. My mother used to weave me things, scarves and the like, whenever she wasn't helping Da' with the flock. But when the Eagle Ameline killed our princess — Tertius declared war on the King-Radiant and thus began the False Kings War between Crata and Lumindal. When the war was declared, hope spread across the land faster than any plague. Even my Da' was on the verge of volunteering to fight, had his pitchfork sharpened and everything." Veil issued a mock laugh.

"What happened?" Raiz dared to ask.

"Well, you've probably heard the stories, I suppose they're accurate enough."

Raiz remained focused on her, unblinking in his desire to help shoulder even a fraction of the burden he knew she was carrying.

"Our king was readying to march on Lumindal. He had gathered an army the likes of which nobody had ever seen before. People from all over the country had flocked to the capital at his call to arms, ready to give their lives so that their family might live free of oppression from an unjust ruler. My Da' had just finished arming himself. He looked ridiculous in a uniform." Veil paused to chuckle to herself at the thought.

"But then it came, white-light so bright it blocked out the sun. They say it came from a black tower rising hundreds of feet into the air at the centre of Lumindal itself. The Last Light they call it, a fitting name, I guess. The Light blinded me and my family as it shot through the air. Then there was the quake. Then the screams." Her hand began to shake, so Raiz took it in his own and held tight.

"One moment all was well, Hirane loomed over our farm like a majestic shadow. The next I looked up and it was gone. Erased like it had never existed. Replaced by thick clouds of smoke and residual Light. Mother and Da' went to help, to find survivors and do what they could. They told me to run, run fast and run far and not to look back. And of course, I obeyed, but I did look back.

"The Light kept coming, pummelling the capital until it was nothing but a pile of rubble and ash. The army was wiped out in an instant. But the threat wasn't over. Even after the explosion, a wall of Light as thin as fog crept slowly across the land, threatening to envelop us all. I watched as it consumed my parents, turning them to dust. It was then that I really ran, without looking back. I'm not sure if I was able to outrun it, or if I was simply immune to its effects. But the next day I awoke in a wasteland, alone and afraid. Everyone around me had vanished, yet I was still alive. But I was not myself, I had changed. I could feel the power lurking within me. Celik believes that's what caused my 'condition' and I'm inclined to believe him. Ever since then I've been able to wield the Light, but am unable to vent it as you do...until, well, you know. That's my story Raiz. That's why I fight them, and that's also why we must be careful who we choose to bring with us on our course to vengeance."

Raiz's tongue refused to move, so caught was he for words. He had been fighting beside her for so long without even a second thought to anything other than his own selfish desires. He embraced her, wrapping his arms around her and refusing to let go. For now, that was all he could do to lend his comfort. But for the first time in a long while, Raiz was beginning to understand the reason behind his father's indecision all those years ago.

Chapter 5
Isha

"W — what is this place?" asked Maitreya over the clash of swords below, her eyes reflecting the light of a dozen different colours ranging across the entire spectrum as her head roamed in semi-circle.

"It's the Luminarium," Isha said. "Don't be fooled by its beauty, this place is a death pit."

"Fanciest death pit I've ever seen."

Isha sighed. "It's nothing but an elaborate ruse, a trick of the light where the sun shines against a series of coloured panes of glass." Isha cleared her throat, staring into the circle of sand below surrounded by rows of empty seats, each higher than the last as they worked their way towards the ceiling where stone met glass.

Her vision rested upon a streak of black stretching into the cloudless sky, the sight of the tower unavoidable, causing her gaze to linger longer than she would have liked.

"And what about that?" Maitreya asked, her line of sight

matching Isha's own. "I saw it from a distance when I was first taken here, but now that I'm up close... I don't even know what to say."

"You needn't say anything. That thing is a weapon. The Last Light of Lumindal. You would do well to stay clear of it."

"But it's so big. I can't even see the top! How does stone reach so high without toppling? Surely there's more to it."

Isha grumbled. Small talk irked her. Though she supposed anything would be better than the mindless task of sitting still and looking proper while her ill-mannered and arrogant pig of a 'master' fraternised with equally self-important and egotistic company. "They say the inside of the tower is moulded with solid white-light and crafted with peridium. Made by the first King-Radiant and his followers over a thousand years ago."

"The idea seems ridiculous, almost unbelievable even. Yet I can't deny the sight before my eyes," Maitreya said.

Isha shrugged, her care for Maitreya's curiosity lower even than her care for the barbaric, testosterone-fuelled violence on display below.

Out of the corner of her eye, she saw Averardus lean over the railing and raise a balled fist. "Marvellous, just marvellous! I have had my eye on that one for quite some time. He will make a fine edition to our company, would you not say Argon?" Averardus said, staring out from his balcony to where one man in a shiny suit carrying a sword had pinned another. Isha rolled her eyes, caring naught for the spectacle and hoping he would pick one already so she could get out of this place.

"Young Kitt will make a competent warrior, I am sure," Argon said, the sturdy brute of a man standing tall in his fitted plate of black and gold.

"Yes yes, a fine addition indeed. Do not hope to steal this one from me Adela. I am afraid he is a touch too unruly for your tastes."

The two Eagles relaxed on their cushioned seats across from one-another. Despite their long-standing rivalry, the two seemed to revel in the competition, finding pleasure in each other's company as they each worked to undermine the other however they could.

"Oh Averardus, but I like my men thick and full of vigour," Adela said with a wink.

To her side, Isha saw Maitreya place two fingers in her mouth and pretend to gag. She couldn't help but stifle a laugh, which was a refreshing change from the constant frown she usually wore.

Panic sparked deep within her chest as she caught Argon staring in their direction, watching Maitreya continue her silent protest. For a moment Isha thought it was all over, that her life was forfeit. But the heavy-set guard did not act, instead he gave Isha a warm smile before returning his attention to the two Eagles it was his job to protect.

Maitreya must have noticed as well, for her face turned pale, all thought of further ridicule vanishing. Isha was beginning to grow a layer of respect for Maitreya. Or was it sympathy? She couldn't tell. Ever since Averardus had revealed how he acquired her, she could think of nothing but her own family dying a bloody death while she was forced to bear witness. It made her feel somewhat better about her own situation. Her family was at least still alive — she hoped. But those selfish thoughts were quick to leave her mind, replaced by a strong desire to protect Maitreya.

Isha wiped a sweaty brow before cuffing her ears with her hands as Averardus chewed on an extra chunky piece of red meat, spitting pieces to the floor as he spoke. "Bring up the next batch! I wish to inspect them myself," he said through mouthfuls.

A slave girl younger even than Isha ran off to convey the Eagle's message. Another ran towards Adela, whispering something into her ear before departing quicker than she had come.

Isha watched as Adela frowned before raising her left eyebrow. She eyed Averardus — who was still caught up in the spectacle below — before rising from her seat. "Ahem, I apologise dear, but I grow bored. The constant racket of metal upon metal does not agree with me today. Will you excuse me?"

Averardus waved a dismissive hand. "Do as you wish, it is not my concern."

Isha watched her go. Was her life here really so bad? There were slaves in this world far worse off than her. She could have been put in the salt mines up north, forced to dig for the rest of her existence, likely dying in some hole no one would ever find. She could have been put on the rice plantations to the east, forced to harvest rice all day every day with little to no rest. And yet here she sat, at the top floor of the Luminarium — the most beautiful building in all of Zapour — doing nothing but existing, her only labour surviving her own self-destructive thoughts.

She turned to her right. Adela had departed in such haste that she had left her prized slave behind. Isha watched as the giant from Wisha fixed Obeyun with a stare so intense she nearly flinched away at the sight. Adela had not been lying about his size. If there were such things as giants, then he was as close as they come. Perhaps not the fifteen-foot-tall giants from her childhood bedtime stories, but his eight-foot frame was enough to frighten even the hardiest children. His skin was deep ebony, a whole shade darker than half of Obeyun's own.

Even in his hunched form sitting against the wall his bulk was overbearing. His limbs dangled to his sides like wide branches from a tall tree. He was a marvel, the tallest person she had ever laid eyes upon.

His stare was unrelenting and Isha could tell it was beginning to unnerve her long-time friend. Finally, he channeled his intensity into words. His common-tongue was broken. He spoke slowly, and took care with every syllable, but his words were understandable enough.

"Prince, live. Is you, yes? Obeyun of Wisha."

Isha's face scrunched as she stared back and forth between the giant and Obeyun.

Obeyun's face twitched, but his focus remained fixed on the small pebble he had been mindlessly using to scratch into the stone. "You are mistaken. I am no prince, I am a slave."

"Is true, I sure. None other have what you have. Long time me seeing you. Many days passed. Many deaths your brother has made."

It was just a moment, a flicker of emotion. But it was all Isha needed to see through Obeyun's careful facade. A moment of hesitation at the giant's words before returning to his pebble. He issued no response.

"I know what eyes see. Ajani sits as War-Chief. Holds wooden crown. Is very bad to be of Wisha now."

The giant man relaxed, closing his eyes as if he had said what he needed to say and that was the end of it. Isha looked over to Obeyun in a new light. He rarely talked about his past, but a prince? Surely this man was mistaken.

Before she had the chance to digest this piece of information, the rhythmic pattern of metal boots pounding on stone flooded the balcony as five soldiers dressed to the neck in polished plate made their way towards the central platform.

Of the five, four were coloured silver. They stood with straight backs, arms to the side, heads stiff as stone. The fourth was outfitted in the black and gold of a Golden Talon. The same as Argon. He held a certain aura of authority in his stance. His groomed facial hair and sharp set of eyes were complimented by the golden crest of an eagle's talon upon his breast. She knew his name from previous meets. Captain Haylin of the fourteenth division.

She had been through this before. Every year it was the same. Recruits and conscripts from the far corners of Zapour would do battle in the arena. The most common, those who failed to live up to expectations, would likely end up as a Blackwing, a regular foot soldier in the King-Radiant's legion. Those who stood above the rest were either recruited by a captain to serve as an apprenticed Knight of the Golden Talon, or were headhunted by an Eagle to serve on their personal guard. Of course, with Averardus' ego, he recruited nothing but the best of the best.

"Lord Averardus," Captain Haylin said, stepping to the side. "I present to you, my students."

Averardus shoved a crisp potato into his mouth before walking over with the gait of a man who had seen the ceiling in his bedchamber more than he had the outdoors. He inspected each closely, his gaze drifting to one on the left. "What is wrong with him?" he asked.

She couldn't see it before, but now she couldn't look away. The man in question did not falter. Long dark hair fell in waves down to his shoulders. But it was his eyes that caught her attention. Blue orbs brighter than a clear sky. However, one was strange, it pointed to sky while the other sat in the centre. He stared into space. His jawline was sharp and well defined, his features hard and rugged. Even with his wayward eye he was quite handsome.

"Has a lazy eye," said the instructor. "I assure you it has no bearing on his skill with a blade."

Averardus looked from the instructor back to the man in question. "What is your name?" he asked.

The man gave no response.

"Do you have a death wish? I asked you your name."

The instructor stepped in, waving a cautious hand. "Apologies, my lord. He is a mute. His name is Puk."

"A mute?"

"Yes, someone who does not speak."

"I know what a mute is, do not patronise me."

Captain Haylin went pale, abstaining from making any response.

"What use to me is a mute with a lazy eye? I expected better from you, Captain."

"W-with respect my lord, Puk will follow any command without question. I purchased him from the Thousand-Shields Company across the sea. All have their tongues cut out from birth and are drilled and disciplined all their life. His loyalty is unmatched. And he does not have the voice with which to protest. Please allow me to demonstrate. Puk," he turned towards his disciple, "draw your blade and cut off your little finger."

In one swift motion Puk's hands were clutching a long knife drawn from his side. He moved immediately to sever a finger from his left hand.

"Stop!" demanded Averardus. "I despise the sight of blood. If his performance in the arena is to my liking, he will do well."

Puk sheathed the blade, returning to his previous stance as if his mind were not his own.

Isha felt a pang of sympathy for him. Was he this way on

purpose? Blindly loyal to any source of authority? Or was he as broken as she was? Battered and beaten until his will to fight vanished along with his voice. Somehow, she knew the answer already. She had a feeling about him, a sixth sense she couldn't explain, yet couldn't deny.

The instructor continued for another few moments, droning on about the abilities and exploits of each of his students, but she was no longer listening. Instead, she focused on Puk, wanting only to figure him out. To see if he had a personality of his own. Perhaps she was just bored and looking for a hobby. Reading people was what she did, and she hated when somebody came along that she was unable to see clearly.

Puk's bout was over before it had begun, with him dismantling each foe like wind to an autumn leaf. She watched with fascination as he was ushered out of the arena. After that, the proceedings were a bore. Isha yawned as steel clashed against steel over and over again, until it was all just one continuous itch at the back of her brain. She didn't care much for sword work, that was more her older brother's game. Come to think of it, she had never quite found her passion in life. Kind of hard to explore and expand your interests with your neck tethered to a chain.

Eventually, Averardus had seen enough, calling in the combatants. Bathed in sweat they rushed over to be judged, each one of them hopeful. Argon looked on with honed eyes, arms crossed as he studied and gauged each of them even as they approached.

Before they could get started, however, a jittery slave girl hastily approached the balcony. She spoke with a shaky voice as she struggled to catch her breath. She knelt on one knee. "My extreme apologies, Master," she said in between breaths.

"What is it?" Averardus snapped. "This had better be worth interrupting my examination, or you will pay with your head."

"It is Lord Saerus, Master."

"Lord Saerus is dead."

"Yes, he is. They are auctioning off his collections as we speak. Eagle Adela is already present. I came here as soon as I found out."

Averardus' nostrils flared. "Why am I only hearing this now? That crafty snake," he said, swiping the air with weak arms. "Argon, Haylin, with me. I trust your students to keep watch over my slaves." He eyed Haylin as he spoke. "This matter is urgent. Not a hand is to be laid upon their heads."

Without another word he rushed down the stairs, nearly tripping on his own feet in his haste, the two knights hot on his heels.

The four remaining students stared at Isha, Maitreya, Obeyun and the giant from Wisha with blank expressions. The moment stretched, growing more awkward as time passed. Eventually they turned, their interest waning into nothing. Only Puk remained, staring at them with a vigilant expression.

One of the soldiers thrust a gauntleted fist onto the railing. "I've had enough of this. I'm no babysitter," he said, his voice thick and grating. He was taller than the others, with broad shoulders and a barrel for a chest. He had a hooked nose and greasy black hair. If Isha were to guess she would pit him as a man from Kogon.

"Easy Ray, don't wanna be get'n on no Eagle's bad side now," said another, moving to calm him.

The soldier named Ray licked his lips, pushing past Puk to hover over Isha. "She's a pretty one," he said. "Could have some fun with her." He looked around, arching his neck to make sure nobody was watching.

Isha withdrew into herself, crossing her arms over her chest as her breaths came short and sharp. She had endured a lot during her time with Averardus, but no one had ever touched her. She hadn't prepared herself for the possibility, not since she was first taken. She tried to speak, to protest, but all she could do was gasp and yank at the chain tethering her to the wall.

Ray took another step forward. Obeyun moved to intercept but was tugged backwards by the heavy metal. "Averardus will kill you if you lay a hand on her," Obeyun said.

"Shut up, Wishan scum," Ray said, descending upon Isha.

Isha closed her eyes, all the fight she thought she had vanishing in an instant. She opened them to see a firm hand grasping Ray's shoulder. Puk thrust the sturdy man backwards with one pull of his arm, sending him stumbling into the railing.

Ray wasted no time recovering, drawing his sword and pointing it at Puk. "You'll pay for that. Ambrose, Leo, you saw what he did. Can't be having that. Are you with me?"

The other two soldiers shared a look and nodded. Ray was clearly their unspoken leader, and they would heed his authority like cubs to a lion.

Nevertheless, Puk remained unmoving.

Ray rushed at Puk, his sword held high. He poised for a strike, but in the last moment side-stepped. He skipped past Puk and swung his sword down straight for Isha. She closed her eyes, preparing herself for death. She opened them to find Maitreya, her body in front of Isha's own, covering her like a bear as she braced for impact. The two of them stood frozen as the sword stopped still, with Puk's hand gripping the assailant's arm.

The attacking soldier stood stock-solid, arms dead-locked in place. A sly grin creased his lips as the other two soldiers moved in to punch Puk in the ribs, doubling him over.

Instead of succumbing to pain as most would from such a blow, Puk thrust a fist into Ray's face before kicking him in the chest, sending him flying to the floor.

Maitreya let go of Isha, the two letting out a breath as Puk watched the soldier scramble to his feet. He snarled at Puk through gritted teeth.

"You'll pay for that, you bastard," he said, spitting blood.

Ambrose and Leo fanned out into a semi-circle around Puk, their blades drawn. "He doesn't have a blade," one of them said.

Isha realised he was right. Puk had left his sword on the sands.

Ray snorted. "I'm not about to give him one." He walked over to the corner where a bucket of utensils sat. He pulled out a large wooden cooking spoon and threw it on the floor before Puk. "A fighting chance," he said.

Puk stared at the wooden spoon and then back at Ray. Defiantly, he picked up the spoon and held it above his head. With his legs spread into a defensive stance he readied himself to face the three men.

In a flare of anger, the three charged. This was no training exercise. Their swords were not blunted, they were sharpened to a deadly edge.

Isha felt her heart pounding in her chest, fearing the new subject of her curiosity was soon to be laid to death.

With the slick movement of a professional at work, Puk weaved his way between each of the oncoming cuts and jabs. He slapped the rounded edge of the wooden spoon hard against the face of the soldier with the already bloody nose, sending him collapsing to the ground.

The other two came at him with increased vigour, keen to

avenge their comrade with a series of sloppy strikes. At least, Puk made them look sloppy as he moved past them with ease, tripping a foot as he swept his leg across, following with jab to the head with the other end of the spoon this time.

The last remaining soldier cursed under his breath. He launched himself desperately, but again found no bearing as Puk stepped to the side, using his forehead as a battering ram to smash into his opponent's temple. Before he could recover, Puk tightened his grip on the spoon and thrust it downward repeatedly until the assailant's face was nothing but blood and cracked skin. He dropped to the floor, his curses lost under a gurgle of murmurs.

When Puk was satisfied the deed was done, he relaxed, walking with calm steps back over towards Isha.

Isha flinched, taking a backward step behind Maitreya. But Puk did not pursue. He simply stood tall, a good five feet before them, his bloody spoon still gripped firmly in his hand.

Isha breathed a deep sigh. She studied him further, her violet orbs meeting his one blue one. She was now more eager than ever to understand him. She wanted to know what made his loyalty so unwavering. The longer she stared, the more Puk began to unravel, as if through her gaze alone she could peel back the layers behind Puk's facade. There was a decent human hidden there. Covered by a lifetime of hatred and neglect perhaps. But if she could find him, she may be able to use him to escape.

Chapter 6
Dazen

A sea of black covered Illidor, sprinkled with a thousand stars that smiled down on the city while Zur slept. Dazen stretched his legs, waiting patiently upon the oaken bench in hope his betrothed had received his invitation to meet. After further thought, it made sense to gain such a powerful ally in the Levic family. And just because he was being forced into marriage, it didn't mean he couldn't at least try to spark up a romantic interest in his bride to be.

So here he sat, in the most romantic place Illidor had to offer — beneath the Shimmer Tree — doing nothing but holding his breath and waiting as the cold of the night stiffened his limbs, and the stretching of time troubled his thoughts. Echo had promised to deliver his letter, so now it was up to her.

The night grew old as Dazen lounged in an awkward slump, abandoning all of his princely postural training as embarrassment seeped into his very bones.

He watched from his high vantage point as the city below slept, the tall curtain wall of stone separating him from the commoners. He used to basically live down there when he was younger. He had many friends in Illidor and not all of them were nobility. But with age came responsibility, and with greater responsibility came a certain neglect towards those of lesser standing. He hated the way of it. The people down there worked hard, much harder than those up here, for their right to live and prosper in times such as these. He would change much when it came his time to rule.

He moved to leave this place of romance, all thought of love squashed beneath the weight of his father's principals, no choice left but to marry for political reasons. Trost and Zuton needed each other if they were to survive the current King-Radiant's regime. Dazen was done waiting for his betrothed to show up, and he was not the sort to give second chances to people with petty excuses and false morals, for he lived and died by the sword.

"Why, I hope I haven't kept my prince waiting," a voice sounded from behind. It was calm and soft, reminding him of his mother.

Dazen bolted upright. Usually, his senses were better than this. How had he not noticed her approach? He could feel the warmth of her breath upon his neck.

He twisted his body, half-stumbling to his feet as he made a mockery of an attempt to bow.

"Lady Sumaya, I thought my letter lost." He looked up with watery eyes. He felt himself fluster as the Shimmer Tree above bathed her in light, highlighting her beauty. Her skin looked soft, reflecting her youth, but its colour was perhaps a shade darker than Echo's own honeyed complexion. She had tied her hair neatly into a bun, piled together with a series of golden pins at its top. If he were to guess, he would say it would flow down to her hips when set free. Her dress was a simple green make, trimmed to fit her tight figure, though loose enough at the bottom to allow her to move freely. She had a regal aura about her, one befitting her rank. Her arms were well defined, even muscular. She held a calloused hand out in greeting, which Dazen took in his own, masking his shock with an awkward smile.

"Echo did as promised. Though if you are wondering at my tardiness, I make no apologies. I was testing your resolve," she said.

Dazen straightened and resumed his princely posture, his clumsiness all but forgotten. "Testing my resolve?" he asked.

"Yes, you see I can be quite temperamental. If a man cannot wait a few hours in the dark of the night for me then I doubt he can handle me when I'm at my most vulnerable."

The outline of his nose twitched upward along with his brows. "You act as if we have a choice in the matter," he said.

Sumaya's lip curled into a teasing smile. "I suppose we might not, but a woman has a right to know the man she is to marry, no?"

Dazen let out a light chuckle. Sumaya was hardly a grown woman yet, though there was something about her that intrigued him as his eyes met her own emerald green.

"What is your first impression then?" he asked, taking a seat on the bench in the garden and gesturing for her to do the same.

Instead of following his lead, she began circling the bench, talking as she did. "Well, you have patience. Not every man would have waited as long as you, even if the lady in question was me. Patience is good, the difference between a rash decision that could prove fatal, and a calculated move that could prove beneficial. But you lack originality." She motioned towards the Shimmer Tree. "I must hardly be the first woman to share your company here. A tree of lights. It's a little cliche, is it not?"

Dazen rose, unsure if he should feel pleased at her praise, or annoyed at her ignorance. Instead, he opted to educate, moving towards the Shimmer Tree before placing a hand on its thick trunk.

Luminescence danced underneath the bark as if it were burning from the inside, only his hand did not falter beneath its touch. He followed the bubbling light along the trunk through to its branches, his hand brushing against the leaves. They shimmered a radiant white, mixing in with the deep green of the leaves' natural colour. "My mother invented Shimmer Trees, before she passed from this world. Did you know?"

Sumaya issued no response.

"It is not an easy task, imparting one's Shine into an object. Even harder to join two opposing forces of nature together so they might exist in harmony. But my mother was no ordinary woman. It was through her will alone that wood and heat can co-exist. She made this very tree herself. Granted her work has little practicality, but it is certainly beautiful would you not agree?"

Sumaya remained calm, but Dazen could tell by the way she looked at it she was impressed. She relaxed her muscles a little, edging closer towards him, causing his chest to tighten.

"So, if it is cliche to court the woman I am to marry beneath the beauty of my mother's work," he continued, "then I must be a cliche. But as to other women sharing this treasure with me," he paused and looked at her, "you are the first."

Sumaya moved with practiced grace as she slid her hand underneath the glowing leaf. "Its touch is both warm and cool. You surprise me, Prince of Trost. My brother told me you were a good man, as well as a competent warrior. I hope you will excuse my assumption that not all great warriors make for good husbands."

"I hope to prove your assumption incorrect." He took her by the hand, gently ushering her back to the bench. "Will you sit with me?"

This time Sumaya sat without complaint, attention focused on him.

"Tell me about yourself?" he asked. "I see Echo's strength of spirit within you."

Sumaya's expression hardened. "If you are trying to decipher which of my brothers I take after, it might satisfy you to learn that I am my own woman. I have neither the cruel persona my elder brothers attempt to portray, nor the soft and fragile heart of Echo."

Dazen laughed. "Point well taken."

He moved to shift the conversation towards a less confrontational topic, when a light caught the corner of his eye. At first, he assumed it to be the Shimmer Tree, but as he turned towards the city, he could see he was mistaken.

New lights flickered in the night, moving together, growing as they drew closer and closer to the palace.

"Torchlights," Dazen whispered under his breath.

Sumaya looked away through slanted eyes, drawn to whatever had caught Dazen's attention. "What is this? Surely this is not another trick to impress me. Because it is not needed, the Shimmer Tree was more than enough --"

"No, this is not me. I swear it. Something must be amiss within the city. They are coming this way."

"What do they want?"

Dazen felt his heartbeat rise as the torchlights gathered closer. "I do not know. I must see to them; they will be at the gates any moment. I hope you will forgive me."

"I am coming with you," Sumaya demanded.

Dazen sighed. "Definitely no Echo in you. I just hope your tongue is not as guileful as the twins."

Sumaya shrugged. "You will just have to find out."

"Fine, but you wait at the gate. And that is non-negotiable," he said.

She nodded. Dazen took off at a frantic pace. Sumaya followed, hands pulling her dress up high so she could run. She had obviously done this before.

Dazen and Sumaya made their way down and around a series of winding staircases, passing by a number of alert guards clad in white plate. Cylindrical turrets rose high from the battlements, each poised with archers and watchmen.

Once at the gate, Dazen motioned for the captain of his honoured White-Swords. "Gale, what is the situation?"

Upon recognising his prince, Gale stiffened, his square shoulders bulging tight against his uniform. "My Prince, the situation is yet unknown. It appears there are a hundred or so men marching towards the palace. They are unarmed but seem to be walking with intent."

Dazen's face bunched into a ball. "That makes no sense. If they truly mean to march upon the palace with a mere hundred, they would at least come armed."

"What are your orders? Shall I send a runner to your father?"

"No, do not bother him. I will handle these men myself. I will take sixty soldiers and meet them outside the gates."

"At once, my lord," Gale said.

Dazen held onto Gale's wrist before he left, looking toward Sumaya and back to Gale. "Mind the Princess a moment, would you? I will not be long."

Gale looked at him longer than a captain should after receiving an order. Gale was more than a captain, he was his friend, and a good man. "Understood," he said.

"Wait a minute," Sumaya interrupted. "You are palming me off, to him!?"

Gale raised a brow but did not speak.

"Would you rather come outside with me to face them?" Dazen said.

Sumaya looked into the blackness outside the gates and then back towards Dazen. "Fine, I will watch from here."

Dazen nodded his thanks. "If anything should go wrong, take her inside the palace and contact my father," he said to Gale.

The captain nodded before standing beside Sumaya while Dazen gathered his men.

The gate swung open with a loud creak as men cranked the lever. "Close it behind me. Do not open it unless reinforcements have arrived," Dazen commanded.

The darkness was eerie. He stood patiently with his men, who had formed into three lines of white, each heavily armed, with Dazen at their head. Archers were poised atop the inner battlements, arrows drawn.

The sound of heavy footsteps filled the dark, torchlight flickering as the mob approached.

Dazen's company held firm. Gale was right, they were unarmed. If it came to combat, there would be a slaughter. But he had no desire to see bloodshed tonight, not on the steps of his own palace. "What is the meaning of this?" he shouted.

The marching mob stopped still. They had no formation, half of them moving into a disorganised bunch, the other half forming a haphazard line.

They issued no verbal response, but it was clear to Dazen they meant no threat. There was no armour, none of the vicious snarling, taunting and hardy expressions you would expect from a rebellion, just panicked shuffling and soft murmurs. They were scared.

"I ask again, what is the meaning of this?"

A man stepped forward, his features hidden in the night's darkness. He wore a black coat and a baggy cap to match, which he removed before he spoke. "We only ask that our voices be heard," he said.

Dazen recognised that voice, his suspicion confirmed as he moved a step closer. "Rich? What are you doing here? If you wish to be heard there are proper channels to go through. This march of yours is edging dangerously close to treason," he said.

"They won't listen!" Rich shouted. "We're patriots, you know this well, my prince. How many times have I harboured you at my inn during your youth? You know me. And you know my brethren. We seek only to be heard."

Dazen hesitated; Rich was right. He owed him this much. To march upon the steps of the palace he must have something important to say. "Very well," Dazen said. "Speak your truth."

Rich nodded. "For one-hundred years Trost has been at war with Zuton. They can't be trusted. You were but a boy when they invaded our lands, murdering innocents and plundering relentlessly. They killed my brother in cold blood, even after the promise of mercy. Many here have similar stories to tell." Others around him nodded and grunted their agreement. "We've tried to speak our truth peacefully, we still try. But Kron won't listen. I fear this sickness has weakened him."

Dazen's expression darkened as he mulled over Rich's words. He thought back to his meeting with Sumaya, to Echo. They didn't seem like bad people to him, just a family caught up in their ancestors' war. "What you speak of is exactly why we need peace. I do not condone what has happened, nor will I forget it. But we cannot live this way. We cannot be ruled by our past. There must be a future without war."

He could see his words having an effect on Rich, though he still seemed far from convinced. "Then what of Lesken?" he asked. "What of the Eagle's death?"

"What of it?" queried Dazen.

"There's more to the tale than you know. I beg of you, hear us out."

Dazen hesitated, then motioned for Rich to continue.

Rich turned, grabbing someone by the cuff of their shirt and gently shoving him forwards. "Go, say what you saw. Dazen is a good man, he'll listen," Rich said to the one presented.

His back was hunched over, and he looked travel worn and in dire need of a wash. He bowed low, coming up awkwardly. "M-my name is Gipp. I was in Lesken when the Eagle perished."

Dazen looked on with curiosity. "You have my permission, Gipp. Speak what you know."

"Y-yes, my lord. It's as I said, I was in Lesken when the Eagle perished. I had business over there, trading to do. The Eagle came for their children, as they often do, but they were attacked by a band of outlaws. These outlaws were strong, extremely strong, led by this 'Red Knight' they called him. His Shine blazed stronger than any I have seen! His right eye was scarred, cut all the way across. An overgrown lizard fought beside him. They were unstoppable!"

Dazen choked on his own breath. It couldn't be. "You saw this yourself?" he said.

"Yes, my lord. Saw him slice through men with my own eyes. But there's more. They were not the one to kill the Eagle. They left him for those in Lesken, encouraged them to take the action upon themselves. Forgive me, but I fear the King-Radiant will seek to lay retribution not only upon these outlaws, but upon Zuton itself."

Gipp filtered back into the crowd as if he had said all he needed to. Rich again took his place. "You see Dazen, this isn't the time to be making peace with Zuton. We can't implicate ourselves in this, for all of our sakes."

Dazen's mouth twitched. News had only just filtered through about the Eagle's death, but if Zuton were somehow implicated in the crime? If the King-Radiant blamed the Levics for the death of his own? The timing could not be worse. They were due to announce his engagement to Sumaya tomorrow. What would the populace think? He clenched his fists, reaffirming to himself he was the sole Prince of Trost, would not be pushed around. Not even by an old friend. But he could sense their anxiety, their fear. He accepted it as legitimate. That didn't mean he had to adhere to their every desire. One day he would be King, and that meant making tough decisions.

"I hear you, Rich, I do. I hear all of you!" he shouted, taking a few steps closer. "But Zuton is to be our ally. If what you say is true, then we will deal with it as best we can, I assure you. I cannot abandon the potential for peace and prosperity with Zuton based on rumour and speculation, even if your man's words are true. There will be an announcement tomorrow. I trust that you will turn to celebration, and not to violence. If you shall choose the latter, I promise you I will not hold back. If you choose the former, then you have my word I will do everything in my power to ensure the safety and protection for all citizens of Illidor and of Trost."

Dazen tightened his jaw, staring each torchbearer in the eye. "Are you satisfied?" he asked.

There was a long moment of silence, then Rich responded, talking on behalf of everyone. "Aye. You are a different man than your father, Dazen. Perhaps a better man than all of us.

We'll lend our support, if that's your decision. But I hope you'll heed my warning. Don't drop your guard, the Levics are a crafty lot, and the King-Radiant has ears everywhere. Best for all of us not to piss him off."

With that Rich and his band departed. "My inn is always open if you find yourself in need of a place to stay," he said, turning back as the torchbearers broke into groups and disappeared into the winding streets of Illidor's inner city.

Dazen let out a large sigh of relief, thankful it was only Rich who he had to deal with and not someone who preferred steel over a levelheaded conversation. Even so, the news from Lesken troubled him. He needed to talk to Sumaya, he needed to talk to Echo, he needed to talk to his *father*. He mulled Gipp's words over in his mind. The description of this 'Red Knight' was far too familiar to simply ignore. But it couldn't be…could it?

Chapter 7
Raiz

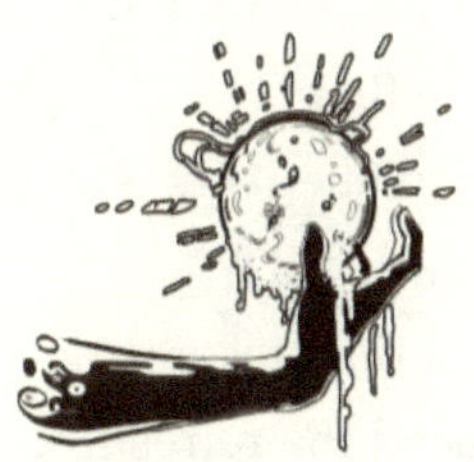

"So, what's the plan?" Raiz asked, poised on a rocky perch.

Veil hummed, arms and legs touching the cold stone below like a frog ready to spring. "What's he even doing out here? Does he know it's raining? Can he even tell the weather through that clump of metal atop his head?"

Raiz shrugged, watching as Draz went through a series of poses. His movements were slow and precise, as if practicing a fighting technique. "He does it before he goes to rest every night. I think it has something to do with where he came from. He'll sit and meditate for a solid hour without moving a muscle some days. He says it helps strengthen his mind. Not for me."

Veil failed at suppressing a laugh. "Anything to do with the mind is not for you Raiz."

He nudged her in the side with a bony elbow, but this only spurred her laughter on.

Once calmed, the two returned to their task. "We could come at him from either direction? I'll pin him down, you force the helmet off?" Raiz suggested.

"Too risky. The rain's made the stone slippery, and the mountain won't prove forgiving if we stumble. We should wait until the light darkens. He has to take it off to sleep, surely."

"I dunno, the man barely stops to eat. And when he does, he just flips open his visor and scoffs his food like a starving pig. I'm sure I've seen him sleep with it on too," Raiz said.

"Doesn't it get hot in there?"

"I'd be more worried about the sweat rash. I'm getting one just thinking about wearing it."

Veil relaxed into a sitting position, letting the rain wash over her face as she embraced the refreshing drizzle. "Why do you want to know what he looks like all of a sudden?"

Raiz's eye twitched, as if he didn't fully understand himself. Perhaps it was just a petty act of defiance against Celik, as if breaking one of his precious rules would anger him. But deep down he knew it to be more than that. Hearing Veil's story the other day had opened his eyes. His companions were more than just people to help his cause, Celik be damned.

Raiz shrugged. "How can I be expected to know someone, to truly trust them, without first seeing their face? Besides, Draz has been a part of this crew for a long time now, I don't want to feel alone anymore. I want to know the people I'm fighting beside."

"We hide who we are for good reason, Raiz. Sometimes it's best not to pry too deep, lest you not like what you see."

"I like you," he said, reaching out with his hand as if he could catch the words and put them back in his mouth.

He noticed her smiling at him before quickly concealing it through narrowed eyes as her expression bore down onto Draz once more. "I must admit, I've always wondered what he keeps under there, though I think an ambush is out of the question. The man is too alert, there's no surprising him, not even if we work together. And a frontal assault won't work either, we don't want to kill the man."

Raiz held out an open palm. "So, we give up then."

"We could always ask him..." Veil offered halfheartedly.

Raiz laughed. "We've tried that a dozen times. The man's hard as stone."

"Ask him nicely?"

"No. Draz is an ex merc. He won't respond to kind words, only swift action. If we want Draz to reveal his true self, we'll have to earn it."

"He'll take it off eventually," Veil said. "We just have to make sure we're there when he does. Meet me back here at full-dusk?"

"Not like I have anything else to do with my time."

Summer's hot breath was fading as the cool winds of early autumn whipped and crashed against the mountainside's sturdy cliffs. Weeks had passed since their battle at Lesken, and still Celik kept them here in hiding. Patience was not one of Raiz's strong points. He wanted to hunt them down one by one, without the wait, without mercy. But if he had it his way, he would most likely end up dead.

Celik was good for him, he was the bow and Raiz the arrow. Even still, there was a growing frustration he was finding hard to ignore. Up until Lesken, they had only ever hunted smaller game. Raiz had been tasked with either the assassination of lowly noble officials or with disrupting enemy supply lines. He was getting quite good in the art of espionage, but he preferred his tasks ending with the blood of an enemy. Not because he enjoyed killing for its own sake, but because he enjoyed the feeling it gave him, knowing their deaths would correct the world and lead towards ending the corruption staining the lands of Zapour. Ever since Lesken, his desire had grown tenfold. Saerus was the big game. He was one of the King-Radiant's Eagles, he was just like the one who took his sister from him.

Raiz was no longer the boy he once was. He didn't have the imposing stature and thick frame of his brother, but his muscles were defined through years of combat training, his reflexes unmatched, and his Shine shone bright.

He had not forgotten his sister's pleas. Her screams still echoed through his mind, fresh as the day he had heard them. He would rescue her, even if he had to march upon the steps of Lumindal by himself. Veil would not be able to stop him next time.

"Raiz," came a whisper in the wind. "Raiz!"

He shook his head, nearly losing balance as Veil crept up to perch beside him. Zur's warmth had long ago vanished beneath the distant horizon, lending her the freedom to do as she wished.

"If Draz is as easy to surprise as you, we're sure to succeed," Veil said. "You're planning something, aren't you. I know your planning face when I see it."

Raiz feigned a yawn. "This is my boredom face, what took you so long? Let's get moving."

The two bounced between rocky surfaces, making their way back towards the cavern, sure they would catch a glimpse of Draz in his pure form. Keeping to the shadows, the pair approached his sleeping quarters with practiced quiet. Their footsteps were masked by carefully dispersing their weight so as to not make a sound above a whisper.

Draz had always valued his privacy, preferring to sleep alone and favouring the metal of his helmet as a friend over others. He slept in an alcove, a small pocket tucked away in the side of the mountain away from the darker depths of its inner sanctum. There was ample footing for the two of them to angle themselves into position, and a reasonably high vantage point for them to stalk their prey. The pale light of the moon shone over Raiz's shoulder, basking the defenceless sleeping form of Draz in a ray of moonlight. A hint of metal glinted against its shine.

"Well throw me in the Abyss, he sleeps with the damn thing on," Veil said. "Always tomorrow, I guess."

"No, we strike tonight," Raiz said, a strange conviction in his voice. This was no longer about unmasking him; this was a testament to his own will. If he could not accomplish the simple task of removing a helmet, then how could he dare to rescue his sister from the depths of Lumindal? "Same plan as before, split and come from opposing angles. I'll try to slip it off while he sleeps. If that fails, I hold him down and you remove the helm, agreed?"

Veil nodded, but something in her demeanour hinted that her dedication was wavering.

Nevertheless, the two parted, moving like assassins in the night. Only they had no intention of killing their target. Killing Draz would have been easier, much easier in fact. Death was natural to Raiz now. He was unafraid to take life. Though he had not succumbed so far that he would kill to amuse his own self-interests. To do that would be to admit he was like *them*. That was a fate far worse than death.

He bent into a low crouch, now level with his target. He crept forward until he was close enough to see the eight tiny swords etched into the black lacquer which coated the metal of the great-helm. It was of simple make, with small rivets outlining its rim where sheets of metal layered on top of each other. Draz currently wore no other armour, though a soft blanket was wrapped around his body. The thick helmet was intimidating, and Raiz could hear the steady pattern of breath against metal as Draz slept.

With hands like a healer, Raiz felt underneath the helm, searching for a strap or a pin he could pull free which would lead to its easy removal. He felt a sudden unexplained weakness take hold of him, similar to when he expended too much Shine. He jerked away from the helmet, the feeling vanishing and his strength returning. He hovered his hand over the metal, watching as it wavered and vibrated, then lowered his arm, again reaching beneath the great-helm for a strap to release.

He smiled as he unlatched the chinstrap with relative ease. He could feel Veil's presence burning into his side from the shadows. She was ready to pounce if needed.

He was tempted to just lift the visor. It loomed ominously beneath his hands. An easy target, all he had to do was lift it and catch a glimpse of his face. But Raiz was not content with half completing his task. He wanted the whole helmet off.

Draz rolled to his side. Raiz hovered both hands in the air as if he were about to throttle the man. Once he was sure he was still asleep, he re-adjusted his fingers, placing them delicately underneath the helmet so that he had enough leverage to pull. His hands physically ached with the task, the Light he had previously stored in his body seemingly non-existent as felt the helm begin to slide.

He was going to do it, all while Draz slept. A knot of guilt swept over him at the thought of unmasking the man so casually. But it vanished as quickly as it had come as his excitement began to pique.

One more inch and he could whisk it away smoothly, his task complete.

His wrist burned as something clasped onto it like a shackle pulled too tight. For a moment the night was still. He remained an inch away from his goal, but he found himself unable to move. Then realisation dawned upon him, Draz was awake.

"If you wanted a kiss from Draz, you could have just asked."

Four bare knuckles crashed into his prone face, causing Raiz to let go of the helmet and stagger backwards. Draz's hand was still firm on his wrist. He bounced back as if on a string, another knuckled fist connecting with his cheekbone even more powerfully than the last.

Instinctively Raiz twisted his body, shaking loose the grip on his wrist. "Veil, now!" he yelled.

Like a cat on its prey, she pounced. She was best with a dagger or a bow, but Veil could be scrappy when she needed to. She clung to his back like a leech, refusing to let go by hooking her arm around his and pinning it in place.

Draz muffled a laugh through the visor before reaching an arm over to catch Veil by the back of her shirt. With a heavy grunt and no small amount of exertion, he flung her forwards, sending her crashing to the ground below and toppling into Raiz.

Draz may have been small, but he was certainly not short on strength. "Draz was wondering when the two of you would crack," he said. "Ain't nobody seen Draz's face in years, not since Celik."

Raiz bounced back to his feet, spitting blood from his mouth. "Celik has seen your face? That selfish bastard."

"Hah! Don't bother. If you can't take Draz while he sleeps, you won't take him while he's awake," Draz said.

"We'll see, I'll turn your precious helmet into a pile of ash," Raiz said as he ran. He feigned an attack to the left before arcing a curled fist from the right. Draz was ready for him, however, blocking his swing with a left-handed chop before throwing a thrust of his own.

Raiz dodged and took a backward step to regroup.

"Use your Shine lad, Draz dares ya," Draz teased.

Raiz stared at him, bemused. Why would he want him to use his Shine? Did he want to die? This fight had already gotten more out of hand than he had expected it to. Now it threatened to escalate even further.

"Use it!" Draz demanded. "Right here!" He pointed a stubby finger towards his head.

He was insane. Raiz's Light would kill him. "You will die," he said.

"Draz will live. Do it! Do it now! If you hit your mark, Draz will reveal his face. Don't be a coward."

"I am no coward!"

"That is not what Draz sees. Do you not want to save your sister? Now be a man, prove yourself worthy."

Raiz saw red. How dare he mention his sister? He knew she was a sore spot for him. Now he was mad. He took one look towards Veil, who had regained her footing. She shook her head vigorously.

Raiz ignored her plea. He raised an open hand and channeled his inner Light. It bubbled in his palm, yearning to be released. The power within him took hold. With a crack, Light burst forth from his palm in a straight line.

Draz did not waver. Raiz felt a great pang of regret. He had killed him, killed Draz, all for the sake of his pride.

But the Light did not penetrate as it did with his enemies. It did not burn, it seemed to... reflect?

Draz braced himself with a wide stance. He let the Light connect with his helmet. It bounced off the metal as if it were elastic, ricocheting into the ceiling and burning a hole straight through the stone.

Raiz blinked with disbelieving eyes. Veil too, looked astonished, her hand covering her open mouth.

"Hah!" cried Draz once the Light vanished. "Told you Draz would be okay."

"You're insane, the both of you," Veil said.

"I — I think I need to sit down," Raiz said, moving towards the mouth of the alcove for some fresh air.

Veil followed, the moon bathing her luminescence.

Raiz steadied himself, his head still dizzy from the helmet's touch. He took a deep breath. "What foreign magic is this?" he called back to Draz, who was making his way over towards him.

"No magic," he replied, tapping his helmet with the point of a finger. "Peridium. Harder than steel, rarer than gold. Strong against white-light."

"Peridium?" Veil said. "I've heard of that before. It's a metal mined in Yagos, extremely valuable even by a king's standards. How did you come by an entire helmet made of it?"

Draz let out a deep sigh. "Long story."

Veil crossed her arms and nodded towards Raiz in a look that said, 'you wanted to know more about him'.

"We want to know Draz, please," he said.

Draz looked from one to the other. "What, first you try to melt Draz's head off, now you want to know Draz?"

Raiz's eyes narrowed. "You baited me."

Draz rolled his shoulders and cracked his neck. "Never tested before now. Good to see it works."

Veil and Raiz again stared at one another with open mouths. "You mean you didn't know if it would work?" Raiz said, bowing his head into his chest.

Draz shrugged.

"How did you come by it?" Raiz asked.

Draz clasped his hands together and cracked his knuckles. "You really want to know?"

"We do," Veil said.

Draz took a deep breath and moved to sit beside the pair of them. "Draz will tell you. But it is not a pleasant tale."

"These are not pleasant times," Veil said.

"Have you ever heard of the Greysword clan?" Draz said.

Veil perked up. "You mean the mercenary group?"

Draz nodded. "Yes, Draz was a Greysword. No, Draz *is* a Greysword."

"But weren't they all wiped out when the Shine-bomb destroyed Hirane?" Veil said, before covering her mouth with her hand. "Oh, Draz, I'm sorry. I didn't think."

Draz sighed, this time Raiz could see behind the mask. There was despair there, even if metal covered his features. "Not all," he said. "Many were killed, yes. But our numbers were high. King Tertius was a great man, but after he failed, and Hirane turned to dust, the King-Radiant branded all who sided with him outlaws. They forced us into hiding as those Golden bastards and the Bloodfeather family hunted us down one by one. Draz's family was the last, we were strong. But even the strong can't run forever. The Bloodfeathers cornered us in Northern Crata. A ruthless lot, cunning and arrogant. They love gold more than any merc. Long have they served the King-Radiant. Draz's father and uncle fought them, fought well. We thought we had won. We thought them all dead. We were wrong."

Raiz leaned closer, not wanting to miss any of the story through his muffled voice.

"Draz's father removed Gallant," Draz pointed towards the helmet on his head, suggesting that was its name, "thinking us victorious. He moved to give Draz Gallant — a relic of the Greysword clan — as a gift so that Draz would grow into it and fight alongside him one day. That was when it happened." Draz paused, leaning his head on his shoulder as he clenched and unclenched his fist. "White-light faster than any arrow ran through his eye. He was dead before he hit the ground."

Raiz and Veil let out a simultaneous gasp, their eyes wide with shock.

"Draz's uncle killed the man who felled him, though he too paid the ultimate price, as did the entire clan. Draz was left alone. If Father had not removed his helmet, he might have survived. We could have rebuilt the Greysword clan. But no, now Draz is alone, and Draz will not make the same mistake."

Raiz withdrew inside himself. All this time he thought he was alone in his anger. In his selfish mindset he believed he was the only one who owed their oppressors a debt of blood. He took heart in the knowledge that there were others out there with similar motives, a similar purpose.

"But Draz keeps his word," he continued, moving two hands beneath his helmet. "Some fresh air will be good spent among…friends."

"No!" Raiz protested. "I mean, suddenly I have lost all desire to see your ugly mug. I think the world is better off hidden from the sight of whatever lurks beneath Gallant a little while longer."

Draz let the helmet drop back to rest upon his shoulders. "Bah! Young Raiz is just jealous Draz will steal all his fame and women!"

All three of the gathered companions burst into a fit laughter, during which Raiz and Draz shared a look of unspoken respect. Step-by-step Raiz was beginning to understand them as more than just people to use as pawns in a game against his enemy. They were his friends. Celik be damned.

"I would raise a cup to drink, but I'm afraid I —"

Raiz stopped mid-sentence, sensing movement within Gallant's reflection. "There is someone watching us."

The three grew still, as suspicion heightened their senses.

"On three," Raiz whispered. "One, two."

They pounced, using their legs to propel themselves backward with extreme speed. A shrill shriek sounded from the direction they headed. A boy no older than thirteen lay crumpled on the rocky mountaintop, his hand clutching at his ankle. The sight of the three charging at him must have startled him.

"I'm sorry, I'm sorry! Don't kill me, please!"

Raiz, Veil and Draz stood in a state of confused readiness. "Who are you?" Raiz shouted. "How did you come by this place?"

Before he had the chance to answer, Draz beckoned towards the expanse of plains beyond the mountain. They were distant and a light fog covered their number, but there was no doubting their banner. Crimson red streaks of silk littered the landscape in organised patterns. It had been a long time, but Raiz would know that standard anywhere. He would never forget the stench of Craw.

"That's the Saelmere standard! They've found us. The boy is a spy!" Veil shouted.

Chapter 8
Isha

Isha stared out into the open city of Lumindal. She stood atop the Forty-Fourth Spear. With fifty Spears in total, Averardus' home was near the highest point in all of Lumindal, rivalled only by the six Spears above and the Last Light itself. Towering works of architecture well beyond their time, the massive pillars of stone shot up into the air, which from an outside perspective made it look like a giant crown, circling around and rising so that the tallest were at the middle, with the King-Radiant's weapon of destruction the centrepiece. The tips of each tower pointed skyward like the sharp end of a spear.

There was a reason people called it the City of Light. The Spears were coated with a thin layer of breen — solid white-light taken from excess Shine. To most, breen had little practicality, but there were rumours its surface protected against ancient magic, including blasts of Shine. The breen coating was like a sponge to light, drawing it in and making it glow. Even in the moon's light it glowed bright, taking on more of a greenish tinge.

Each Eagle held residence in their own Spear. The higher the Spear, the greater that particular Eagle ranked in terms of importance.

Isha cared naught for politics. In her mind they were all animals. She didn't even think it mattered which one bore a higher ranking, they all held the same power, were all as untouchable and as rich as each other. But to them it was all a game.

She pursed her lips and sighed, her breath trailing out into the city winds. She would never tire of looking at such a majestic work of art, the city's beauty tainted only by the people within.

She closed her eyes and began to whistle. It was a soft tune; she much preferred the graceful melody of a slow and meaningful song to that of an upbeat one. It reminded her of peaceful times, when she was a child unburdened by responsibility and, well, slavery. Her mother had sung her this tune, Three—

"Three Birds and a Fly," came a voice.

Isha's lips tightened, her song fading to nothing as she whipped her head around. She gawked with an open mouth as she saw Argon standing there, frozen as if he had never spoken a word. He was dressed in a padded black arming coat, emblazoned with the crest of a golden eagle, which had been stitched into its breast, feathery wings outspread and stretching towards his neck. He had short-cut brown hair and wore no readable expression. His eyes burned into her own with an intensity she likened to her father.

"What did you say?" she asked.

"Three Birds and a Fly, the tune you were whistling," Argon said.

She gave him a puzzled look before shaking her head and making herself look busy by fumbling with an ornament laid on the balcony table.

What had that been about? Was he talking to her now? She was his captive. She a slave and he a captain of the most prestigious company in all of Zapour. Why speak now? After all this time.

Her curiosity piqued, she turned back to face him, but found herself short on words.

Eventually she found her courage. "My mother sung it to me when I was very young, before she passed from this world."

A hint of movement touched Argon's lips as they twitched upward. "Aye, my sister would sing it to me in our youth. Poor fly never had a chance."

Isha arched an eyebrow before huffing a surprisingly not forced laugh. She studied Argon. Now that she looked at him properly, he was likely only ten years her senior. Though his square head, firm jaw and deep-sunken eyes coupled with his large frame added a few extra years to his look.

"So, is this a thing now?" she queried. "We can talk to each other? I was beginning to think you a statue, another decoration for His Holiness' house of leisure."

"I would advise against such talk," he said. "If the wrong set of ears were to listen, I would be forced to take action."

Isha's eyes hardened into a cold stare. "Forced? Is your mind not your own? Do you not have free choice?"

"You have a strong will, child. But be careful how you speak. There are things you do not know."

"Then teach me what I need to know. You are not like the others. I can see it. You are not evil, despite what you do. What strips you of your ability to choose?"

She was playing a dangerous game. One wrong word could

cost her. But she held her gaze nevertheless, confident her gamble would pay off.

"It was a mistake of me to speak. You should choose your words carefully when 'he' is around," Argon said, lowering his head as if the conversation was over.

Isha took in a deep breath, accepting his decision. She moved for the second balcony where Obeyun and Maitreya were sifting through Averardus' latest acquisitions.

"Surely these can't be real," Maitreya said. "This painting alone would be worth more than my entire village back home."

Obeyun placed a careful hand on her shoulder. "That is why we must handle it with soft hands," he said, taking the painting from her and setting it down on the table.

"Didn't know you were one to care," she said.

Obeyun sighed. "My opinion means little. What matters is that we do not break what Averardus trusts us to handle. The last slave to mar one of his artefacts met with a slow death."

Maitreya pulled at the collar around her neck. "What about you, Isha? Do you care for his collection?"

"Not in the slightest. I prefer practicality over decoration," she said.

"And yet the two of you are in charge of one of the biggest collections of historical artefacts and artworks in all of Zapour? Staggering."

Isha shrugged. It was true Averardus was well known for his collection and display of anything deemed rare or expensive in this world. Whether Isha had somehow managed to gain his trust, or he just gave her the task to keep her busy, she didn't know. She was the centrepiece of the entire gallery after all. "Good eye for organisation, I guess," she said.

Maitreya eyed her suspiciously. "You know in Craw we have a theory. They say those born with violet eyes are Mystic, or special."

Isha sighed, she had heard that before.

"To be taken in by a Mystic's glare is to be gripped by their spell. Said to hold power over desire, they can coerce even the hardiest of men. If they're strong enough, of course."

Isha listened, her jaw slack.

"I can see that theory doesn't hold water though," continued Maitreya. "Or you wouldn't be here. Even so, there may be some truth to the tale yet," she said with a wink.

Isha mused. What did she mean by that? She couldn't control anyone, could she? She couldn't even handle her own emotions half the time.

"Maitreya, I've been meaning to thank you," she said.

"Thank me? Thank me for what? I should be the one thanking you for getting me this job. Sure beats being on show all afternoon," she said, looking around to see if anyone was eavesdropping.

"For standing in front of me," Isha continued. "When that man came at me with his sword."

"Oh that. It was nothing. The damn thing would have just bounced right off, remember? I would have loved to watch his reaction though; reckon he would have wet his pants!"

Isha grinned. "Do you know why? I mean, do you know why you are the way you are?" she asked.

"Not really," Maitreya said. "Found out what I could do when I was little. It's not very useful, not for a woman like me anyway. My family kept it a secret, for obvious reasons. They told me it had something to do with the sulphur mines back home in Craw. I got stuck down there as a child."

Maitreya turned from her then, fingering a tapestry atop the table. It was clear that memories of her past pained her. "This is amazing," Maitreya said, changing the subject. "Is this a real battle? Surely these creatures are just made up to scare kids."

Isha leaned over towards the tapestry in question. It was a famous piece. Long coloured threads woven with an expert hand depicted a battle of great proportion. "It's the Battle for Lumindal. The last battle of the Shadow Wars."

"Who's this man?" Maitreya asked, pointing towards a man practically glowing with a red light, sitting atop a dragon in full flight, its wings stretching nearly the length of the tapestry.

"That is Gallion Lightfire. He was the first King-Radiant. And this here is his Krono-Dragon, Scale."

Maitreya focused, scanning the picture in a state of awe "Do dragons really exist?" she said, perking up.

Isha turned her head as she laughed. "No, no. Well, I don't believe so. At least no one has seen one since the Shadow wars. I gave my brother a Pricket when I was younger. They are said to be cousins of the great Krono-Dragons of old. But he was the size of a small mouse, nothing like what is depicted here."

Maitreya bit her lip, continuing to scan the tapestry. "Then what are these creatures? The ones he is fighting?"

Isha scrunched her face. "Have you really not heard of the Shadow Wars? It's what our whole religion is based on..."

Maitreya shook her head. "My parents weren't big on religion. Didn't believe any creator ever existed and didn't think to teach me about one neither. The whole concept of Zur and Light and all that never made sense to them. Guess they thought, why believe in something that don't make sense, ya know?"

"Fair enough," Isha said. "Well, I don't know if I believe it myself, but these here are called the Skae." She pointed towards the human-like creatures woven with dark, shadow-like threads who were clashing with Gallion's army. "There isn't much information about the Skae, but they're supposedly born of the shadows. Made by Cova — the moon — or the daughter of Zur. They say Gallion and his followers — who would become the first Eagles of Zapour — used Zur's Light to defeat the Skae over a thousand years ago." She traced a hand towards the top of the tapestry where a black tower loomed above all else. A series of white threads poured from its top, aimed menacingly at the army of Skae. "That's the Last Light," she said.

Maitreya moved a hand over the threads of black back up towards Gallion and Scale. "If Gallion was so mighty, then why is Evanon so guileful?"

Isha waved two hands in the air. "Who knows really. It was a long time ago. The world is a different place now. A lot can change in a thousand years."

Isha's attention shifted towards Obeyun, who was holding a painting under his chin as though it were a long-lost child.

"What is that to you, Obe?" she asked.

Obeyun looked but did not respond.

Isha arched her neck to get a better look. It was a natural self-portrait of a man black in colour. His head was ringed with a crown of a simple wooden make. No precious gemstones studded its width, no golden plate lined its rim. His features were hard and stern, he practically glowed with authority. "Has it something to do with what that man said about you the other day? Were you really a prince?"

Obeyun opened his posture, holding the tapestry so they could again see it. "This is King Augus Sarr. He is my ancestor, yes. Dead for an age, he was the first King of Wisha, crowned by Gallion after he split Zapour into the Six Kingdoms. I do not want him displayed here. It would dishonour his name. These people are not deserving of his watchful eye."

Isha placed a steady hand on Obeyun's arm. "I will see to it he remains under lock and key."

Obeyun nodded.

"Hold up," said Maitreya. "So, what that man said is true? You're a prince?"

"*Was* a prince," Obeyun corrected. "Now a slave."

Isha felt a wave of disorientation wash over her. How could she not know Obeyun was royalty? Eight years the two had lived together, grown together. And he had been keeping it a secret the entire time. It made her wonder if she really knew him at all.

No. Of course she knew him. Obeyun was her friend. So what if he preferred to keep his past in the past? So did she. Rarely did she speak of her time as Princess of Trost. Why should she then expect him to, especially if his memories were laced with as much pain as her own?

Isha felt a sudden need to confess, to spill all of her secrets. "I was a princess, once," she blurted, more for Maitreya's sake than Obeyun's.

"W-w-wait a minute. You're telling me that the both of you are, *were*, royalty?" Maitreya said.

"It would appear so," Obeyun said.

"How in all of Zapour do two royals end up with a chain around their necks in a place like this?"

"It is not uncommon," Obeyun said. "Averardus is a vile man with an appetite for the extraordinary. If there is a prince or princess born special, their royal lineage only increases their value to him."

Isha clenched her fists, knuckles going white.

"Averardus must be powerful then, to get away with something like that," Maitreya said.

"Hardly," Isha said. "It's all a ruse. I've been here for eight years. Their power is blanketed by history. As long as people believe they are figures of 'God', they hold 'His' voice."

Maitreya frowned. "I see. Which kingdom were you from? If you don't mind my asking?"

"Trost. I was taken from Illidor when I had just passed my twelfth year."

"So, a Prince of Wisha, and a Princess of Trost. You have to tell me how you came to be here, or my curiosity will end me," Maitreya said.

"Mine is not a pleasant story," mouthed Obeyun.

"Nor mine," Isha said.

"Worse than having your family slaughtered before your eyes to test a theory?"

Isha and Obeyun looked at each other.

"If you don't want to share, I won't hold it against you," Maitreya continued.

"No," said Obeyun. "I have hidden from my past for long enough. It may be good for me to unburden my shame."

Isha and Maitreya settled into a seat.

"Before I begin, you must understand that Wisha is not like other countries. The high peaks of the Weeping Mountains and the thick forests shelter us from the outside world. We still hold to the old law, and are answerable to the King-Radiant, but many in Wisha resent that fact and wish to be free of his tyranny. As a result, we have been known to be rather 'unwelcoming' to outsiders."

Isha nodded her understanding.

"With the King-Radiant still holding Wisha to ancient oaths and demanding such a high price for our mere existence, many from Wisha hold with them a hatred for those not of Wishan colour.

"I was not always this way," he motioned towards the patchy line where his skin split between light and dark.

"I was born unblemished, my skin the natural black of my culture. I was a great warrior, and my family had high hopes for my future. It wasn't until my eleventh year my 'condition' arose." He motioned towards the white half of his body.

"It started with my hand. I dismissed it as a mere mark, possibly a wound that had incorrectly healed. But as time wore on, it grew. I was forced to wear gloves to cover it. The imperfection had no effect on my health, but the whiteness would not stop. My mother searched all over Wisha for a cure, but no medicine or secret remedy was enough.

"The whiteness spread as I aged, becoming too obvious to conceal. As a prince, and the first in line for the Crown of Wood, people naturally began to question my condition.

"My brother had always been jealous, with me being the firstborn. When my father was killed by wounds suffered early in life, I was to be crowned. But by then I was as I am now. My body, half the white of our subjugator, living in a world dominated by black.

"My brother used this as an opportunity, gathering clans together who shared a similar mind to his own. He shamed me in front of my own people, denouncing my claim to the crown and labelling me one of 'them'. A lie of course. But with my colour and my country's superstitions, an easy lie to believe when told by one with a tongue as sharp as his.

"There were many who supported me still. Wisha was on the brink of a war that would have broken us in two."

"What did you do?" asked Maitreya, leaning on the edge of her seat.

"I did what I thought was right. I left Wisha in order to save it. Perhaps I could have defeated my brother and claimed the Crown of Wood as my own, perhaps not. But what price was I willing to pay? How many lives would be lost in a senseless blood feud?"

Isha clutched her chest, feeling a deep sense of loss. She yearned to see her brothers again, to share her burdens with them. She wanted to see her father, to ask him why, why he did not protect her? Why had he not come to save her? To reclaim her as his own and free her of this chain around her neck. She bowed her head, but found Obeyun's touch beneath her chin, his warm smile lifting her spirits once again.

"Do not despair, it is I who learn from you every day not to give up hope," Obeyun said. "This life will not be our end." He motioned towards their surroundings. "One day I will venture back to my homeland. I must set my brother onto the correct path. It would honour me greatly if I could one day share Wisha with you, Isha."

Isha leaned back. "I would like that very much. I'll have to introduce you to my brothers! They'll like you."

Isha's thoughts turned again towards her brothers. She wondered at their wellbeing. She wondered how they turned out. Was Dazen as tall as Father now? Had Raiz finally managed to control his Shine? Were they both together? Were they even still alive?

Her heart began to race at the thought. She needed to find out for herself, she was sick of merely surviving. She needed to escape, to find them again. Her gaze drifted outward onto the high walls of Lumindal. The city was like an endless bucket. It circled her position all around, stretching for miles until it hit the overhanging outer walls, trapping everything within. She leaned over the balcony.

The Fifty Spears were built atop an enormous stone mound at the centre of Lumindal. She felt as though she were in one gigantic birdcage with no escape possible. She huffed an exhausted sigh, returning inside.

In her haste, she stumbled over a balcony step, her momentum thrusting her forwards. She braced herself for the impact, closing her eyes and hoping her outstretched arms were enough to absorb her weight. But she did not strike the ground. She felt the smooth texture of metal as she thudded into a chest. She thought it to be Argon, Averardus' ever watchful guard was always around. She immediately recoiled, not wanting to give him the satisfaction of helping her. But to her surprise it was not Argon. It was Puk.

He stood tall in his black uniform. Isha tilted her head to see the same eagle stretching the width of his arming coat as Argon's. Puk smiled as he lifted her back to her feet. He was a full-fledged Knight of the Golden Talon now, his golden pin shining bright above his coat of arms.

She quickly patted herself down, offered her thanks and scuttled away. She hadn't forgotten what he had done for her. She would repay her debt to him, even if it meant unburdening him from the false sense of honour whoever was controlling him had made him believe.

Chapter 9
Isha

The streets of Lumindal were a maze, though instead of high-trimmed hedges and winding pathways, the landscape consisted of endless alleyways in between an array of densely packed buildings and too many people to count. Isha stood out like a rabbit in a cage full of lions, her metal collar choking her with each step.

She had no idea why she was here, only that her 'master' requested her presence and was too lazy to come and fetch her himself. She was not complaining, it was a rare occurrence. The chance to walk around the outer city did not come often, and she intended to make the most of it. Every turn she made a mental note, memorising each street and landmark.

She looked over her shoulder towards the Fifty Spears, which were majestic as ever. It felt odd to be outside Lumindal's inner sanctum. She had grown so used to her life high in the sky, it was no wonder the Eagles rarely left their nest.

Lumindal was separated into three major sections. There was the crown — or the Fifty Spears — where only those of holy descent and their army of slaves and guards lived. Next there was the Middle Sector, a ring around the central crown where the 'upper class' citizens or those with more than enough coin to fill their pockets lived. And last there was the Outer Sector. No real barrier separated the middle from the outer, so the lines were blurred. Every time Isha came here she always heard arguments between the citizens of each about who lived where, as if it were the only thing that mattered in the world. Of course, the Outer Sector of Lumindal was the largest, and where the bulk of the population lived, but that didn't stop anyone from aspiring to greater heights. It was protected by a giant wall of stone so high it would take half a day just to climb. She remembered when she had first been taken here, staring up at the Fifty Spears and the Last Light as they poked over the top of the battlements.

Isha struggled to comprehend the sheer size of the place. It must be at least ten times that of Illidor.

Of all people, Puk had been tasked as her 'escort' around the city as they made their way towards wherever it was he was taking her. Flanking him were two Blackwings. Citizens of the Middle Sector clung to the walls as they passed, none daring to venture within ten feet of the esteemed soldiers.

Puk was never more than half an arm's length away from her. It was a rather awkward transition. He was kind, in his own way. He didn't pull too tight, didn't push her forwards or gawk at her through sinister eyes like some of the other guards did. She wanted to talk to him, but what does one even say to a mute? Was she even still interested in him?

She thought back on Maitreya's words to her the other day. She knew it had just been a tale, that she held no real power, but she couldn't shake the feeling there might be an element of truth. Ever since she was a child, she had a talent for reading people, could tell good from evil and draw out the best in a person. She rubbed her eyes as if trying to activate some lost magic before laughing at the absurdity of the idea. She had no more control over people's emotions than she did her own life, else why would she be here?

She stared at Puk through her violet eyes, watching as he went about his task meticulously. She felt as though she knew him. It was similar to the way she looked at Argon, like he was a pure soul trapped behind layers of deceit and oppression, and then shrouded within a well of darkness. Both were good men forced into a life they did not choose.

It was possible she was just being a naive girl, searching for hope in a world full of nothing but anguish and sorrow, but she would not let her situation define who she was. She would not be beaten.

Isha stopped still in the middle of a street, the two Blackwings eyeing her with irritation. Puk nudged her in the back with a light finger, but she refused to move. She turned to face him. "Why do you work for them?" she asked, knowing he could not answer.

If Puk's expression was anything to go by, he didn't understand the question. But she could tell he did. He placed a hand on her shoulder, turning her back around before nudging a little harder this time.

"Hey!" Isha protested. "What if I run?" She turned her head. "Would you run after me? Chase me down the street? I could do it you know."

Puk said nothing, grasping onto her wrist with a firm grip. It wasn't a rough grip, he didn't dig into her flesh, but she could sense the strength in his arm.

The thought did cross her mind to run. If she really wanted to, she could. Hide in the bustle of the crowd, find an alley and wait it out until she could formulate a plan. The city was certainly big enough. But the idea was hopeless, and she knew it. Lumindal was not like Illidor. Blackwings patrolled every street. Working men and women would betray her without even a second thought if it meant escaping the punishment of the law. The King-Radiant showed no mercy; no justice, no trial, just death to any who opposed him. There was no need for the high walls and thousands of soldiers. They were just an illusion, the face of fear. The real fear was what lurked beneath. The fear of losing one's life, losing their business, their family. Punishment keeps people in-line.

"Ugh, fine," Isha said, resuming her march, "but only because you were gentle."

Puk nodded, his one good eye flicking towards a corner where it seemed people were gathering.

For a moment Puk's grip relaxed, and Isha took the opportunity to slide her arm up his wrist so that her hand was now in his. She leaned towards him, pressing her body against his. "I think you deserve better than to be someone's puppet," she whispered into his ear.

Without waiting for a response — or lack thereof — she resumed her walk towards the cluster of people.

Averardus was waiting for her, donning a plain white robe threaded with gold stitching. Wrinkly fingers curled around his golden sceptre as his lip curled into a frightening smile. He was a man who's heart was tainted beyond repair, she did not need a sixth sense to see that. There was no remorse in his character, no compassion, not even respect. He was a man fuelled by lust and want.

He beckoned her over. "My Violet, come, sit by my side while I sentence these sinners and remind those who would betray the King-Radiant what is to become of them should their thoughts turn to action."

The two walked up a series of steps until they were atop a large central podium fixed into the middle of the street. She took her place behind Averardus on a cushioned chair, staring out at the muddled crowd. Most of those gathered were caught up in the Eagles' spell, too narrow minded to see them for what they truly were. Or perhaps they revelled in the malice, Isha didn't know. The others, usually the ones lurking at the back, were here only to show face. They wanted no part in the business that was about to play out but feared for their family and their reputation if they were to be seen as showing sympathy to conspirators.

As the crowd grew, Isha began to grow nauseous. What was she doing here? Who was being punished? She forced herself to look on, though as her senses heightened, she became fully aware of her surroundings.

Sitting adjacent from their own podium was a long beam of metal flanked by dozens of Blackwings standing as a barrier to the crowd. Isha's chest tightened, her breaths coming in short. She knew what that strip of metal meant. There was about to be an execution.

"People of Lumindal, I bid thee welcome," Averardus said as he rose, his outstretched arms as wide as his heinous smile.

The ever-growing crowd roared a cry so loud Isha had to cover her ears. It made her sick to think of other people actually enjoying what was about to happen.

Averardus lowered his hands, silencing the apprehensive crowd.

Isha rolled her eyes until she saw the black of her eyelids. She hated when he spoke publicly, acting all high and mighty as if he were the most important person in the world. She knew the serpent beneath the facade.

"My name is Averardus," he said, booming his voice across the courtyard with uncharacteristic vigour. "I am the Eagle of the Forty-Fourth Spear, and I welcome you all here today, to bear witness to justice."

Again, the crowd roared.

"I am a vessel of Zur, his own Light shines through me. To harm one of us is to harm Zur himself!"

He paused, watching as the once upbeat crowd turned towards each other in a wave of murmurs and hushed voices.

Isha suppressed a scoff. Averardus was well versed in pretending to be powerful. He surrounded himself in an aura of faint light, providing the illusion of a deep power beneath, but Isha was aware of how empty the boast was. Even so, it was enough to draw every eye in an ignorant crowd.

"To kill the God of Light's chosen is an unforgivable crime. It is one that will have ramifications across all of Zapour! Every day that passes without Saerus' presence, this world becomes harsher. We provide the balance necessary for us to survive. Without the King's Eagles to watch over Zapour you risk another age of shadows! Without us, the sun will crack and fade, the moon will rise, and the darkness will return."

Isha watched with a curious eye as people covered their mouths with their hands, turning to one another with panic in their eyes.

"The people of Lesken have committed heresy of the highest order, and those responsible must be punished."

The synchronised march of a Golden Talon company made their way through the crowd as if on cue. In between them walked a line of men and women connected by a thin line of near solid white-light, which curled around their necks and wrists. Isha's mouth hung agape. Shine collars were a brutal form of punishment. Those skilled in weaving Shine could bend and shape it to their will, creating all sorts of objects and tempering the heat as long as their energy and source did not run dry. The sun was high in a cloudless sky, providing plenty of fuel for whoever had control of the collars. Isha couldn't even imagine the pain they must be in. Dirt and grime covered the prisoners as they stepped towards their impending death.

"Let their deaths be a warning to any who should think to defy Zur," Averardus said, returning to his seat upon the podium.

A man stepped forwards from within the ranks of the Golden Talon. He was enormous, towering over the others. He held one hand in the air and wiggled his fingers, smiling as he regarded the prisoners. He must be the one controlling the collars.

As the crowd watched on, their cheer returned. People were throwing rotten fruit and vegetables at the prisoners with no remorse. One unlucky woman was spat upon, a mouthful of tomato splattering over her face.

A silence took hold as the condemned cast their final glare. Averardus inclined his head, nodding his approval towards the executioners.

"They speak lies!" came a cry from one of the prisoners. It was the lady with tomato pasted over her face. She paid it no mind, speaking through the spittle of red. "These beasts are not gods. They are barely even human! I killed him with my bare hands. They bleed just as the rest of us, red blood!"

Isha leaned on the edge of her seat, basking in this woman's courage.

"They preach lies! There is a better way. The Red Knight showed us! They can be defeated! You need not suffer in their wake anymore."

Averardus' lip quivered, his arm shaking as he rose from his seat. "Bathe them in Zur's Shine!" he said, thrusting his arm downward.

The large knight held his hand higher in the air, curling his fingers into a claw. A scream came from the metal beam, soon followed by half a dozen more as the prisoners echoed a painful last cry for help. Isha could see the skin sizzling upon their necks as it burned away the flesh. In a quick motion the knight clenched his fist tight. The screams faded into nothing as the chain of Light burnt right through their necks, severing heads from bodies and sending them plummeting to the floor.

Isha squirmed in her seat at the sheer brutality. But Averardus was not done. His eyes bulged as he turned to face her.

"Show this so-called Red Knight what it means to fight against us. Bring on the children!" Averardus shouted.

Isha's mouth hung open. What did he mean, the children?

Her jaw dropped another inch as a dozen children hooded in sacks with collars of Light were herded onto the metal beam, their shaking forms standing over the headless corpses of their parents.

The cheer dulled, the people of Lumindal's earlier enthusiasm dying and morphing into a silent expression of sheer horror. Averardus wasn't here just to send the people of Lesken a message, he was here to send the world one.

A deep-set panic flowed like a river through Isha's veins. They were going to kill children? She had to do something. She looked over at Argon, his face a picture of disgust just as hers. She looked at Puk next. He was closer. His remained impassive, but she could see the pain beyond, his tears hidden beneath whatever ordeal they had put him through.

"You have to do something!" she pleaded to Puk. "They're just children!"

Puk's good eye shifted to look at her, but only for a moment. He bowed his head, closing his eyes as if it would shield him from the horror.

Her heart pulsed, wrought with the sudden urge to run, to get away from this situation no matter the consequence. There was no chain attached her neck, only a collar. She could do it.

Without giving herself the chance to second guess, she leapt out of the chair and dashed in the opposite direction. She wasn't sure if the high-pitched screams were real or just an image imprinting into her mind. Either way, she cupped her ears with her hands. She ran until her legs ached. In the commotion, none had followed. She ran without purpose, without destination. She thought she was strong enough to sit through such tragedy, thought she could handle it. But as she ran, she found she no longer wanted to be that kind of strong. She embraced the sickness in her stomach, for without it she would be a monster, like them.

As her emotions curtailed, she began to comprehend the seriousness of her situation. She was alone, disoriented in a section of the city she was unfamiliar with. Escape would be impossible. As soon as they noticed her disappearance the entire city would be after her. But she couldn't go back, not now.

Fortunately, her feet had taken her into a more secluded section of the city centre. In place of the bustling crowd and decorated buildings were empty streets and dark shadows. She tugged at her collar; she would never be able to fit in with the chunk of metal acting as a constant beacon. Eventually she gave up. Without a key it was pointless.

She began walking more cautiously, peeking around corners, glancing behind her every spare moment. For some reason the scene reminded her of Raiz, though this time it was her turn to run and hide. If only he were here now. Though she was sure her father and Dazen were taking good care of him.

She stumbled down a shady street, passing a cluster of men shrouded in shadows and watching as their seedy eyes followed her. She quickened her pace, vaulting over broken boxes before darting left and then right through the alleyways. She suspected some were following and risked a glance, proving her suspicions correct. She searched for a weapon, anything that could be of use, but nothing was forthcoming. Instead, she picked up the pace again, turning into a sprint.

Her pursuers were not deterred. Footsteps echoed against the walls of the otherwise silent alley. Her foot landed in a puddle, splashing water over her dress and soaking her shoe, making each step heavier and the ground slippery.

She could hear their grunts and groans now, all sense of stealth and secrecy lost amidst the heat of the pursuit. She began panting, taking quick breaths as she reached the end of the alley and emerged into the open.

Her stomach dropped. All hope of an escape was dashed as she nearly ran headfirst into a solid wall of rock. She looked in either direction, both seeming to stretch for an eternity.

No time to hesitate. With a sure foot she burst to the right, hoping for a miracle. A sharp pain began to form in her side. She was not the runner she used to be, eight years as a captive does that to you.

They were gaining on her. She could see them clearly now. Four delinquents -- likely homeless, chasing her with all the vigour they could muster. Their shaggy trousers and dirt-stained shirts flapped loosely in the wind.

A flicker of movement blurred in the distance. Isha wasted no time, pushing through the pain, forcing one leg in front of the other. The blur became more apparent the closer she stumbled, but the wind hindered her vision and the threat from behind caused her to forgo any sense of caution.

She was almost there, could see forms moving. A sneer from behind fueled her steps. She stumbled again, rising to see a line of children march into a passageway carved into the rockface. She crashed lightly into two older children. They stared back at her with a mixture of fear and shock. One flinched, as if expecting to be punished for something. They were all tied together by a long rope connected to collars around their necks, similar to Isha's own. The scene was similar to the one in city-centre, only she could see their frightened faces this time, and they were bound by metal and not Shine.

"What's going on over there? Why have you stopped?" came a cry from the back of the line.

Isha clutched at the pain in her stomach. She might not have it in her to run any farther.

"What's all this then?" A soldier dressed in the common blacks of a Blackwing approached from the rear. He looked her up and down. "Hey Harris, come have a look at this one, would ya?"

Isha kept her eyes low to hide her identity. She glanced quickly to her pursuers, watching them scatter, not wanting anything to do with Blackwing business. She issued a sigh of relief, but now a new dilemma presented itself.

"Where's your rope?" he asked her.

She responded with a shrug.

Another Blackwing pushed his way through the line.

"What do you make of her?" said the first. "Found her without the rope. Has a collar like the rest of them. But she looks a little old, don't ya think?"

"Bah, never know with these Shine folk. Sometimes they bloom late," the man named Harris said. "Rare, but happens.

We don't have time for distractions, Cap'n said the tower's about ready to pop. This here should be the last lot before it happens. Just shove her in with the rest of 'em, tie her to the back of the line."

Isha moved to protest, but where would that get her? These men didn't know her. She could say she was with Averardus, that might scare them into letting her go. But it was just as likely they would turn her in, and she would be back where she started. She had to admit, she had been curious about the tower ever since arriving in Lumindal. Eight years of living in its shadow, and never allowed to go in. This could be her only chance to see what it was. So, she held her tongue. She would have to figure out a way to free herself later.

The soldier ushered her towards the back of the long line of kids whose fate she now shared. She looked to the mouth of the small passageway; had she run from one tragedy straight into another?

She hated them, hated everyone, hated the world. Who gave them the power to dictate these children's future? To sentence them to whatever cruel horror lurked beyond in that dark tunnel. They were just children. They deserved to decide their own future, to forge their own path in life. She had been stripped of that right. Why should they be too?

Her boiled up anger soon turned to fear as light gave way to darkness. Foot by steady foot they made their way down the slimy tunnel. The tang of wet stone clogged her nose. Rats scurried about their feet. The only audible sounds were the odd shout from a guard and the continuous thrum echoing from deeper within the cavern.

It seemed to stretch for an eternity. The air grew hot and sticky the further they went, as if they were walking into an inferno. Isha's already sore feet flared with pain and her knees began to buckle. They were handed to another two soldiers who shared whispers before squeezing them through a narrow doorway and forcing them to climb a steep set of stairs.

The stairs wound upward in a spiral like fashion. A boy five or so years younger than herself tripped on a slippery step, jerking her neck forward in the same motion. She managed to catch him in her arms before they caused the entire line to tumble backwards in one great crash.

"Just a little farther, I'll see us through this yet," she whispered into his ear.

She didn't know why she made such a promise. She had no means of keeping her word, but it seemed to work, for the boy pushed forward.

Another rough prod poked into her back from behind. "Move!" insisted the sandy haired guard.

Dizziness overwhelmed her as the spiral continued, but dizziness was the least of her problems. What did they want with a bunch of younglings in a place like this?

"In," said the guard once they reached the top.

Isha scowled, keeping her eyes in line with his chest.

"In!" The guard cut her rope before shoving her into a small pocket carved into the stone, shutting the wooden door behind him.

Isha fell to the floor, using her hands and elbows to brace her fall. A man stared down at her, a wide grin spread across his face. He was old, really old. Isha scanned for a weapon, but the man moved for her.

She shied away. The darkness helped conceal the violet of her eyes, but she would rather not risk it, not yet.

"You are much older than I was expecting," said the man, pausing to snort a nose full of snot onto the stone. His features were dim in the dark, but she could see he held a wooden cane in his right hand, which he used to hold himself up. He leaned over, clasping her chin with soot covered hands. Isha squeezed her eyes shut, balling her fist ready for a strike, but the man grunted and backed away. "Usually Shine manifests during the early stages of adolescence, but I admit there are circumstances where the Light comes in the later stages."

Isha bit her lip. What was he talking about? Shine? She couldn't use Shine. That was a skill only her two brothers had inherited. Of course, it was entirely possibly that she would have manifested the Light as they had, but Shine was a fickle concept, often skipping a sibling or sometimes even a generation. According to the texts, white-light used to only manifest in the offspring of Gallion's original Eagles. These days it was much more common, though whether that was because Zur decided to continue to share his gift, or the Eagles just bred like rabbits to a point where Shine became diluted within the general population, was up for debate.

The elderly man clasped his hands, placing the knuckles beneath his chin. "Now, show me your Shine," he said. "Come."

He moved for a small metal hatch fitted into the wall, opening it with a heavy tug. The light was near blinding, Isha had to avert her eyes. The heat was overbearing, her skin prickled, and her nose twitched as the smell of liquid fire filled the chamber.

"Look, see what we have created. You should feel lucky, we are almost ready. Your Shine will be the last," the man said.

Curiosity overwhelming her senses, Isha moved for the hatch. She peered into the pit of light. Her eyes widened. Solid crystalline breen walled the cylindrical chamber. It wound around the inside of the tower, stretching high and low. A couple dozen feet below her sat a bubbling pit of white liquid. She likened it to a volcano ready to explode. She looked around to see similar open hatches just like the one she was peering through. Fresh Light oozed from patches of darkness beyond, pouring into the pit like a molten waterfall. She turned back to the man, who began nodding vigorously.

"Empty your Shine inside, see." He pointed towards the other hatches and grabbed her by the hand. "Empty, everything. I will know if you hold back," he shared a wink with her. She cringed, wanting to plant a fist into his already crooked nose.

Her hand remained stagnant. "I — I don't know how," she managed to say.

"Why it is quite easy, the Light wants to come out, see. Just place your hands into the hatch and will your Shine to its natural course."

"Why children? Why are you doing this to us?"

The old man rolled his eyes, and Isha could tell he was getting frustrated. "It is not your place to question. But if you must know, the Light is more potent in those who have only recently broken. Children soak up extreme amounts of sunlight, so they are much more useful to us than adults. Now don't make me get my instruments, neither of us would like that, I assure you."

Isha began to panic, her mind struggling to formulate a plan. She was about to be tortured for not doing something she was completely incapable of doing. She doubted expressing her lack of ability would change his mind.

"I grow impatient," he said. "You don't want to know what happens when my patience thins! Empty, now! Through your palms."

Isha held out her hands and willed something, anything to happen, but of course it did not. She took a deep breath, fighting off her fear, refusing to believe that this was even happening to her.

"Ahhh, stupid child." He slapped her across the face with a strong backhand. "Looks like I will need my tools."

As soon as the man turned, Isha wasted no time, lashing out with a fist, imprinting four knuckles onto his nose. He rocked back with a shriek, hands over his nose as a fountain of blood ran through his fingers.

"Guards! Guards!" the man cried through muffled hands.

Isha lashed out again, kicking him behind the kneecap with her shin. She thought about throwing him into the pit, but she doubted she could muster the strength, and the hatch wasn't very wide. With another knee to his gut, she burst for the exit.

Before she could get there, the door swung wide and a guard stood in her way.

She looked up. He had long hair down to his shoulders, was strongly built and one eye was strange.

Puk?

Puk moved his index finger up to his lips and motioned for her to follow.

Not having any other choice, she followed his lead, closing the door and leaving the wounded man in her wake.

Puk led Isha back down the spiral staircase, which was surprisingly easy to climb down now that she had been through the pain of walking up it. The two travelled unhindered out into the dark tunnel back towards where she had come from, none daring to stop a Knight of the Golden Talon.

"Wait!" she cried. "Where are we going? I can't go back there. I can't go back to him."

Puk said nothing. He fixed her with a keen stare before tugging on her arm. She had no energy left to fight back, he was far too strong.

Exhaustion began to take her. The tunnel seemed endless, and her muscles would carry her no further. She stumbled, moving to collapse on the cold stone before Puk caught her fall. Without hesitation, he lifted her onto his back and continued forward. There was a sense of urgency in his step. Was he trying to get her back before Averardus noticed? Or was he just determined to do his duty and save his own skin?

She felt his dagger sheath dig into her side. The temptation was there to pull it out, to slide the blade underneath his throat and continue on unburdened. But something stopped her. Perhaps it was the exhaustion, perhaps it was something else. She felt comfortable with him, well, more comfortable than usual at least.

Finally, Puk reached the exit. A tiny sliver of light grew into a larger one as Isha covered her eyes to shield herself.

Something didn't feel right, the atmosphere had changed. Heat lingered in the air and stuck to her skin. A light rumble sounded from below.

Puk placed her on her feet, confident she either would, or could no longer try to escape. They stared up at the Last Light, its height stretching into the clouds. Was she really just up there?

The rumble grew louder and turned into a visible shake. The ground began to tremble, loose stones jumping up and down.

Isha was thrown off her feet as a sudden explosion of Light erupted from the tower with a force greater than a thousand charging horses. Heat radiated from its top, as an intense beam shot forth in a horizontal line. The Light seemed never ending, its velocity causing vibrations that prevented Isha from finding solid footing.

Puk kept his feet, but he too stared in awe as the massive surge of energy poured from nearly the exact spot she had been mere moments before.

Her stomach dropped, churned and then tightened all at once. What was this? Where could such power possibly be heading? Who would even be cruel enough to unleash such devastation? She took a steadying breath. She knew exactly who would be cruel enough to exercise such a vicious assault. In fact, she knew many people, if she could call them people at all.

Chapter 10
Raiz

Raiz was on top of the boy quicker than Veil could draw an arrow, his dagger pitted against the soft skin of his neck.

"How much do they know? How many do they number?" Raiz questioned, drawing a drop of blood which trickled onto his loose linen shirt. He moved the trembling boy towards the edge of the mountain. "Speak now unless you want this view to be your last."

The boy's mouth quivered as he looked to the sharp stone edges below.

"Raiz!" called Veil. "Let him go, he's just a child. He's sprained his ankle, he's not going anywhere. You're not going to get any answers out of him shivering like that."

Raiz relaxed, shocked at his own lust for blood and the feeling of his Shine bubbling beneath the surface. Is this what he was becoming? So enraged that he would threaten a mere boy?

He moved him back onto the surface, watching as he shuffled to a nook in the rockface. Raiz moved to the edge. The mass of soldiers were steadily making their way closer. "They're crawling all over the mountain down there. How did they get the drop on us?"

"I — I'm not a spy. I came to warn you."

Raiz turned, the boy was still shivering, but now that the threat of imminent death had been removed, he had found his voice. Raiz tilted his head. "Why should we believe you? Who sent you here? Was it Ancel? That fiend has always been cunning."

"Wha — who? I told you I'm not a spy! I came to warn you," said the boy.

Raiz studied him further, Veil and Draz taking an uneasy quick glance below before moving to stand beside him. "What's your name?" Veil asked.

"Hector," said the boy, puffing out his chest.

"If you are not a spy, then what is your business up here?" Veil continued.

Hector lowered his head and hummed.

"Speak!" Raiz demanded.

"I'm from Lesken!" Hector shouted. "I saw what you did, to the bad men that came for me. You saved me. Mother was ready to give me up, hand me to the bad men for good. She didn't want to. But I don't think she had a choice."

Raiz leaned in, inspecting Hector with more intent this time. He looked over at Veil. "He looks familiar."

Draz stepped forward. "The boy is of Lesken. One of the children handed to the Eagle. Draz is sure, his shaggy hair and bushy brows give him away."

Hector combed a nervous hand through his hair before plucking at a brow.

"Then he can use Shine, correct?" Raiz asked.

Draz nodded. "He should be sensitive to the Light, yes."

"Show me," Raiz said, turning back towards Hector. "If you are who you say, prove it to me. Show me your Shine."

Hector hesitated. "I — I don't, I'm not sure how to, really. Mother told me never to use it."

He reminded Raiz of himself as a child, burdened with an unfamiliar power that's sole purpose was death and destruction. He watched as a small spark flickered in Hectors open palm, lines of concentration forming on his face.

"That's enough!" Raiz said, moving to cover the boy's hands with his own. "Say I believe you, there is still the question of what you are doing near our camp, halfway up the side of a secluded mountain."

"I want to join you!" he spurted. "They call you the Red Knight, because of your Shine. The people in Lesken, I mean. They think you're a hero! I followed you here weeks ago, when you first left Lesken. I can fight! I'm not good yet, but I'm a quick study! And I'm sneaky. Followed you here and back without being noticed. Well, until now," he added.

Raiz raised a brow towards Veil and Draz, who nodded and shrugged.

"And you say you came to warn us?"

Hector nodded. "Yes, they came into Lesken. Men, lots of men. Too many. Started asking questions. I heard them speaking of you. They're searching for you. They started taking people away, my mother and father and..." The boy lowered his head. "Then they left. All of them. I climbed the city walls and saw their banners, more this time. But they were headed this way. I had to come warn you, you have to leave. And take me with you."

Raiz stared at the clouds. "And did it occur to you," he said at last, "that instead of helping us, you might have led our enemy directly to our doorstep?"

Now it was Hector's turn to stoop in silence. He bowed his head, shaking it slowly.

Veil rose. "We must leave. It's no longer safe. I'll fetch Aroha and Cel —"

Her voice cut off as loose stones tumbled down the side of the mountain, followed by two figures. Aroha was first, her hulking leg muscles sending pebbles both small and large sprawling in random directions. Celik followed, his legs acting as springs as he bounced from rock to rock, his dead arms dangling uselessly at his side. It always amazed Raiz how agile he was for a crippled old man.

"What is the meaning of this?" Celik asked, landing on their level with all the grace of a professional dancer. "Can I not have one night of peaceful sleep without the three of you blowing up half the damn mountain? And who is this?" he nodded towards Hector.

Raiz sighed, guessing the fight between himself and Draz had been louder than anticipated. He looked away guiltily. Here he had been blaming the boy for leading them to the mountain, yet it was more likely they had been drawn by his fight with Draz.

"This is Hector, one of the boys from Lesken," Raiz said.

"Oh, so you're taking in strays now, eh?"

"Wha -- no! He followed us here, I only just met him," Raiz said.

Celik grunted. "No matter, either way you must get rid of him." Celik moved towards the cliff's edge, spitting a fat lump of drool and watching as it drifted in the wind. "Saelmeres, always were too eager to please. They will be on us soon because of your incompetence. What were you thinking, using your Shine in a place like this?" He looked to Raiz, his scowl digging into his soul. "Quickly, we must go. This place no longer holds any value to us. Pack your things, we're leaving."

"And what of the boy?" Raiz asked.

"Throw him off the edge, cut his throat, whatever is easiest. But we can't have him at our backs, he'll only slow us."

Veil stepped in front of Hector. "He's just a boy! He is no enemy!"

"Everybody who is not us, is an enemy, Veil. We are outcasts, nobody will think twice at our deaths. Best you leave your conscience behind, lest it get you killed in the future."

Veil's mouth dropped, clearly not expecting such unwarranted brutality.

Raiz stepped ahead of her. "First you question me about my actions having consequences and now you would kill a mere boy purely because he is inconvenient?"

Celik's mouth bubbled with spittle. "There is a difference, Raiz. Between one small child, and an entire city. Or are you not strong enough to do what must be done?"

Raiz balled his fist. "Why do you fight against them, anyway?" he spat. "What did they do to you that was so terrible it would turn you into this?"

"My reasons are none of your concern. Now if you are done, we must be going, unless you want to fight the nation of Craw all by yourself, hmm?"

Raiz looked back to Hector. "The boy will stay with me," he said with all the conviction he could muster. Whether he really did want to protect the boy, or whether he just wanted to ease his own guilty conscience, he couldn't tell. "He's sensitive to the Light. He could be useful to us in the future, I'll train him myself."

Celik paused to consider, eyes narrowing as he looked from one to the other.

"Let me take a chance on him like you took a chance on me,"

Raiz continued.

"As you wish, but he's your responsibility, I will take no part in his training. Should he slow us down I won't hesitate to leave him to starve."

Raiz nodded, accepting Celik's decision for what it was.

Hector's face lit with excitement as he jumped to his feet, pretending he had not just sprained his ankle.

Raiz couldn't help but give a mock smile. The boy had guts, that was for sure.

Before Raiz's band had the chance to recoup and depart, a line of white-light flashed over the horizon in the distant corner of the landscape.

"Look, a shooting-star," Draz said. "Where Draz comes from, to see one means good luck."

"T — that's no shooting-star Draz," Veil said, her eyes going wide with fear. "That's..."

The mountain began to tremble as an unknown force of nature took sudden hold. The group watched on dumbly as the 'shooting-star' failed to come and go as the stories told. The whiteness intensified, gaining bulk as it drew closer.

Before any of them could comprehend the source of such a volume of power, it crashed into the ground in the near distance. The mountain shook with the impact, chunks of rock rained from above, smashing into the hard stone beneath them.

Raiz lost his footing, scrambling and clasping onto anything he could just to keep himself steady. The sound was deafening. Even from their distance and vantage point he could hear the crackling as Light pounded into the surface like one enormous bolt of lightning, only instead of vanishing, it continued to pour into the ground, pounding it with such force it made Veil's outbursts look tame in comparison.

Veil clutched at her heart. Raiz reached out to take her hand, but she fell to her knees. She had been through this before.

Columns of dust billowed into the air, filling the atmosphere as far as the eye could see. It became hard to tell whether the Light had stopped.

"That's where Lesken is!" shouted Veil over the chaos.

Raiz watched as Hector scrambled to his feet, his eyes deep with sorrow. Tears poured from them like a stream. His hands were trembling so hard they could not even move to wipe them away.

"This is our chance," cried Celik. "We must slip out the side of the mountain while the enemy is pre-occupied."

He spoke with such callousness, showing neither concern nor care for the thousands of people caught up in whatever horror was taking place in what was left of Lesken.

Raiz looked on with bleary eyes. He grabbed Veil's wrist and tried to pull her away, but she wouldn't budge. She sat there, staring. Her eyes grew glassy, as if her soul had been ripped in two and there was nothing left. He pulled harder, lifting her limp form over his shoulder before following Celik's lead down the mountain.

Each step was filled with regret. A city was gone, and it was because of him. Because of what he did. He tried to pass off the blame, to tell himself it would have happened regardless. But he was only fooling himself. He had known about the Last Light and its power. But that had only been theory. He'd had no idea the weapon was this powerful.

Thousands of people were dead, and he was the one responsible.

Chapter 11
Dazen

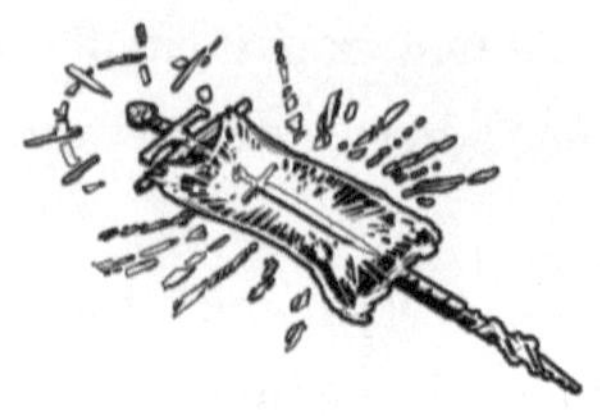

Kron Glaive sat at the head of the high table, his barrel-like chest on full display as he puffed it out with all the composure he could muster. His sickness was a worry of the past as far as anyone present could see. But Dazen saw his confidence for its falsity.

Behind the golden crown glittering with a dozen jewels, behind the tailored silk and leather, behind the bravado, sat a dying man.

The Glaive end of the high table felt empty, with Kron and Dazen being the only two remaining members of the immediate family. His mother was dead, taken at a young age. His sister was lost to a world he would rather not picture, and Raiz had run away — was probably dead. Though he found Gipp's story about this 'Red Knight' interesting. He thought about telling his father his suspicions but decided not to. Not until he was certain. Besides, Gipp's story was likely played up, drawn from his imagination or glorified by Rich to persuade Dazen against aligning with Zuton.

It was now plain to him why his father sought an alliance.

The throne of Trost needed another heir. They needed to expand their reach. The White-Knights of Illidor were stretched too thin. With the limit placed on Shine wielders in each kingdom dwindling to a mere five-hundred after the False Kings War, Trost's strength had been cut in half. The King-Radiant demanded too much. They needed the help of Zuton.

He constantly glanced across the table towards Sumaya, her pleasant smile providing him warmth in an otherwise awkward situation.

Where before her youth was a deterrent, he was beginning to see it as a blessing. Her skin was still soft and pure, hazel eyes bright with energy, and her soul was yet untainted by years of courtly intrigue and deceit.

His stomach dropped as his innocent exchange turned sour when Rayner Levic's hardened expression bore down on him like a lion protecting its cub.

Dazen gave an awkward nod before pretending to stare into empty space.

The Levic end of the high table consisted of the King of Zuton, Rayner Levic, Dazen's wife to be Sumaya seated beside him, and resting beside her were her twin elder brothers Petros and Huet, wearing their characteristic sinister smirks as they peered out into an apprehensive crowd of Glaive nobles. Echo rounded out the Levics, shadowed in the image of his elder brothers as he watched on. He held his head a little higher though. He looked stronger somehow. Not physically, but he seemed more sure of himself, if only a little. His back arched straighter and his eyes were more focused, as if the emptiness beneath had been lifted.

Kron stood, causing Dazen to snap back to attention. Within moments, the chatter in the hall dissipated into less than a whisper as the wine stopped flowing, all those present frozen and ready for the king's address.

"Welcome, family! And all of those I consider family!" His voice boomed across the hall, arms wide in a welcoming gesture.

"Today is a call to celebration! Long have Trost and Zuton been neighbours. Long have we fought one another over petty disputes ending in a tentative peace." He paused to cough, and for a moment Dazen thought his sickness would get the better of him, but he continued unhindered.

"But my ancestors' quarrel with the Levics need not be mine any longer. We can choose to place the burdens of war behind us. Today we announce a treaty of long-lasting peace. An alliance sealed in marriage. The marriage between my son Dazen, and the Levic daughter Sumaya."

The hall grew still as the gathered nobility paused to mutter amongst themselves. Not all would be willing to place their grudge against the Levics behind them. For some, their hatred ran too thick. But Dazen was pleased to see most nodding in approval.

After one started clapping, the hall erupted in cheer, mugs of ale clashing against each other, spilling alcohol across the tabletops. A bard began to sing, dancing atop a platform, his lute strumming with an upbeat chorus befitting such an historical moment between the two kingdoms.

Hungry revelers devoured plates upon plates of food filled with red meats, boiled potatoes, and fresh fruits, bonding over the notion of peace.

Dazen took the opportunity to further showcase his quality by standing and offering his hand in dance towards Sumaya. Her olive face turned a deep red as she placed her hand in his. The two moved around the dance floor as if they had been practicing together for years.

"I was unaware you could dance as well as fight," Sumaya commented, twirling underneath Dazen's arm before returning to embrace him.

"Ah, but dancing is just another form of fighting," he replied. "Only without the blood." He shared a wink before bending her over, her dress dangling mere inches from the floor.

His heart pounded as he pulled her up and drew her close. He felt her taut, muscular arms curl around his own. There seemed to be more to her than met the eye. Her breath was warm on his neck. A light citrus fragrance emanated from her like its own aura of Shine. His breathing halved, the desire to hold her tighter near overwhelming.

He was staring too long. Her left brow twitched as the awkwardness of the moment grew. "Uh, how is your brother?" he asked to cover his bashfulness.

"I have three brothers, Dazen."

"You know what I mean."

Sumaya wrapped her arms around his head. "Echo is well, you are a good influence on him. I was wrong about you, Dazen, and I am glad to be proven so."

Dazen moved a smooth hand from her waist and clasped her hand in his own. "Come, let us speak with him."

The two made their way to the high table. A small round of applause rose from the onlookers as more couples and would-be couples flocked to the dance floor.

King Rayner and the twins looked deep in conversation with Dazen's cousin Estevan, leaving Echo alone.

"You look brighter this evening," Dazen said upon approach.

"Thanks," Echo said. "I feel much better. Congratulations, by the way."

Sumaya looked up at him. "Thank you, little brother. You

had better be careful now, you are almost a grown man. Any day now the ladies will be knocking down walls to get a chance with you."

Echo tittered. "Yeah, right. I am the fourth child, and I cannot even wield the Light."

Sumaya scowled, the look of which reminded Dazen never to get on her bad side. "All you boys, Light this and Light that, as if it were the only thing in this world that mattered. I cannot use it, does that make me any less worthy to find a match?"

Echo retreated a step. "N — no, that is not what I meant. "

"Take note little brother, there are more important aspects that make up a person than the ones they are born with."

"Y — yes Sister. You are right."

Dazen placed a hand on his shoulder. "Do not fret, you are more than capable a man, Light or no. Now, any news from Lesken?"

Echo shook his head. "Father refuses to speak of it. He acts as if it is no concern. But I can tell he is stressing over it. Apparently, they have seized the city. No one allowed in or out until they decide what to do."

"Decide?" Dazen said. "What is there to decide? His death was the work of outlaws. Why would an entire city be punished for the work of so few?"

"Have you ever known the King-Radiant to be merciful?" Echo said. "The capital's lust for power has grown out of control. Ever since the False Kings War they have tightened their grip. It has become even worse now that Urion's son, Evanon, has taken the title of King-Radiant. I have heard the stories and studied hard. I would not want to come between that man and what he wants."

Dazen was about to speak out against the King-Radiant, but he bit his tongue. You never knew who was listening in such a large setting, even if those gathered were your own.

The conflict in Lesken was enough for Dazen to doubt the union of the two kingdoms, and he had not forgotten the confrontation with Rich and the protesters the other day. The people needed reassurance.

He took a reassuring breath, confident that all would be well, his worries only hysteria.

Before he could right his thoughts, Kron, Rayner and the Levic twins came bounding over, towering over them like they were ants.

"We must talk," the Zutonian King said, his voice deep and rigid.

"Is something the matter, Father?" asked Sumaya.

The two respective kings moved to sit next to Sumaya and Echo, leaving the twins to make themselves comfortable next to Dazen.

Dazen shifted in his seat but refused to be intimidated by the two bullies.

"If this alliance is to survive, if this marriage is to take place, we must first seek permission from the King-Radiant," Rayner said.

"So, we send him a letter," Sumaya said, though Dazen knew her words to be naïve.

"We cannot afford to disrespect him, especially given our situation," Rayner continued.

"Disrespect him?" Sumaya said. "Are we not our own nation? Are we not allowed to choose who we can and cannot marry?"

Rayner waved a dismissive hand. "You are young, you do not understand. This is the way it has always been. The King-Radiant is our high ruler. One King-Radiant and six kings. The city of Lumindal protects us. Without it we are vulnerable."

Dazen could see Kron grimacing, as if those words were poison to his ears, but it was Sumaya who spoke up. "Protect us? Protect us from what? And do I need to mention there are now only five kings, not six?"

Rayner stepped forward, grabbing Sumaya by her arm. "Keep your voice down," he said through gritted teeth. "It was not always this way. The rebellion in Crata has shaken them. When one ruler dies, and another takes his place, there is always a period of adjustment. We need his favour, now more than ever."

Sumaya withdrew her arm with a heavy wrench, moving to stand a step behind Dazen.

Kron spoke next. "We have discussed the matter at length, and we have decided to send the three of you north to Lumindal," he said, pointing toward Dazen, Sumaya and Echo.

The twins simultaneously planted open palms upon the table. "You would send Echo to the capital over us?" Huet barked. "He is not worthy. He will ruin us."

"Enough!" Rayner bellowed. "The two of you have important business with me in Nanta. Echo will travel with Sumaya to the capital to plead forgiveness and ask for the King-Radiant's blessing in their marriage."

Huet and Petros settled back into their seat, seemingly content with their position of importance.

Dazen turned to Kron. "You would have me leave? I will be gone a long time, and you are not well."

"My health is of no concern. I have had no issue running a kingdom over the past two decades. I am sure I can manage a few moons without my hero of a son to tend to my every duty," Kron said. "You will leave in two days. That should give us enough time to gather a party and supplies. We will postpone the wedding until you should return with his blessing."

"And what if he does not give it?" Echo said, asking the question on everybody's lips.

The table grew silent.

Finally, King Rayner spoke. "You have my permission to give him whatever he asks. Double our usual output for a year if it will persuade him either way. But do not insult him. Probably best you stay clear of his Eagles while you are there as well, lest you should stare at one the wrong way." He inclined his head toward Echo.

"Double?" Echo said. "But he has already taken more than half of our soldiers, we cannot afford --"

Rayner fixed him with an intense stare Dazen likened to his own father's when a temper struck him. "If you do not grasp the seriousness of our situation, I will send the twins. Give him what he wants. We cannot afford to upset him further."

Echo lowered his head. "Yes, Father."

"We will talk more on this in the morning," Rayner said. "For now, let us feast in celebration."

King Rayner ripped a drumstick from the platter of food on the table and shoved it in his mouth before departing. Kron too, hobbled away.

That left the twins sitting idle in their stupor, foreheads red, as though they had overindulged themselves in wine. Petros fixed Echo with a malicious stare. "You realise Father only lets you go because you are expendable."

Echo shared a blank look with Dazen.

"Think about it," Petros continued, "you can't use the white-light like we can, you cannot even harness it at all. What use is a spineless prince? With Lesken in the shit and an Eagle dead, there is every chance the King-Radiant will look to take out his frustrations. Who better to punish than a lowly prince begging for forgiveness?" Petros' lips widened until they could stretch no more. "You will be dead the moment you walk in there, and Father knows it."

"Petros, enough!" Sumaya said.

But Petros remained unmoving, his eyes not leaving Echo's.

Dazen grit his teeth, expecting Echo to crumble, expecting him to cower and run away as he did the last time his brother mocked him so. But he remained still. There we no tears running down his cheek, no quivering lip, just composed anger.

"Maybe you are right, Brother. Maybe Father has sent me to my death. Or," Echo said, holding a finger out in front of him. "Father refused to send either of you on such a diplomatic mission because one whisper from either of your foul tongues falling upon the wrong ears will see our country ended. Either that, or they will take one whiff of your odour and send the both of you to the depths of the Sea of Sapphires with rocks tied to your feet."

In unison both twins rose, fists banging on the table. Their brows knotted and their muscles tensed so tight that Dazen could see each individual sinew in Petros' outstretched arm. The only thing keeping them from jumping the table and throttling their younger brother was the fact that they were in a room full of Glaives.

Echo was not finished though. "I may be just a lowly prince, never to sit on our father's throne, but hear this. A throne cannot fit two kings. So, who shall it be? Father will not be around forever. Who will take his spot at the head of the family? Which brother is more deserving? I heard Petros was born an hour before you Huet, does he now gain favour ahead of you?"

Petros and Huet stood stunned, each watching the other's movements as if suddenly in deep competition with one another.

Dazen couldn't help but gawk at Echo after his brave and calculated retort. With a flick of his tongue he had managed to turn the brothers against each other, or at least cast a growing doubt into their minds that they would not soon forget.

The twins' anger boiled, their fists clenched, ready to unleash. Not even the threat of ruining their sister's wedding announcement was going to be enough to contain them after their brother's brash insult, so caught up were they in a world where they controlled each outcome. Huet threw back his chair in a display of disgust and lunged for Echo, grabbing him by the cuff of his shirt. Petros was not far behind, raising a balled fist, ready to swing.

Dazen moved to intercept, the table still separating the three brothers. Before their outburst could reach further than the high table, the doors to the hall swung open with a loud bang. The entire hall stopped still. The music ceased, Huet dropped Echo, and everyone present stared motionlessly at the entrance.

A man walked in, unfamiliar to Dazen.

"It's gone!" the man shouted across the hall. "Lesken is no more. Nothing but a pile of dust!" The man bent to his knees and wept.

Interlude
Evanon

Evanon sat cross-legged atop the Last Light, his presence a vision of power as he cast a threatening gaze over Zapour. The high winds buffeted his exposed body, flowing like a river down each patch of charred and scarred skin. Hot rays of light reflected against the black iron. The metal was surprisingly cool to the touch, despite the gathered Shine beneath its surface.

Evanon tilted his head into the cloudless sky, exhaling as he soaked up Zur's warmth to replenish his strength. He felt the refreshing Light pulse through his veins with every gasp of breath. He was the King-Radiant, and he would protect Zapour from those who threatened it, no matter the cost.

The air still tickled with residual heat from the force of the blast. A transparent line of fading Light stuck to the sky like a cloud where Evanon had directed the bolt of energy. His body ached and his head burned with fever, but he paid the pain no mind. He had done what needed to be done.

All magic has a cost. Directing such a large volume of gathered Shine took a toll on his body. He had to impart his own Shine into the tower before siphoning its contents into one giant ball of molten white-light, held together only by his will and the peridium coils protruding from the towers tip, which curled until they met in the middle — marking the highest point in all of Zapour.

Look at me now, Father.

It pained him. To think back on the person he had been. He

was a different man now. No longer was he the weak little boy unable to wield the Light, forced to suffer through beating after beating as his predecessor sought to draw the power out of him.

He stood, looking at the energy cloud which had wreaked so much destruction, and felt no remorse. His soul was tainted, and he knew it. But his father was right, he had been weak. Weakness had to be punished. Insubordination must be punished. He was the King-Radiant. These people were his to control, his to mould. And now they knew the cost of betrayal.

Is this what you wanted me to become, Father?

PART 2

Chapter 12
Raiz

A cloud of insurmountable guilt hung over Raiz, as if it were tethered to his very soul. It threatened to rain down upon him at every turn. He sulked forwards with slumped shoulders, dragging his legs with each step, his body unable to contain the emotions within.

It was his fault, and they all knew it. He didn't have to involve them. He could have killed the Eagle himself, as planned. Perhaps then their lives would have been spared.

Spike had found him during the commotion of the blast that had shaken the mountainside. The pricket and Raiz had always shared a mental connection of sorts. No matter where Spike wandered off to, he would always find his way back.

Hector lay sprawled atop Spike's scaled back, his mood even darker than Raiz's own. Spike did his best to try to cheer the boy up, however, taking every opportunity to arch his serpent-like neck backwards to lick at Hector's hands with his spit-covered blue tongue.

Raiz couldn't bear talking to him, couldn't bear talking to anyone right now. He was responsible for his family's death. Did he have a brother caught up in that explosion? Perhaps a sister? He didn't even know. And yet Hector still followed. Did that mean he didn't blame Raiz for what had happened? Or did he just have nowhere else to go? It didn't matter, nobody could blame him more than he blamed himself.

After long hours of travel, Celik called them to a stop at the bottom of a small grassy knoll south-west of where Lesken had been. "We rest here. Don't get too comfortable. We leave once our breath is recovered," he said.

The party dropped their packs before relaxing into the grass. Veil's face was grim with black shadows of exhaustion. Raiz couldn't imagine the pain she was going through, reliving the horror. Old wounds re-opening and fresh ones forming. She had been a wreck the entire journey, had barely said a word to him. Usually she was distant, but this was more than that. "Are you okay?" he said, moving close to her.

She clutched at her chest. "I can feel it, like I did back in Hirane. It's like a cage around my heart, growing tighter by the day. I can't live like this Raiz."

Raiz looked her in the eye. "Just hold on a little longer, we'll find a way to break the cage."

"What *was* that?" Aroha said, interrupting as she stared into the distance where clouds of smoke and dust blacked out the sky. Cool air rolled down the hill, whipping into bare skin as an eerie silence engulfed them.

"It was a Shine Bomb," Veil said.

Aroha gasped, holding a hand to her mouth. "You mean to say Lesken has met with the same fate as that of Hirane?"

"The blast was smaller, but yes. Like the one that took my homeland from me," she said, her hands shaking.

"How does someone even possess such powerful Shine? To wipe out an entire city? There is no being powerful enough," Raiz said.

"That blast was not the result of a single person's Shine," Celik said, as if sensing their confusion. "It was the work of many. It was sent from the Last Light, but the weapon was not built for such a purpose, it is not to blame. It is the person behind the weapon we must destroy."

"You speak of the King-Radiant?" Raiz said.

Celik nodded. "He must be killed, he has poisoned Zapour. He no longer knows what it means to be its protector."

"And who is he to you?"

"He is nobody, just another person on my list of people to kill. Now come, we must burn what happened in Lesken from our minds. There's work for us to do."

Raiz's anger boiled. "Burn it from our minds? An entire city lies in ruin because of what we did! That's no simple memory to forget."

"No Raiz, the city is in ruin because of you. Because of your decision to take matters into your own hands and involve others in our cause. Look on if you must, but if you want the real people responsible for their deaths, if you want true justice for their murder, then you will turn your attention towards our next course of action."

Raiz wanted to speak, to rebuke him, to ask how it was possible to have such disregard for human lives in the face of such tragedy, but his guilt was too strong. Instead, he lowered his head, taking comfort in the soft grass.

"We were all there." It was Veil who spoke for him. "We all took part. We could have killed the Eagle ourselves if we wanted to. But we allowed Raiz to speak, we helped him inspire those people to take justice upon themselves. If anyone is to blame, it is all of us." She paused to look from Draz to Aroha.

"Yes yes, very inspiring, blame who you like," Celik

muttered. "But we must move on. There are plenty more Eagles for us to kill. I will bathe in their blood before I meet my end, be sure."

Raiz's cheek twitched. "Why do you hate them? You know my reason for wanting them dead, but what's yours? Such hatred isn't born from nothing."

"I've told you before, Raiz, it's none of your concern! We don't speak of our past. We are merely tools, we don't share our feelings, we stamp them out."

"Tell me why and I'll never speak of it again, I swear it."

Celik gave a low growl. "Watch it, boy."

"Tell me!" Raiz shouted, no longer able to follow a man he did not truly know.

Celik twisted his head to the side, pursing his lips before exhaling slowly. "They took my son from me," he said.

Raiz's next words caught in his throat.

"Now enough of this, can we move on?" Celik said. "Put Lesken in the past."

"And if I can't go on?" Raiz said, finding his voice. "If my conscience won't allow me to kill if the result is this," he pointed towards the sky, which was still a smokey haze.

Celik took a step towards him so that Raiz was close enough to feel the warmth of his breath. "I didn't take you for a coward. I took you in as a weak and frail boy who had run away from his daddy. I trained that weakness out of you!

"Your potential is endless, your control over the white-light is unrivalled. And you would piss it all away over a battle with conscience? What of your sister? Who will provide justice for her death if not you?"

"My sister is alive!" Raiz snapped.

"You are deluded, Raiz. She was dead the moment your father let her be taken. You have always known it to be so. You mustn't let your fantasies cloud your judgement. Let your hatred take control. The same people who took your sister burned that city to the ground. Let the deaths of those responsible be your goal, purge the weakness from your body so that you may become the man you were born to become!"

Raiz's anger threatened to overwhelm him. He refused to accept Celik's words for truth. "I was born a Glaive. My sister is alive, and I will find her."

"There's more at stake here than your sister! Zapour is in danger, the world will suffer if that tyrant remains in power."

"Go and kill him yourself then," Raiz said, brushing past Celik and walking up the hill. There might have been calls for him to stop, but his thoughts were too loud for him to take any notice.

Two white-red orbs of energy levitated over Raiz's palms, radiating power as they vibrated. A solitary patch of grass stuck from the soil, long blades of green staring at him innocently. An image of Lesken came into his mind as he stared, the power in his hands the Shine Bomb. He imagined each speck of soil a person, and each blade of grass their home.

His hands shook with the thought, his control faltering to the point where the two orbs grew unstable. He clenched his fist, dispelling the Light and heat.

"Can you teach me how to do that?"

Raiz twisted his head to find Hector standing over him. He had expected the boy to be angry. To blame him for the destruction of his home, the death of his family. But there was something in his stance that told him otherwise, a sense of purpose.

"You would still learn from me? I'm a monster," Raiz said. "It's because of me that your family is dead."

Hector stood unmoving. "You mean my mother, who would give up her own child to 'them' to save herself? Or my father the drunk, who would beat me whenever he came home after a night at the tavern. I'm sorry they're gone, I'm sorry for all of them. And I'm angry. But I would rather be angry at the real reason my parents acted the way that they did. I would rather take my vengeance against the real enemy."

"And who is the real enemy?" asked Raiz.

"Fear."

Raiz raised an eyebrow. "Explain."

"My parents, they weren't always bad people. My mother used to sing me songs, take me places. She wanted to see the world. And my father, he wasn't always so brutal. He used to teach me things; how to harvest crops, how to run the family business. But then 'they' came. Every year the men in black would come, they would take Da's money, claiming he owed it to the King-Radiant. Da' didn't take it well. He'd spend what little we had left on drink. Mother's songs faded in time. She no longer wanted to travel, save to get away from Da'. They were just scared, you see. Scared of the men in black. Scared of the King-Radiant. Scared of themselves, I think.

"So, I want to eliminate fear from the world. If that means learning to use my power from a monster, then so be it."

Raiz looked the boy up and down. "And how old are you again?" he asked, refusing to believe someone so young could be filled with so much maturity and resolve.

"I'm older than I look, fourteen this summer," Hector replied.

"Show me your hands," Raiz demanded.

Hector looked at him with a puzzled expression. He grudgingly lifted his hands from behind his back and held them out for Raiz to inspect.

Raiz grabbed him by the wrists and leaned forward. He had the soft skin common for one of such youth, but his hands were blemished with burn marks and charred chunks of skin. They were not blackened to the state of Raiz's left hand, or to that of Celik's arms, but it was only a matter of time before they were, unless he learned to control his shine.

"When did you first use the white-light?" Raiz asked, the two of them joining eye-lines.

Hector mused for a moment, touching his fingers to his chin as he thought backwards. "Must be over a season ago now, at least."

"And how did it happen?"

"It's only ever happened once."

Raiz pursed his lips. "Curious, are you sure it only happened once?"

Hector nodded.

He reached for his hands once again. "You have quite serious burns for just one blast, you must have quite the power tucked away there. Tell me how it happened."

Hector looked down at his hands. "I was out in the fields with mother, harvesting the season's crops, and it just sort of, happened. My body started to shake, like there was something inside of me wanting to come out. I felt it pressing against my skin, sizzling. I told Ma, but she brushed me aside as if I was complaining about the common cold. Anyway, eventually I couldn't take it, I had to release it. Once I decided it needed to go, it just came out of my hands like one big rush. I burnt a hole in the ground as wide as a small house, but it just kept coming. I had no control over it. Ma started screaming, but I could barely hear her. I burnt the whole field to a crisp. It was all I could do not to singe Ma with it."

"What was the weather like on that day?" Raiz asked.

"The weather?"

"Yes, the weather."

"Uhh, well it was hot I guess."

"So, the sun was out?"

Hector nodded again.

"And what happened after? Once you ran out?"

"I don't remember," Hector replied. "The next thing I remember is waking up in my basement surrounded by nothing but darkness. My parents kept me there day and night for…I don't even know how long. I hadn't seen sunlight for the entire harvest season. I think they tried to keep me a secret, I could hear them talking above me sometimes. But there were others in the field that day. I was seen for sure."

Raiz bowed his head, struck by the cruelty this boy had to endure simply because he was born with a power people did not understand. Shine was common enough, though it was more common in those of royal lineage, and less so in the peasantry. Those few less well-off people who were born with the Light were quickly identified and sought by the capital to be processed and either filtered into the army or disposed of with little empathy.

Raiz placed a reassuring hand on his shoulder. "Your Shine is not something to be locked away in darkness. You were born special, as was I. Together we carry the light of the sun within our bodies. It is a gift from Zur."

"Isn't that what 'they' preach?" Hector asked.

The brash nature of the question caught Raiz off guard. He scoffed at the notion of being compared to them. "They speak only in half truths. They believe themselves gods among men. They spread the false ideology that if one of their own is to die, then part of Zur dies with them. They hide under a blanket of superstition, pretending to be something they aren't in order to keep hold of their power over people. We are all born of Zur, not just them. I will prove their ideology false. Only then will people believe in independence. Only then will people see they are free to live their own lives —"

"Away from fear," Hector interrupted.

Raiz could see the fire in his eyes, a once-dim light now bright with energy.

"I will share in your goal," Hector said. "I'll hunt them down with you, show the world they're nothing but fakes."

Raiz smiled for the first time all day. "First we must teach you to use your Shine."

Chapter 13
Isha

Isha blew a lock of hair from her eye, standing perfectly still like the doll she was supposed to be. Her head ached. Hours spent in the make-up room while servants laboured over every blemish covered the tiredness she felt, at least on the outside. She hadn't slept a wink. How could she?

She was still trying to piece together what had happened. What had she been a part of? What were they doing to those children in the tower?

Deep down, she knew the answer. She just couldn't believe it. They were siphoning children's Shine into what seemed like a never-ending pit of molten Light. She was lucky to be alive. That man would have killed her when he found out she was not Shine sensitive. If Puk hadn't been there, she would likely be lying in a ditch somewhere.

She looked to her feet, wincing at the beige polish on her nails, matching perfectly with her open-toed shoes that glittered with a dozen moonstones. This was not her. Even when she had been a princess, she had spent her time studying in her room or chasing Raiz around the palace. She had never enjoyed the spotlight. But that was a lifetime ago.

Her thoughts turned to Puk. Of what she had put him through. Averardus had been ready to execute him when he had returned with her. He had been furious. But Isha had told her story. She told him why she fled, and about how Puk followed her into the Last Light and saved her from the man within.

Averardus was far from a reasonable man, though when it came to her, he was…different. She used to think it was because she was too valuable for him to lose. His prize jewel in a mountain full of them. But as time wore on, she began to see things differently. He genuinely cared for her. Not in the tender way a father would care for his daughter, far from it. But there was a connection between them. The thought of it brought bile to the top of her throat, but it had saved her on more occasions than one. He couldn't harm her, and he knew it.

And so, he took out his frustrations on others. The man in the tower had been found and executed immediately. The two guards who had captured and failed to recognise her had also been located and killed. And Puk, although he had saved her, had been given half a dozen lashes as punishment for letting her slip from his eye. Isha bit her lip, grimacing at the thought of him receiving pain on her behalf. She hadn't seen him since and wondered if Averardus had been true to his word and spared him.

And now they celebrated?

Hardly a person walked by without a goblet of wine in their hand, smiling and laughing with each other as if they actually cared that their fallen Eagle had been 'avenged'.

It took all of her will not to lash out at the nearest reveller, her fists clenched, ready to strike at the next pompous Eagle to approach her.

Averardus was busy escorting groups of partygoers through the maze of artworks in his gallery below, likely taking his time to gloat about each famous piece. That left Isha on display as the final piece before they entered the true party on the top-floor of the Forty-Fourth Spear.

Isha wasn't the only centrepiece on show today, though. Across from her in the wide-open space of the hall rested the bones of Scale. The remains of Gallion's own Krono-Dragon stood rigid atop a steel framework with metal poles and platforms underneath to keep them in place. The bones were pieced together with some form of adhesive, and arranged to resemble a dragon about to take flight. Isha couldn't help but marvel at the creature. Its large breast stuck out, the bones around its neck twisting as the head arched like a snake ready to pounce. Its wings were long and wide, spread out and held into place by a series of metal poles rising from the ground.

Eagles, old and new, circled around the dead creature in groups as they fraternised. Even amongst the King's Eagles there was a formal ranking. Those in greater favour with the King-Radiant were placed in a higher building. As the forty-fourth highest Spear in Lumindal, that made Averardus perhaps the seventh most powerful person in all of Zapour. But that didn't stop him from aspiring to grander heights.

Isha looked to her left, taking comfort in both Obeyun and Maitreya's presence. Despite her initial hesitation, she was coming to like Maitreya the more she got to know her.

She moved to try to talk to Obeyun but found her voice wouldn't carry. As always, he was half naked, his skin bare and on display.

"Please, make yourself at home. My home is your home," sounded a voice from the stairwell. She could tell from the high-pitched drone it was the old man Averardus himself.

He came into view, wearing his fake smile as he escorted a couple of lower ranked Eagles into the hall.

"There is plenty of food and drink. Go, fill your bellies! Make Saerus cry out from the heavens in envious gluttony!" He followed with a cackle of laughter that made Isha's ears shrivel.

She looked around. It seemed the only Eagle in Lumindal not in attendance was the King-Radiant himself, though it wouldn't surprise her if he did show up. In his stead, he had sent his mother. Lady Sephare stood alone, though she didn't seem lonely. She held her head high, her gloved hands clasped together as she idly gazed at a painted portrait of Gallion himself. Nobody dared stand within ten feet of her, as if in doing so they would burn to ash. Her head twisted slowly around to face Isha, as if sensing her glare. Isha caught her breath, eyes widening before quickly looking away. She cursed under her breath as Sephare walked over to her, each step placed with specific purpose.

She stopped before Isha, close enough to see each individual wrinkle lining her forehead. "I never quite understood the appeal towards one such as yourself," she said. Isha looked to her feet. She assumed Sephare was talking about the colour of her eyes. "You need not be afraid of me girl," Sephare continued. "You have grown much since I first laid eyes upon you in Averardus' hold so many years ago."

Isha remained still, not daring to look her in the eye.

Sephare let out an amused sigh. "I do not blame you, to want to remain inconspicuous. This life is ill suited to one of your lineage and beauty. Though I suspect this is but one wayward step in a long life. You are destined for greater things, Princess of Trost."

Isha snapped to attention just in time to see the back of

Sephare's neatly trimmed gown disappear into the growing crowd. What did she mean, destined for greater things? She was a slave, and she was beginning to think she would always be one. She had tried to escape, to run away, but she had been caught. Maybe this was her destiny? Maybe there was no hope after all. She barely had time to gather her thoughts as Averardus approached, using his sceptre as a walking cane that clinked on the marble floor.

"My treasures! Look alive, look alive!" Averardus encouraged.

Isha clenched her fists, suppressing the urge to claw at him. He seemed in an unusually gracious mood. Not that Isha cared. He was a murderer.

"This is a time for celebration!" he said, placing a greasy hand underneath her chin and squeezing her cheeks. She thought about spitting at him, but she more than any knew how his temper could go from cold to hot in a matter of moments. There was an unspoken tension between the two of them, a lingering cloud of mistrust. But he couldn't do anything about it. Not now at least. Not while he played host. Instead, he dropped back into his comfortable facade, lips in a wide grin, back and shoulders straight as a flagpole.

"You are my gems, and I would have you shine," he continued.

Obeyun and Maitreya took another deep breath, their faces grim with exhaustion.

Averardus reached for a whip that was not there, taking a step closer to the three of them, his mouth hovering between a smile and a frown. He leaned forwards and whispered. "This is an important day for me. You three will be present, and you will look alive!" He turned his gaze towards Isha. "You have already disappointed me once. I will not be so forgiving the next time."

Isha gave a weak, defeated nod.

Averardus paused, and something seemed to change within him. Their eyes locked, his expression faded, as if he could see the pain within her, feel the despair. He placed both hands on his sceptre and leaned forwards. "Tell you what. Saerus' death has put me in a pleasant mood. I shall give the three of you one day. One day free of chain and free of duty to roam my household unhindered."

Isha's face came to life, her chin perking up. She glanced at Obeyun, who had edged a little closer. He too was a picture of curiosity.

"Yes yes. I am magnificent, am I not? One day I give you. A day of your choosing. You will still be under guard, of course, I would not have my most prize possessions sneaking out on me again. But I trust that this will please you?"

Isha risked another look over her shoulder before nodding.

"Excellent, all I ask is that you look alive! Greet my guests with a smile. And stand up straight for Zur's sake. I will not deprive my guests the joy of seeing such precious violet jewels. Lift your head girl!" He ran his still greasy fingers over her eyebrow, pulling at her skin. "You do this for me, and I will give you a day. And do not think me soft. It is not every day we have cause for such celebration."

Isha nearly choked on the thought of celebrating such an event, but she was not about to give up the opportunity. She straightened her back, standing taller than she had in years, and curled her lips into a smile.

"There we are! Wonderful! Much better."

Obeyun and Maitreya followed, putting on a display of acting which looked so practiced one could mistake them for performers in a play.

"Well well, Averardus, it seems good quality does not diminish over time after all!"

All eyes flickered towards the newcomer. Salador was his name, Eagle of the Forty-Sixth Spear. He was younger than Averardus by many years. He ran a hand through dark hair, which was neatly combed and tucked behind his ears. He clasped his host's hand before slinking back into the company of two young females wearing such frivolous clothing that they could hardly be called clothes at all.

"Salador, welcome to my home," Averardus said. "And with such fine company." He paused to gawk at the brunette to Salador's left, who was showing far too much leg.

"I remember this one as a child," Salador said, gesturing towards Isha. "She is just like a fine wine grown sweeter with age. And you get to taste her all for yourself! You surely are selfish sometimes Averardus. What would it take for me to procure her services from you? I am a very wealthy man, as I am sure you are aware."

Isha refused to let this man's vile nature and commentary get under her skin, her resolve stronger than her urge to cut his throat. Instead, she placed an image of Salador away in the back of her mind. Some day she may have need of her hatred again, but for now she smiled.

"As always Salador, your admiration is appreciated, but I am afraid I will not part with her for any price. For it is as you say, I am a selfish man."

Salador leaned back into a glowering stare. "Very well, I know when to concede defeat, though I do believe we have business to discuss. Tell me, Averardus, have you any interest in Peridium?"

Averardus' eyes widened. "That metal is as rare as the sun shining in the night."

"Maybe in Zapour. Though my contacts in Yagos suggest a new vein has been found. They are mining it as we speak."

"And why should I believe you? Why tell me this now?"

"Search for yourself if you do not believe me. As for why I am telling you, well, I am soon to be coming into a great deal of the metal. More, you might say, than I will need. And you quite by chance have something that I desire."

"The girl is not for sale," Averardus said with a stern expression.

"No no, not the girl, though that trade would prove acceptable. You see, I have a certain buyer who is very 'particular' with his purchases. He requires a collection of stones once hoarded by our dear Saerus. Saerus however proved quite reluctant to relinquish his possessions to my care. Of course, after his unfortunate demise I sought to acquire them for myself but found another had already acquired them." He inclined his head.

"You seek the Koshaki Stones," Averardus said.

"My, my, you are as perceptive as they say. You are correct. My partners in the west have a certain interest in the Koshaki Stones, and they have something which I very much desire."

"We are the King's Eagles; nothing is beyond our reach. If you want something, why not simply take it?"

Salador's face contorted, lines of frustration forming on his forehead. "My partners in the west are isolated in their mountains. Unfortunately for me, force is not an option."

"So, you are desperate," Averardus said, a sly smile creasing his lips.

Salador tensed, unslinging his arms from the ladies' shoulders. "I come to you with a fair offer of trade. Something you desire, for something I desire. The chance for a score of peridium does not come along often. I would suggest you consider the consequences before you brush my offer aside. Perhaps Adela will be interested —"

Averardus waved a hand dismissively. "Do not involve her. Say I was to give up the Koshaki Stones, there is something I want in return, even more so than peridium."

Salador raised his left brow. "And what could be so rare that its value exceeds the rarest metal in existence?"

Averardus leaned closer. "I seek the black powder," he whispered. "I know you took what was left from Crata after the war."

Salador's face tightened. Isha found herself drawn into the conversation as if she were a part of it herself.

"I know nothing of black powder. That stuff is illegal even by our standards."

"Do not play me for a fool, Salador. I do not wish to turn you in."

"Say I did have some of it hidden away, what use would explosives be to you? I did not pick you for the type."

It was very subtle, but Isha knew Averardus well, and for the barest moment his eyes flickered towards Adela, who was at this very moment leading people away from Scale's bones. "My reasons are my own," he said. "Was it not your ancestors who built the Last Light? It is dangerous for you to horde such material so close to their creation. Let me take some off your hands."

Salador cleared his throat and took a step closer. "We have a deal."

"Excellent, I will begin preparing the stones. I will have them to you by —"

"There is one more ah, slight detail I forgot to mention. One that requires your discretion."

"Huh! And here I thought we already were being discreet.

Speak your piece."

Salador sighed. "You see, much as you rival with the Lady Adela of the Thirty-Eighth Spear, so I share in a rivalry of my own with Lunet of the Forty-Second."

Averardus huffed, crossing his arms as he again eyed Adela. "What are you asking?"

"It is a simple enough favour. You see, Lunet also desires the stones. I suspect her spies lurk within my walls. I am sure that her men will pounce upon anything I export from Lumindal. If I give you the information, I will need you to transfer the stones for me."

Averardus leaned forwards. "And this favour...I would hope it comes with compensation."

"But of course, I will send a runner for you at a later date to discuss details but be sure you will be rewarded handsomely."

"Then we are in agreement."

Salador nodded and bowed before taking his place between the two ladies and departing.

Averardus turned his attention back towards Isha, who had been too caught up in the conversation to remember to smile. "Best to put that smile back on your face, or maybe next time I will sell you to him," he said before leaving to bask in the company of other guests.

It was an empty threat, and she knew it, but even still, the prospect of a day's freedom was too good to ignore.

However boring the brief interaction between the two Eagles seemed, it had sparked an idea within Isha. It was a shallow one, merely the base of a plan, though it was something. A small ray of hope, perhaps her only chance.

Isha spent the rest of the evening smiling and greeting onlookers as if she were indeed the centrepiece of the entire gallery, all the while her mind ticked over, formulating a plan that would see her and her friends away from this place, and to true freedom.

Chapter 14
Dazen

The City of Light sat idle in the distance. Lumindal was painted like one giant white silhouette against a landscape of blue sky and green grass. Weeks of travel had only worked to further dampen the mood of the travelling company.

Dazen ran a hand through the smooth coat of his horse's neck before feeding him a carrot and patting him for all his hard work. "Just a little farther, Brock," he whispered into his ear.

Echo rode beside him, his back slumped and his face red-raw. He clearly wasn't handling the fast on-and-off pace of a long journey well, though he tried to hide it. Every time Dazen thought he was near to falling off the side of his horse, the youngest Levic would suck in a deep breath and straighten himself.

With the news that Lesken was no more, King Rayner was forced to backtrack on the idea of sending Echo and Sumaya alone. The situation had become grave. Lesken was their city, second in importance to their capital in Nanta, but it was their domain and like it or not the Levics were responsible for what happened there in the eyes of the King-Radiant.

Everything had changed since the news from Lesken. The day had turned from celebrating the end of a century of mistrust and warfare to a desperate plight to seek forgiveness for a crime they did not commit.

The King of Zuton rode at the front of the troupe, his daughter and two eldest sons at his side. Dazen hadn't had many chances to talk to Sumaya on the trip so far. He didn't like to admit it, but he found her father quite intimidating, and he could never seem to find a lasting moment alone with her. But there was something between them. He was sure. Their distance from each other only served to strengthen his curiosity.

"I think that's enough staring for one day, don't you think?" came a voice from his left.

He swung his head around, nearly losing control of Brock, shaken from his reverie.

"I uhh, what?" he said as Echo drew closer.

"Please, you do not have to hide it from me, I mean you are betrothed, after all. Just maybe save your gawking for when you are face-to-face," Echo said.

Dazen couldn't help but choke out a laugh. "I, uh, noted," he said. He reined Brock in so that he rode side by side with Echo. "Are you nervous?" he asked, looking to change the subject.

"I would be a fool not to be."

"A wise answer," Dazen replied.

"Why did you come?" Echo asked. "This is not your battle to fight."

Dazen took another look at Lumindal spiralling above the skyline in the distance. "I am sick of fighting. It is all I have ever known, and it never ends well for any party. If my presence can help to forge an alliance between our two nations, then I will gladly walk into the City of Light with you."

Echo shifted in his seat, correcting his posture. "You are a good man, Dazen. I am glad to have had the chance to meet you."

Dazen didn't know how to respond.

"How much longer do you suppose we have left on the road?" Echo said.

Dazen mused, taking another look at the silhouette. "I would say we will be there before nightfall. Think you can last until then?"

Echo grunted, shifting his position on the saddle. "I will manage. Think they will give us time to rest? A nice bed and some warm soup would go down a treat right now."

"I hardly think the King-Radiant will be in the mood to wait upon our health and wellbeing. It is more likely he would see us crawl on hands and knees. My father does not speak fondly of him."

"What does he say?" Echo inquired. "Mine refuses to comment whenever I ask him. Have you met the King-Radiant?"

"I have not had the chance, no," Dazen answered. "But Kron is not himself whenever his name mentioned. He has made me swear to be cautious around him. I think something happened between the two of them years ago, but I cannot be sure."

Echo stared out into the clouds, deep in thought.

"What is it Echo? What troubles you?" Dazen asked.

"Nothing," Echo said. "Just, do you really believe we should be apologising? If what I hear about the Eagles is true, then the people of Lesken had every right to fight back. They took their children. What kind of person would not fight to keep their own kin safe? It does not sit well with me, grovelling to make peace with people such as them."

Dazen grimaced. His words hit a sour spot, the memory of his sister's screams still as fresh in his mind as the day she had been taken. "The matter is more complicated than that," he managed to say, though he didn't really know if he meant it or not.

"Maybe it should not be," Echo said. "Maybe things need to change."

Dazen rode Brock to a standstill, placing a hand on Echo's shoulder. "I hear your words, Echo, but now is not the time to display your courage in such a manner. Where we are heading will require a different kind of courage. Keep your sentiment if you must, I will not discourage your right to think for yourself. But keep in mind the consequences of such talk before you have the mind to speak it openly."

Echo let out a heavy sigh, though his eyes still brimmed with conviction. "I will hold my tongue. You have my word. For the sake of our two kingdoms. But we will find a way to end this. We must."

Dazen accepted his words as honest, marvelling at the way Echo was beginning to hold himself. He just hoped his newfound sense of justice would not get him killed, or worse.

Chapter 15
Raiz

Zur was out in full strength, the sky a sunburned blue, as if the dust storm had scared away the clouds before settling. Hot rays of sun beat down upon them, prickling at open patches of exposed skin.

"You must first learn how to control the flow of white-light through your body, and how much to take in," Raiz said, watching Hector struggle to cross his legs on the grass.

"Your awakening in the fields was caused by an overflow of Light in your body. Think of it as a sunburn, only on the inside. Over time, your body soaks in sunlight, and without the proper means to release it, the Light builds up until it bursts."

Hector inclined his head, staring directly at the sun before squinting and shielding his eyes with his wrist.

Raiz shook his head and smiled. "Zur doesn't like people staring."

Hector gave a guilty half-nod and scratched his head. "So how do I release it?" he asked.

Raiz paced the grass, the hilly landscape providing a good pocket for the two of them to begin training. "Tell me how you feel," he said.

"How I feel?"

"Yes. We've been in the sun for some time now. How do you feel?"

"I, uh, I'm not sure. I feel kind of strange. There's this tingling, like an itch I can't scratch."

"Good, then you're almost ready. That tingle is your Shine. Now you have two options. The first you are already familiar with, expending your Shine. Dangerous for one who doesn't know how to control how much to release, or how to release it. This is why children suffer from the burnout before they have the chance to mature." He lifted his blackened left hand as proof. "Even the most skilled in the art of white-light manipulation were once novices struggling to contain a power they did not understand."

Hector stared at Raiz's blackened hand and then back at his own. His gaze drifted over Raiz's shoulder. "Then why was she unharmed?"

Raiz craned his neck.

"I saw what she did," Hector said, pointing to where Veil sat in conversation with Draz. "How is she still alive after releasing so much Light? How is it possible she even has that much power? Will I someday be able to do that?"

Raiz took a steadying breath. "The short answer is, I don't know. Veil is special. Her power was shaped by events beyond her control. But all power comes with a cost. She has no control over how or when it comes. It took everything she had just to direct it."

Hector's eyes widened before narrowing as Raiz snapped his fingers. "She is not your concern," Raiz said.

Hector gulped and nodded. "What's the second option? You said there were two."

Raiz dropped his shoulders. He was not used to playing teacher. He was used to learning. He looked towards Celik. The old geezer's hateful gaze burned into him worse than any ray of sun could.

Celik may have been right, it was foolish to take on a student in a time like this, he would likely be a burden too heavy to carry unless he learned to control his Shine, and quickly. But the delicate art of Shine manipulation is not something you can teach in a day. He still had flashbacks to his time in training. Celik's lessons had proved both mentally and physically straining, bordering a line between cruelty and necessity.

Raiz didn't have time to train a student, he had to rescue his sister, and there were many people he needed to kill before he could achieve that. But he couldn't just leave him here like this. His family was dead, his home a wasteland. He would inevitably end up dead as well, whether by his own doing or by bandits on the road. Raiz had a responsibility toward him, it was his fault he was on his own. So, he would help him, at least until he could hold in his Shine.

"Once your Shine is at capacity, you need to stop your intake of sunlight. Shine users are much more powerful during the day when Zur is at the peak of His cycle. Then, they can replenish their power. This is why small raids and assaults are usually done during the daytime, and during summer. When not in battle, it's best we try to avoid the sunlight. This is likely why your parents locked you in the basement after your awakening."

"Well, I hope there's another way," Hector said, his voice hopeful.

"Wearing protective clothing helps. Long sleeves, cloaks, anything that covers the head. Exposed skin is the easiest way to soak up Shine." Raiz indicted towards Veil once more, her body covered head-to-toe in black cloth.

"Then why don't you dress like her?"

"Because I am confident in my control over my Light. There is only so much that clothing and avoiding the sun will do. If you want to drain the Light safely from your body, you need to learn how to Shine drip."

Hector's face contorted, his left cheek twitching higher.

"But before I teach you that, you must learn the exit-points, and the different variants of Shine," Raiz said.

"Exit points? Variants?"

Raiz sighed and rubbed a hand over his face. "How much of my fight did you watch?" Raiz asked.

"You mean when your arm became a weapon?" Hector said, his eyes alight with energy.

"Well, yes. But don't hope to accomplish a technique like that just yet. You're a long way off. But do you remember where my Light came from?"

Hector stared into the sky. "It came from your palm!" he said after a time.

"Correct. Hands are the body's most natural exit point for Light. Makes it easier to direct. Fingers work too, but they aren't capable of holding much Light."

"What about the rest of your body?"

"Well technically, Shine can leak from any open pore. There are those who live deep within the highlands of Crata who are quite proficient using their Light in combination with their feet. I never had the knack for it though. Once you learn how to manipulate Light, you can create your own style."

"And how do I manipulate my Light?"

Raiz offered a teasing smile. "Well, before you learn to manipulate Shine, you first need to create it. I suppose I can teach you the basics now, but don't expect to be able to do it first go."

Hector leaned forwards. He was more eager than Raiz had anticipated. Raiz obliged him though, holding out his palm as he concentrated, forcing the Shine within to the surface in a show of will. A sphere of Light flickered into motion, rotating rapidly and hovering an inch from his open hand. "This is Shine in its liquid state," he said. "From here I can do a couple of things with it. I can send it out in a blast, the result of which can burn through just about anything. But this uses a great deal of Shine. My preference is to manipulate it." Raiz reached over with his other hand and physically grabbed hold of the ball of floating light.

Hector gasped, as if expecting the heat to burn through Raiz's fingers. Raiz smiled. "Don't worry, the white-light I produce is a part of me. As long as it's my own I'm touching, I'll be fine."

Raiz stretched the gooey, lava-like substance until it reached the length of his arm. With a concentrated twist of his hand the liquid began to straighten and solidify. Its surface glowed a bright white, a line of red streaking its centre. "This is Shine in its solid form," he said, grabbing hold of it like he would a spear. "It keeps its heat but becomes usable as a weapon."

Hector's eyes widened. He reached out to touch the spear like object.

"No!" Raiz said, slapping Hector's arm away with his free hand. "You'll lose a finger."

"Sorry," Hector mumbled. "I got carried away."

Raiz threw the stick of Shine onto the grass, watching it sizzle and then fade into a wax-like substance, its light diminished. "Once you lose control over your creation, Shine turns into breen. Breen is mostly useless, though people seem to find a way to make the most of it. And Spike loves it.

At the mention of his name, Spike came bounding over on all fours, his heavy bulk shaking the ground with each step. The pricket bent his neck low so that Raiz could stroke it before licking at his face. He nestled himself into a nook in the grass, his long tail wrapping around Raiz in a protective circle.

Raiz reached for Hector's arm again, grabbing hold of his wrists with a firm grip. He closed his eyes and began to concentrate. He could feel the blood pulsing through his veins like rapid water down a stream, only it was hot to touch. "I would say you'll have another incident before the sun drops below the horizon this day if you fail to drain your Light in time."

Hector flinched, withdrawing his hands with a jerk that sent him off balance. "W—what? I can't go through that again! I just can't! You have to help me."

Raiz remained still, showing no sign of emotion as he watched the boy panic and shake his hands as if the Light would just fall out.

He continued to shake, growing more aggressive with his hand gestures. Raiz shook his head in disappointment. He was not ready. Even so, he had to intervene, for if he did nothing the boy would spiral.

"Calm yourself. You'll never master your Shine through uncontrolled anger and frustration."

The words seemed to snap him back to attention. Hector inhaled a deep breath. "I'm sorry. I don't know what came over me." He grimaced. "Please, tell me what I need to do, I promise I'll listen this time."

Raiz rubbed at his chin. "Close your eyes."

Hector did as he was told.

"Those born of a certain lineage have Light running through their veins, as well as blood. It cannot harm us, at least not while on the inside. Do you know where blood is pumped from?" Raiz said.

"Your heart."

"Correct. Light is no different. Are you familiar with the tale of Gallion Lightfire?"

Hector hummed. "I've heard the name before, but I don't know who he is."

"Well, he is long dead now. He was the first King-Radiant."

"So, he was bad then?" Hector said.

"Not necessarily. Not all King-Radiants were evil. In fact, if the stories are true, most of them ruled with honour, their strength rivalled only by their integrity."

"Then what happened?" Hector said, scratching his head.

"I couldn't tell you, but the current King-Radiant is a shadow of what Gallion stood for. Gallion was the first person to wield Zur's Light. It was said to be a gift to Zapour's greatest warrior to aid humanity in their fight against the Skae — who were ancient creatures born from the shadows of Cova's wrath."

"W-w-wait a minute. Skae? Cova? You've lost me."

Raiz exhaled a deep breath. Was he this bad of a student when Celik taught him about the Shadow-Wars?

"I'll slow it down for you then. Over a thousand years ago, humanity shared this world with the Skae. You see, while we are children of Zur — the God of Light, the Skae are children of Cova — the goddess of darkness, or the moon."

"I see, well what happened to the Skae?"

"History tells of humanity fighting countless battles against the Skae for control over Zapour. These were known as the Shadow-Wars. With humanity on the verge of defeat against the Skae, Zur blessed the bravest of humanity's warriors with a fragment of his will so they might draw power from his Light.

Gallion became known as the first King-Radiant, and the other blessed became his Eagles. Together they created a weapon strong enough to hold all of their Shine and used it against the Skae, taking back their lands and wiping them from existence."

Hector sat with his mouth half-open, hanging on Raiz's every word. "So, they're no more?"

Raiz nodded. "That's what is taught, though Celik has a different theory."

"What's his theory?"

Raiz waved a dismissive hand. "It's not important. But now that you know the origin of our magic, it is my hope you will grow to understand it."

Hector lowered his head, squinting towards the ground as he curled his lip into his cheek.

"What's the matter?" Raiz said. "Do you still not follow?"

"No, I get it, I do. But what I don't understand is why we can still use Zur's Shine today. I always guessed we were born with it. But if we get our Shine from our parents, then that must mean..."

Hector stared at Raiz with a blank expression.

Raiz sighed. "You're correct. We are descendants of Gallion's original Eagles. Shine has been heavily diluted over the past thousand years. Zur's Light has spread across all corners of Zapour, perhaps even farther."

"Then why can't we claim to be an Eagle? Why do they get special preference?"

"The world doesn't work that way, unfortunately. There must only be fifty Eagles at any given time, and those bastards breed like rabbits. Only first-born children may inherit the title. Others are given lesser roles of importance. Some go on to forge their own kingdom, or usurp another. That's where I come from. Others bear bastard children who then go on to breed on their own. Shine sensitive humans are too numerous to contain, so the King-Radiant sets a limit on each kingdom. Those who are found to exceed that limit and don't have proper documentation are sent to Lumindal to become part of his army. That's likely where you were headed had I not intervened."

Hector clenched his fists. "That's wrong! They can't do that. They take away our choice."

Raiz didn't respond. Hector had every right to be frustrated, and he was allowed to vent it.

"Teach me. Teach me how to use this gift, and I swear I will only use it to set the world right again."

"Very well. Close your eyes."

Hector did as he was told.

"Now picture the Light pumping from your heart. Listen as it flows through your body. That tingle from before, find it and grab hold."

Hector squinted, and Raiz could tell he was struggling internally just as much as he was externally. "I think I've found it!" he said, tensing as if he were physically holding it.

"Great, now follow it through to your arms, and then to your hands. Feel its flow and direct it to where you want it to go."

Hector was silent for a moment. His fingers twitched, his hand curling into a claw.

Raiz leaned back, impressed by his ability to harness his power so quickly.

"Uhh Raiz," Hector called. "What's next?"

"Release it slowly. You want to drip your Shine, not expel it all at once. Picture water dripping from a pipe. You don't want to flood the ground, just a few droplets will do."

Raiz watched as a tiny droplet of white-light formed on the tip of Hector's index finger. Spike followed Raiz's line of sight, moving in to lick the droplet of shine from his fingertip.

Hector recoiled. "W-what's that!"

Raiz laughed. "That's just Spike. He feeds off Shine. It's like food to him, makes him grow."

"You mean he eats the stuff?"

"Mhm. He was so small he could fit in my pocket when I was younger, now look at him."

Spike issued a low growl as if in response, still nibbling playfully at Hector's fingers.

"How big will he get?" Hector asked.

"Honestly, I don't know, I didn't think prickets could even grow this big. I don't think anyone did. Now keep going, you still have Shine to drip."

Hector shook his head, welcoming Spike's involvement as he re-doubled his efforts. Light came in a stream now, almost too quick for Spike to take it in.

"Slow down Hector, you're going too fast."

"I can't. It won't stop, Raiz!"

Raiz grabbed his wrist, to no avail. His arm vibrated as if there were some beast trapped within who wanted out.

"I don't think I can hold it any longer!" Hector said.

"Calm yourself!"

"I can't, I'm sorry. It's too hot. It burns!"

Hector was convulsing now, his muscles contracting at the strain of keeping such power at bay. The Light was nearly visible through his pale skin as it reached its boiling point. A splash of molten liquid burst out from his palms, burning through the grass below with a resounding crackle.

The veins in Hector's neck were popping out of his skin. "It's too hot, I need to let it out!" Hector closed his eyes, placing his hands together with open palms. With a loud pop a wave of Light burst forth at a blinding speed. It soared through the air over the top of the grassy knoll they now lay in.

Realising his mistake, Raiz rushed in and struck Hector on the back of the neck. The force of the blow sent him plummeting forwards. He caught the boy mid-fall, his Light melting into breen as his unconscious body sunk into the comfort of Raiz's embrace.

"You fool!" came a cry from a distance, though the husky cackle in the voice almost certainly belonged to Celik. "What have you done? You have compromised our position." He ran up the knoll with surprising speed, arms flailing behind, caught in the wind.

He stood there a while, peering out into the distance, searching for any sign of their pursuers. Their position was concealed, though the hilly landscape was sure to provide cover for their pursuers as well as for themselves.

Eventually, Celik made his way back down. "We must go. And leave that idiot child behind will you? He has done nothing but slow us, and now he threatens the safety of our retreat."

Raiz fixed him with a defiant glare. Draz, Veil and Aroha were on their feet now and fully aware of the situation. He looked to them for support, but only Veil offered him sympathy.

He lifted Hector's limp form above his shoulders and walked off without a word. Before he could go more than a few steps, however, a soft thud sounded on the grass beside him. He looked to find the shaft of an arrow protruding from the soil. At first, he thought it was Veil playing at some trick. But as he turned, he saw a shower of black dots raining down from above, their pointed heads like tiny instruments of death. He stepped to the side, narrowly avoiding a deadly blow as an arrow buried itself in the soil where he had been a moment ago.

"They have found us!" cried Celik. "Retreat! Over the hills, we will lose them in the canyon."

A flurry of footsteps came rushing past Raiz, leaving him in a daze as three forms pushed up the hill. Celik came after, whispering in his ear. "Leave the boy and save yourself, he is a burden you aren't yet ready to carry."

But the old man's words had no effect. He planted a boot firmly into the ground before pushing off into a run, Hector dangling uselessly over his shoulder.

Celik issued an exasperated sigh, but did not argue his decision further. More arrows landed just short of their position. Raiz had to cock his head, but he could hear the faint sound of soldiers issuing orders in the background.

The light crunch of soil beneath his feet soon gave way to a hard thumping as the terrain turned rocky. Raiz tried to keep pace with his companions, though he was lagging further and further behind with each step.

The enemy was visible now, a large line of red trailing along the horizon.

Raiz had always hated the Saelmeres. He was just a kid when he last visited Craw, but his one visit had told him all he needed to know about them. Craw was a cruel and unforgiving place, led by a callous king and his demon-spawned son.

"Ditch the boy or these rocks will be your grave Raiz!" called Celik from out in front, his words drifting towards him in the wind.

Celik's words only sought to double Raiz's resolve. It was his fault Hector gave away their location, his fault he was unconscious. It was his fault his home and family were no more. He owed him this much. He would not let another child fall victim to the crimes of their so-called protectors.

He whistled again through tightened lips. Spike -- while not quite as fast as a horse -- was still faster than Raiz. He hauled Hector's unconscious form over the pricket and onto the makeshift saddle he had made. He wound the leather strapping around the boy's thin waist and fastened it tight. Hector looked awfully uncomfortable, his legs dangling to the side and his head rocking back and forth at a strange angle. He could apologise for the sore back later. He slapped Spike on the side of his tail, watching as the pricket sped off. Raiz thought about jumping on the back with him, but Spike was not yet large enough to carry both of their weight.

His legs ached with pain as the others became more and more distant. His breathing turned from practiced control to heavy panting, his lungs at capacity.

Thankfully, they were nearing the canyon. A formation of tightly packed rocks arched overhead like one giant gateway. He spurred himself forward. If he could make the formation, he could lose them in the maze.

Arrows continued to drop several lengths short, his legs barely able to outrun them. A searing pain struck his side as a projectile tore through his sleeve, grazing flesh. He looked for the instrument but could see no arrow. He risked a glance over his shoulder once more to see a solitary figure leading the pursuing pack, his hand outstretched and pointed towards him.

It was Ancel, he was sure. There was no mistaking his Light. He stood taller than Raiz remembered, but his hair was black as the night itself. His crimson red uniform stood out like a bear in a library, his black cloak billowing in the wind. The Prince of Craw had found him.

Raiz was almost tempted to turn around, to rid the world of another worm, but he had a duty to the boy, and the pursuers numbered too many.

Veil slowed to match his pace. He followed her into the formation, throwing projectiles of Light over his shoulder, providing temporary cover as they weaved their way further into the canyon.

The rocky road forked into three different routes. Raiz spotted Celik and without hesitation followed him down the middle route, distancing the gap between their pursuers.

Celik and Draz had stopped for a moment to catch their breath. Raiz doubled over, gasping for air before checking to see that Hector was okay.

"They will lose their strength of number as the canyon narrows. If they choose to pursue we can cut them down one-by-one," Celik said. "Any room on those broad shoulders of yours?" He turned towards Aroha. "This old man could use some comfort, seems to be the way to travel these days."

His rebuke towards Raiz did not go unnoticed, though Raiz was too exhausted to care.

"You have lost the use of your arms, not legs. Now move, or shall I cripple the rest of you and leave you behind as bait?" Aroha said.

Celik had only begun to laugh when a bolt of Light flashed through the passageway. "We must make haste, no time to rest."

Raiz ushered Spike forward and charged through the split in the rock.

"Get down!" Draz cried.

Instinctively, Raiz threw himself against the stone column as a volley of arrows forced their way down the narrow stretch. They whistled past his ear to clatter uselessly to the floor.

All five of them clung to the wall, stiff as statues as the barrage continued. Spike changed the colour of his skin to match the murky brown of the rockface before darting behind a gap in the stone.

"What's the plan?" Veil said, raising her voice over the commotion.

"Open to ideas," Draz shouted.

"Risk it?" Veil responded.

"Are you insane?" Draz said. "Those arrows will cut us down before we make it halfway down the stretch."

"We could wait them out?" Aroha offered. "Let their quivers empty."

"No," Celik said, projecting his voice. "They will only draw closer, and the passage is still too wide to hold off against a frontal assault."

"Then I will use my Shine. It is the only way," Veil said, unburdening herself of her protective clothing.

"No, Veil you can't!" Raiz shouted, nearly throwing himself at her before pulling back at the sight of a soaring arrow. "You'll lose control. You could kill us as well as yourself!"

"Well, I don't see any other options!"

"I have a plan," Raiz said.

"I don't know if I like your plans, Raiz," Veil said.

"Just trust me on this one, please. Move on my mark," Raiz said before anyone could question him further.

He waited patiently as a fresh volley flittered past his eyeline.

"Now!" he shouted, stepping out into the open.

"Raiz no!" He heard Veil call, but it was too late, his mind made up.

Ancel's face was a picture of surprise as he thrust his arm downward, sending more arrows flying over his shoulder.

Raiz's reaction was quicker, however. He waved his hands in a flurry of movements, Light leaking from his fingertips with practiced control.

It melded together, forming into a sheet of near blinding transparent white-red Light. He opened his arms wide, expanding the sheet until it blanketed the entire fissure. Arrows turned to ash as they passed through Shine in its liquid state. Prickling specks of charred metal and wood fell to the ground.

Raiz shuffled backwards, at the same time maintaining control of the blanket of Light, edging further and further away from the approaching bowmen.

The scuttle of steps behind gave him fresh confidence. All he had to do was hold his position and his friends would escape.

His hands began to tremble as his Shine ran low. This technique required a constant flow of white-light, and was much more taxing than using his glaive. He looked up towards the sky but found no help from Zur. The rocky slope was now angled too high, and the warmth of the sun dipped too low for it to be of any use.

If he kept this up much longer, he would likely lose the use of his already blackened left hand. He grit his teeth through the pain and held firm, frustrated soldiers still firing uselessly into the ever-narrowing fissure.

Time no longer held meaning as the battle ensued, the drain on his Shine his only measure. Surely he had held them enough for his friends to escape. His mind flashed with images of his friends trapped against a wall of stone, forced to stand, knowing it would be their last fight.

He shook those thoughts from his mind, sweat pouring from the tangled mess of hair on his head. Finally, he could take the strain no longer, the sheet dematerialising, breen flooding his feet. He expected an arrow to pierce his heart at any moment, sending him to his rocky grave. But none were forthcoming. Had they run out?

Through exhaustion filled eyes, Raiz looked up. Ancel was closer now, grinning as he ordered his men to step back. The fissure had narrowed to where only maybe three men could come at a time. At full strength he would have liked those odds, though his legs were threatening to cave in, and he could barely lift his arms over his head.

Ancel clasped his hands together, reaching behind his back as he gathered his Shine into a singular orb of Light.

Raiz knew what was coming. This was the end for him. He just hoped his friends had made it. Maybe his life had been a waste. Maybe his quest for vengeance had been futile. He closed his eyes, waiting for the inevitable, waiting for it all to be over.

He felt the familiar heat of somebody charging their Shine. It came in waves, radiating through the air in such a cramped space. He felt, more than saw, Ancel release the blast. He opened his eyes, welcoming death. A beam of pure energy as bright as the sun itself came at him faster than any arrow. Raiz had no defence against such power, not as he was now.

Something tugged at his elbow. Rough hands wrapped around it and pulled. He flew to the side, his back smashing hard against a rocky edge.

Draz stood before him, charging headfirst into the bolt of white. Quicker than he could comprehend, Light met metal in a blinding flash. Pillars of Light ricocheted in different directions, slamming against stone. The ground shook with the impact, heat cutting boulders the size of Aroha from the rockface, which rained down from above in a rockslide.

Now he understood how the soldiers in Lesken felt as Draz dropped a bell tower upon their heads.

He scrambled away from the blast radius as quickly as he

could manage, dragging a dazed Draz with him, peridium helmet and all.

The rubble piled up in-between them and Ancel, stacking head-height and blocking off the pathway. Dust clogged his senses, causing him to cough several times into his shoulder. The fist-sized gap that remained was too tempting for Raiz not to peer through once the dust began to settle. At first, he saw nothing, only charred rock. But as the scene became clearer, it was impossible to miss the agonising wail of a man in pain.

Ancel's right arm was crushed. Blood, flesh, and bone mixed together in one big mess of hurt. "I know who you are!" he shouted above the agony. "Glaive! I know your face!" He gargled on his own blood, choking out the words. "Raiz! Son of Kron. I will make sure they know."

He began coughing as dust clogged up his mouth. "Mark my words Glaive. Trost, will be no more!"

Raiz went to spit on him through the gap but found his mouth too dry.

A cackle of laughter soon replaced the coughing as Ancel leaned back to look him in the eye. "I've seen your sister, too. Sweet, sweet Isha Glaive. Shame what they have reduced her to, she had promise. Be assured she is suffering. Oh, how she suffers. I would rather this stone had crushed me whole than be left to her fate."

Raiz surged with anger, his body lighting up with a reserve of Shine he never even knew he had. He glowed with energy, ready to unleash his full might just to wipe this man from existence.

"Raiz, we must go!" cried Draz. "Hold your temper! You'll bring the fissure down on us! We will get her back, trust Draz."

In a motion that went against every instinct, he let his friend take hold of him and drag him away from the rubble. Ancel's sinister laughter echoed in the air.

But Isha was alive. If she was alive, then he would find her. It was just a matter of time.

Chapter 16
Dazen

Dazen craned his neck, blowing out a breath of cool air as a curtain of white stone dwarfed him from above. Cylindrical turrets rose high into the night sky, mocking natural law in their immensity. He leaned closer, squinting as he noticed multiple forms moving across the crenelated battlements. They looked like ants, but he supposed he was the ant from their point of view.

Above it all, above the circle of stone that made up Lumindal's outer walls, rose the Fifty Spears — the Eagle's Nest, as some called it. They shot out of the ground like giant white fingers.

Large metal-barred gates stopped the travelling company in their path. Rayner Levic waited patiently as a sharp click sounded from beyond their sight. Soon after, the two columns of metal parted, opening wide. The gates halted with an ominous thud.

An official walked from within the depths, draped in red velvet, hands loosely clasped together. He had a long egg-shaped face devoid of age lines despite his greying hair, which was tied into a neat knot.

Following the official was a mass of soldiers clad in black plate. A banner-man stood tall at the front of their ranks, holding a standard with a golden eagle perched atop a cliff, pitched against a sea of red cloth. The soldiers parted, marching in a synchronised movement as they surrounded the skeptical Levic and Glaive guests.

Brock issued a nervous neigh before Dazen's reassuring hand settled him. The official approached Rayner. "Greetings, warriors of Trost and Zuton. On behalf of the King-Radiant, I welcome you. My name is Yvain. Before you venture any farther, I must insist you lay down your arms. I am sure you mean no harm, but His Radiance does not permit your kind to bear arms in the holy city."

Dazen leaned towards Echo, his face tightening at the high-pitched wail of the official's voice. "Your kind?" he said. "Are we not human?"

Echo rolled his eyes but said nothing.

Rayner held out his arm and lowered it, giving the order to disarm. Blackwings came from all sides, ripping weapons away with no sense of care.

Dazen let them frisk him, dismounting as a man with more freckles than stars in the sky took away his steels. He watched him walk away, memorising his face in case the time came to make a quick exit.

"You will get your weapons back, provided the King is satisfied," Yvain said. "If you would please follow me to the keep, His Radiance is expecting you at his banquet this evening."

Dazen cursed under his breath. Provided he was satisfied? What sort of nonsense were they willingly walking into? He sighed. There was no turning back now. He jumped back into

Brock's saddle and followed the official into the capital.

An overwhelming brightness greeted him. Had he been mistaken? Was the sun still out? He squinted and raised an arm over his face. He forced himself to open his eyes, adjusting to the light. Sumaya rode in stride with him. She moved to poke at a small spherical globe glowing bright with white energy. It was attached to a string and hung from a large metal pole. Similar poles lined the entire length of the street. White cobblestone pavement weaved its way around the city, which was littered with an abundance of exotic flora. Multi-coloured flowers and peculiar looking trees were everywhere, mixing in with the infrastructure and set alight by the shining balls above.

"What are they?" Sumaya asked, recoiling at their touch.

"Watch it! They are hot," Dazen said. "They are called Shine-globes. A marvellous invention. Think of them as ever-burning lanterns. It takes a skilled craftsman to make one, and one with great control over their Shine."

Dazen wove his hand around the sphere of light, feeling its warmth radiate through his fingertips. "They coat the outside with glass, then smother a thin layer of breen over the inside, then they have someone pour fresh Shine into its centre and seal it up."

"So, these never burn out?" Sumaya said.

"Not unless they break, or maybe after a very long time. I am not too sure."

"Amazing! There must be thousands of them here," she said, staring out into the city beyond where indeed thousands of Shine-globes truly gave sense to the name 'City of Light'.

Lumindal stretched for miles, and they followed Yvain in a direct path, Blackwings flanking them on every side. People of all kinds scurried away, preferring to gawk from the safety of their own homes.

It was impossible to miss the massive black streak towering over even the Fifty Spears. It stretched high into the sky like the god of all buildings.

Dazen stared in a mixture of awe and disgust at the instrument of destruction. He had no idea how it generated so much power, but he had heard the rumours, and could now see they were not exaggerated. The tower's mere presence was enough to intimidate and incite fear in the hearts of men.

Beside him, Echo clenched his fists. Dazen couldn't imagine the emotions coursing through him right now. That tower was responsible for so much death.

Eventually, Yvain led them to another high wall, which circled the inner sanctum of Lumindal. Guards ushered them past the gate only for them to come face-to-face with a mound of stone. Carved into the rockface were numerous sets of stairs leading upwards to where the Fifty Spears settled on a large plateau in the centre of the city. The Eagle's homes were a marvel, each column of rock and metal varying in size. A glowing white layer of breen coated the upper half of each structure. The breen shimmered in the moonlight and cast a luminous gleam over the entire sanctum. They were all interconnected, stitched together by a series of long overarching walkways devoid of railings, which acted like bridges between each monument.

Dazen's heart rate quickened. He had only ever seen an Eagle in the flesh once in his lifetime, and that incident had given him nightmares ever since. He wasn't sure if he could maintain his composure. He looked back towards Echo. He had to set an example for the young prince. Had to keep himself calm. But what sort of example was he going to set? How to grovel? How to beg? The thought irked him.

He marched up the stairs on weary legs, all the while

wondering if the Eagles had to climb such a distance every time they ventured out, if they ever did come down.

"Here we are," Yvain said once they were all gathered. "I must ask that you wait here. I shall return once he is ready for you."

Dazen collapsed, the climb taking its toll. "It is no wonder this place has stood for so long," he whispered into Echo's ear. "This place has more fortifications than deaths during the plague."

His comments only seemed to frustrate Echo further, his gaze never drifting from the Last Light.

"I wonder how the people from Hirane planned to take it. You know, before they were destroyed," Dazen said.

This caught Echo's attention. "You think they had a plan?"

"They must have, it would have been foolish not to," Dazen said.

"Foolish to try in the first place."

Dazen grunted, eyes flickering to the surrounding Blackwings. His stomach growled. Reaching for his pack, he plucked out an assortment of dried fruit. The thought of dining in a place like this troubled him. He had heard too many tales of peaceful ceremonies turning treacherous, poisonous wine and tainted food at the centre of each tale. The very air seemed to taste of poison the closer he got.

The sun was well below the horizon when Yvain returned. Dazen pushed himself up on stiff legs, his muscles aching from the cold of the night.

"His Radiance requests that only those of royal blood enter."

A number of grumbles and groans came from tired travellers. It was an expected request, though surely they could have found lodging for them in the city instead of making them wait out in the cold.

Dazen walked alongside the Levic family as a representative from Trost. He didn't officially have to be here. This conflict was between the Levics and the Crown. Though if he wanted to solidify Trost's newfound alliance, he first needed to seek the King-Radiant's permission to marry Sumaya.

Yvain escorted the six of them through a long hallway, passing by a number of vacant rooms furnished to the brim with historic tapestries and ornaments. If the building itself was this intimidating, he found it hard to imagine being in the presence of so many figures of power.

He sucked in a deep breath, walking through yet another arching doorway. They came to a stop before two stone statues. Twin eagles stared down at them from their perch atop a marble mound representing a cliff. Their beaks were the size of Dazen's head. Their wings were folded, covering the lower half of their body, leaving their barrel-like breasts exposed.

"What is it with these people and eagles?" Sumaya wondered aloud, brushing her hand against a wing.

"Eagles are apex predators. No animal their match," Dazen said.

"You mean besides dragons?"

"Well yes, but they are long extinct. Some say the great eagles of old grew to be larger even than some Krono-Dragons. Though there hasn't been a sighting in years. If I had a guess, I'd say that's who the modern day 'Eagles' modelled themselves after. They even built their fortress high in the sky, like one giant nest."

"You are correct," Yvain said, who had been quietly listening in on their conversation. "Though I would be hesitant to mention the fact in their presence. They do not take kindly towards acknowledgment of their ancestors' long-lost companions."

Dazen nodded, taking his word for it.

"Step this way please," Yvain said, ushering them onto a large platform built into the wall in between the two statues.

Dazen and the Levic family stood on shaky ground as the platform began to move. Only Rayner and Yvain held their composure.

"What is this?" Echo said.

"It is a lift," Yvain said. "Do not concern yourself, we are perfectly safe." He pointed towards a series of moving ropes attached to mechanical counterweights.

Slowly, the lift rose, Echo pivoting each time there was a small jolt.

After a time, it came to a stop, Yvain taking them across one of those bridge-like archways Dazen had seen from the ground. He looked over the edge, gasping at how high up they were suddenly. The bridge was wide enough, sure, but that didn't stop him from walking straight down the middle.

Another set of iron-barred gates opened, and they walked into a wide, open hall similar to that of the great hall back in Illidor.

His stomach dropped. Perhaps fifty sets of eyes followed their every step, their weight tearing a metaphorical hole straight through his chest as he walked into the throne room.

Dazen had lived his entire life as a prince. At home, he was the authority, and everyone worshiped him as though it were law. He didn't ask them to, but they did anyway. Now, as he walked forward in the presence of so many of the King-Radiant's Eagles, he felt as they must have.

Behind the facade he attempted to convey, he looked at them with disgust. He hated all of them. But to them, he was a light breeze in a sea full of hurricanes. He was nothing but a peasant in their eyes.

He tailed Rayner, who bore the brunt of their hosts' snide remarks. Some were vocal, calling out a series of bizarre insults. Others were less verbal, but just as demeaning, their glares shooting arrows of pure hatred.

They all donned blood red robes as if they were part of some cult. Their faces blurred into one as Dazen focused on putting one foot in front of the other.

Evanon himself sat leisurely upon the Light-throne. He wore a thick fur coat which seemed to bolster his presence, or at least give the illusion of masculinity. Dazen had never seen the King-Radiant in person. But he would not forget the way his father shivered every time he heard his name.

Evanon looked strong. Not just physically; he projected an aura of strength that was nearly visible. It radiated from him like a glow, as if his mere presence could force a man to bend the knee.

Dazen had seen this before. It manifested in those with strong Shine. The Flare, some called it, an innate ability to harness the sun's energy and project it outward without having to expend any Shine. Dazen thought of it more as a force of will. Kron had been capable of a similar sense of authority, intimidating visiting merchants and messengers simply by using his will to dominate the room. Sometimes Dazen himself wondered if he were capable of such a feat.

His legs grew heavy. He felt as though at any moment he would sink into the ground and that would be his grave.

The Queen-mother sat at Evanon's side, her villainous stare biting into him like a snake toying with its prey. Dazen matched her intensity, the two locking eyes. There was something behind her stare that he couldn't comprehend. She was studying him. Dazen was mixed in with the crowd now, but her eyes did not leave his own, watching as if she knew something that he did not.

Eventually, Dazen turned his attention away. He didn't want to go picking fights, not here. This was not about him, it was about the future of Trost.

The King-Radiant stood, his glare alone enough to silence the crowd of gathered Eagles. "Herald!" he called.

"At once, my lord," said Yvain, shuffling towards the podium before clearing his throat. "Standing before you are King Rayner Levic of Zuton, his sons Huet, Petros and Echo, and his daughter Sumaya."

Evanon's eyes flickered towards Dazen.

"Ah yes, accompanying them is Prince Dazen Glaive from the Kingdom of Trost."

Evanon crossed his arms, his face an unreadable mask.

Rayner bent down onto one knee, bowing low before his children followed suit. "Your Radiance, may I speak?" he said, his words addressed towards the ground rather than Evanon himself.

Evanon waved a hand, indicating it was okay for him to speak.

"I offer you my most sincere condolences. Though I was not there, Lesken is a city of Zuton--"

"Was. Was a city of Zuton," the King-Radiant corrected.

"Yes, of course, Your Radiance. *Was* a city of Zuton. And therefore, I must take full responsibility for the actions of my countrymen. But I can assure you that any action or belief held by the accused is not a result of my country's teachings, nor is it acceptable. If you had not taken it upon yourself to see to their punishment, I would have taken apt measures to reform and discipline the heretics."

Dazen winced. It was hard to watch a man of Rayner's standing reduced to a grovelling mess.

"We do not reform heretics, we purge them," Evanon responded. "Their actions did not deserve discipline, they deserved death. Our system has stood for a thousand years. Only once more has there been an incident such as this, and I will not repeat the mistakes of my father before me. I allow you to govern yourselves. I allow you to squabble like children over petty disputes. To have your own armies, your own rulers. All that I ask in return is your loyalty and your faith."

Dazen nearly fell to the floor, his mind bubbling with a thousand different retorts. But he kept his composure.

"My Eagles are the law. Their holiness second only to my own. Their divinity is sacred, their very lives linked to Zur's. An attack on one of my children is seen as a direct attack on Zur himself! We are what binds his light to our world. Without us there will be no more light. Is this what you wish, Levic?"

"Of course not, Your Radiance," Rayner said. "I would never dare to harm you or your Eagles, but with Lesken no more, the heathens responsible are all dead. I beg you to spare my kingdom further disaster."

Evanon let out a distressed grunt. "I have heard those words before! From the King of Crata himself. To him, my father showed mercy, and what did he get in return?

"Rebellion. I had hoped their erasure from existence would mean the end to these petty acts of rebellious behaviour and disrespect. My will for mercy wanes thin."

Dazen could see sweat pouring from Echo's brow. All five of them knelt motionless, awaiting their fate.

He had never held much love for the Levic family, considering them a rival more than a friendly neighbour. But times were changing, he did not want to see their country turned to dust, to become a barren wasteland like Crata. He wanted them to live, he wanted the peace to last, to see their two kingdoms prosper together.

"My lord, may I have permission to speak?" Dazen said, looking from Evanon to the Queen-Mother and back again.

He was expecting Evanon to berate him, to chastise him for speaking out of turn. Instead, the Queen-Mother spoke. "I was wondering when the famed Prince of Trost was going to announce himself. Please, speak your mind."

Dazen squared his shoulders.

Evanon clasped his hands together, not bothered by his mother's choice to speak for him.

"The Levics were under my family's care at the time of this horrific attack," Dazen said, projecting his voice so that all could hear him. "To the best of my knowledge, they were not aware of any such heresy among their citizens. The people of Lesken acted upon their own free will. I do not believe any form of collaboration was present."

The Queen mother laughed, placing a gloved hand across her lip. "That is a bold statement from a Glaive. My son does not often burden himself with the disputes between Zapour's kingdoms. That burden rests upon my shoulders. I am well aware of the long-lasting feud between the Glaive and Levic families. Your two countries have been at war since even I was a child. I must ask, why the sudden change of heart? Old Kron losing his touch?"

Dazen studied Rayner. For a man usually so imposing, he looked on edge. He had played all of his cards and his fate now rested upon the tongue of his old enemy.

"The time for war between our nations has come to an end. It is my father's hope to look towards the future. I came here today to ask your permission for Lady Sumaya's hand in marriage so that our two countries may be joined together in blood."

This time, genuine surprise crossed the Queen-Mother's face, though Evanon remained unreadable.

"You wish a union with the Levics?" she queried.

Dazen nodded. "My kingdom has ever been loyal to Lumindal. We adhere to all of your demands and have never failed to please Your Holiness. I speak these words not to seek admiration, but I would ask this one favour of you. Allow me to marry Sumaya. Allow our countries to join as one so that we may eliminate any further blasphemy against you or your Eagles. I will see to it myself that they recompense for the crimes committed by the people of Lesken."

Dazen felt as though he was swallowing a hard stone. It was a desperate plea, and it sapped his strength. He was not one to grovel, but he could see the fragility of the situation. He would sacrifice his dignity if it meant sparing lives.

The moment stretched for an eternity as Evanon pondered his decision.

The King-Radiant puffed out his chest and smiled. He took in a deep breath. "How is your father, Glaive? Tell me, why does he not come himself?"

Dazen tensed. "My father has taken ill. Sickness has rendered him unable to travel. I speak with his full authority."

The King-Radiant snickered. "You know we were close once, Kron and I."

Dazen furrowed his brow. Kron had never told him this.

"It saddens me to think of him taken to his bed," Evanon said, pausing to ponder his own thoughts. "When you see him again, please remind the King of Trost, that ambition comes with a cost. If he is once again trying to seek that which was never his, the consequences will be dire."

Dazen again twisted his brow into a knot. What was he talking about? What history did his father have with the King-

Radiant?

Evanon waved his hands. "Your political alliance does not concern me. If you wish to align yourselves with Zuton, you may do as you please, but know that the price will be high. I grant you your permission to marry the Levic girl."

Dazen let out a sigh of relief, the invisible cage restricting his breathing, finally breaking.

"Thank—"

"I am not done speaking!" the King-Radiant grumbled. "You may marry her as planned, but I cannot simply forgive such a treasonous crime. It may be true that you played no part in the death of my brethren, but your people are your responsibility!" He shot a deadly look towards Sumaya's father. "I cannot allow such ill-management to continue, nor can I trust the man who sits upon the throne of Zuton."

In a movement so subtle and casual, Evanon lifted his index finger. A streak of red Light flashed through the air almost faster than the eye could see.

The room grew deathly still. Everyone stood motionless, Dazen trying to comprehend what had just happened.

It wasn't until Rayner dropped to the floor that true understanding occurred.

Dazen still knelt, his limbs frozen with fear. Sumaya issued a loud shriek as she rushed towards her father and turned him to face her.

Echo, Huet and Petros were as Dazen, eyes wide with shock as they sat staring at the dead body of their father, a scorch mark still sizzling where his heart had been. The bolt of Light had pierced his chest, he was dead before he even hit the ground.

"I am done with you, take his body and find yourselves a King fit to lead. My underlings will send you instructions in terms of payment for your crimes. Now begone from my sight," the King-Radiant commanded.

Sumaya lay atop her father, refusing to believe in the reality of what had just happened. Dazen rested a hand on her back. She leapt into his arms, tears streaking down her face and wetting his shirt.

"Come, we must leave this place now," he whispered into her ear.

How could he even ask her that? Her father had just been killed, and he would have her move? But there was no time. If he did not act, then they were all dead. He grabbed the motionless body of Rayner Levic and thrust him over his shoulders. He shot Echo a daring look, hoping he would have courage enough left to rally his brothers and sister to depart.

Echo took his sister by the hand and ushered her across the throne room. Petros and Huet were swarmed by rush of black and gold as Knights of the Golden Talon swept them away down the corridor.

Dazen followed, his legs no longer so weary as adrenaline rushed through his veins. Knights closed in on him, a line of spears forming either side, leaving him with one direction in which to walk. He was nearly out of this place of terror when something caught his eye. His body stopped still, as if refusing to function.

A flicker of violet light clouded his vision. He waited for his bleary eyes to clear, Echo, Sumaya and the Knights pressing in close and forcing him to continue. But as to what he saw before him, there was no doubt. His chest tightened, the cage returning even smaller this time. He choked on his own breath as all sense of time and space vanished. It seemed like forever since he had seen those fluorescent violet eyes, but there could be no mistaking their owner. His sister was here. His sister was alive. Isha had survived, and she was in chains.

Chapter 17
Isha

Isha tapped her feet violently. All of her planning, all of her patience, came down to this day. But her determination was infinite. Nothing would change her mind. Nothing was going to stop her from becoming a free woman.

The image of her brother's face fixed in her mind. He was so tall and handsome now, every bit the man she knew he would become. A wash of old forgotten emotions came through her like an arrow to the chest. She often wondered about him, and about Raiz. Had they tried to rescue her from these tyrants?

She knew the answer already. Of course they had. They were just unable. How could she expect a fifteen-year-old and a ten-year-old to take such bold action? Her father was another case altogether. But that worry was past her now. She was just glad to see Dazen's face once more.

If she wanted to see them again, she had to take matters into her own hands. The time had come to create her own destiny, to change her own future.

She had a single day to make it happen. A senile old

cockroach of a man Averardus may be, but he was also true to his word. He had given Isha, Obeyun and Maitreya their day free of chain. No duties to fulfil; no housekeeping, no visitors to please, just time to kill. And Isha planned to use it just for that.

Ever since Saerus' death, Averardus had been in a plentiful mood. Out of every eagle in the Fifty Spears, he stood to benefit the most from Saerus' venture into the other-world, or wherever it was 'holy' beings went when they passed. Today was just another profitable business deal for the master collector. And it was no coincidence Isha chose this day as her one day of relative freedom. She recalled the conversation between Averardus and Salador. They had been foolish to talk of such dealings in her presence, but then again, who would ever expect a mere slave to use it against them.

"I don't know about this Ish," Maitreya said, taking in a series of panicked breaths. "It's way too risky. You could get yourself killed."

Isha shot her a confident smile. "This coming from the woman who was ready to rip chain from wall and run through the throne room half-naked to escape not so long ago?"

Maitreya shrugged.

"Don't tell me you're having second thoughts. I can't do this alone."

"It's not me I'm worried about."

Isha's mouth opened and then shut. She'd had no idea Maitreya had come to care for her so much in such a short span of time. But she supposed they were stuck in this prison of a house with nothing but each other as company. It was only natural they would grow closer.

She placed a reassuring hand on Maitreya's shoulder and lifted her chin with the other. "I can't promise you this will work," she said with a smile. "But I can promise that if we don't try today, we won't get another chance, not ever. I don't want to drag you into this unless you're one hundred percent willing to live with the consequences should it fall to pieces."

Maitreya bit her lip but gave a semi-confident nod. That would have to do.

Beside her, Obeyun shifted his feet. The Wishan prince was usually composed, but she was placing a lot of weight on his shoulders. Was she forcing him into something he didn't want to do? He offered her a reassuring smile. "I know what you are thinking," he said. "Do not fear. I should have done this a long time ago. We do not belong here. I will see this through with you. All or nothing."

Isha relaxed. Obeyun always knew how to calm her nerves. She turned her attention to the task at hand. Averardus and Salador had come to an agreement. Isha learned that today was the day Averardus was to transport the Koshaki Stones. Only, if she had anything to do with it, that wouldn't be all he was transporting.

Getting to the stones was easy enough. She knew the Forty-Fourth Spear more than any other, and she knew where he kept artefacts that were soon to be exported.

The only problem was the guard detail left watching them at every turn. Two guards stood at the foot of an arched doorway. They had been instructed to let her pass if she pleased, but they would follow her anywhere she went. If she wanted to escape, they needed to be taken care of.

Her hand shook. She had never killed before. She ran a finger over the silk at her thigh to where she kept a concealed dagger. Averardus was always cautious about leaving sharp objects around, especially since one of Adela's slaves had taken his own life with a blade not so long ago. But Isha was smart.

She had taken the dagger from a collection purchased at Saerus' auction. The dagger was ancient, more rust than metal. But it would have to do.

She studied the two guards. One, Ray, was fairly new. His nose was still crooked from where Puk had hit him with the spoon. She remembered him well, remembered his lust for her.

The other, Deryk, was much older and more experienced. He stood tall, his arms crossed and his usual bored expression hanging on his face. They needed to be separated if they were to stand a chance.

"Maitreya, you know what you need to do," Isha said.

She gave a half-nod. "Please be safe."

Maitreya bashed her knee against the stone parapet with enough force to graze and draw blood. She screamed, hopping around as if it was the worst thing to ever happen to her.

Isha looked to the guards, watching as Deryk made his way over to the commotion, Ray staying to watch over the door.

She brushed her hair behind her ear, straightened her posture and walked out into the open. Immediate regret and anxiety hit her like a punch to the gut, her earlier confidence shattered. What was she doing? Was she actually about to go through with this?

She clenched her fists to stop her hands from shaking. She would not fall victim to vulnerability. She was no coward. Her determination was infinite, she would suffer this indignity if it meant being free of this place. No ordeal would be worse than another ten years living like this. She needed to escape, and this was her chance.

Her confidence renewed, she sucked in a deep breath. She locked gazes with Ray, batting her lashes to gain his attention.

She thought back to her conversation with Averardus, and to Maitreya's theory on her eyes. There was something to it. She didn't know what, or how it worked, but somehow, she had always felt it. It was the same with her father, with Puk, with Argon. Men were drawn to her, turned soft in her presence, and it had nothing to do with her looks. Even so, she called on the power lurking within her violet eyes. She threw her will towards Ray, drawing him toward her like a bee to honey.

Her chest tightened. She hated herself for doing it, but she bent over, loosening her gown at the shoulder, revealing more than enough of her cleavage before standing straight and lifting her dress to show her bare leg. With a casual grace, she lifted the dress even higher, leaving Ray staring with wide eyes and an open mouth.

She ran a hand along her open skin before moving towards the spare room they had planned for. Taking one more glance over her shoulder, she beckoned Ray with an elegant wave.

Her anxiety heightened as he followed. She took fast shallow breaths, telling herself that this was okay, it was the plan.

Sooner than she expected, Ray was in the room with her. He pressed his body close to hers. "I've been waiting for this," he said. "About time you chose yourself a real man."

He began kissing her neck. Isha bit her lip, cringing internally. She kept her composure, however, feeling for the hilt of her dagger below her dress. She tried to grasp it, but Ray twisted her away, pinning her arm against her side as he pawed at her.

She wiggled free of his grip, responding with a kiss of her own. She needed him to let his guard down completely if this was to work. Ray took the bait, his shoulders drooping as if under her spell. She clutched the hilt of the dagger, sliding it free.

Her hand shook as it hovered over the back of his neck. For

a moment she thought she couldn't do it, that this had all been for nothing. But she soon recaptured her resolve. She brought the dagger down in one swift motion, feeling the tip dig into flesh, tearing the skin apart. Crimson blood spurted from the wound as Isha withdrew the blade.

Ray opened his mouth to scream but only released a low gurgle as blood filled his throat. He placed one hand to the wound, his other reaching out for Isha in a weak show of defiance.

Before long, he fell to the floor, dead.

Isha dropped the dagger, the blade ringing as it struck the floor. She placed a blood-stained hand over her mouth, watching as a red pool began to form at the base of Ray's neck. She shook her head, carefully stepping around the body. She felt oddly numb, expecting to feel remorse but finding none. She took one more glance at the corpse of the guard before leaving him to rot.

The sound of Maitreya screaming echoed around the chamber as Isha re-entered the room. It seemed Obeyun had not been as successful in his attempt to take out Deryk. The knight was wounded. Blood seeped through his fingers as he held a hand over his shoulder. Obeyun stood tall, his feet wide in an offensive stance. He snarled through gritted teeth, Deryk's own sword raised high in the Wishan's hand.

With his free arm, Deryk held a knife to Maitreya's throat. "Back off slave," he barked at Obeyun. "He will have you all killed for this."

Isha froze. She wanted to intervene, but there was nothing she could do. Obeyun shared a knowing look with Maitreya, and then he advanced.

Deryk stumbled backward, a look of pure shock crossing his face as he pressed the knife closer to Maitreya's neck, only to find his hand rebuffed, the metal glancing off some unseen barrier. Maitreya thrust an elbow into his gut, finding enough room to wriggle free as Obeyun's stolen sword swung down in a jarring motion, cutting into Deryk's exposed neck.

The guard gurgled just as Ray had, and then he too, fell to the floor, dead.

The three of them stood still for a moment to catch their breath. Isha motioned forwards. "Come, we have a few hours before the next guards are scheduled. The crates should be due to leave within the next hour, we don't have long."

Isha grabbed her pack of pre-planned supplies and led them down a series of empty corridors and stairwells. Averardus was a private man when he wanted to be. When he was not playing host to hundreds of guests, he preferred his own company, so they were met with no resistance.

She stopped briefly to wipe away a drop of blood leaking from her dress. "It's this way," she said, leading them down another long corridor and another set of winding staircases. She held up her hand and crouched low. They were at the base of the Fourty-Fourth Spear now.

The air down here was damp, and there was a distinct metallic smell. They crept along the shadowed hall, sticking to the wall where the darkness was thickest. The trio weren't exactly inconspicuous, but they continued forwards nevertheless.

A series of grumbling moans sounded all around them.

"Are we in the dungeon?" Maitreya whispered.

"Not quite," Isha said. "This is the gladiator's quarters. It's where Averardus keeps his contestants for the games in the Luminarium."

Maitreya clasped her hand around Isha's arm. "You can't be serious."

"Relax," Isha said. "We'll be fine. They're under lock and key. This is the safest way through if we don't want any trouble."

She could physically hear Maitreya swallow a nervous lump.

"Help me," came a voice.

"Free me," came another.

Isha turned to see a bearded man press his body against iron bars.

"I don't belong here. Free me, please."

She lowered her head, pretending not to notice him. It pained her, but she couldn't bring them all with her. It was sick, what these men had to go through. Waking up every morning knowing it might be their last, forced to fight simply to survive, usually against overwhelming odds. A gladiator's life was a short one.

She continued through the dark corridor, each ignored cry for help tearing at her soul. A faint flicker of light filtered in through a grate in the ceiling, illuminating the exit. "The stones should be kept two rooms over after this one," Isha said, forcing the gladiators' pleas from her mind.

Obeyun nodded, quickening his pace. Isha raised a hand against the light, placing her other on the door frame. She turned and stared into the cell beside her. The man within did not cry for help, did not even move. His arms were held upright by a tight rope, his bare chest stained brown with dirt. Long hair draped over his face, which sagged low in defeat.

"Isha! What are you doing? We must go!" Obeyun insisted, taking her hand.

She ignored him, instead angling her head to get a better view of the man within the cell.

"Isha!" Obeyun cried.

She held up her hand to silence him. "Puk?"

The man within the cell lifted his head, sending his mop of wet hair tumbling back to reveal the sky-blue eyes beneath, one a shade lighter than the other, its focus elsewhere.

"Puk!" Isha said. She thrust her body against the iron bars in a useless attempt to pry them open. When that failed, she moved for the lock, searching for a key she knew was not there.

Obeyun closed the gap and grabbed her wrist again. "Isha, we don't have time for this. We have to go. Leave him."

She jerked her hand backward, snatching her arm and fumbling for some way to see him free. Puk just stared at her, unmoving. "I can't just leave him here, Obe, he saved my life."

"He saved your life because it was his job to do so," Obeyun said. "It is foolish to think otherwise."

"I owe him. I won't leave him here. It's my fault they punished him like this."

"He is broken. Likely from birth. The Thousand-Shields, they strip their soldiers of emotion before selling them. He is husk, a shell built for one purpose only."

Isha turned, her entire body tense. She refused to believe that. Refused to believe there was no hope for him. "I'm not leaving without him. Will you help me or not?"

A firelight flickered in the distance from which they had come. Isha continued to struggle against the mechanism locking Puk inside the cell. She looked to Obeyun through hope-filled eyes.

He huffed and brushed her aside. "Step back."

Isha did as she was told, though what Obeyun could do that she could not was beyond her.

He placed a hand on the metal latch keeping the door locked. His arm vibrated, his ebony skin glowing, as if there was a light within wanting to come out. The metal melted around his fingers, chunks oozing to the ground beneath the heat. Isha and Maitreya watched on with wide eyes. "You can use Shine!" Isha exclaimed. "Eight years I've known you, and you never told me! How did you get away with it? Does Averardus know?"

Obeyun dripped the remaining Light from his hand, pushing the door open with the other. "What I am and how I have survived is not important right now. Do you wish to free him or not?"

Isha didn't bother to argue. She rushed into the cell and cut Puk down with her stolen dagger. He fell heavily into her open arms. He stunk, and his back was scabbed red with long marks. He looked down at her, confusion wrought on his bony face. "It's okay, Puk," she said. "We can leave this place now, for good."

He didn't respond, couldn't respond. Instead, he let Obeyun take most of his weight and did his best to walk with them from his cell.

Together they made it through the door and towards the adjacent room and then into the store house.

The sound of muffled voices sounded ahead. Isha tightened her grip on Puk's hand, reassuring herself and strengthening his resolve. "No more blood is to be spilled. We need everything else to continue as normal. If they suspect anything, the plan is over."

The others nodded. Together they crouched, waiting with patience for the voices to filter away into the darkness.

"There they are," she whispered, pointing towards a series of brown crates already loaded onto a wagon and ready to be transported.

She had often accompanied Averardus down here as he supervised the departure and arrival of his assets, though in recent times he had grown lazy, instead relying on others to do it for him.

She grinned. All they had to do now was slip inside.

Illuminating the room were six Shine-globes dimmed to a lower light by a thicker casing of breen. They hung from the walls in an ordered fashion. She reached out and grabbed the thin sliver of metal attached to a globe and held it aloft.

She hopped onto the back of the wagon, pulling out a set of keys she had stolen from one of the workers. She fiddled with the glass, pushing the globe closer and feeling at the edge of each key before placing it into the hole, repeating until she heard a sharp click.

With a yelp, she turned to her friends. She did the same with the crate beside the first, it too clicking open. Her luck turned at the next, however. She tried every key twice, failing each time. With time against them, there was no choice. "We'll have to share. Me and Puk will hide in this one, you two take the second."

She helped Maitreya and Obeyun squeeze into crate, forcing their heads down as they struggled to manoeuvre their bodies between the hard edges of the stones. The Koshaki Stones did not seem very special. They looked just like regular rocks, though supposedly they were blessed by Zur and contained magical properties only a select few could harness. "It's not going to be a comfortable journey, but it'll be worth it in the end," she said. "Can you get yourself out with your Shine?"

Obeyun hesitated, as if he hated using Zur's gift, but nodded.

"Let us pray this works." Isha closed the lid, listening as the mechanism locked itself once again.

She looked at Puk. "Are you ready?"

Puk looked at her with more intensity than any flame. He eyed the door they had come through for a long time. His fist clenched. Isha knew his confliction. "Puk, listen to me," she said. "I know you understand me. These people," she gestured above, "they are wrong. You don't have to fight for them anymore. You can be free, make your own choices in life. Just come with me, please."

She forced him to look at her, placing two hands around his neck and locking his gaze with hers. She felt him begin to lose himself in her eyes. She didn't want that, didn't want whatever power she may or may not have to be the reason he came with her. But there was no choice. She gently ushered him into the crate, slipping him a loose shirt from her pack. Taking his hand, she lifted herself into the crate and found a reasonably comfortable spot to rest. Puk wiggled his taut and muscular frame closer to hers. They huddled side-by-side, Puk's long, wavy hair pressed tight against her cheek. An inevitable sense of claustrophobia washed over her as she lowered the lid.

The darkness was unsettling. Rocks poked and prodded her at all angles. She wasn't sure how much air they had left with the two of them constantly sucking it in. She felt as though they had been buried alive, left to die at the bottom of a grave. But this was the price of freedom. She would suffer through the indignity if it meant she could breathe a breath of free air once again.

The silence was deafening, the wait heightening her anxiety. She couldn't be sure how long they had been lying in the dark, but the tension was building. Had the bodies been discovered? Had their absence been noticed? What was taking so long?

Puk began work on a breathing hole, carving the sharp edge of the dagger into the side of the crate in a way that was not obvious, yet allowed air to flow in and out of the casket-like box.

Isha grabbed his hand, holding it tight as the sound of footsteps rang in the distance. Low, muffled voices followed. She couldn't make out what they were saying, but she could only assume the time had come. Her plan would live or die riding upon what happened next.

She held Puk tighter. The voices grew louder and a spot of light touched the darkness where Puk had carved the hole. Hooves stomped in the background as she assumed horses were brought in, likely being loaded and strapped for the journey ahead.

Her excitement rose. They were really going to do this. She was going to pull it off. Her heart pulsed, every inch of her body on high alert, anticipating some kind of setback.

But none came.

More voices joined in the conversation. She felt the wagon rock as they loaded more items into the back, thumping down next to her. She focused on her breathing. The wagon began to move, rocking back and forth. Nausea began to overwhelm her at the thought of being trapped in this space on the road, but she would bear through it.

A familiar, commanding voice rose above the muffling.

Isha went numb. A chill rose from her gut causing her throat to close up. Puk felt it as well, his muscles tensing as his body braced itself for failure.

"Hold up!" came the voice, loud enough so they could hear. "It has come to my attention that a set of keys has gone missing. I must insist upon inspecting the merchandise one last time before it leaves."

Isha's heart dropped in her chest. It was all over. Argon was here.

She prepared herself mentally for a fight. She knew she had

no chance against the captain, but she would not go down easily.

She heard the jingle of keys as the messenger handed his own set over. A shiver shot through her spine as failure dawned upon her. She had been so close.

Again came the click of the lock, and Argon lifted the lid.

Two giant hazel eyes stared down at her crumpled form. All of her mustered fight vanished in an instant at the sight of the man who had watched over her for the past eight years. She blinked at him pleadingly through her tear-stained eyes, knowing too well that it was a hopeless cause.

There was nothing they could do, even If they were able to untangle themselves and find room to strike, he could end their lives in an instant.

But Argon did not act. He stood, staring. She watched as his mind ticked over. What was he waiting for? Why hadn't he called for reinforcements? Why wasn't he ripping her away from his master's merchandise like the monster he was supposed to be?

"Everything in order then?" a man called from the seat of the wagon.

Isha watched as Argon's expression took several forms. She could see the conflict wrought on his hardened face. He wanted her to go. He stepped back from the crate, sparing one last glance at her and Puk before closing the lid. "Everything is as ordered. You may proceed."

She felt the lock click as darkness enveloped her once more. Silence ensued, the only audible sound the soft whistle of a man walking away. Isha knew that tune: Three Birds and a Fly.

Chapter 18
Raiz

Not a single day passed that Raiz didn't think about his sister. The image of her capture lingered in his mind like an invisible scar. He had been young back then. Too young and too weak to stop them. He could not use that as an excuse any longer.

He felt a new strength growing, his Shine was becoming more powerful. Every day there was a subtle change, a pulse of energy that refused to fade. It struck him as odd. Celik had spoken of Zur's power fading, and the evidence was clear; the longer winters, the colder nights. Why then was he growing stronger?

There were many theories about Zur's decline. Some believed Zur to be dying, that this world had run its course and the Skae would return to reclaim Zapour. Of course, this was a more extreme belief. But not one without some merit. Then there was the more common theory, tied to faith. The King-Radiant and his Eagles constantly preached of their divinity. They believed themselves directly linked to Zur, and any harm befalling them had an adverse effect on the world. They used the carnage of the False Kings War to solidify their claim, stating Eagle Ameline's death had broken part of that link, causing a rift between Zur and Zapour. Raiz supposed they would probably do the same now that another was dead.

There were other theories, but Raiz didn't really care for any. The one which made the most sense was Celik's idea that there were simply too many people out there able to wield Shine. He believed that Zur was indeed dying. Not by some unforeseen anomaly, but by humanity's own hand. Every new child born with the potential to use Shine was another person drawing from Zur's not-so-infinite well of energy. Shine was a gift, given to defend his creations against the Skae. With the Skae no longer a threat, natural evolution had multiplied his gift until it became too much to handle. At least that was what Celik believed.

The sound of Spike splashing in a puddle shook him from his reverie. He took a breath of fresh air through his nose. Isha was alive. For the first time since the incident eight years ago he had clarity. It broke his heart to hear of her struggles, especially from a man he hated. But Isha had always been stronger than him. If she could just hold out a little longer...

"We've been following this trail for a week!" Aroha complained. "When will we reach the border?"

Celik turned to face her. "Unless you want the entire Saelmere army at our backs, we keep moving."

Aroha grunted. She was of a similar mind to Raiz. They should be running towards a fight, not away from it.

Celik led the small band of outlaws through all sorts of terrain. The rocky mountaintops of Grayshire and narrow canyons of Silent Valley were far behind them now, replaced by open fields of lush greenery. Raiz moved ahead of the travelling group, cresting a large hill to peer over the top.

"It's there!" he shouted above the wind. "I see it, the Golden Forest!"

While the others scrambled to catch up, Raiz couldn't help but bask in the nature of his homeland. His father would often take them on trips into the Golden Forest that bordered Zuton and Trost, and Raiz had fond memories of learning to hunt and climb the tall trees. His eyes lit up as he skidded down the hill towards the base of the forest. Tall trees of maple and black gum towered over him, and splashing waves of yellow and scarlet leaves rustled beneath his feet. It had been too long since he had seen this place. For a moment he forgot about the rest of the world.

His joy was short-lived, however, as Celik and Aroha rushed in behind him. "You see," Celik said. "I told you we were close."

Aroha ignored him, instead drifting towards Draz. The two of them had been growing closer lately. It was a subtle change, but one that had not gone unnoticed, much to Celik's displeasure. Every evening Draz would take the time to walk Aroha through his routines. Raiz had since learned he called it the Shuku, a set of techniques passed down from each generation of his clan. Aroha hadn't taken to it though. The movements required one to complete a set of stances that just weren't created for someone of her size and bulk. Raiz chuckled to himself as he watched Draz mock Aroha by imitating her attempt to perform one of the movements as he made his way down the hill.

Raiz inclined his head toward Veil beside him. "What do you make of these two?"

"What do you mean?" she asked. "They're just Draz and Aroha, same as they've always been."

"You don't think... you know?"

Veil leaned back. "Huh! No way, look at them. They couldn't be more opposite. I mean, Aroha is tall as a tree, and Draz is so... Draz," she said.

"I think they're perfect for each other."

"You and nobody else. How would that even work? For one, she'd have to bend down several feet just to look into his eyes, and she best get used to the taste of metal, because that's all she'd be getting for the rest of her life."

"Not every relationship has to be based on physicality," Raiz said, gawking at the two of them.

Veil punched him on the arm playfully. "Didn't take you for a romantic, Raiz. You continue to surprise me."

Raiz blushed, shying away so she couldn't see the redness in his cheeks.

"Do you know something that I don't?" Veil pressed.

"And what if I do?"

Veil punched him harder. "If you know something and aren't telling me, so help me..."

"I don't, I don't," Raiz said. "I was playing. You know Draz, he wouldn't go telling me something like that. But I think he likes her. I can just tell."

"Well, who wouldn't like her? Aroha's beautiful."

Raiz averted his gaze, realising too late that he was staring at something he shouldn't have been.

He recoiled as Veil's knuckles imprinted upon his already dead shoulder.

"Maybe I deserved that one," he said.

"Damn right you did."

He shook his head clear. This talk of love only sought to distract him from his goals. He had no time for such games.

Even so, the warmth of Veil's breath next to his could not be easily ignored. She smelled like apricots. The two had been dancing around each other for months, though neither were willing to admit anything to the other. Veil was older, perhaps she still saw him as a child? Like a little brother. The tension was becoming too much. If only his Shine granted him the ability to read minds.

He placed his feelings aside as Spike issued a deafening screech, diving head-first into a pile of golden leaves. He rolled around on his back, panting like a dog and frolicking from pile to pile as if he had never seen a leaf. Raiz couldn't believe how huge he had grown, and he grew by the day. He wished Isha had warned him, but then again, how can one prepare for raising such a creature? It was his Shine that was making him grow. A couple more years and who knows how big he might get.

A groan sounded from behind. Hector dragged himself forwards, his shoulders slumped, head to the ground. He had been this way ever since his incident. It wasn't as though the boy was complaining. His young muscles and bony frame just weren't yet up to using so much Shine. Plus, the boy had never ventured outside of his city. So much time on the road had to be exhausting.

He had kept quiet for the past few days, distancing himself from the others without falling too far behind. Guilt troubled him, Raiz could see it plain as day. His outburst had nearly seen them killed, and he hadn't even been awake for the aftermath. But Raiz had only himself to blame. He had destroyed this boy's home, his livelihood, his very identity.

Raiz tried to continue his lessons, teaching him how to use his Shine, but he refused to listen, too scared of another outburst. He was content keeping to himself, though he had resorted to covering his entire body with a loose cloak, tying it to his head to avoid any direct intake of sunlight.

After a few hours of traversal, the golden hue of the forest began to dim as the darkness of the night took hold. The Golden Forest belonged to neither Zuton nor Trost, growing where the border between the two nations blurred. It was often a cause of conflict. In fact, the battle for the forest's resources was actually the catalyst which set in motion the hundred-year conflict between the two neighbouring nations. People often referred to it as the 'Blood Forest' instead of Golden.

"How long has it been since you've seen your homeland?" Veil asked.

"Too long," Raiz replied, almost under his breath.

He stared in awe at the beauty of the land he had called home for the first ten years of his life. Animals scattered back to their hiding holes as the rough wind berated their homes. Tree-trunks as tall as the Illidoran Palace towered above them, the canopy blanketing the stars.

Throughout the growing darkness, Raiz spotted a tiny speck of light shining in the distance. Raiz strained his eyes, turning to Veil, who confirmed his suspicion with a firm nod. The pair rushed for Celik. "Firelight, we're not alone," Raiz reported.

Celik followed his line of sight. "Take Veil and scout. We must know how many they number and which banner they follow."

Raiz nodded, keen for action again after weeks of nothing but walking. He grabbed Veil and made for the fire. Hector tried to follow, but Raiz waved him off, ordering him to stay with Spike and the others.

The two moved like panthers in the night, their dark clothing and shadowed steps masking their approach as they rounded the campsite, finding an area of elevation riddled with fallen foliage perfect for observation.

The bustle of blue uniforms scuttling around campfires was

unmissable. There was no mistaking the bone-white crest of a longsword stretching the length of their arming coats. These men were the White-Swords of Illidor.

He squinted. In between the mass of blue and white was the green crest of a serpent stitched onto a sea of yellow.

"Those are men of Zuton," Raiz whispered. "They bear the crest of the Serpent of the Twin Lakes. What are they doing with soldiers of Trost?" His hand bubbled with Light, preparing for conflict.

He was surprised, however, to find the men sharing drink with one-another. There was no joy to it, though. They seemed exhausted. He scanned the rest of the camp, finding much of the same. The soldiers walked like Hector had, dragging one foot behind the other. There was no conversation flowing, no friendly banter, just silence. Were they returning from battle? What events could possibly lead to this?

He turned to Veil, who shrugged.

He surveyed the area for a sign, an indication as to why two opposing nations would be here, together. Reflexively, his entire body tensed, pulling his muscles taut. His throat closed as if some invisible gate had been shut. A man paced the length of the camp. Raiz's gut wrenched as recognition dawned upon him. The tall frame, the sharp jawline. It was as if his father's face had been moulded onto a younger body. Raiz hadn't seen him in nearly a decade, but there was no doubt in his mind. This man was his brother. Dazen was here.

"What is it?" Veil said.

Raiz ignored her, unable to part his focus. The world around him narrowed, his mind overflowing with images of the past. The past he had left behind.

"We must go," he said. "We have to leave this place, now."

"Raiz, what's wrong? Has something spooked you? Do you

know them?"

Cool metal pressed against the side of his throat, causing him to freeze.

"Do not move," came a voice.

Raiz cursed under his breath for letting his mind drift so far as to lose himself and his surroundings.

"Stop! You move but a single inch and my brother and I will redden the leaves with your blood."

Raiz obeyed, eying Veil, who was in an identical situation by his side.

"Unhook your belt, slowly! Both of you," came the voice again. Raiz could feel the assailant's hot breath on the back of his neck. He had a masculine voice, but not an old one. Most likely he was a few years Raiz's senior.

The two obliged, Raiz unhooking his belt and placing his weapon on the grassy soil. Veil gave him a subtle smirk. They were fools if they thought she held all of her metal in plain sight.

"Turn around and place your hands behind your head. Make a move, and my brother shoots a bolt through your little girlfriend's eye."

Biting his lip, Raiz did as told. Their second mistake was threatening Veil in front of him. None had ever done that and lived.

"Petros, you are too close, you are going to get us killed. I have them covered."

Raiz craned his neck. Now that he could see them clearly, he noticed they were twins. Not overly large, one an inch taller than the other.

"Shut it, Huet, I know what I am doing. You just want the glory for yourself."

The one named Huet glowered at his twin, crossbow still

pointed awkwardly at Veil's chest. "The only glory you will get is a sword through your chest," he warned.

"You would like that would you not, Brother!"

Raiz and Veil needed no signal, the two moving in unison. Raiz kicked at the shin of the closest assailant, causing him to gasp and fall to the ground. A mechanism clicked, and a bolt went soaring through the air. Veil whirled around in a blur of black, the bolt loosing harmlessly into the darkening night where the soldiers had made rest.

Raiz fell on top of his opponent, muffling his mouth with his palm. "Make one sound and I will turn your insides into a boiling pot of stew."

Veil was not so lucky. Because of the distance between her and her target, he managed to let out a shrill scream of panic before being subdued.

"Do not kill him!" Raiz spat.

"Why?"

Raiz couldn't come up with an adequate response. What could he say? That these men travelled in the company of his brother?

Before Veil had the chance, the sound of armour clinking and boots on soil caused them both to jolt. Instincts kicked in, and Raiz looked for an easy escape. The sound grew closer, and men began to close in around him from every direction. He pulled his dagger from beneath his cloak and held it at one of the twin's throats.

The soldier called Petros croaked as Raiz pressed the tip further into the groove of his neck.

Veil did the same, pressing her knife even harder into the other's, neutralising any thought of heroism.

"What is this madness?" came a shout as more soldiers in blue began circling them.

Raiz hid behind Petros, not wanting his brother to recognise him.

"Release these two at once! I am Prince Dazen Glaive of Trost. If you should harm them, know that you will make a most powerful enemy."

Raiz forced himself not to laugh. Oh, how humble you have become, Brother.

An eerie silence overshadowed the scene as neither party showed any sign of backing down.

"S-she is crazy, g-get her off me!" Huet cried from beneath Veil's blade.

Dazen let out a groan of discomfort. "Name your terms, bandits. If it is riches you seek, I will have my men gather what little we brought with us upon our journey. But if you strike, know that your lives are forfeit."

Petros slumped, lowering his body before Raiz could tighten his grip.

Dazen twitched, leaning forward, his eyes narrowed. He shook his head, shuffling to the side to get a better angle.

The scar, damn it, he was going to see the scar. Raiz lowered his head deeper behind Petros.

"It cannot be. Surely it cannot be," Dazen said.

"W—what are you doing? Get this criminal off me," Petros squawked.

"Show yourself!"

Veil looked towards Raiz for support, but he ignored her.

"Tell me you are not who I believe you to be! Tell me my brother remains lost to this world! Tell me I am seeing a ghost!" Dazen said.

Raiz said nothing.

"Show me your face, Raiz!"

The game was up. Raiz stood up straight, keeping his

dagger at the twin's throat. "It's been a long time, brother."

Dazen took a step forward. "Put down the blade. Let us talk as men."

Raiz tightened his grip, drawing a line of blood. He felt a well of emotions rise to the surface. A thick, bottomless pit of past hatred began to overwhelm him, driving him into a state of mind that was not his own. He hated Dazen simply because he had stayed. He knew it was irrational, that he had still been a child himself. But now that he was grown, the resemblance to his father was too great. He had let them take her and did nothing.

"Fight me for him," he said. "Or will you sit and cower as Father did?"

Raiz wasn't sure what he was doing, but he needed to know the sort of man Dazen had become. Was he his own man? Or was he their father reborn?

Dazen's face contorted. "What are you doing, Raiz? We are kin. We thought you dead! Come back to Illidor, let us be brothers once more."

"We ceased being kin the moment you and Father let them take her!"

"Raiz, this is madness. Put down the blade!"

"Fight me for him!" Raiz repeated.

Dazen grimaced, waving his men backwards and raising his sword high. "Let them go, and you will have your battle."

Raiz looked to Veil. He could see from the look on her face she was struggling to comprehend the situation. He removed the knife from Petros' throat and kicked him forwards, sending him stumbling towards the line of men. Veil did the same, adding an extra oomph to her kick.

Raiz grit his teeth, drawing energy from his well of Shine. The sun was past the horizon now, he would find no aid from

Zur. He clenched his hands, crafting his Shine glaive as if it were natural to him. The rod of white glowed, a thin line of red at its core.

To his surprise, Dazen stayed firm. He drew another sword from his belt, this one smaller, and closed his eyes in concentration. A vibrant burst of energy erupted from the hilt of each sword, the Light wrapping around the blade's edge like a coat.

Their eyes locked in a fierce battle of will.

Raiz charged first, putting years of pent-up aggression into an overhead slice. His glaive met Dazen's heated blade in a clash of energy. The sound resonated, sending sparks of Shine into the air, the liquid turning to breen the moment it touched the ground.

The two fought a dance that seemed to go forever, neither finding advantage.

"Coward!" Raiz spat as he moved in for a sideways slash.

"Deserter!" Dazen said as he blocked and countered with a strike of his own.

Raiz took a step back to recover his breath, eyes never leaving his brother's. "It is you who is the deserter, not me!" he said. "You left her to die in the hands of that monster! For that I will never forgive you."

"I was fifteen, Raiz! Not yet a man! Do you not think I tried? I begged Father, I begged!"

"It was not enough, you gave up! You stopped searching, continuing your life of leisure with our coward of a father. I never gave up, I will never give up on her!"

Dazen's emotion was plain for all to see. Tears streaked down his face as he came at him.

Raiz was no different, fighting through bleary eyes as the two clashed. Throughout the battle, Raiz felt a new strength growing inside of him, one born of sheer anger. His chest tightened. It burned with an unfamiliar sensation. He clutched at it with his blackened hand, trying to suppress it. But it was like he was a kid again, with no control over his Shine.

Raiz glowed with a white-hot energy he neither could, nor wanted to contain. The energy was like an aura surrounding his entire body. He gave in to the sensation, pushing outwards in a sudden burst. A near-invisible wave struck his brother, pushing him to the ground and keeping him there as if he were tethered to it.

Raiz hovered over Dazen's prone form, his glaive vibrating beside his open neck.

Dazen stared up at him. "T—the Flare. Since when can you use the Flare?"

Raiz ignored him. He didn't know what his brother was babbling about. He wanted to strike him down, to kill him for what he had — or rather had not — done. His arm shook with uncertainty. He felt the rage hidden below continue to surface, his Shine taking control as if his body were not his own. "Admit it!" he screamed. "You failed her! She still suffers because of you! Admit it! I want to hear you say it."

He felt tears begin to stream down his cheeks, emotion pouring out of him.

"Raiz!" came a call. It was Veil.

Her voice brought him back to reality. What was he doing? Was he about to kill his own brother? He let out an angry gasp before dispelling his glaive, placing his head into his hands.

For a long moment the two sat there, weeping.

"I'm sorry," Dazen said. "I should have done more. I should have protected her. I should have brought her back."

Tears dripped from Raiz's eyes like Shine from fingertips. "No. It's my fault. It's all my fault. She wouldn't have been there if I had done what I was told. If I didn't disobey. I just wanted a better look. And she, she was just looking out for me. She didn't deserve this! She didn't deserve this life!"

Dazen embraced him, pressing his head into his shoulder. All sense of the outside world vanished as Raiz gave in to a warmth he had thought lost forever. "We will get her back," Dazen said. "I promise."

Chapter 19
Dazen

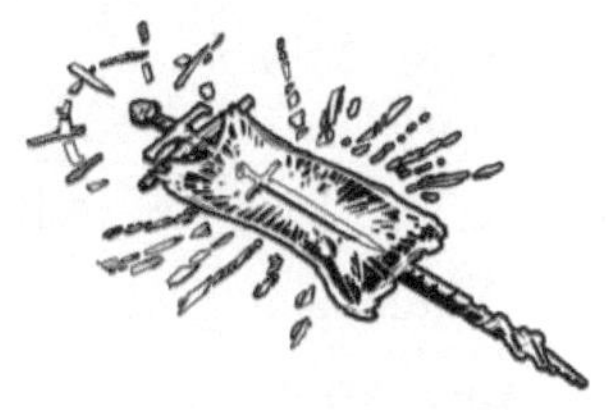

An intangible tension gripped the room. Dazen had invited Raiz and his companions into his command pavilion for supper, hoping to put the past behind them and move forward as brothers. Though, drawing conversation out of them was like prying a nail from wood with nothing but your fingertips.

The elderly man travelling with Raiz watched him like a hawk through dark, beady eyes. He was the most unusual person Dazen had ever seen. A long, unkempt beard covered his chin. His arms were dead and dangled at his sides, most likely from Shine burnout. He had thick, powerful legs and a burn mark in the shape of a hand across his face, making his stare look even more sinister.

Dazen ignored him, instead turning to the mountain of a woman to his left. He found no comfort with her either. Raiz had introduced her as Aroha. A long silver broadsword draped across her back, resting against locks of braided brown hair. She cracked her knuckles, filling the silence with the click of bone against bone.

Three more of his brother's companions rounded out the table. The woman named Veil sat at the end, a bored expression never leaving her face. There was another who refused to remove his helmet, no matter how hard Dazen insisted, and the last was a boy. Dazen raised a curious brow, wondering how someone so young managed to get mixed up with this lot, but he thought better of questioning it.

Then there was the pricket Isha had gifted to Raiz. By the looks of it, the beast had grown to an unbelievable size. It lay next to Raiz, its barbed tail curling around him. He wondered if Isha knew just what her gift would turn into.

Dazen withdrew inside himself. Thinking of his sister always pained him. He still hadn't built up the courage to tell Raiz what he had seen in Lumindal. He still couldn't comprehend it himself. Isha was alive. All of these years, she had survived. And once again, he had done nothing. But what could he have done? A king had just been executed. He could have tried to save her, torn the chains from her wrists, but that would have just seen him killed. He could do nothing for her if he was dead.

Dazen shook his mind clear. "So, Raiz," he said, "how did you come by such friends?"

The entire room turned to look at Dazen before settling their gaze on Raiz. Petros and Huet huffed derisive sighs before turning their attention back to their food. He supposed he couldn't blame them, Raiz had held them hostage.

"Celik found me wandering the forest when I was a boy," Raiz said, gesturing towards the elderly man with the charred face. "He taught me how to fight and how to control my Shine."

Dazen's left cheek twitched. He should have been the one to teach Raiz to wield his Shine. It was his duty as an elder brother. He should have been there. There was nothing to do about it now. He didn't force Raiz to run away, that had been his choice.

"Aroha and Veil were already with him when he found me," Raiz continued. "Draz, we picked up a few years back in the mountains."

"And what do you do with yourself? Are you part of the mercenary guild?" Dazen inquired.

"We don't fight for coin," Raiz said, planting a hand on the table. "We fight for what's right. We fight for justice."

Dazen leaned back in his chair. Beside him, Sumaya's knuckles grew white. He could hear her snarling through gritted teeth.

She stood up. "It was you!" she said, directing her accusation at Raiz. "You are the Red Knight. I could see it in your Shine. You are the one who murdered the Eagle in Lesken. You are the one responsible for my father's death!"

With a blur of motion the room was in chaos. Petros and Huet moved to their sister's side, weapons drawn. Raiz and his companions bunched up, the pricket issuing a rumbling growl. A stilled silence settled as both parties eyed one another cautiously.

Dazen was left to play mediator, standing between the two groups with outstretched arms. "Stop this," he insisted. "They are here upon my invitation and shall not be harmed."

The twins lowered their weapons but did not drop them. "What my sister says is true, you know it Dazen," Petros said. "These people cannot be trusted."

Dazen's head snapped to Raiz. "Is it true? Are you the outlaws responsible for what happened there?"

He could see by his expression that Sumaya was right. "Oh Raiz, how could you? Do you know what you have done?" he said.

Raiz stood. "I know what I have done."

Sumaya turned to Dazen, grabbing his arm in a firm vice. "We should take him in. We will be shown mercy if we bring Evanon the true culprit."

Dazen shook her hand clear. "We will do no such thing! He is my brother!"

Sumaya bent over and slammed her fist into the table. "He is not your brother anymore. Look at him. He is a criminal, an outlaw."

Dazen grimaced, turning from the scene and placing hands over his temples as if they were about to burst.

"Look at yourselves," Raiz said, gesturing towards Sumaya. "Your king has just been executed, and you wish to kiss the foot of the executioner."

Sumaya's face changed into a deadly scowl, but she said nothing.

"I saw what happened in Lesken," Raiz said. "And I am sorry for my part in it. I truly am. I will have to live with that image for the rest of my life." Raiz paused, glancing at the boy before continuing. "But such destruction should not be possible. Such power was not meant to be held by one man. I refuse to live by their rules. I refuse to bow down while children are taken from the arms of their crying mothers. While cities are wiped out in the blink of an eye. Call me a criminal if you must, but the Eagles will burn."

Dazen's mouth hung open. His body shook with the force of gravity weighing him down. He didn't even think Raiz realised he was projecting his Shine.

The tension broke as a black bird fluttered through the opening. The raven squawked, landing atop the shoulder of the man with the charred face. Raiz released his hold on the room, relaxing back into his seat.

The woman named Aroha untied a piece of parchment from the bird's foot and rolled it out onto the table before them.

"What is this?" Dazen said.

"I demand an answer," he insisted when nobody responded.

"Hush, child," the elderly man said, as if he were the prince and Dazen the outlaw. "This here is Fulcrum. He is perfectly harmless."

"This isn't the time, criminal," Petros said. "Send your bird away before we put it in the ground, along with the lot of you."

"Is that a threat, Prince of Zuton? Because I would heavily advise against it. Besides, are we not currently under your protection, Dazen Glaive?" The old man eyed him.

Dazen moaned. "Just send it away, I'm sure the bird has better things to do."

"Sending me messages is precisely what Fulcrum is supposed to do," Celik said, eying the letter as he spoke. "I have him trained to track the scent of Raiz's Shine. He would not come here unless it was important."

Dazen watched as Celik's face changed. His eyes grew wide, and he spared a look towards Raiz before reading the letter again.

"What is it?" Raiz said.

Celik turned to face Dazen. "It seems fate has a sense of humour, Glaive. You may be forced to change your stance. An Eagle has left the nest."

"So what," Dazen said. "That is of no concern to me."

"Would it concern you then, to know he is chasing a certain violet-eyed individual?" Celik said.

Dazen's stomach dropped. His limbs refused to move as the words struck him like a physical blow.

Raiz leapt to his feet. "Isha has escaped? Where is she?"

"She is travelling west of the capital. We should catch her if we leave now," Celik said.

Raiz was ecstatic, barely able to contain himself. "Brother, we must go to her, we must!"

Petros stepped forward. "It is a trick, Dazen. You know it to be so. Where could he have come by this information? They are making you look the fool."

Petros' words may as well have been lost in the wind, for Dazen's focus was on one thing only.

"Are you with me, Brother?" Raiz said, holding out his arm. "Or will you abandon her as Father once did?"

Chapter 20
Isha

Isha's lips kissed wood, the rough texture grating against her chapped skin, softened only by her own drool pooling into a wet puddle.

She felt sick. The constant racket of hoof beats on hard soil and wheels turning over and over itched at her. The sounds melded together into one big, consistent drone that she was growing ever certain would end her sanity. Even worse was the ongoing fear that the wagon would hit a divot or run into some kind of pointed stone, causing the whole crate to jolt. She forced herself to swallow, refusing to let her bile come to the surface.

The acidic smell of ammonia filled the crate. A day and a half they had travelled, and she had been forced to relieve herself. She was thankful her bowels had not caused her too much concern, though she was beginning to feel nauseous.

The caravan had kept a furious pace, stopping only for a brief rest during the night. Averardus was not one to mess around, sending the stones on a direct route towards western Craw. Isha knew she was walking a fine line. He would send riders the moment he noticed she was missing, but she needed to gain as much distance from Lumindal as she could, and this was the fastest way.

Puk was her one comfort. She felt his strong arms bulge as they wrapped tightly around her, reminding her that she was not alone. As glad as she was for Puk's embrace, she found the silence to be quite disturbing. All she wanted was to talk to someone again, to have human interaction. She knew it wasn't his fault he was the way he was. But even so, it would have been nice to fill the void with some light conversation.

She opted to speak anyway, talking to Puk about her past and about her present. She told him of her brothers, and of life back in Illidor. She told him about the day she was taken, and of the things she had seen and witnessed in her life as a slave. This must have paled in comparison to what Puk had been through, but he didn't seem to mind, tightening his grip around her waist.

She wanted to find out more about him, so she worked out a way the two could communicate. She would whisper him a question, and he would answer by poking her softly in the ribs. It was all they could manage within such a tight space. One poke meant yes, two was no, and no response meant he was not comfortable answering, or he did not have one to give.

"Is Puk your real name?" she asked.

One poke.

"Do you have a family?"

Two pokes.

Isha placed a hand on his arm. "Do you want a family one day?"

Puk's hand hesitated, and for a moment she thought he was going to let the question slide, but she felt a soft finger press into her ribcage.

So, she was right. He was not the mindless servant people

made him out to be. There was a soul there, and a good one. The notion gave her confidence. If someone as scarred as him still held hope for a better life, then there was no reason for her not to.

She wanted to pry further, to ask him deeper questions so she could begin to understand him. But wounds were still fresh, and now might not be the appropriate time to delve into his past. Instead, she opted to turn the subject back towards herself. "Are you angry at me for getting you into trouble?"

The question was risky. She didn't want to make him reconsider the situation, but she needed to know. The lacerations on his back were only just starting to scab over, and she still felt guilty. It was her fault he was punished so.

Two pokes.

She let out a sigh of relief, adjusting her head to a more comfortable position. She owed him, more than once, and she was not done repaying her debt just yet.

She had to commend the horses at the yoke of the wagon. They kept a fierce pace. Isha smiled to herself in the darkness, pleased at her own mind. She not only managed to outwit her — now former — master, but she had escaped out of perhaps the most heavily guarded and fortified city in all of Zapour.

She centred her mind. The deed was not done. They had been patient, but Averardus was no fool. He would discover the bodies. He would notice she was missing. Her gut twisted as she recalled the image of Argon dropping the lid. It still baffled her. What had she done to deserve such an act of kindness? Argon had always been nice to her, it was true, but that wasn't it. There was something more. Had he come to care for her more than she thought? Or was he too just another good man trapped within the chaotic cog of Lumindal's hierarchy?

A chilled breeze filtered through the hole in the crate,

freezing her bones and signalling Zur's decline for the day. Communication with Obeyun and Maitreya was tricky. It wasn't as though they could jump out and have a leisurely chat about their escape. But it was her plan, and she had to trust that they would follow her lead and stay put until she decided it was time.

The wagon wheeled to a stop. From the muffled conversations overheard on their brief breaks, several guards escorted the small convoy. She waited until the talking grew distant, and then finally non-existent. The time was now. The urge to pee was too great, and she couldn't suffer the indignity twice. "Are you ready?" she whispered into his ear.

One poke.

"I would rather not leave an obvious trail, but if it comes to blood, are you able?"

One poke.

"I think most of them are asleep. We should start carving," she said.

The two went to work, poking and prodding at the hard timber, cutting away chunks and prying at others with bare hands until she could fit her fist through it. Their escape had to happen tonight now, lest someone discover the hole.

"Can you crawl down a little so I can fiddle with the lock?" she asked.

Puk obliged, wriggling his taut form lower into the crate.

Isha held her breath as his body rubbed against her. She was now keenly aware of his face directly in line with her behind.

Thankful for the darkness, she placed a bony forearm through the gap, careful not to catch a splinter from the sharp points. She manoeuvred her fingers so that her thumb, index and middle fingers clasped tightly around a particular key on the chain. Her remaining two fingers were used to feel for the cool metal of the lock. She moved the mechanism around until she found a small indent.

Sweat trickled down her brow. She had only one chance. If she dropped the keys, she would not recover them.

With a steady hand she placed the key into the hole and twisted, listening again for the click. With another sigh, she and Puk pressed against the lid of the crate, slowly lifting it away.

She welcomed the fresh breeze. Never again would she take the outdoors for granted.

She bit hard into her lip as all of her aches and pains became apparent. Her back was as stiff as a flagpole, and her neck was bent out of shape. She cracked it back into place with her hands in an unladylike fashion. She had long since left her courtly mannerisms behind. She was no longer a Lady of Illidor, and no longer an object to be admired. She didn't know what she was anymore. But the thought of finding out lifted her spirits.

The snap of a twig beneath her boot brought her back to reality. Her head jerked sideways as she stared into the darkness. Two silhouettes stood outlined in the light of the moon against a pitch of black.

Sentries.

She knocked three times on the other crate and watched as the wood surrounding the lock began to burn away. She pressed a hand to her mouth. A strange aura of energy emanated from the now open crate. The very air itself seemed to vibrate as Obeyun and Maitreya untangled their limbs. A couple of the Koshaki Stones levitated in the air above Maitreya's prone form, glowing a deep blue. Isha reached out to touch one of them. Its surface was cold. The rock bobbed up and down but did not fall. "What is this?" Isha whispered.

Maitreya shrugged. "They just started glowing a few hours ago. I think it might have something to do with what I am. The stones move away from me like metal does. I think they respond to me, but I can't tell for sure."

Isha grabbed the closest stone and pocketed it. "We'll have to figure this out another time."

Maitreya nodded, carefully helping Obeyun out of the crate and onto the soft soil. Together, they placed the lids back on and pushed them closer to the side of the wagon to cover the gaping hole they had carved into the front. When satisfied, the four of them crept away from the wagon.

As if in tandem, they all sucked in a deep breath of fresh air. Isha looked around. The landscape was barren, nothing but a few half-grown trees and dry leaves. They moved towards the two four-legged silhouettes to their left, approaching the tethered horses with caution.

Firelight flickered in the background, highlighting the banner of Lumindal, the feathered eagle billowing in the wind, warding off would-be bandits.

Obeyun ran a hand along one of the horse's coats before untying the knot. He mounted it with relative ease, casting his arm down for Maitreya to grasp. She tucked in neatly behind him.

Puk began to mount when a raspy voice cut through the air. "What the -- thieves! Thieves in the night! Guards! Thieves! To me, you fools!"

Isha's limbs froze. Puk's arm whistled like an arrow as it drew back and thrusted forward.

"Thie--gahhh."

Isha couldn't see what had happened, but by the loud gurgle, she knew Puk had struck true. It was too late, though, the camp had been roused. Sentries were closing in.

Isha reached for the horse, remembering her time riding as a child as she flung herself over the saddle. Puk did the same, kicking the horse into motion before the guards had time to orient themselves. Together they joined Obeyun and Maitreya as they galloped their way across the dark plains.

Her earlier panic turned to excitement as they travelled further and further away from the camp, the guards nothing but grey dots on the horizon.

They had made it! Though she couldn't help the overwhelming sense of dread. Averardus would not let her go. He would come for her. Wherever she went, he would follow, she was sure. She was too important to him.

She fixed her gaze forward, refusing to look backwards anymore.

Let him come.

Isha's stomach grumbled. Days turned into weeks as the four of them traversed the wilderness of Craw. Thankfully, she'd had the foresight to pack food and drink before making her escape, but their supply was dwindling awfully low, even after rationing. Their water was basically gone, and Maitreya had just eaten the last of their fruit. They scavenged a few berries along the way, but Craw was not like Trost. A wave of dunes lined the horizon, blocking their path further west and forcing them to go around. Much of Craw was an infertile desert, devoid of vegetation. They were very much a seafaring nation, with most of their cities lining the coast and most of their wealth generated from trade with the Darkwater islands.

She tried to calculate their location in her head. Without the horses they would be lost, but without food and water, they wouldn't make it much farther.

"We must be out of their reach by now," Maitreya said, leading her horse by the reigns.

"Don't underestimate him," Isha said.

"Isha is right," Obeyun called. "Averardus is not the type to let this go. His pride will not let him. He will have every soldier in Lumindal searching for us soon."

"I wouldn't be so sure," Isha cut in. "Think about it. Averardus is a man of pride. But what he values above all is his reputation. There's no way he would want our escape to become public knowledge, not if he can help it."

"So, you don't think he will come then?" Maitreya said.

"Oh no, he will come. But he'll use only his own resources, no other."

"Then let us be far away from here when he comes," Maitreya said. "But uh, where are we exactly?"

Isha stared idly at the landscape. "I'd say we're about halfway between Lumindal and the Sapphire Sea. If we take this route around the dunes, we could reach the sea in a few weeks. Then we can look for safe passage across."

Obeyun rounded his head. "You wish to venture across the sea to Yagos? Trost stands but a few days travel south, are you sure?"

Isha lowered her head, slumping into her saddle. "I've been thinking. Maybe it's best for me to not return."

"But that is your home," Obeyun said. "It is all you have talked about since I have known you. Your father and brothers are waiting for you there!"

Her mind rattled with indecision. "And what if I return to find I'm no longer welcome? What if my return brings further harm upon my family? It will be the first place Averardus looks. I can't go back. I'll put them all in danger."

Isha looked up to see Obeyun had closed the distance. He placed an arm on her shoulder. "I understand your pain, but do not come to a rushed decision. Think on it some more."

Isha nodded, the heat from her friend's hand warming her.

"Why didn't you tell me you can use Shine?" she asked.

Obeyun withdrew his hand. "It is not because I do not trust you. I have told no one. As much as I hated the way we were treated, there are worse fates out there."

Isha couldn't help but feel a little annoyed that her friend had hidden such an important detail of his life from her, but she couldn't blame him. She would have done the same. "How did you keep it hidden?" she asked. "My older brother used to have to drip his Shine into a hole, he showed me once."

"Shine only comes to us from light," Obeyun said. "Averardus kept us indoors for the most part. Other times I had to be creative."

She turned her head to Puk. "Can you use Shine?"

He shook his head.

"Puk is from overseas," Obeyun interjected. "Shine is much less prevalent in Yagos. It is likely why their empire has kept its distance all of these years."

Puk stretched an arm into the air, pointing out a mark on the horizon. A small dot of black against the bleak landscape of brown and yellow.

They picked up the pace, watching as the shadows multiplied, forming into the shape of houses.

Puk reined in the horse as Obeyun and Maitreya caught up to them.

"Any ideas?" Obeyun said.

Isha's stomach rumbled. "We have no choice. We'll starve if we don't get food and water."

"We have no money and nothing to offer for trade," Obeyun said. "Unless we sell the horses, but the burden may be too much to bear without them."

"Maybe they will take us in? Offer us refuge?" Isha offered.

"No. We cannot take the risk. Lumindal has agents

everywhere, even in remote towns like this," Obeyun said. "And the people of Craw do not take kindly to people of Wisha wandering inside their border."

"Then we starve," Isha said.

"Wait! I just remembered," Maitreya said, ruffling around in her pack. She pulled out a pin that glinted gold in the sunlight. The metal was circular, with four claws of an eagle's talon etched into its centre.

"Where did you get that?" Isha said. "That's the pin of the Golden Talon."

"I swiped it from the guard back in Lumindal. He won't be needing it anymore."

Obeyun took the metal and held it in the air. "Well, this will get us something, but we cannot sell it. The item is too prestigious, it will draw attention."

Isha dismounted and stretched her aching limbs, taking the pin from Obeyun as he and Maitreya did the same. "What if we melt it?" she suggested. "Not all the way, just enough so the symbol is indistinguishable. You can use your Shine." She gestured to Obeyun.

"My Shine is not a tool for you to use like a torch," Obeyun snapped.

Isha recoiled and took a step backward. "I — I'm sorry. I didn't mean..."

Obeyun waved a dismissive hand. "In Wisha, Shine is forbidden. It is seen as an instrument of destruction and nothing else. It is the tool which enslaves us, which forces us to hold our oaths to the King-Radiant. For that, it is despised. A person found capable of wielding the Light is sent to the capital as a sacrifice so the lowlanders will leave us in peace."

"I'm sorry Obe. I didn't know," Isha said. "Did your clan know? About your ability?"

Obeyun shook his head. "Unlike my skin, my Shine was easy to hide. I did not need another attribute for my brother to use against me, not that it mattered in the end."

Isha bowed her head, letting her hand and the golden pin slump to her side.

Obeyun took her hand in his own, prying the pin from it as gently as he could. "I will do it. Just this once."

Isha offered a faint smile. She watched as Obeyun's focus shifted towards the metal. He placed it between his thumb and two longest fingers. He closed his eyes. A bright, white Light centred around the tips of his fingers, radiating heat as the metal slowly began to bend out of shape. The four talons melded into one, the perfect circle of the pin losing its shape and turning into an unclear blob.

He paused just before the metal began to fully melt. "This should do," he said. "When it cools, we should be able to sell it. But we cannot go. Between your eyes and my skin, people will notice. It has to be someone else."

"By someone else, you mean me," Maitreya said, rolling her eyes.

"You are the only one who can do this," Obeyun said.

"You want me to go in alone!?"

"We don't have a choice," Isha said. "We'll starve or freeze to death in a few days."

Puk stepped forward, grabbing Isha by the arm. He nodded towards Maitreya and tightened his grip.

"Are you sure?" Isha asked.

He gave a confident nod.

"Take Puk," Isha said. "He'll follow, keep his distance. If you suspect danger, clasp your hands behind your back. That will be the signal for him to come. Take the nugget of gold and trade it for food and clothing. Don't worry about a fair price, just get the supplies and get yourself out of there."

Maitreya sucked in a deep breath. "Okay, I've got this. You can count on me."

She took the now cool metal and disappeared into the growing darkness. Puk followed behind, keeping at least ten paces distance, but never leaving sight.

The icy sting of the night's wind brushed against her open cheek. Isha rapped her leg on the dry soil, the tempo growing faster the longer she waited. She hated putting her friends in danger. It should be her risking her life. But she and Obeyun were too recognisable. One look at either of them from the right angle and it would doom them all.

Time went slowly as they waited for Maitreya and Puk to return. They perched themselves on top of a small ridge about a hundred yards away from the town. It was no more than a couple dozen houses thatched together with whatever wood they could find. The village inn stood out among the rest, a slightly larger building at the edge of the town. A billow of smoke rose into the sky.

She turned to Obeyun. "They've been gone too long."

"They will be back, do not worry," he said.

Isha groaned, but she trusted her friend's word.

"What's that?" she asked, startled.

A grey blur moved along the outskirts of the village before darting towards them. It grew in stature, separating into two, causing Isha to jump with excitement. "It's them!"

She rushed to greet them before pulling herself back under the cover of the night.

Puk's hair blew in the wind as he bolted up the ridge, closely followed by Maitreya's bony frame, tensing as she struggled to lift a sack.

"Success?" Isha asked, moving to help her.

"Success. You should have seen his face when I offered him the gold for such a low price," Maitreya said, struggling to suppress her joy. "Reckon I could have got us a little pocket change too, but best not to be too greedy."

"You did wonderfully," Isha said. "Now, let's get out of here before we draw any more attention. What did you —"

She stopped mid-sentence as more grey blurs appeared in the distance.

"Were you followed?" Isha asked, her voice quivering and frantic.

Maitreya looked behind, her face slack as the multiple forms became clear.

They formed a haphazard line. Some held tall pitchforks aloft with both hands, others clung to pickaxes, shovels and whatever they could conjure by the looks of it. Some in the back nocked arrows as the advancing villagers moved to surround them.

"Seems there was something he liked even more than gold," Isha cursed.

"Or feared," Obeyun grumbled. "We must leave, now!"

Without further consideration, the four of them sprinted down the ridge, not bothering to check what their haul contained.

Isha slung the two sacks over the horse and moved to mount. A feint whooshing sound passed her. She ducked, peering into the distance, looking for the source.

The sound came again as four arrows landed at her feet. They thudded into the ground, one skidding along the surface and nearly impaling her ankle. She stumbled to the side, tripping over her own feet. Puk's stone-like arms lifted her up. He jumped on the horse's back and held out his arm. She grasped his forearm in a firm grip and felt him pull.

Her thigh pulsed with a sudden impact. Her grip faltered, and she fell to the ground. She clutched at her thigh, which was now sticky and wet. The shaft of an arrow lay embedded in the soil beside her, sticking out like a nail ready to be hammered, her blood staining its edge. She looked down at her wound, it was only a graze, but there was no time.

Obeyun and Maitreya were on their horse. They were speaking, but Isha was in too much pain to comprehend.

"Go!" Isha screamed. "Leave me, save yourselves!"

Her words fell upon deaf ears. The pair dismounted, moving to aid her and Puk.

The villagers rushed forwards, surrounding the four of them in an impenetrable circle.

"I'd be staying still if I were you lass," a tall man with a long, black moustache called. "Don't get many people sell'n gold in these parts. S'pose yeh don't mind tell'n me where you got it from, eh?"

"Please," Maitreya said, "that's all we had, I promise. Just leave us be, we're simple travellers."

"Don't think so lass," he said. "No simple travellers gonna be walk'n round with gold in their pockets, then trade'n it for bread'n water. I'd wager you'se are thieves. I reck'n yeh stole it, an someone's gonna come look'n. Now, yeh gonna come quiet? Or do we have to make yeh?"

Puk began to rise, drawing the dagger from his side.

"Hold Puk," Isha said. "These men are not our enemy. We'll find another way. Trust me, please."

Puk looked from her wound and back to the man. He grit his teeth before throwing the dagger to the ground.

"That a boy," the m   ' "

Chapter 21
Dazen

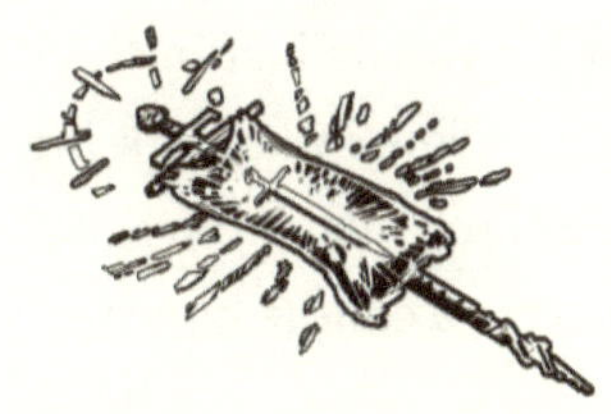

"Raiz stop! This is madness!" Dazen called over the clamour of his galloping horse.

He spurred Brock onwards, knowing the seasoned war horse to be quicker than Raiz's pricket, if this creature could even be called one anymore. A full day had passed since news reached their ears of Isha's escape, and Dazen had still not come to terms with it.

The pricket was a marvel. It was slower than a horse, but seemed to have endless stamina, carrying Raiz on its scaled back for miles without reprieve. It ran on all fours like a hound, its barbed tail and serpent-like neck bobbing with each stride.

Brock snorted, keeping his distance from the creature as if sensing Dazen's own hesitation. He had never seen a pricket this large before. They were said to grow no more than a few feet in length, and yet Raiz's had grown to be nearly as big as Brock.

Dazen stood in his saddle and turned to face him. "Slow down! You are going to kill your animal! And then where will you be? Stuck on your own two feet while our sister runs for her life?"

"Don't underestimate Spike's strength," Raiz said, refusing to even look his way.

"Then think of your friends. Think of us. We cannot keep this pace, and you cannot do this alone."

His brother's determination seemed infinite, and for a minute he thought his words lost in the wind. He breathed a sigh of relief as Raiz pulled Spike back into a canter. Likewise, Dazen placed a soothing hand on Brock's neck. He looked behind. The others were a couple hundred yards back, but they were following.

"What was that?" he asked his younger brother as they came to a stop.

"Our sister is out there. I've waited long enough."

"Do not think you are the only one who wants her back," Dazen said.

Raiz dismounted and looked at him through tired eyes. "You don't get it. We may never have another chance."

Dazen leaped from Brock and grabbed hold of his brother's shoulder. "I know what is at stake, believe me. But there are things we must talk about first."

"Such as? What could possibly be more important than saving Isha?" Raiz demanded.

"We could be starting a war! Do you not see that?" Dazen explained. "If we murder an Eagle and the word passes, it will be Trost who suffers for it. I know you no longer care for your country, but I have a duty to protect Trost."

"So, you would leave her again?" Raiz said.

"That is not what I am saying," Dazen replied.

"Then speak plainly."

Dazen wiped a bead of sweat from his brow. "If there is a way to free Isha without the Eagle's knowledge, we must take it. Or is your lust for revenge so great that you would risk all of Illidor for a taste?"

Raiz bit his lip and clenched his hands before letting out a long sigh. "Yes. If there's a way, then I'll take it. But if that proves impossible, I won't hesitate. Isha is my first priority. If that's too much for you, then you should go back to Illidor. I'll do this alone."

Dazen paused, the weight of the decision a near unbearable burden. He thought about his sister, remembering their conversations about philosophy and the world. He remembered her smile and the way it made him feel. He remembered her passion, her conviction, and her sense of justice, even at a young age. If there was anybody worth fighting a war over, it was her. He held his arm out in front of him. "We do not leave Craw until she is in our arms, live or die," he said.

A smile stretched high into Raiz's cheeks as he clutched Dazen's arm in his own. "I am with you," he said, and then nodded over Dazen's shoulder towards the horses dotting the distance. "What of them? This isn't their fight. Why do they follow?"

Dazen took another look over his shoulder. Petros and Huet had broken into a fight the night before, disagreeing over their course of action. Huet had decided to join them, though whether through genuine compassion, or through the desire to solidify the peace between their two nations, Dazen couldn't tell. Petros had left in a rage, taking his father's body back to Nanta. Echo too offered to join them, and Dazen suspected his lust for justice and revenge almost rivalled Raiz's. Sumaya's presence was the most surprising, given her apparent hatred towards Raiz, but still she followed, continuing to impress him.

"They are good people. They can help us get her back,"

Dazen said.

"Good people?" Raiz said. "For a hundred years Trost has been at war with Zuton—"

"That was a long time ago!" Dazen interjected. "You have been gone a while. Much has changed. The conflict between nations was born before us. It does not have to be our future. Father and the King Rayner have come to an agreement."

"And now their King is dead, and they blame me for it," Raiz said. "They'll turn on us, I can see it in their eyes."

Dazen stamped a foot on the ground. "And who are you to talk of trust? Who is this man you blindly follow? Where does he come by such information? How do we even know he speaks the truth?"

"Celik has taught me more than Father ever could have. And I don't question what brings me closer to my goal."

"He is using you as a weapon Raiz, can you not see?" Dazen said. "Whatever agenda he has against the Eagles, let this be the last. Once we free our sister, come home with us. Let us be a family again."

Raiz snorted. "While Father lives, I can never come home."

"Well, you may just get your wish," Dazen muttered solemnly. "Father is dying."

Dazen watched for a reaction from Raiz, a hint of emotion that might suggest sympathy, or even regret, but he showed nothing.

"Will you become King?" Raiz asked.

Dazen paused. "I had not really thought upon it, there are more pressing concerns."

"Well, you should think on it. Kron is set in his ways. His eyes are closed, they see nothing beyond the high walls of Illidor. If you are to rule, you must open them."

"I am not as blind as you might think. I see how the King-

Radiant poisons our lands, I know Zapour cannot sustain these restrictions and limitations forever. But there is a way to go about these things, Raiz. The weight that comes with a crown is heavy, and that is what you do not understand."

Something changed in Raiz's demeanor then, a subtle shift as he lowered his head.

"There is something you must know," Raiz said. "Ancel, the Saelmere prince. He saw my face. He knows who I am, and what I want."

Dazen bit his lip and cursed under his breath. "Are you certain?"

"Yes. Draz and I broke his arm, he wants my blood."

Dazen interlaced his hands behind his head and exhaled. "Ah...you are a fool sometimes."

"What's done is done," Raiz said. "I thought you should know. One way or another, they'll come for us."

"I suppose we have no choice now. Though, do yourself a favour — do not tell the Levics. They are already hesitant as it is, and we may need them to save Isha."

Raiz laughed. "And face the wrath of the Princess again? Not likely. She's a feisty one, you'll have your hands full there. I like her."

Dazen ran a hand over his hair before shaking his head at Raiz's comment. "You are not wrong there, Brother. Seems we both have an eye for the dangerous type," he said with a wink, watching as Raiz's gaze dropped before drifting toward the traveling company as they closed distance.

Chapter 22
Isha

Isha woke to a searing pain in her thigh. She clutched at her side, the wound calling to her like a baby in the night. She placed a hand against the ageing bandage, which had now turned a sticky greyish colour. As had become her routine, she scratched at the bonds of rope around her wrists with her growing fingernails. The rope was frayed in several places after days hard at work, but still she made little progress.

The four of them were prisoners once more, but instead of the wealthy high walls of the Forty-Fourth Spear, they were held in some kind of inn, forced to sit quietly while the innkeeper and several villagers gawked at them over hunched shoulders. Come to think of it, this was not so different from the capital.

A plank of wood was nailed atop the arch of the entrance with the words 'Hot-Pot Inn' painted over it. A fireplace carved into woodwork kept the place warm at least, and a cauldron of stew, cooking at all times, gave off a pleasant smell. Wooden tables set on trestles lined the length of the inn, illuminated by the flickering light of tallow candles and oil lamps.

The village speaker planted a single chair on the floor before them, sitting on it backwards and letting his arms rest against its top. She had come to know him as Speaker Tomi.

"Right," he said with an exasperated sigh. "Last time I'm gonna ask youse. Who are yeh and where'd yeh get this metal?" He held the chunk of gold between his thumb and index finger.

Isha said nothing, turning her head away from him. All she had to do was delay until she could formulate another plan of escape.

"Silence's s'not yer friend here lass. Gold ain't so common out in these parts yeh see. When word passed of someone flashin' it round and selling it for nothin' but a few scraps, I can't help but be curious. Now, where did yeh find it? Better me askin' than Gillet here, trust me lass." He gestured to the man named Gillet, who puffed out his chest and slung his hammer over his shoulder.

Isha looked to Maitreya, who had refused to make eye contact with her since their capture. She felt a pang of guilt. It wasn't Maitreya's fault, it was hers. Everything was her fault.

"I'd be careful 'bout this one," Gillet said, pointing towards Isha. "She got them violet eyes. She's one them Mystics I heard 'bout. She'll bewitch yeh if yer not careful."

The Speaker edged closer in his chair, holding up his hand to reach for her chin.

Before he could do so, however, a flurry of footsteps sounded from the entrance.

"Speaker Tomi!" shouted a voice. "Got company, the Golden kind."

Tomi's face twisted, his mouth hanging open as if he had forgotten to breath. "Don't play with me boy, don't got time for yer nonsense today."

"I'm not kidd'n 'round this time! They're really here!"

The speaker's mouth twitched. "How many?"

"A whole lot of 'em! Can't count them on me fingers, sir."

Tomi grumbled. "Yeh can't count on the best o' days, boy. Let me see n—"

A large thump cut his voice off. The door smashed open, breaking one of the hinges in the process.

A wash of black and gold plate burst through the entrance, shoving the village guards into the corner as though they were nothing. They filled the room, pushing tables and chairs out of the way. They bounded up the two spiral staircases, flushing out any villagers before reporting to their captain, who removed his black helm and shook his face free of sweat.

Isha shied away, knowing what was to come but praying for some kind of miracle.

She recognised this man. She didn't know his name, but she could tell by the way Puk shied his head that he did.

The captain took slow steps forward, his boots clinking against the wooden floorboards as he came to a stop less than a foot away from her. He bent over, grabbing her chin and twisting her face towards him. Isha squinted, refusing to let this man see her for who she was.

"Open your eyes, girl," the captain said.

Isha couldn't hold any longer. She felt his mead-fuelled breath sting against her cheek as he pried her eyes open with greasy hands. She opened her eyes, snarling as she did so.

"It's her," he said.

"Shall I let him know, sir?" one of the other soldiers asked.

"Wait a moment," the captain said, striding a step or two to his left to where Puk sat motionless against a metal pole, hands bound behind his back. "I know this man. He was one of us."

Before Puk could react, the captain swung a furious

backhand, cracking into Puk's cheek and sending him reeling, spitting blood onto the floor.

"This man thought himself better than us," the captain said to everyone in the room. He cut the rope binding his hands and grabbed Puk by the cuff of his shirt before throwing him across the room. "He thought he could escape, and with a princess! How noble of him."

A synchronised chuckle resonated through the line of soldiers as they shared a laugh at Puk's expense.

"Well, I for one, demand justice." The captain kicked Puk hard in the ribs before drawing his sword. He cut at Puk's shirt, shearing it all the way until it fell off, his bare back showing towards Isha. If she had the use of her hands, she would have clasped them over her mouth. His back was a canvas of marks both old and new. Some were ancient. Chunks of white flesh protruded from his skin, some stretching the entire length of his back. Others were more recent, scabs from his suffering under Averardus' cold whip. Blood poured from his latest head wound and trickled down his back, working its way past the scars like a bead through a maze.

The Blackwings peered over him like a pack of hyenas before a slaughter. They snickered and sneered, glad to have the chance to implement their own twisted form of justice.

They took turns kicking him, each boot landing harder than the last. Puk could do nothing. He had no weapon, no way out.

She forced down a scream. She wanted so badly to help him, to save him as he had her. But she once again found herself useless. There was nothing she could do but hope for a miracle, for justice to correct itself. She swore then that if she were to be freed from these bonds, they would be the last to bind her. She would be helpless no longer. Never again would she be the flesh. She would be the knife.

"I'm sorry," came a voice from her right. It was Maitreya. She spoke to the ground, refusing to look up at her. "It's all my fault, I didn't know I was followed. If only I —"

"Hush, Maitreya, you did nothing wrong," Isha said, interrupting. "It was my plan, not yours. I'm the stupid one.

Isha winced as another soldier struck at Puk's prone body.

"Right then," the captain said. "Now that this place is safe from this scum," he paused to spit on Puk, "go and get His Holiness."

A sense of dread washed over her, melting her insides and turning them to mush. She knew what was coming. Who was coming.

More guards clad in polished black armour filtered into the room, forming two lines before standing at the ready. Averardus marched into the room as if he were the King-Radiant himself. He forced his shoulders to straighten — a hard task given his age and sheer lack of any physical bearing. Lines of terror formed into a tight bunch atop his brow. He held his golden sceptre in his left hand and seemed ready to use it for once. He strode over in his white robe to where the four of them lay prone, and stood over Puk's body.

For a moment everything was still. Nobody dared speak a word for fear of risking Averardus' wrath. Her heart wrenched as Argon walked up behind him. His broad shoulders and tall frame towered over everyone, including Speaker Tomi, who was now quivering in the corner like a child who had misbehaved.

Her first thought was that Argon had turned her in, but that didn't make any sense. Why let her go just to catch her again? It could have been a game, some cruel fetish where he enjoyed the chase. But one look at his sombre face and she knew it not to be true. He was disappointed. Through some misplaced sense of kindness, he had given her the chance, and she had failed.

She silently tried to plead with him one last time, blinking tears through her violet, hypnotising eyes. But she knew it to be fruitless. There was only so much he could do.

Averardus' anger flared when he noticed the bandage upon her thigh. He tried to calm himself, taking slow focused breaths. "Who did this? Who marred my artwork? I demand to know."

The silence stretched longer than anticipated, but eventually Gillet stepped forward. The smith had been stripped of his hammer, and the apron around his neck was smeared with grease and dirt. "I did yer holiness. They be steal'n the gold. I was just take'n it back yeh see. Shot 'er down me'self."

"Argon, cut this man's throat," Averardus said.

Without hesitation, Argon slid his knife underneath Gillet's beard and pulled. Blood poured from the open wound as he collapsed — lifeless —next to Puk, his apron now doused with red.

The Blackwings stood as statues, watching as the knight wiped his knife on his victim's trousers before sheathing it as if nothing had happened.

Averardus moved towards her, taking her chin in between his fingers and turning her head to each side. "I should kill you," he said. "Look what you have made me do. I have not left Lumindal in years. Years! And yet here I find myself, in the middle of this shit of a country. In this shit of a town, because of you. And yet, I cannot kill you, you are far too precious to me. You are my most dazzling jewel, the centrepiece of all of my wealth. Do you not understand your value? Do you not appreciate what I have given you?"

Isha went numb, too overwhelmed by both internal and

external pain to care for his nonsense.

"You will live, but know that your life will no longer be pleasant."

No longer be pleasant? What did he think her life had been? All rainbows and sunshine?

"No more roaming around unchecked, no more managing my affairs, no more seeing your pretty little friends here. You will be like a painting on a wall."

Despite listening as he rambled about her impending doom, she found herself laughing. A big belly laugh, pausing only to cough as her delirious mind faded between sanity and insanity. She laughed louder, so that all could hear. She barely even noticed Averardus' face as it boiled until it was redder than a tomato. It was only when a hard backhanded fist cracked against her cheek that she came to herself once more.

"You insolent little..."

"You cannot touch me," she said through bleeding teeth. "You are nothing. You are a false god. You think yourself mighty, you think yourself holy. When in reality, you are neither. You are not Zur's chosen, you never were. You are just a simple man who happened to be born into a position of power."

His lips pressed into a thin line as rage seared through his entire body. He attempted to compose himself, even forcing a smile before backing off. "Perhaps a demonstration is in order then." He turned to Puk. "I see you have come to care for this man."

Isha's delirious confidence faded, her face shrinking like smelting iron.

"He means something to you, does he not?"

Isha said nothing.

Averardus issued a shrill, agonising laugh. "I may not be

able to bring myself to harm you, but this young man is a traitor. And one who has caused me great grief. I do so despise bloodshed, but I suppose I can make an exception here."

He raised his sceptre high, the metal wings of an eagle at its tip pointing like a scythe. He poised for a strike, hovering in the air for an eternity before she heard a sharp ring. She closed her eyes, not daring to look at the inevitable corpse of her friend.

Chapter 23
Raiz

Hills rose and fell, each distinctive, yet all seeming to mould into one. "How much further?" he asked, wheeling Spike to face Celik.

Celik looked odd on the back of a horse. Without arms, he was as useless as a fly without wings while riding. To compensate, Aroha had strapped him to Draz. A tight rope was slung around their waists, much to Draz's discomfort. Even the horse seemed to protest, sagging behind and snorting every time they rose up an incline.

"Do I look like I have a bloody map?" Celik said, kicking at the horse's side. "This is precisely why we always travel on foot. These beasts are all stink and shit. Too much trouble for their worth."

Veil trotted up beside them, looking comfortable on the back of her stallion. "What was that?" she said. "I think I just saw Draz roll his eyes."

Despite the seriousness of their mission, Raiz found himself laughing. The ex-mercenary just shrugged, tapped his metal helm, and moved on, Celik muttering a bunch of curses to himself at the rear.

Soldiers wearing the traditional blue-white uniforms of the White-Swords of Illidor constantly flanked Raiz. He stared at them, trying to discern their intent. He looked for a familiar face, but found none. It was clear who they followed, huddling around his elder brother like a protective shell.

Soldiers bearing the green crest of the Serpent of the Twin Lakes rode in a similar formation, grouping around the royalty. They seemed a mixture of emotion, hovering between Huet and Sumaya as if not quite sure who to follow.

Sumaya was a mystery. She had challenged him, called him out in front of everyone. Her vexation towards him had simmered, but it was still there. She didn't trust him, nor did he trust her. He did respect her though. She was strong, like Veil. She didn't rely on others to speak for her, and she carried her sword at her hip as if she knew how to use it. You didn't have to trust someone to respect them.

Hector seemed to have taken a liking to the youngest Levic prince. The two rode together, and often Raiz would catch them deep in conversation. He felt a sliver of relief. Maybe the boy would be better off with his own people. That would leave Raiz to focus on more important matters. But even he had to admit, Hector was growing on him. It was a surreal feeling, teaching someone else to use Zur's gifts.

As if sensing his thoughts, Spike grumbled through gnashed teeth.

"Don't worry, boy," Raiz said, stroking the scaly skin between his two snake-like eyes. "You'll never go hungry while I'm around." He lowered his arm to Spike's mouth, letting his excess Shine drip from his fingertips and feeling the familiar tingle of Spike's tongue licking it away.

He pulled up next to Dazen. "Any news on her

whereabouts?"

Dazen sighed. "It is akin to shooting an arrow in the dark here. We have no way of determining which direction she headed."

"What's your opinion?"

Dazen raised a brow. "So, now that you are lost you want my opinion?"

"I'm done playing games, I just want to find her. So yes, if your mind will bring us closer, then I'll gladly eat my pride."

"Very well," Dazen said, pulling out a rough map of the area. "These are only estimates, but I take our position to be about here." He pointed towards a spot on the map. "If your friend is to be trusted, then our sister left Lumindal anywhere between ten and twelve nights ago, following a direct route towards the coast. It is impossible to tell whether she continued upon this route or ventured off on her own. My guess is the latter. She is smart. She knew her captor would be hot in pursuit. Now, there are only three known villages between Lumindal and the coast here," Dazen said, drawing his finger along the line of the map. "This part of Craw is fairly remote. We can cross Doonatal off the list, it is too far west and beyond their capacity to reach given the time frame. If she is to have any chance of surviving, she would have needed to make it to one of these two," he pointed towards two dots on the map. "Keld is the larger and more populated, but it is a way up northwest. My guess is she stopped at Speakers Hollow," he relayed, pointing to the closer dot on the map.

"That's close!" Raiz exclaimed, Shine building beneath his skin.

"I put us no more than a day east of the Hollow. We must be prepared for anything."

"Then what are we waiting for, let's ride!" Raiz urged.

"Wait!" Dazen cautioned. "You must not get your hopes up. The likelihood we find her there is slim. Best we can hope for is information, anyone who has seen her."

Raiz grinned. "Don't worry, Brother, I have a good feeling about tomorrow."

Shadows curled at his feet, his body hidden from the pale light of the moon as he crept atop the bluff overlooking Speakers Hollow. He wriggled closer, squinting to give himself a more direct view. Dazen crawled up next to him. "Do you see anything?" he asked.

"This is a ghost town. Why did they name this place after people speaking?" Raiz said. "I'm going to go take a look."

Dazen pulled at his shoulder. "Wait a moment longer," he insisted.

Raiz obliged, though his body twitched with an urge to move that was almost beyond his control.

"There!" Dazen said, pointing towards one of the larger buildings. "Watch."

Raiz followed his line of sight but saw nothing. "What is it? Did you see her?"

"Just watch," Dazen said.

A streak of black with a glint of gold moved against the grey outline of houses. Dozens more followed it.

"Blackwings!" they said in unison.

Raiz rose to his feet before the word finished rolling off his tongue. "They might have her! I'm going."

He moved to attack, but Dazen's hand jerked him back, pulling him close enough to whisper. "Remember what I said. If they have her, we must free her quietly."

Raiz wrenched his shoulder free. "I'm not a fool. I've been doing this kind of work longer than you. Veil and I will do reconnaissance and return with more information. If our situation should turn dark, look for Light in the sky."

"Zur is sleeping, are you sure?" Dazen said.

Raiz spread his lips into a grin. "You've seen what I can do with my Shine. Do you wish for another demonstration?"

Dazen shone a brazen smile in return. "I see the years have not turned you humble, little brother."

"There's no time for modesty. I've waited too long to hold back now," Raiz said.

The others drifted up the hill behind them. From his pale face, Huet looked as though he had just seen a ghost. "Those are Blackwings," he said. "Maybe even a few Knights of the Golden Talon. This is not what we agreed to, Dazen."

Raiz scoffed and shook his head. "Of course."

The furrow on Huet's brow deepened. "Watch your tongue, outlaw," he warned.

Raiz rolled his eyes, but Dazen placed a hand on his chest and pushed him back a touch. "This is not your fight, Huet. If you wish to leave, do so now," Dazen said.

Huet stepped forward. "You two are mad. You wish to fight them? I did not come here to do battle with Lumindal. We are in enough trouble as it is."

"Then what did you come here for?" Raiz interjected.

"Dazen, shut your little shit of a brother up before I put my sword through him myself," Huet said.

Dazen put his arm in front of Raiz. "Enough, Brother," he said. "The Levics have no business here. This is our fight." He turned to Huet. "Huet, even if you leave here, I will honour our fathers' deal. Our nations can be united."

Raiz snorted. "Coward," he said.

Huet jumped at Raiz, but Dazen caught him mid-flight and held him back.

Raiz had no intention of holding back, however. "You can't tell me you have no desire to see your Father avenged," he said. "Well, this is your chance."

"I will avenge my father right here and now," Huet said, lunging at him.

A woman slipped between them, tugging at Huet's collar and pulling him backwards. "Quiet, you fools. Do you want to get us all killed?" It was Sumaya.

Huet calmed a touch, brushing his coat clean of dirt.

"We are with you," came a voice. Raiz bit his tongue as the youngest Levic made his presence known. "Forgive my elder brother, he is simply concerned about our country's standing. To the Abyss with the King-Radiant! And his followers! We will fight for what is right," Echo said.

Huet's face flamed red. "You do not speak for me! Shut your mouth before I close it for you."

Raiz expected the young prince to cower, but to his credit he stood firm. "I always took you for a coward, but now I have proof," Echo said.

Huet threw an open palm at Echo but fell short as a blur moved from the shadows and struck him in the gut.

Sumaya looked up at Raiz, a fire in her amber eyes. She rolled her shoulder in its socket. "Go, find your sister."

There was a pain in her voice. She had not yet forgiven him for his role in her father's death. But unlike her elder brother, she was stronger than her own convictions.

Raiz was one with the wind before Huet could utter his word of protest, Veil close behind as they bolted down the bluff and climbed onto the closest rooftop.

The houses of Speakers Hollow were not like that of a densely packed city. They were spread thin and scattered randomly, with no sense of formation. A series of dirt roads set the places apart, making it hard to scout. Instead, they made do on foot.

"There's no one here," whispered Veil. "Has this village been abandoned?"

Raiz sniffed the air. "No, I smell fresh meat and spice, wood-smoke too. People are here, they're just making themselves scarce."

"A contingent of Blackwings will do that to you," Veil said.

Raiz grunted. At least it made for easy spying. The two climbed one of the larger buildings at the heart of the town. They peered across the top of the triangular shaped roof and watched as patrolling Blackwings made their rounds through the village. The clinking of armour and heavy boots squelching in the damp soil was all Raiz could hear.

He looked back towards the bluff where Dazen was waiting for him before signalling for Veil to follow.

He needed to get closer.

The two landed with sure feet, clutching the shadows as best they could. He looked over at Veil and knew she was in her element. Darkness was her friend.

The Blackwings seemed to gather around one location, the soldiers not on patrol guarding what he assumed by the buttery smell of ale extending from within to be the village inn. The guards stood stone still with ever vigilant expressions, their sharpened halberds pointed towards the night sky.

"What do you think is in there?" Veil asked.

"You know I'm not going to wait around to find out," Raiz said, moving to cross the road.

Two hands pulled at his waist, jerking him backwards and sending spit flying onto the road. "Hold," Veil whispered in his ear, covering his drooling mouth with her open palm. "There's someone coming."

Raiz relaxed, the warmth of her embrace culling some of his anxiety as dozens of Blackwings crossed the road mere feet from where they hid. They knelt in the shadow of a thatched house as a figure emerged from the darkness, his pale skin practically a shining light amid so much black.

Raiz's skin crawled, his hands curled into claws. His heart beat heavy in his chest, and he was suddenly thankful for Veil's soft hand covering his mouth; the urge to scream was almost unbearable. He looked down at his hands. Shine leaked from his fingertips, dripping down to the soil and singeing the grass upon impact.

It was him. There was no doubt. His image had come and gone in a flash, flanked and hidden by a number of Blackwings, but he had felt more than seen the presence of his prey.

Veil seemed to sense his bloodlust. "Calm Raiz, calm."

She held him tight, locking his arms to his waist with her own. He could break free easily if he wanted to. His target was just in front of him, the one who he had been searching for all these years. All it would take was one swift swipe of his blade, one bolt of Light through the chest. He channeled Shine into his good hand, letting it build until it was the size of his fist.

"Raiz, no!" Veil grabbed his wrist, gripping it with all of her strength and forcing it down.

Raiz tensed, his whole body convulsing with energy.

"Not yet! Think of your sister, if you do this now you may end her life."

He felt the warmth of her breath heavy on his cheek, the touch of her hand upon his wrist, the smell of her scent drifting under his nose. He relaxed, releasing the Light in his hand and easing into her open chest.

"He's heading towards the inn. Let's take a peek at what is within before we make any further decisions," Veil said.

"Fine. But my mind is made up. He dies tonight."

The pair waited for the Eagle to enter before striding across the road and hugging the wood wall with their backs. Flowered vines draped down the side of the building. Raiz and Veil grabbed hold and pulled themselves up. A wooden shutter lay open to the side, making for an easy access point. Together they crawled through, knives at the ready. Fortunately, the small bedroom was empty.

"They must have cleared the rooms," Veil whispered.

Raiz nodded, slowly opening the door and creeping out onto the balcony overlooking the inside of the inn.

The room was still. Men in black armour stood at attention, lining the outskirts of the room as if their very lives depended upon them standing as motionless as possible.

Raiz's eyes locked onto one in particular, his right hand instinctively running over the now smooth scar across his eye. The man who had made that scar now stood before him, within killing distance.

Raiz wasn't sure of his name, and he didn't much care. What use is a name to a dead man?

He was taller than he remembered, a giant among men with short-trimmed hair and cold, ever watchful hazel eyes. Raiz clung to the dark, holding the edge of the rail and waiting for the opportune time to strike him down.

His vision was hampered, he could only see so much from their position. He tugged at Veil's side, and the pair crept along the balcony.

Slowly the picture became clear. A man in his undergarments lay motionless before a line of soldiers, black, beaten and bruised. Another man lay by his side, red blood pooling from his neck and gushing over his apron.

He circled the room, watching. His breath grew shallow and

the Light inside his body convulsed, threatening to overwhelm him like it had the other night. His body tingled with an itch he could not scratch. His sister was here. Isha was alive.

The room went grey, all colour forming into one big blurry mass with Isha at its centre, her violet eyes blinking like an orchid in full blossom.

He felt at his face, finding his cheeks to be damp. He wiped away the tears, but they streamed down his face like a river down a waterfall. After years of searching, of training, of fighting, he had found her.

No longer was he the weak little kid, unable to protect that which he held dear. His body was a weapon sharpened finer than any sword, and he intended to use it.

Suddenly, the Eagle slapped her.

Raiz was so caught up in the moment that he didn't react as the back of the Eagle's hand connected with his sister's cheek.

And then he saw it: the bonds, the bandage around her leg.

He began to glow, red and white Light surrounding him in an aura of Shine.

The Eagle backed up a step. There were words between them, but Raiz was not in the frame of mind to listen. He watched as the Eagle hovered over the near unconscious man stripped of clothes, sceptre in hand. Raiz couldn't hear what was said, but whatever it was, he would end the conversation.

The Eagle raised the sceptre, ready to bring it down with a deft swing. Raiz felt his sister's distress as if it were his own. She cared for this man, or at least wanted him to live.

He aimed his index finger towards the Eagle's heart, felt Light froth at its tip, and let loose. It streaked across the room and for a split second Raiz felt relief.

It was short lived, however, for his streak of Light ran into another, deflecting its course and sending it through the Eagle's hand. His sceptre dropped to the floor with a sharp ring.

He felt the cold stare of the man who had given him his scar bearing up at him.

So, he could weave the Light too.

The Eagle screamed, clutching at his hand.

Raiz poised himself, shooting a projectile of Light up into the air, burning through the roof and into the night sky.

Veil wasted no time, moving along the balcony and drawing her bow.

Blackwings looked around in confusion, some scrambling to protect their master, who was writhing in pain. Likely the only pain he had ever known. "Argon!" he called. "Protect me!"

The giant-man Raiz assumed to be Argon readied himself for an assault, signalling for his men to charge the staircase.

Raiz took a quick look at Veil and leaped off the balcony, flipping in the air and landing in a roll at his sister's feet.

Isha stared at him with an open mouth. There was no time to speak. That would come later. He burned through the rope around her wrist and lifted her into his arms. He turned and moved for the door, but found his path blocked by Argon and at least a dozen Blackwings.

Veil's arrows shot like darts through the air, felling man after man and causing panic. Argon used his Shine to deflect an arrow, giving Raiz the chance to sneak past.

"We can't leave them," said a whisper in his ear. "We must turn back. I won't abandon my friends." Isha squeezed his arm in a tight grip.

Raiz hesitated, caught between the urge to see his sister to safety and her plea to save her friends.

"I'll come back for them, I promise. But first I need to get you to —"

He was thrust backwards as a shield crashed into his side,

sending him flying and Isha tumbling into a wall.

He rose, clutching at his rib. The Blackwings had gathered around him, now aware of his presence and of Veil's, a group of them holding up their own curved shields in defence against her deadly arrows.

He watched as six of them raced up the stairs in pursuit of her, the others' attention firmly fixed on him. There was no way out, he was trapped. He backed up to protect his sister, arms glowing with spheres of Light. Veins he didn't even know he had popped out from his forearms as he waved them at the enemy, daring them to come a step closer.

Argon drew his sword — the same sword that had given Raiz his scar — and coated it with Light. It shone like a beacon of pure energy. He should have expected nothing less from a member of the Golden Talon. There was no hatred in his expression, only duty. Raiz couldn't say the same for himself. His nostrils flared red. "How would you like to die?" he said.

Argon glanced at the Blackwings by his side and nodded toward Raiz. An unlucky one took a step forward. Raiz thrust his palm, sending a thin line of Light streaming towards him. A smokey haze curled around Raiz's open hand as the guard dropped dead at his feet, a hole the size of a fist in his chest. The remaining soldiers trembled before his aura. Even the might of the capital's best was no match for the sheer intensity of his radiating heat. Only Argon remained unaffected.

Raiz risked a look over his shoulder, finding his sister no longer there. At first, he turned to Argon, thinking he had pulled off some form of trickery, but as his wits gathered he found her running back to her friends. She had taken advantage of his distraction. Soldiers were swarming towards their injured master. There was no way Isha would make it. She was practically running into their arms.

A soldier reached for her, his fingertips brushing against her blouse when a loud crash sounded from the entrance to the inn.

A blur of blue, white and yellow rushed into the fray. Within seconds, the room was chaos. The ringing of swords clashing and the exertion of men fighting for their lives filled the room. Several against Raiz were forced to retreat to cover their comrades — and were probably glad to. Only Argon stayed.

A sly grin touched Raiz's lips as he witnessed Dazen cull two Blackwings with smooth strikes of his Light-coated steels. Sumaya issued a war-cry, rushing into the fray and slicing into her nearest assailant with surprising skill.

The two brothers locked eyes, and without hesitation each understood their role. Dazen bolted towards Isha, flanked by the two Levics and Draz. Aroha stood by the door, bashing two assailants' heads together as if one was the hammer and the other an anvil.

The air split with a large roar. Raiz watched through proud eyes as Spike came crashing through the doorframe. He thrust his barbed tail like a whip, sending three Blackwings tumbling, breathless, into the woodwork. The pricket moved for the closest soldier, biting into him with his huge maw, shattering bone and metal. Blood seeped through cracks in the armour as Spike searched for his next victim.

Raiz faced Argon with renewed intensity. He sent a line of Light into the wooden floorboards, focusing as he moulded it into his glaive and solidified it through years of practice and sheer willpower. Its energy glowed vibrantly. A glaive for a Glaive.

Together, the bitter enemies danced. Light flashed, sending sparks of molten residue to the floor where they melted tiny holes into the wood. Frustration came in the form of a series of low grunts as Raiz found his glaive unable to cut through the

Argon's coated blade.

Raiz was quicker, but Argon was stronger, and on more than one occasion he found himself forced to backtrack as the knight's wild swings threatened to tear him in two.

Dazen and the others engaged the soldiers protecting the Eagle. Meanwhile, Isha had draped her body over the near-unconscious man, holding a stray dagger above her head and growling at any who dared come near.

Raiz felt a gash graze his arm as the point of Argon's sword cut into him. That would leave two scars on his body from the same sword.

He shook his head, annoyed at himself for being so careless, before shooting a beam of Light from his blackened hand. The manoeuvre seemed to catch Argon off guard, for he only barely managed to dodge, a line of red forming on his shoulder.

The two resumed their stare-off as a hulking form came crashing into Argon's back, sending him plummeting to the floor, head banging hard against the floorboards.

Aroha stood before him and shrugged.

Raiz shrugged back. Nobody said it was a fair fight.

He thought about finishing him, but his sister's call was more urgent. He rushed to her side. He had no clue who this man was, or why she was so protective of him, but if he mattered to her, then he mattered to him. He watched on as the Blackwing numbers thinned.

Echo and Huet Levic flailed about, swinging wildly at anything that moved. Hector was not present, likely watching from afar with Celik.

Raiz sliced through black plate and listened as the man screamed in agony, clutching at where his arm used to be. The man's cries were the last as the inn grew silent. A mass of sweat and blood stained the floorboards, which could barely be seen underneath a sea of red, green and black.

Raiz whirled, listening to the heavy breathing of the Eagle. He was hunched over, hands covering his head as he rocked back and forth.

Raiz had been waiting for this. Finally, he could sate the ever-building rage inside of him, and all it would take was one quick flick of his hand.

The fallen Eagle began blubbering to himself, looking up at the carnage.

"Any last words, demon?" Raiz said.

"Y-you cannot touch me," the Eagle cried. "I am a vessel, chosen by Zur himself. Do you not know what will happen to the world if I perish?"

"You're no god, you never have been," Raiz said.

"You are him, are you not?" the Eagle said. "The one who slew Saerus."

Raiz paced the floor, circling his prey. "So, that was his name. You're all the same to me. Monsters among men. All will fall to my Light."

The Eagle growled through gritted teeth. "You are nothing! The King-Radiant will place your head upon a pike for what you have done. The only monster here is you."

"You're right," Raiz said. "I am a monster. You should know, you created me."

He swung his right hand down to end him, but paused as the Eagle muttered something under his tongue.

A flash of pure white burst from the Eagle's prone form, blinding Raiz and the rest of the men who stood before him.

He tried to blink free of its embrace, but it was too late. He felt — no — heard the sound of a knife sinking into flesh.

Raiz opened his eyes, thinking himself dead. But to his surprise, his sister lay over the Eagle, slashing and hacking at his lifeless body, blood staining her blouse and making its original colour unrecognisable.

Over and over the blade carved its edge into the pink, squelching its way through blood and tissue.

As her hunger subsided, her strokes grew slow. She came to a stop and goggled at the now staring crowd of surviving Glaive and Levic soldiers.

The three Glaive siblings stared at one another in disbelief. A tear trickled down Isha's cheek. Both Raiz and Dazen rushed to her side, embracing her in a blood-stained hug that was long overdue. She welcomed their warmth, dropping the knife and wrapping her arms around them.

"It's over," Raiz whispered. "He can harm you no more."

A stir came from their rear, and Raiz whirled his head around to see Argon regaining his footing in the corner. Raiz rushed over, ready to end what should have been ended.

"Raiz, no! Wait!" Isha cried. "Please, do not harm him!"

But Raiz was already halfway across the room, dagger drawn.

To his surprise, Isha leapt between them, hopping on one leg as she put her life in Argon's hands.

Raiz was expecting him to take her life, to run her through with his sword. But no such action occurred.

"I beg of you, spare his life. This man saved me. If it were not for him, I would not be here today."

Raiz scrunched his face. "This is the man who took you! This is the man who gave me this scar!" He tilted his head and moved a lock of hair so the lump of uprooted skin stood out. "I've waited years for this, and you would have me spare him?"

"Yes, I would," she said. Her glare was infinite, equal if not more intimidating than their father's own.

Raiz wavered, hand still tight around his dagger.

Before he could muster the courage to come to a decision, Aroha brushed past him, standing wide eyed, her face a picture of surprise. "Brother?"

Argon stared back at her as if she were a ghost. "Sister? You are alive!"

294

Interlude
Evanon

Evanon Lightfire sat leisurely on the Light Throne, his hands curling around the solidified column of breen-coated metal that made up the arm-rest. He exhaled, watching closely as a white plume of steam filtered from his mouth out into the open air of the hall. "It is not yet time. Has winter's cool touch come early?" he asked the only other person present.

Queen Mother Lady Sephare sat by his side, wrinkles parting her once perfect skin as she scowled at him. "Perhaps this so-called Sun Prince from across the sea had a sliver of truth to his words? Perhaps we are overusing Zur's Light?"

Evanon laughed off the comment. "Choose your words carefully mother, you sound more and more like Father. Shall I deem you a heretic too? Zur's Light is infinite. This imposter from overseas is nothing but a tyrant seeking power through misdirection and fancy words."

"It seems he also has an army at his back to go with his fancy words."

"He is of no importance to me, if he comes, the Last Light shall burn his ships and feed his troops to the serpents of the Abyss."

Sephare turned towards him and clasped her hands together in one calm motion. She looked up at him through cold, black eyes. Her dark hair was tinged a light shade of grey. "You are a king like no other, my son. But you are losing your touch. Using the tower on Lesken and executing the Zutonian

King was too much, the people of Zuton are angry."

"My rule is absolute. If their new king should prove unworthy, then he will meet the same fate."

"A fitting punishment, of course, for an unforgivable crime. Strike a man down once and he will learn his lesson. Strike him down twice and he will learn it double. But strike him down thrice, and a man's reason begins to wander into the realm of insanity. Insanity breeds foolishness. Trap a rat in a box and it will have no choice but to try and claw its way out."

Evanon huffed his disinterest. "Always one for wordplay, you are. I will not forgive those who seek to destroy the order of the world. The Eagles are Zur's true vessels. If I cannot protect them then this world will be at the mercy of Cova and her shadows. Any malice towards them is to be treated as treason of the highest order and will be punished as such."

"I thought you did not believe in Cova and the Skae?"

"I don't. The Skae are a myth. My words were merely a figure of speech."

"Your father thought differently."

"My father was a liar. And he is no longer here. I will hear no more talk of him, am I clear?"

"As you please, Your Highness. I should inform you that Averardus has left the capital in pursuit of the female prisoner."

Evanon tensed his thick muscles. "Which prisoner?"

Sephare stared at him, unblinking. "You know of whom I speak."

His throat constricted, veins popping from his forehead as blood looked for an escape.

"You are a cruel man for withholding the girl's imprisonment from *her*," Sephare said.

"I withhold nothing. It is not my fault she locks herself in her room away from the world."

"Blame whoever you will, but in the end, there are consequences for the lust of your former self!"

"I do not need a lecture on cruelty and lust from *you*, Mother! What I am today is a result of your twisted words and Father's fists."

Sephare snapped her neck towards him. "Then will you shame me as you did your father?"

Evanon's Shine began to leak from his hands. "Do not tempt me."

"Do you think I care for my life anymore? I live only to see you succeed. If you find me no longer of value, then dispose of me. But you will not, because you need me."

Her words rung true, hanging in the air like an arrow ready to fall. He needed her. But even so, he couldn't shake the feeling that her loyalties drifted elsewhere. "Do not think me a fool! I know where your true allegiance lies. I know you wish Father was still here."

He could see the shock beneath her calm facade. It was a subtle moment, a simple twitch of the eye, but he could see his words had struck a chord.

"Urion was a great man once. Though, an unforgiving one, it is true." Sephare said. "But he is no longer the King-Radiant. My loyalty remains solely with you, my child."

Evanon scoffed. "And what would you have done if I remained impotent? What if my Shine never shone? Would you have been of one mind with Father? Would you have accepted his beatings as just? Evanon Lightfire, son of the great Urion Lightfire, Shineless."

"You cannot believe that to be true. You were always my son, Shine or no."

"Save it Mother. I know of your infertility. I know you could have no other children. I was his only hope for a successor, and

I was a failure."

"That is not true, Evanon! Look at all you have accomplished!"

"It must have been quite a shock to you both when Zur's Light touched me. But too little, too late. I am a better king than Father ever was. I will bring order to this world once more. All will fear me and bow as they once did to Gallion."

"Of course, you are the true heir."

A knock sounded at the door, breaking the tension.

Evanon cleared his throat, turning away from his mother. "Enter!" he bellowed.

Yvain's egg-shaped head pushed its way through the doors atop the Fiftieth Spear and bowed deeply. "Your Radiance, sir. Ancel Saelmere, Prince of Craw is here to see you."

Evanon rubbed at the hairs on his chin. "Has he brought me the culprit?"

The Herald's voice quivered with a shaking fear. "I — I do not believe so, Your Radiance, but he brings with him information about the person in question."

"Send him in and begone," Evanon said with a flick of his wrist.

The Herald rushed out the door and was soon replaced by the broken figure of Ancel Saelmere. His right arm hung limp at his side, draped in cloth to hold it upright. He walked up to the platform with the gait of a defeated man, his uniform in tatters, hair a mat of unwashed mud and gore.

"You are a brave man to come back here without our enemy's head on a spike," Evanon said.

"My apologies, Your Radiance," Ancel said, bowing as deeply as he could muster. "He proved more elusive than I expected."

"Tell me of this news you bring."

"It is true I was unable to capture or kill the band of outlaws. But I was able to determine the identity of their leader."

He opened his palm, gesturing for the prince to continue.

"The man in question is Raiz Glaive, third born to the King of Trost, Kron Glaive. My lord, I am positive. The scar on his face was unmistakable, and I heard the voicing of his name in conversation. It is the same boy who ran away from his family eight years ago. He is the one who killed Saerus in the city of Lesken."

Evanon went to speak, but no words came out. Instead, his mouth hung agape. He stared at Ancel, red Light tingling underneath his fingertips, threatening to pour out at any moment. He tried to suppress his emotions, to hide his outright shock and horror at hearing that name after so long. After so many years...

"Leave us," he said, finally.

"My lord, the Cratons? My father —"

"LEAVE US!"

"As you wish," Ancel said, scuttling out of the chamber, carrying his broken wing in tow.

Sephare raised a curious brow his way.

"There is someone I must have a word with," Evanon said.

Servants parted in his wake, clinging to the walls and pretending they had important business elsewhere as Evanon walked the halls of the Fiftieth Spear, a red aura trailing him like a smokey haze. Those who failed to part in time were forced to sink to their knees, so intense was the raw power and heat radiating from his body.

He approached a long archway stretching across the crown of interconnecting Spears, his steps nearly melting the stonework below. He stopped outside of a door, his destination lying within. It had been a long time since he had mustered the courage to enter this room.

He bit his lip, anxiety threatening to get the best of him. But he was stronger than his past self, stronger than the weakling he used to be. He was a changed man, and his queen awaited him.

He turned the key and felt it click. Slowly, he pushed open the door, light touching the darkness within as if it were a long-lost friend.

A woman's form sat crumpled at the desk, back towards him. A mountain of half-read books and parchments engulfed the room, scattered randomly into piles upon piles of disorganised paper. A forest of artificial greenery lined the outskirts of the room, the lush vegetation glowing with the faint aura of a Shimmer Tree.

But he paid them no mind, his focus centred entirely upon the woman.

She turned her head, and he knew instantly she knew it to be him.

Nearly two decades the woman he had taken as his wife had locked herself in here. Despite all of his pleas, all of his attempts at persuasion and seduction, she would not come out. And still, he couldn't find the strength to force her.

Her hair dangled low, brown locks years in the making curled towards the ground. High cheekbones cut into her smooth and flawless skin as she moved towards him, eyes closed.

He felt the air leave his chest as her presence began to overwhelm his own. She inclined her head and moved her lips into a half-smile. Finally, she opened her eyes. Bright violet orbs stared back at him like shining stars, brimming with life and energy.

Finding his courage, Evanon spoke at last. "I come here to talk of our son."

PART 3

Chapter 24
Raiz

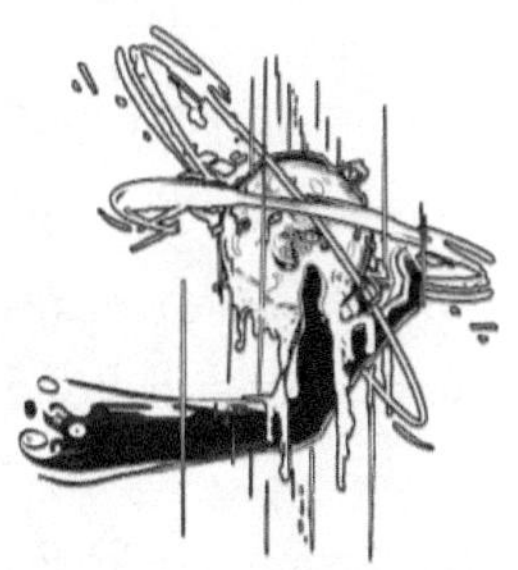

Each step brought Raiz closer to his past. The familiar dewy softness of the soil and grass beneath his feet, the scent of wildflowers blooming atop the sun-warmed earth, the sight of his long-lost sister now safe and back in her own country — back with him. He breathed a heavy lungful of fresh air but came up shallow. There was still an emptiness within him, a hole he couldn't seem to fill.

It irked him. He had saved his sister from the clutches of an evil man. He had fulfilled his lifelong desire, corrected the mistake he made all those years ago. Why then did he still feel empty? Why then was his lust for blood not sated?

He looked towards his open hands, one blackened and scarred, and the other pure and white. It was as if they represented the two parts of his soul. He could feel the rage continuing to build inside of him. It grew stronger and fiercer every day as his Shine morphed. Every day the white in his Shine faded, the fraction of red growing steadily more potent with each use. The change in colour was nothing compared to the change in the power he felt, the power lurking beneath the surface of his skin. If his Shine kept growing at this rate, he would soon match Veil's own, though the thought of becoming so unstable unsettled him. Why was he different? Why did his Shine grow while everyone else's faded? He made a mental note to ask Celik about it later, though he doubted he would find answers there.

He took a glance towards Isha. He had not let her stray further than his vision could see the entire trek home. She was still the same Isha. Taller and leaner now, but her mannerisms were the same. Her violet eyes still stood out like a white swan in a blue lake.

Illidor loomed in the distant background, a ghost hidden in a cloud of mist. He walked on in quiet contemplation. Who was he now? Was he Raiz the assassin, cold-blooded murderer hell-bent on vengeance? Or was he Raiz Glaive, Prince of Trost and loving brother?

"What's wrong? You seem lost," Isha said, looking up at him from the bank of the river.

Raiz looked back at her with a reassuring smile. "Nothing is the matter. I am just glad to have you with me again is all."

"Ahh yes, I'm sure you've missed my annoying shadow following at your feet around the halls of the palace every time mischief calls. How have things been back at home anyway? Is Father well? I can't get anything from Dazen," Isha said.

Raiz gulped, his head aching with the burden of secrecy. Isha was still unaware of his long absence from Illidor, and he couldn't bring himself to tell her the truth. Not yet anyway. "I am sure my brother just wishes for you to see for yourself," he said. "We are nearly there after all."

Dazen walked up alongside him, cupping river water between his fingers and splashing it over his face. "I heard the word 'brother', is Raiz sullying my name already?"

Isha let out a gentle laugh before hiccuping, her head jerking back as if choking on her own laughter. After a slight pause, all three Glaive siblings burst into a fit of long overdue laughter, pointing and doubling over as Isha's barrage of hiccups grew louder and more frequent.

Raiz leant back, enjoying the moment for what it was. After so much intensity and heartbreak, it felt unnatural to actually enjoy himself. But he didn't let his insecurities hold him back. The trio continued poking fun at one another, trading bites of banter back and forth as if they were children again.

Attracted to the joy, Spike came charging up the riverbank to nestle under Raiz's arm, forcing his long neck in between his shoulders.

"I still can't believe how big he's gotten!" Isha said. "When I gave him to you, he could fit in my palm. I know they grow by feeding on Shine, but I don't think I've ever seen one this large before! Your Shine must be incredible, Raiz."

Raiz, not used to such praise, simply shrugged his shoulders, patting Spike where he liked it between his eyes. "Spike and I have been through a lot together, haven't we boy," he said.

Isha smiled back at him, and he could tell by the way her lips stretched wide into her cheeks that it was genuine. He wondered how long it had been since she last smiled like that. A silence gripped the air like some invisible hand and held on tight. Raiz looked towards his sister again, trying to imagine her pain. No matter what he had been through, no matter his setbacks, he knew she had suffered worse. He could see it on her lips. The smile was genuine, she was glad to be home, but there was a layer of pain buried beneath it that would not break so easily.

Isha broke the silence. "So, tell me dear brothers, how long have you planned such a well co-ordinated and executed rescue?"

There was a playful tone to her voice, but it only caused tension between Raiz and Dazen, the two locking guilty eyes while holding their breath. Neither of them said anything.

Isha raised her brow, confusion wrought on her honeyed skin.

"I am sorry it took us so long," Raiz finally said. "But we both never stopped looking. Dazen and I spent every spare moment thinking of a way to see you home where you belong."

Dazen shot him a wide-eyed look, but quickly disguised it. Both understood it was best to keep both Raiz's disappearance and Dazen's lack of action a secret for at least a little longer. Isha needed to be welcomed back by a happy family.

"I knew you both would," she said. "And what of Father?"

Both Glaive brothers again went silent, but Raiz could not bring himself to cover for his father as well. An unforgivable hatred still lingered close to his heart. He now understood the reason behind his father's inaction that day, but he had not forgotten, and he would not forgive.

"I take your silence to mean he did nothing then," Isha said. "I thought as much."

"Isha he —" Dazen moved to say, but she placed a hand on his arm.

"Do not try to lie to me about this," she said. "I may not have been able to complete my education, but I am not so stupid as to believe him a loving father. We have always played second fiddle to his patriotism. If he was going to act, it would have been the moment he saw me being taken."

"Isha —" Raiz began.

"Save it," his sister interrupted. "Being a slave gives you lots of time to think. And I have agreed to let the past be the past.

So, I ask you both, can we move past this and be a family once again?"

Raiz nodded, but he knew it to be a lie. She might be able to keep the past in the past, but he could not.

As light faded and Zur's reign over the day ended, so too did darkness rise as Cova's watchful eye ascended into the night sky.

Raiz gathered wood for a fire, striking the flint until it sparked to life. He cupped his hands over the flame, feeling its warmth battle with his own inner heat. If he wanted to, he could easily use his Light to warm his shivering body, but too much reliance on his gift was dangerous. He need only take one look at his blackened hand or Celik's dead arms as an example. He had been far too reckless lately, and he could feel the toll it had taken on his body.

The sound of snapping twigs turned his attention. It seemed his fire had attracted more than a little company. Gradually, everyone had made their way to the fire. The travelling company had grown quite extensive, comprising a mixture of backgrounds and strong personalities — few of which actually got along.

Celik sat on a log behind him, his heavy beard clouding his chin and hooded cloak pulled tight to conceal the black handprint marring his face. He seemed content taking a backward step for now, allowing Raiz to take the lead. These were not his people, but Raiz supposed that as long as their interests aligned, Celik had no need to intervene in their affairs.

Hector made himself comfortable beside the youngest Levic boy, whom Raiz had come to know as Echo. He seemed a capable lad; calm and collected in his thoughts, at least when compared to his twin elder brothers. Spike had taken a shining to the youngest Levic too, his tail resting between him and Hector as he relaxed near the fire.

Sumaya, his brother's apparent wife-to-be, sat by Dazen's side. She held herself with an aura of authority. Not in the way Raiz himself did, there was no magic in her bones, but sometimes the right expression mixed with a certain passion could be magic on its own.

Veil was a comforting presence, sitting by his side with her usual calm, bored demeanour.

Next came Isha, her violet eyes a beacon in the night. The fact that she was here, sitting before him under his ever-watchful eye, filled at least one of the holes in his heart; one that even Zur's Light could not furnish.

The man known only as Puk stood before her. Out of everyone here, he was the most surprising. His glare was iron, his body steel. Gone was the frail looking man, near-naked and beaten. Replacing him was a hardy looking man with long hair and a lazy eye. It would be foolish to underestimate him, he hovered over Isha like a dog protecting its owner. Isha had given her explanation of his identity, and despite him having been an inducted member of the Golden Talon, Raiz couldn't deny his role in her escape. His defensiveness towards her was further proof of his loyalty, though Raiz was ever suspicious of anyone he did not understand, and could never fully trust one of those Golden bastards.

By Isha's side sat the man from Wisha known as Obeyun. If his sister's eyes were a beacon, then his skin was a bonfire. His body was an abstract canvas, an even mixture of milky white and charcoal black. Raiz remembered him from the day Isha was taken. The memory of that monster's whip rising and cracking onto his back still made him twitch to this day. Behind him sat a small woman. Nothing unusual stood out about her, but Isha seemed comfortable with her, and that was enough for Raiz. It filled him with warmth that even in such times as these, his sister had made so many reliable friends.

Draz landed on the log beside Veil with a thump, his arms crossed, body unmoving. Raiz could practically see him scowling behind his helmet.

It didn't take Raiz long to understand why. Aroha came strutting up the hill, her brother in tow, tightly bound and under the close watch of a couple of Dazen's White-Swords from Illidor. The Golden Talon were responsible for the murder of Draz's entire clan, it was no wonder he was so tense.

Raiz shared in Draz's discomfort. He wanted to see this man dead at his feet. "What is he doing here?" Raiz said, his tone reflecting his anger.

Aroha looked around at the gathered crowd. "He is my brother," she said. "I will not have him eating off the floor like some stray dog! You have my word he will not move against us."

"This man is a cold-blooded murderer. We should have ended him back at the inn," Raiz said, unable to hold his tongue.

"You will do no such thing!" Raiz turned to see Isha on her feet, hands clenched at her sides.

Raiz grumbled, but turned his head, not wanting to disrespect his sister.

To his surprise, Draz rose from his seat and pointed towards Argon. "This man is an abomination," he said under his helm. "His order hunted Draz's family down like animals and slaughtered them all. Draz will have his vengeance."

Aroha puffed out her chest, pursing her lips as she snarled through gritted teeth. "You know nothing about them, Draz. What they go through. What Lumindal does to them."

"You speak as if you know," Draz said.

Aroha went quiet.

Draz squared his shoulders. "Tell me you are not one of them!"

Raiz spread his arm out as if to calm him. "Do not be absurd, Draz. Aroha has killed even more of those bastards than me."

Draz turned to him. "Then ask her yourself. We want the truth. No lies."

Raiz thought about stamping the notion down. He knew Aroha. She couldn't have been one of them, could she? "Just say it is not so," he said, turning to her. "I will take you for your word."

The gathered company turned their heads towards Aroha, but her expression told him everything he needed to know.

She bowed her head. "I was once, but I am no longer," she said.

A collective gasp sounded around the campfire. Raiz was the first to speak, throwing his arm backwards in a wild gesture. "You cannot be serious. All this time hunting them, and you were one of them all along."

"*Was* one of them," Aroha said. "No longer."

"Why?" Raiz said, trying to temper his breathing. "Why would you choose to be one of them?"

"Fighting for Lumindal is not always a choice, Raiz," Aroha said. "You should know that well."

Raiz gulped a lump down his throat. He spared a glance towards Argon, though the heavy brute seemed preoccupied, staring idly in Celik's direction. The old man ignored him, pulling his hood tighter and turning his head. Draz brought Raiz back to attention by stamping his foot.

"This is unforgivable," Draz said. "Draz will not work with a Golden rat."

Isha stepped forwards, spreading her hands wide in defence of Aroha. "That is enough," she said. "I have lived in Lumindal. Eight years I have suffered under their thumb. I know how evil they can be. But there are good people among them. Puk risked his life to save mine. And Argon could have turned me in. He had every chance. But he showed mercy. Not all are heartless killers. Not all are tainted. Give your friend a chance to explain. Or does she mean nothing to you?"

Raiz stared at his feet. Isha always knew the right words to speak. "I — I am sorry, Aroha. I judge too quickly. You have more than earned the right to speak your piece," he said.

Draz harrumphed, sitting back on his log, arms crossed.

Aroha relaxed her shoulders. She placed a hand on Isha's arm and proceeded to take a seat on an empty log by the fire. Raiz did the same as Aroha cleared her throat.

"It was a long time ago," Aroha said. "Me and Argon were barely past our fifteenth summer when they came to our village seeking men to fight in the False Kings War. We were a small village, no more than a couple hundred of us. But that didn't stop them. They wanted more.

"My brother was one of the first taken, and when they ran out of young men, I guess they chose the next closest thing. I don't think they expected much of me, but I was big for my age. Strong, too. When they realised what I could do I was sent to train as a Blackwing. It was there that Argon and I were separated. Once his Shine came forth, he was expedited and placed in the Forty-Fourth Spear. Not long after, Hirane was destroyed and Evanon took over from his father as King-Radiant. Everything changed from there."

Raiz dug his nails into his palms at the mention of the King-Radiant.

"I was trapped in a world I neither understood, nor wanted

to be in," Aroha continued. "My company were sent to kill the remaining members of the alliance who had not perished in the Shine bomb."

By his side Veil tensed, and he could hear Draz gasp across the fire-pit.

"I watched them burn villages, and pillage innocents who had done nothing more than associate themselves with the rebellion," Aroha said. "I watched them rape and I watched them murder until eventually I could watch no more. We were tasked with finding and killing a group of women and children who had fled from a neighbouring village to warn another. 'Bring me their fingers as proof they are no more' is what my commanding officer told me. Can you believe it, children's fingers! They wanted me to cut off their fingers simply to prove the deed was done. I don't know whether the others were more broken by their training than I, or if they were just evil at heart, but they went without hesitation.

"We found the villagers foraging for food in the nearby forest. They were surrounded, on hands and knees, begging for mercy. There was an elderly lady with them. She placed herself between us and the children, and was run through with a sword for her efforts."

Aroha's hand began to shake, but she continued. "I still remember it like it was yesterday, the memories refuse to die. I couldn't let them do it, it wasn't right. It wasn't just.

"So, I stepped in. I slaughtered them all, my fellow soldiers. I thought it would be hard, I thought the pain of killing my own would eat me from the inside, but instead I felt alive! My sword cut like butter. Never before had I swung with such purpose, such tenacity. I was my own justice.

"I let the women and children escape, swearing them to secrecy before I too fled, later to learn I was assumed dead,

Lumindal none the wiser to my betrayal. That is when I found Celik and set my course to ending the suffering of those caught in Lumindal's web."

The fire hissed and crackled with growing intensity, matching the tension in the air.

Raiz slumped his shoulders. Guilt flowed through him in a wave, an emotion he was becoming too familiar with. "I am sorry, I did not know. The things you must have been through. That sounds horrible. But you should be proud. Many people ignore the wrong in the world, it takes courage to act upon it."

Aroha nodded, a faint smile touching her lips.

Draz was less impressed. "Then what of your brother's suffering?" he said. "Should you end his like so many others?"

Isha hobbled to her feet, clutching at her thigh. "There is goodness in him! I have seen it. Please, I beg of you, hold in your anger."

Draz settled into his seat. It pained Raiz to see his two friends at each other's throats, especially given how close the odd pair had become over the past few months. But he understood Draz's anger. His whole family had been murdered by agents of Lumindal. And Aroha had been one of them.

Aroha shot Draz a glare that would rival Zur's own, but she let his remark fade.

For a long time, nobody spoke. Raiz poked at his meal, chewing on a stringy piece of meat. He watched as Dazen stood to address the group. "We must come up with a plan," he said.

To the side, Huet scoffed, spitting a chunk of his food before speaking. "You are not my king, Glaive. I do not obey you."

Raiz watched as Dazen's jaw tightened. "I am not asking you to obey me," Dazen said. "Only that we speak openly."

"Speak openly?" Huet said. "And what is there to say? We killed another Eagle. You saw how forgiving the King-Radiant is. What is there to do but run and hide?"

Dazen grit his teeth and hesitated. Raiz watched on with a curious eye. He wasn't sure how his brother would react. Yes, Dazen had acted against Lumindal, but that was in the interest of saving their sister. He wondered, if a peaceful opportunity presented itself, would he choose it? Or would he take up the fight against Lumindal alongside him?

He didn't get the opportunity to find out, as Veil spoke next. "What if we take down the tower?" She sat leisurely on her log, hands busy twirling her dagger around her fingers in a non-threatening show of skill.

"What?" Dazen called, as if speaking what was on everyone's mind.

"What if we take down the Last Light?" Veil said. "Remove their weapon, they lose their power. Simple."

"That is a suicide mission," Huet said.

"You cannot take down the tower!" a voice called over the rest.

Raiz turned to see Celik standing on his two feet, his features still shaded by the night and his hood.

"Why not?" Veil cried. "It's clearly the easiest way to cripple them."

Celik grumbled. "The Last Light is an ancient relic built by the first King-Radiant to defend Zapour from the Skae. To bring it down would put all of Zapour at risk."

Snorts of derision sounded from all corners of the campfire. "The Skae are a fairytale," Dazen said. "They are a myth. And even if they were real once, they are long extinct. The Last Light has lost its purpose."

"So, you will help?" Raiz said, trying to judge his brother's intentions.

Celik interrupted, stamping his foot. "You are young and

naïve, master Prince. Do not claim to know what you don't understand."

Dazen leaned back into the log, his words caught in his throat. Argon stood, glowering at Celik through the flickering light. He seemed to be studying him.

Raiz turned to Celik, the man who had taken him in and raised him as his own. He knew him to be callous, but to deny Veil the goal she desired most in this world...

There was something he wasn't telling them.

"Ancient threat or no, I am bringing that tower down," Veil said.

"I will stand with you," Raiz said, watching as Celik's hateful glare burned into his side.

"Don't be a fool, Raiz!" Celik snapped.

"I cannot see the world changing as long as The Last Light stands," Raiz said.

Celik's scowl intensified, the mark on his face seemed to darken, his other features shrouded in the cloak. "This is not the plan. This is not the way."

"Then what is the plan?" Raiz asked. "Because so far all we have done is piss them off. When are we going to strike a fatal blow? When are we going to make a real difference?"

"Ignorant child," Celik snapped again. "You know nothing of what we are up against. So much power, so much strength, and it is wasted on a child like you with such a false sense of bravado. I got you your sister back, now you will listen to me."

Raiz rocked onto his back foot. He felt anger boiling inside of him, an anger he never realised he had. It rose to the surface in a sudden rush. Celik had done much for him, it was true. He had guided him when no one else would, mentored him and taught him to fight. But he was not his father. And Raiz was no longer under the delusion that he did so with the kindness of his own heart. Raiz was his tool, he was the arms that he had lost, and nothing more.

He suppressed his anger, focused it. "Me and Veil are not just tools for you to manipulate anymore," he said. "We have our own minds, and we will choose our own path if you refuse to help us."

Celik glowered at him, and Raiz thought he saw the old man's mouth twitch. He said nothing, turned, and stalked off, cloak billowing in the air behind him.

"Well, that was intense," Huet said. "What is his problem?"

Raiz ignored him, instead turning to Dazen. His brother approached him and spoke. "I am afraid you must put your plans on hold for the moment, there is a more pressing issue we must deal with."

Raiz eyed him with a questioning expression.

Dazen took a steadying breath. "How to deal with Father."

Raiz's skin crawled, his Shine itching to be free even this deep into Zur's rest. He paced the length of his tent, searching for a release for his anger but finding none. Veil was a comfort, even just her presence was enough to sooth his frustration enough to think clearly.

"This isn't how I pictured events playing out," Raiz said.

"Oh, and how exactly did you picture it then?" Veil said.

Raiz groaned, searching for the right words but finding none.

"Not everything can be controlled," Veil said. "Celik had too strong a hold over us for too long. Maybe it'll do us good to get some space from him."

"So, you think I was right? To speak to him the way I did?"

Veil exhaled a heavy sigh. "I owe Celik my life, more than once over. But he is arrogant, self-centred, and egotistical.

We're just pawns to him. I never planned to stay with him forever."

"What will you do?" Raiz asked.

Veil shrugged. "I don't know. But I'm too dangerous to be around people, and you know it."

"Veil, that's not true. You can control it. I've seen you."

She waved a dismissive hand. "No Raiz, I can't. We've exhausted all options. Sooner or later my condition will cause me to hurt someone, or myself. I'm better off alone."

"There are always more options!" Raiz protested. "When my sister is safe, we'll travel to northern Crata, to the source of the problem. There must be others like you there, they'll know what to do. They can help you."

"No. There's no one like me. I've searched. I'm alone."

Raiz slumped. "So, you're leaving then?"

She nodded. "I want you to come with me. You're the only one who understands me, the only one I can't hurt."

Raiz stood motionless, trying to process what he had just been asked. "Veil I — I want to, believe me. But my sister. I've only just got her back. I can't abandon her again."

Veil cupped his hands in her own. "I know, Raiz. All I ask is you think on it. Do you really want to go back to Illidor? Be a prince again? That is what awaits if you return, not to mention your father."

Raiz went to speak, his mouth beginning to form words before Veil pulled him close, her cold lips pressing against his own. She pulled away, placing a finger over his now wet lips. "Don't make any decisions now," she said. "Stay with me tonight, I don't want to be alone."

Raiz forgot to breathe. It was as if his lungs had suddenly stopped functioning. His body yearned for another taste of her, if only a bite. It was all he could think about. Celik, Dazen, his father. None of them mattered anymore, not now.

She took hold of his hand, pulling him closer as she moved to the sleeping pallet. He slipped in beside her, the light touch of her pale leg rubbing against his own. It took him a moment to realise he had been holding his breath, but as her hand joined his own, he exhaled, relaxing into her embrace.

Together they intertwined, locking legs, arms, fingers, waists. Raiz grabbed a handful of hair as she ran her mouth over his neck, leaving a trail of burning kisses. He felt her Shine grow hot beneath her skin. It flared wildly, matching the intensity of the moment. The two rolled around in a fit of passion. Raiz twisted his body until he was on top of her, his mouth refusing to leave hers for longer than an instant.

She wrapped her legs around his, pulling him closer still. Raiz was so caught up in the moment he nearly didn't realise that something was wrong. Her body grew hot, extremely hot. Her breathing doubled, hands clasping the sheets as if there were something inside that was longing to come out.

Raiz recoiled, and suddenly he knew exactly what was happening. He lifted his body off of hers, taking her hand and kneeling by her side. "Calm Veil. It's okay, I'm here. Let it pass."

She struggled still, writhing and wriggling in the sheets as she fought to keep her Shine in check. She began to physically glow, emitting a radiant white light above the pink of her skin. Raiz refused to leave, knowing full well what would happen if she failed to contain it. "You can do it. Press it down, I won't let you lose control," he said.

He didn't know if his words were having an effect, but he kept speaking, repeating the same thing over and over, his hands never leaving hers despite the growing heat. He pressed his Shine against hers, similar to what he had done to his brother the other day. It held her in place, his Shine and her own clashing in an almost invisible battle of forces. He felt connected to her then, in a way he had never been before. Their Shine seemed to mix, melding into one as the two forces joined together.

Veil relaxed, her breathing returning to normal as the heat within began to dissipate. She rolled her head back, exhausted. She wiped a bead of sweat from her forehead with one hand and grabbed Raiz's with the other. "Thank you," she said, "but this is why I must leave."

Chapter 25
Isha

Sleep was an illusion, a concept Isha had grown accustomed to either going without or having very little of. Now that she was free, she found old habits were hard to break. She tossed and turned in her pallet, shivering underneath the cloak Dazen had given her to use as a makeshift blanket. How could she be expected to sleep with so much playing on her mind?

She looked down at her hands. On the outside they looked clean and unblemished, but to her they would be forever stained with the blood of her captor. She felt no guilt for what she had done, if anything she felt elated, as if she had finally taken the reins of her life back. But even though she knew in her heart it was the right thing to do, she was still a killer, and her actions had consequences.

She rolled around on her pallet, placing sinister thoughts aside.

Dazen and Raiz were every bit the men she knew they would become, both so handsome and powerful. She burned with the desire to know more about them. What had they been up to in her absence? Was Father treating them well? Did Illidor still prosper? How was one supposed to sleep with so many questions yet unanswered?

She opened her eyes, giving up on the idea of sleep entirely. She peeped through the slit in the tent-flap. Puk still hovered outside, his expression dark and ever vigilant. She wondered what she had done to make him so loyal to her. Did he love her, perhaps? Or is loyalty the only thing he had ever known? Maybe Maitreya was right, and it was all the magic of her eyes.

His protectiveness was occasionally overbearing, but she didn't mind. She owed this man her life more than once over, and if his companionship was the only price, then she would gladly pay it.

She heard footsteps approaching; boots crunching against scattered rocks as a man made his way over towards where she slept. He was met with Puk's hand pressing against his chest.

Isha tilted her head, pressing her ear into the air in order to decipher any words spoken.

"I wish to speak with the princess," came a voice softer even than a whisper. "Please, the matter is quite urgent. I will not be long."

Isha was expecting Puk to turn the man away, but to her surprise he stepped aside, allowing the man to come close.

Any anxiety was quickly quashed, however, when Obeyun stepped forth from the shadows and knelt by her side.

"Isha, are you awake? I apologise for disturbing you, but I need to speak with you before I go."

She turned to face him. "Surely you know by now that myself and sleep are not on friendly terms."

Obeyun issued a low belly laugh. "I am well aware of your feud with it." He sniffed the fresh air before turning to her with an expression she was unfamiliar with.

"I did not think I would live long enough to smell the scent of nature once again. It is a surreal feeling, would you not admit?" he said.

"I will never take the outdoors for granted again, that is for sure. Now what is this talk of leaving? You cannot leave now; we are so close to my home."

"Ah, but that is exactly why I must leave, young one. I have much desire to see your homeland, it is true, but it has been long since I have seen my family. Just as you must return to face your father, I too must return to face my brother. I am burdened with the guilt of my country's suffering under his rule. Wisha needs me, and so I must return."

Isha sat upright in her pallet. "But he will kill you! You cannot go! I need you here, Obe. What will become of me without you?"

"Hush now, you have never needed me, and you know it. It is I who drew strength from you all of these years. Do not despair, this is a journey I must take alone. To move forward in my future, I must first confront my past. Puk will watch over you while I cannot. I was wrong to doubt him so, there is strength within him, of that I am now certain."

Isha pouted, groaning with discomfort at the thought of her best friend leaving her side. But there was nothing she could do. This was his decision to make, and he would not be moved.

"Promise me you will return one day so that we may feast in the halls of Illidor together!" she insisted.

"Or perhaps I shall invite you to my country, where we can dine in the Hall of Songs. I am sure Mother would love to meet you."

Isha could not hold back her smile as she gazed upon her friend for perhaps the final time.

"You must watch over Maitreya in my absence," Obeyun

said. "She is lost, I can see it. Watching you become reunited with your family has only furthered her depression. I fear she will again be hunted when knowledge is released about what she can do."

"I will welcome her as a sister, do not worry."

"I bid thee farewell then, know that I stand with you against the King-Radiant if our paths should meet again."

Obeyun turned to leave, but Isha reached out, pulling at his cloak. "Obeyun wait! Please be careful, and have a plan," she said with a wink.

He met her gaze with a warm smile before turning to walk away, "Always," he said as he left.

She watched his body shrink as he walked further and further into the darkness of the night until he was one with the shadows.

A dreaded worry sunk into her bones at the thought of never seeing him again. Zapour was dangerous for those who travelled alone, and he had a long trek if he wanted to make it all the way to Wisha. She shook her head, casting the doubt from her mind as she settled herself back into the relative comfort of her pallet.

Her head had barely touched the floor when she heard a woman shouting in the distance. She sat upright, hand clasping tightly around the hilt of her knife — the same knife she had used to kill her former master. She crept out into the night to find Puk holding out his arm to block her off.

"Puk, I must see what the matter is, someone could be in trouble."

The mute grudgingly obliged, keeping her close as the pair made their way towards the commotion. It seemed they were not the only ones drawn by the sound. Nearly half the camp was on their feet in the middle of the night, weapons drawn.

A blur of blue and yellow shapes descended the slope, ready for combat.

"Raiz!" came a shout from down below.

"Raiz! Come out here! Show yourself! How could you?"

Isha laboured to a stop. Aroha knelt on her knees clutching at her brother's limp body. Argon's head lolled over her massive forearms. His mouth hung agape, face lax with the typical expression of a dead man.

Aroha was distraught, hissing at any who dared venture too close, suspicious of everyone.

"Argon!" Isha half-screamed before covering her mouth with her palm. She ran to his side despite Puk's reluctance and Aroha's intense glare. "Is he…?"

Aroha nodded. "Slain in his sleep. You had best keep that brother of yours on a tight leash. Raiz!" she screamed again. "Come out here."

It wasn't long before Raiz showed himself, rubbing sleep from his one good eye as he stumbled his way through the bustle of gawking onlookers. "What is the matter? Are we under attack?"

"Don't play dumb!" Aroha snapped. "You know well what it is you've done."

"What are you — is that the prisoner?"

"You should know, you killed him!"

"I did no such thing. I have been abed since our gathering."

"Liar!"

"Aroha, calm yourself. It is true I feel nothing for his loss. If he were not your sibling, and my sister had not pleaded for his life, I would have ended him back in Speakers Hollow. But I promise you I did not kill your brother."

"Then how do you explain this?" She turned Argon's body over, exposing the charred clothing covering an arrow sized hole in his chest. An empty space now sat where his heart had been. "Man over there said he saw a red flash." She waved a hand towards one of Dazen's White-Swords. "Came over to find my brother like this, and the culprit nowhere to be seen. I know of no other whose Shine flashes red! Now drop your act and just admit you killed him!"

Isha turned to her younger brother, nostrils flaring. "Is it true, Raiz?"

"Wh — you too sis? Isha, I swear by Zur's Light I am not the one who did this."

Dazen — who seemed to have already been up and aware of the situation — stepped forwards. "Gale, is it true? What did you see?"

The captain of the White-Swords stood at attention, "It is my fault sir, I should have been watching closer. You must reprimand me."

"Gale, this is not the time, what did you see?"

"I saw a red light shine from within. It came and went quicker than I could move. By the time I made it inside, the deed was done, and the assailant gone. Even burned himself a hole out the back."

All eyes, including Isha's own, turned to Raiz.

"You'll pay for this!" Aroha cried.

Raiz took a backward step, his face twisted in what seemed to Isha as genuine surprise. "Aroha, I did not... I did not do it, I swear."

"It's true." A woman stepped forward from behind her brother's shadow.

Isha had come to know her as Veil, and though she was happy Raiz had found himself someone to rely on in her absence, she still did not trust this woman.

"Raiz was with me tonight. He couldn't have harmed your

brother."

All eyes shifted toward Veil, who, even wrapped in a bundle of fur, still looked like she could use a good meal or two.

"The man was scum!" cried an onlooker, a Levic soldier by the look of him.

"We're better off without him!" said another, this time bearing the crest of a White-Sword.

Aroha's eyes darted from place to place but were met with the same response.

Isha's heart broke for her. It seemed the soldiers of both Lesken and Trost carried with them no sympathy for the death of their enemy. It made her wonder if they were any better.

Aroha stood, lifting the carcass of her brother over her shoulders before moving away from the crowd. "Don't follow me, I won't be back," she said.

Isha turned back toward Raiz. If he was the murderer he was being portrayed as, there was no regret in his eyes. No remorse. *How much have you changed while I've been gone, Brother? Are you still the innocent boy I grew up loving? Or are you something else entirely?*

Chapter 26
Dazen

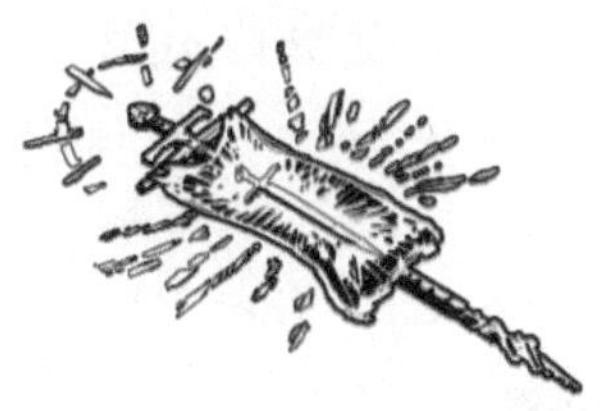

D azen stood atop a high hill. The bright, multicoloured leaves of the Golden Forest were behind him now as he stared out into the open fields of his homeland. The tip of the Moon-Spire spiralled into the sky like a giant white arm. Cradled by thousands of glittering stars, it stood as a symbol of protection and provision. Though, compared to the Last Light in Lumindal, it seemed less majestic to him now.

Raiz did not seem to share his opinion. He gawked at the structure in the distance like a lost puppy who had found its mother. "How long has it been since you set foot in Illidor?" Dazen asked.

Raiz's gaze did not falter. "Too long."

"How do you suppose Father is going to react when he sees not one, but three of his children return to him?"

Raiz snorted. "You should tell me, you have lived with the bastard."

Dazen searched his brother's expression for any sign of the child he used to know, but came up short. "Are you sure you want to come back?"

"I am not scared of Kron anymore."

"He did not take it well when you left. Do not expect him to forgive you quickly."

"I do not seek his forgiveness," Raiz snapped. "And I will not ask for it. It is he who should asking for mine. He was a coward, always will be. What choice did he give me? He could barely look at me after Isha was taken. He blamed me, and I blamed him. There was no life for me here, and you know it."

Dazen let out a long sigh. "Then why come back at all? Why not remain a vigilante?"

"Because, unlike you, I spent my entire life training to become strong enough to free her. I will not let her walk away from me again. And besides, I need to see Father's sickness for myself. If the old man is truly dying, I would not miss it."

Dazen grimaced. It seemed this 'Celik' had twisted his brother's mind further than he thought. Or maybe this was just who he was now. It made him wonder. "Raiz," he said. "I must know, was it you who sent your friend's brother to an early grave?"

The air stilled, and Raiz's silent glare turned from Illidor towards Dazen. "Do you think I did it?"

Dazen hesitated before hardening his expression. "No. I know you to be a cold-blooded killer, but I would hold hope you are an honest one."

A hint of a smile touched Raiz's lips. "A fool's hope, but no, I did not kill him."

"Any idea who did?"

"Can any of your men use white-light?"

"A couple, yes, but with the King-Radiant restricting our number to a mere five hundred, I could only afford to take a handful with me. And none have Light that shines red."

"What of those guarding the prisoner?" Raiz said.

"No, Gale is my most trusted captain. He would not betray me; you have my word."

"Then perhaps one of the Levics?"

"Huet is a handful, and I wouldn't put it past him, but do you truly believe them capable? His ability with the Light is novice at best."

Raiz gave him a smug look. "Compared to the skill of Illidor's finest prince you mean? I see you have borrowed Mother's technique."

Dazen laughed. "Trust me to turn Mother's creation into a weapon. Though I fear it pales in comparison to your own concoction. Tell me, how long until your arms turn to ash? You flirt with death every time you call upon that much Light."

"Death and power are one and the same, you cannot achieve the latter without risking the former."

Dazen raised a brow. "Be careful, Raiz. I would hate to see you become that which you have spent your life trying to destroy."

"Do not worry about me, I am true to myself."

Dazen hesitated, unsure whether his brother's remark was meant as ridicule, or just a statement of fact. "What of your friend?" he said after a time. "I have not seen her since the death. Has she gone?"

"Aroha? She will be fine. I will seek her out when the time is right."

"The death of a family member is no easy obstacle to overcome. Be sure that you do. When the time is right, of course."

A shadow formed in the corner of his vision, followed by a cloaked figure. Dazen jolted, hands at the hilt of his short sword as he turned to face the newcomer.

The one known as Celik stood before him, his face an ugly mess of black marks. Dazen sheathed his sword, realising only too late he had been staring.

"Celik, what is it?" Raiz said.

"I need to speak with you." He glared at Dazen through sceptical eyes and turned back to Raiz. "Alone."

"Whatever you need to say you can say to my brother," Raiz said.

Celik righted himself, gritting his teeth as he scowled at them both. "We do not belong here, Raiz. Illidor is not safe."

"That is not true," Raiz said. "My brother will protect us."

"Your brother," Celik said, pausing to offer a mock smile Dazen's way. "Cannot protect his boot from the shit on the road."

Dazen said nothing, just gripped the hilt of his sword a little tighter.

"Our place is out there," Celik continued, inclining his head away from Illidor. "Your sister is free. You have fulfilled your duty to her. Hiding behind these walls only provides a bigger target. Let us be gone. There is work to do."

"Work to do?" Raiz protested. "Veil suggested a plan, a great one. And you fought against it. I am sick of hiding in the shadows, picking off targets one-by-one. I want to do more. We can do more."

Celik physically hissed, his face twisting into a snarl. "The tower must not be touched! There are other ways to fight against Lumindal. You do not understand."

"Then make me understand," Raiz said. "What is so important about the tower? It is a weapon of destruction and nothing more."

"The Skae —" Celik began.

Dazen stepped forward. "The Skae are a myth," he

interjected. "An afterthought. A tale to scare children."

"The Skae are very real," Celik said, eyes narrowing. "And they will return."

"And how do you know so much?" Raiz asked.

"That is not important."

"Of course it is important," Raiz snapped. "You ask me to trust you, except you will not tell me why! I have made up my mind. I will return to Illidor, for the time being at least. You can come with me, or you can wait for me. The choice is yours."

"Our job is not done simply because you have your sister back. We have work still to do."

Raiz stepped forwards so that his body was nearly pressing against Celik's, "I have not forgotten anything. I have run from my father for too long, the time has come for me to face him. Once I am sure my sister is safe and I have dealt with him, I will find you," he said, looking Celik in the eye. "Now forgive me, but there is someone I must see before I leave."

Chapter 27
Raiz

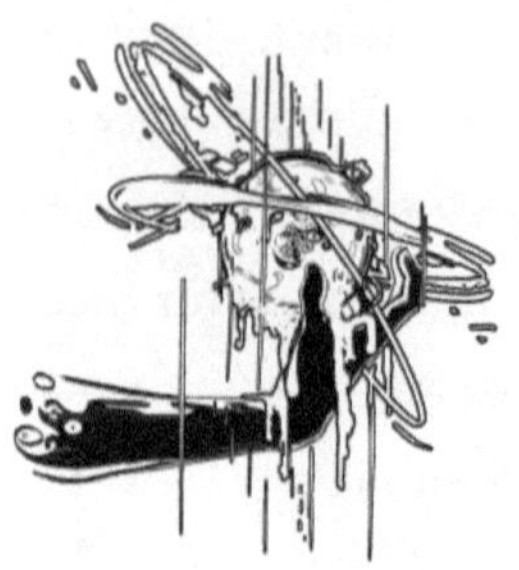

Bright blue eyes peered back at him. Veil bit her lip, the muscles around her cheekbones tightening as she voiced her concern through sheer force of will alone.

"Don't look at me like that," Raiz said, avoiding her gaze.

"Like what, hm?"

"Like you're disappointed in me."

Veil crossed her arms, tucking her fists deep into her chest. "I'm not disappointed, you can go wherever you wish."

"Sure, and the sun isn't bright. I see through you."

Veil rolled her eyes so high her pupils were no longer visible. She moved to leave.

"Veil, wait!"

She turned back to face him. Raiz grabbed her by the wrist and tugged her towards him. "I don't want to go. I don't want to leave you."

"If a man doesn't desire to do something, then he doesn't do it. Simple."

"I have to go back. I must face my father, and I must see that my sister is safe."

"You already know the answer you seek. Your father won't have changed. You won't be welcomed with open arms. You don't belong here Raiz."

"Then where do I belong?" Raiz said.

Veil's limbs stiffened, her words lost, as though her vocal cords had been severed. Everything was so complicated now. Raiz wanted to be with her. Of course he did. He had always wanted to. But after the other night, he didn't know anymore. He had always been her calming presence, despite his own hotheadedness. She was good for him, and he, her. But the moment they got physical, things changed. She nearly lost control. Raiz couldn't do that to her, not every day. Sooner or later, she would pop, and it would be his fault. He thought of his sister. He couldn't leave her, not now anyway.

Veil relaxed, her shoulders dropping low. "You're right. Maybe this is where you should be. I was never enough for you, I shouldn't have—"

"Veil stop, it's not like that."

"No, I get it, don't worry. You have your family back now. You should go, be with them. I'll be fine. I'll search for Aroha with Draz and Celik."

Raiz sighed. "I will return, I promise."

Veil gave a half smile. "You'd better, we have a kingdom to topple."

Raiz let go of her hand. "Take Spike with you, he doesn't belong cooped up in a city."

Veil nodded. "Don't be too long playing happy family." And then she left, leaving nothing but her scent as she disappeared into the distance.

Raiz spun, positioning his body to hide the redness in his eyes. He shook his head, cursing himself for not saying more.

So many words left unsaid. But what could he say?

He rubbed at his eyes as Draz approached. "No need to hide from Draz," he said. "Trust Draz. Draz knows all about hiding." He tapped the peridium metal atop his head.

"That obvious, huh," Raiz said.

"She'll come around. Don't keep us waiting, 'Your Highness'. Got people who need you out there," Draz said, gesturing behind him.

"I'll be back, don't you worry. What are you going to do about Aroha? I know you two were close."

Draz shrugged. "Not much that can be done. She made her choice."

"But you need to find her! She's one of us."

"Not by my standing. She was one of them. Once a Golden bastard, always a Golden bastard, it seems."

"You don't really believe that do you?"

Draz shrugged again. "Doesn't matter what I believe, she's gone, Raiz."

Raiz paused, studying Draz through narrowed eyes. He didn't say anything. He didn't need to say anything. Draz was suffering, just as he was. Raiz could see through his facade.

"Right, Draz better be off then," Draz said. "Take care of your sister this time, will you?"

Raiz laughed. "I will, don't worry about that. Keep a watchful eye on Veil for me while I'm gone?"

Draz turned to leave. "Aye, Draz will watch over your little girlfriend while you're gone, but she can take care of herself."

He wished then that Aroha had been here to say goodbye to, but their next interaction would have to wait.

Raiz returned to Dazen, well aware of the fact he had been eying him in the back the entire time.

"I trust all is well?" Dazen said, the two walking in step with one another.

"It will be," Raiz said, before his focus turned to Isha. He sighed as he watched her attempt to communicate through hand gestures with the mute she kept close by at all times.

"She will come round. Let us allow her to process life away from the capital in her own time," Dazen said.

"I feel her heart is too pure for what is to come," Raiz said.

Dazen scoffed, choking on a mouthful of wine. "Clearly you did not see what I saw back in the Hollow. Her knife cut that piece of filth into a pile of ribbons."

Raiz swallowed his words, forced to accept the truth. Isha was as hardened as he, perhaps even more so.

"Years spent in captivity have done nothing to sully her character," Dazen continued. "But I pity her next victim, and pray her wrath does not fall upon the wrongly accused." He tilted his head, puffing his lips into a grin.

"I do not need to continue to plead my innocence," Raiz said. "She either believes me, or she does not. The truth will come out eventually. In the meantime, keep your eyes open." A figure caught his eye. "I will be but a moment, there is one last person I must speak with."

Raiz moved for the young lad he had taken into his care after his family had been eradicated. "Hector, a word."

The boy shuffled out from behind the youngest Levic boy to confront Raiz.

Raiz looked him in the eye, and for a moment he saw himself when he had first met Celik. A lost boy, in search of a home. "Hector, I must apologise to you."

"Apologise? Apologise for what?" Hector asked.

"I agreed to take you in, to train you as my master did me. But my path leads me down another route. Celik was wrong. I did the right thing taking you in when you had no other. But he was also right. I have no business taking you under my wing when I don't even know my own path."

Hector bowed his head. "I understand. What'll happen to me?"

Raiz's chin rose in a show of pride before his gaze turned to Echo. The youngest Levic was likely only two years his junior, but there was a glint in his eye, a flicker of determination that Raiz found was a rare trait. "That is where I was hoping you will lend a hand, Echo."

Echo stood forward, thumping his fist into his chest. "I will take him in. You have my word. The boy is of Zuton, he falls under my protection."

Raiz nodded his appreciation. "Hector here is strong with the Light," he said, patting him on the head and ruffling his wavy hair. "He will prove his worth when he comes of age, of that I have no doubt."

Hector took one more pleading look at him before he turned to leave. "Raiz!" he called.

Raiz twisted, cocking his ear to the side, but did not move his body.

"Promise me you'll conquer the fear. Promise me that my family didn't die for nothing."

Raiz smirked beneath the cover of his shadowed face. He lifted his blackened hand into the air as if to wave as he trailed away from the boy. He needed no promise to keep his mind on his goal. He did not need to conquer fear, he was the fear.

His friends were nothing more than indistinct shapes in the distance as he approached the majestic iron gates of Illidor. Surrounded by acres of agricultural farmland and orchards, Illidor was a place like no other. The smell of fresh vegetables and herbs was almost enough to make him regret leaving in the first place. They trudged down dirt paths lined with pruned trees in orderly rows, some laden with nuts and fruits. Figs, pears, peaches and the like were scattered around the trunks of the trees, and Raiz basked in the atmosphere.

Cries of 'the prince returns' echoed throughout the land as citizens rushed to greet Dazen. Raiz wondered if they realised that not one, but three Glaive siblings walked among them this day.

Mutters and murmurs rose the closer they drew to the gates. Many of the older looking onlookers pointed and clasped hands to mouths, running to find a better vantage point as Raiz, Dazen and Isha walked in sync through the gates and up the cobblestone. Dozens of white-coated guards flanked their position, more flocking towards them the further they went. The Levic family trailed behind, playing second fiddle to the returning Glaives.

Another set of iron gates blocked their path but were soon opened after a quick word from Dazen. The palace of Illidor was as he remembered it. A pang of anxiety hit him like a horse's kick as he walked the steps leading towards the courtyard. He looked to Isha, her hand pressed hard against her heart as she too felt the pressure of returning to the very place she had been taken.

Raiz lowered his head. He swore he could see his own blood still splashed against the stone tiling at his feet. He ran a finger over his mangled eye, pulling it away, expecting to see red. The stone was polished to a sparking gleam, as if the whole event had never even happened. His sister's screams echoed in his mind, the shrill shrieking of a child whose voice had not yet matured. Panic flared in his chest. He felt a cool touch on his hand and was ready to lash out, only to find Isha's hand pressed into his. A calm washed over him then. He was reassured by her warm smile as the two reminisced over their past terrors, intent on battling them together. Did this mean she had forgiven him for the crime he had not committed?

There was no time to speak of it now. The wide doors swung open. A contingent of Illidor's finest, dressed in silver chain coated with pale blue doublets, threaded with the white stitching of a sword into the breast, poured out into the courtyard. They marched past, forming two lines, three body lengths apart before coming to a halt, their statuesque expressions devoid of emotion.

Raiz tiptoed, pausing to take in the spectacle, hand fingering the hilt of his blade beneath his coat. Dazen waved him down, waltzing through the line of troops with all the confidence in the world.

They allowed him to pass, Raiz and Isha not far behind. The three siblings waited in the entrance hall. Raiz stared up at the tiling where the stone had been replaced after his outburst of Shine during his youth.

The thick ironwood doors of the Great Hall edged open, creaking eerily as the light from beyond seeped through the cracks.

The Great Hall was a marvel. Rows upon rows of neatly organized tables and chairs lined its length. Countless ornaments, tapestries and trophies of the past decorated the walls. This life was a world away from the damp, rat infested caverns Raiz had been living in for the past eight years. It disgusted him, the fact that they had been living this lavish lifestyle while people suffered poverty beyond belief. While his sister suffered.

His eyes drew away from the finery as a faint but familiar aura pressed against his. His attention fixed towards the throne at the end of the hall.

Pressure built behind his temples like a headache, growing stronger with each step. His father sat on his throne of red velvet, his scowl every bit as intimidating as he remembered. He looked a vision of his youth, nothing as Dazen had described him. Veins popped from his forearms, which were tensing with anticipation. A neatly trimmed beard of black tinged with a shade of grey dangled from his chin, reaching down to his chest. Lines of age wrinkled his brow and outer eyes, but they did nothing to weaken his overbearing presence — if anything, they strengthened it.

Raiz looked to Dazen, hoping for some sort of explanation as to his remarkable recovery, but judging by the look of shock on Dazen's face, he would receive none.

The three siblings stood before the dais, Raiz only now acknowledging the vast multitude of palace guards flanking Kron, others moving to block the path they had just traversed.

The hall grew silent as the last footstep settled into position. Kron rose, silver rings shining as he stretched his fingers. He stalked down a step towards the three of them. Raiz heard Dazen gulp beside him, head lowered to the floor.

Raiz took a deep breath but fixed his glare towards Kron. He would not cower beneath this man. He would not show any sign of weakness. Light boiled under his skin, wanting to come out, wanting to be set free. He pressed it down, focusing instead on matching his father's presence. His attention faltered, if only for a moment, as a puff of almost red steam clouded around him, pressing against an invisible barrier, matching his father's own cloud of white. The two opposing auras of Shine met, each attempting to gain hold over the other. Raiz didn't exactly know what he was doing, or how he was doing it, but he was holding his own.

Kron's expression remained unreadable. He walked past

both Raiz and Dazen before coming to a stop before Isha. His guard lowered, his shoulders slumping as he gazed upon his long-lost daughter. He moved to embrace her, but Isha inched away as if his very touch was poison. Kron continued his advance, wrapping giant arms around her as if to strangle her. Instead, he gently pressed her head into his chest. "My daughter, you are returned to me. I knew this day would come."

Raiz could practically feel his sister's anger boiling beneath the warmth of her father's arms. He pictured her mind burning, her tongue on the verge of lashing out with the words, *'and yet you did nothing to help me'*.

But she remained silent, accepting his embrace without complaint, without scolding him as he certainly deserved.

Raiz thought about doing it for her, about tearing down his father from the pedestal he put himself on, but it was not his place. Isha could fight her own battles, and if he was to act rashly, it would only give cause to weaken her resolve.

"Father, I see even sickness cannot defeat you," Dazen said.

Kron turned to Dazen then. He reached for his hand and planted a kiss upon his knuckles. He took a deep breath and exhaled, as if boasting of his renewed health. "You did this? How? How is it that after so many years my daughter is returned to me?"

"I — uh — we found an opportunity and took it. Me and Raiz, with no little help from Isha. She was incredible, she managed to escape Lumindal all on her own."

Kron scowled at Dazen. "You know what this means for us? What danger this places us in?"

Dazen straightened his back. "I am well aware. But I could not let them take her, not again. I made my choice, and I do not regret it."

Kron seemed to relax, clasping his hands together. "And the Eagle?"

Dazen froze, refusing to meet his father's eye-line. "Dead," he whispered.

Kron's eyes grew wide, his breaths coming in short and sharp. "You fool! Were there any witnesses?"

"The Levics were there, and perhaps some citizens of Speaker's Hollow, but they will not talk! They have fled."

Kron scrunched his face, his aura flaming.

Raiz stepped forward. "That bastard deserved to die! I would see him dead a hundred times over if I had the chance!"

Kron's glare settled on Raiz. "Of course, the false son returns. Only with you would such a burden arise! You have forever troubled myself and Trost. You should never have come back here!"

Isha placed a hand to cover her mouth. "What are you saying Father? Raiz is my brother, he is your son! He is every bit a Glaive as Dazen or I."

"I have but one son," Kron said.

"What is this nonsense? What happened between the three of you while I was gone?" Isha pleaded.

Raiz and Dazen looked each other over, their distrust seemingly reignited.

"Ahh," Kron said. "I see you haven't told her yet. Not unwise, given the circumstances. But you must have known how this was going to play out."

"Father, what are you talking about? Raiz, Dazen, explain," Isha prodded.

Raiz bit his lip, hand edging closer and closer to his hidden blade. Dazen was none the wiser. Words seemed to be stuck in his throat every time he made to speak them.

"Very well," Kron said. "I shall explain. You see after your dear brother so foolishly led you into the Eagle's open hands, after ignoring my explicit instructions to stay inside the palace, he *then* lacked even the courage to face up to what he had done."

Isha leaned in closer, her jaw slack and her eyes wide.

"He ran! Like the coward he is, he ran!" Kron said. "Not brave enough to face the consequences of his own actions. And now he returns. An outlaw. A *murderer*."

Raiz no longer had control of his own body. His heart thumped, pumping both blood and Light at such a rapid pace that it threatened to burst at any moment.

"Do you think me unaware of what you are, Raiz?" Kron continued. "Of what you have become? I know what you do, and so does Lumindal."

Raiz's feet shifted, Light wilting from his fingertips, ready to be used.

"But all is not lost," Kron said. "Raiz still has a chance to make up for his mistakes."

"You bastard," Raiz spat. "Liar! Hiding your shame behind the misgivings of a ten-year-old boy. You did nothing while she was taken. You stood and watched as your only daughter was taken and enslaved on your very doorstep! And you still believe yourself righteous?"

"Do not speak of what you do not know!" Kron bellowed. "Every action has consequences, boy! As I am sure you are now aware. Or have you not seen the crater that was Lesken? I believe you were there. Is this not true?"

Raiz looked at the ground and then back at his father. "The people of Lesken died for a just cause, a noble one. Their deaths will not be in vain, I swear it!"

"Bah! Thus is the dribble of a madman. Can you not see, Dazen? Can you not see through his false promises? His ideals are a fantasy, a concept from a past that has no bearing on the present and the future. We are the future. The Glaive family will live on, we will see through this mess he has created, and Raiz will help us do it."

The three siblings looked towards their father with tilted heads.

Kron reached into his belt and pulled out a curled parchment, throwing it at Dazen. "The King-Radiant has called for a Council of Kings. This has not been done since the fall of Hirane. Raiz's identity has been revealed, and I am sure he means to seek vengeance. Fortunately for us, his vengeance has been delivered to our doorstep on a silver platter. There is only one person who shall take the blame for the fall of Averardus! Guards, seize this abomination at once!"

Raiz pounced, his blackened hand drawing the blade from his coat, his other hand dripping with molten Light.

"Raiz, no!" came a cry. He turned and saw Isha, tears pouring down soft cheeks. "Please, do not kill any of them. We will sort it out. Do not prove you're the man he thinks you to be."

Raiz tensed, his entire body shaking with energy. He could probably kill half of the guards here, or at least enough to see him to an exit point. He shook his head. He knew it was a mistake to come back. He never belonged here. He belonged with Veil.

A mass of blue and white circled him, sharpened blades pointing his direction.

"Father, please," Dazen said. "I brought him here under my protection, you cannot do this."

"Be quiet!" Kron said. "You are not king yet. To be a true king you must learn what it takes to survive in this world."

The men continued to circle Raiz, drawing closer with each

careful step. He looked towards Kron and then towards his sister. Against every instinct in his body, every urge, every lesson Celik had ever taught him, he bent down to his knees. His blade clattered to the marble floor beneath his feet. All Light faded into the dark depths of his body, to be used another day.

Chapter 28
Isha

Isha sat cross-legged atop the tiling of the Moon-spire. She stared out into the haze which had taken hold of Illidor. Not much had changed since she had last been here. The hundreds of houses below seemed like tiny pebbles at the bottom of a stream, flowing around the great boulder that was the palace.

Nearly a full season had passed since her escape from Lumindal, and winter was almost upon them. Yet she felt no better for it. She had simply exchanged one prison cell for another. Granted, her current status was self-imposed, for she refused to leave the Moon-spire until Father released Raiz from his shackles. She could come and go as she pleased, but she was a fool if she thought Kron would let her out of his sight for long.

She was angry.

Angry at her father for having the guile to imprison his own son. Angry at Dazen for letting him do it. She was even still angry at Raiz. What kind of world did she live in? Was everyone at the mercy of their own selfish desire? Would Zapour even be better off without the King-Radiant in power?

She dismissed her last thought as foolish. There was no excuse for the merciless killing of thousands of men, women, and children. Her father was cruel, but even he would not stoop so low.

She had to get to Raiz. The thought of him sitting in a lonely cell for over a month while her father made plans to hand him over to the King-Radiant didn't sit well with her. He had devoted his entire life to her. Now it was her turn to repay that debt. But she had no tools at her disposal. The Council of Kings was due to meet soon, and every day that passed gave her less opportunity to break him free.

Puk guarded her room as he always did. She didn't ask him to. She didn't want him to. She wanted to give him the choice to make something of his life. To show him he didn't have to stay here, with her. But she supposed protection was all he had ever known, and his presence was comforting.

A shadow moved from over her shoulder and Maitreya poked her head through the ornate window. "Isha, your dinner's waiting for you. It'll go cold if you leave it too long."

Isha waved her away, continuing to stare at the grey haze beyond, despite her stomach barking at her to provide sustenance.

"Very well, as you please. But don't expect me to spoon feed you. I'm not your room slave you know," Maitreya said.

Isha swung her head around. "I'm sorry, I didn't mean to be rude. It's just, I have a lot on my mind is all."

Maitreya relaxed her shoulders, moving to sit by her side. "You trouble yourself with too many burdens. There's nothing you can do now. What plays out will happen regardless of your feelings, I'm sorry to say, Ish."

Isha snapped her neck to the side, glaring at Maitreya as if she had drowned a pup. "While I yet draw breath, there is always something I can do. I just need time to think."

Maitreya shuffled backwards. "My apologies, of course. Your brother's strong, I'm sure he'll find a way free of his predicament."

"Or I'll find one for him."

A knock came from the hatch, or more like a rough thump. She made her way back inside the tower and edged closer. A shuffle of footsteps caused her hand to hesitate, but she pulled open the wooden hatch, regardless.

Two forms wrestled together in a tangle of limbs. "I, must, see, my, sister!" cried one of them through gritted teeth.

"Dazen?" Isha said.

Dazen looked up. He pushed himself free of Puk's grip and patted his tunic. "Isha, I wish to speak with you. Can you please order your oaf to move aside?"

Isha smiled at Puk before gesturing for him to step aside. He did so without hesitation.

"If you wish to remove me from my hole, you will find your time wasted," she said.

"Isha please, I come in peace. I just want to talk."

She moved back, allowing him to climb the small ladder before the two made themselves comfortable on a pair of old wooden chairs.

"Stubborn, that one," Dazen said, motioning towards the hatch where Puk stood guard below. "Where did you acquire him?"

"I did not 'acquire' him. I do not ask him to protect me. He just does. A story for another time."

"Well, then I shall be glad to hear it when you are ready."

Isha bit her lip. "So, what is it you wish to speak to me about, dear brother?"

Dazen clasped his hands, taking a steadying breath. "Father

is worried about you."

"Oh, I am sure he is! I am certain he is just dying to cradle his little girl in his arms again. I am shocked he even remembers who I am."

Dazen exhaled, his cool breath visible in the dark of the attic. "I share your concern, believe me. But nevertheless, he is worried."

"And what are you, his lap-dog? Can he not say this himself? Does he have the emotional spectrum of a stale loaf of bread? You can inform Father that he shall never set eyes upon me again until my brother is safely free of chains."

"Isha, he will not budge! I have tried."

"Well try harder."

"But can you not see the consequences? The King-Radiant thinks it was Raiz who killed his Eagles. He likely knows we were involved in Averardus' death. If we do not hand Raiz over, then what happened to Lesken we will surely be our fate next!"

"What, are you agreeing with Father now? Was this your plan from the beginning? Rescue me and blame it all on Raiz?"

"No of course not, I—"

"You disgust me. You are not the man I thought you to be. If you believe for even a second that sacrificing your own brother so we can live happily ever after is a good idea, then I do not want to have anything to do with you. "

"Isha..."

"You were willing to risk everything that day you stormed the inn, ready to throw it all away to see me to safety. But now you will not do the same for Raiz?"

"Raiz is not like you and I. What he has become, the things he is capable..."

"He is our brother, Dazen! You and Father are one and the

same. Leave! Get out! I want nothing to do with you anymore."

"But—"

"Leave!"

Dazen scrambled to his feet, running a hand through slick hair. He took one last lingering gaze toward her before returning down the hatch.

Chapter 29
Dazen

A sharp pain split down the centre of Dazen's head. It was as if the two halves of himself were at war. He pressed a finger upon each temple, but the pain persisted.

He walked in a slump through the narrow halls of the palace, dragging his feet step-by-step towards his father's chamber, head bowed low. Was it true what she had said? Had he really become like him?

He came face-to-face with a high wooden door. He knocked and a servant answered, bowing deeply before ushering Dazen into the decorated room. Kron sat on his bed with his back to the entrance. He turned as Dazen walked in, clinking his silver rings against the wooden frame at the end of the bed. "What ails you, son? You look to have seen better days."

Dazen shied away from his father's scolding. "She will not budge. I fear she is lost to us."

Kron grunted, lifting himself off the bed before walking towards a platter and stuffing his face with a heavy piece of chicken leg, chewing with his mouth open. "She will come around," he said between mouthfuls. "Just give her time. Once this business in Lumindal is over, life can resume as normal."

Dazen's eyes narrowed into slits. "You mean after we sanction my brother to his death."

Kron reached over the table and grabbed a goblet. He took a lengthy pull of wine, washing down the chicken before bearing down upon Dazen with a harsh stare, red staining his lips. "We have been through this! Raiz gave up his right to call himself a Glaive the moment he ran out on us. He is no son of mine." Kron took another sip from his goblet. "He never was."

Dazen stared at the table, unable to look his father in his eye any longer. But everything he spoke was the truth. Dazen had known. Isha and Raiz may have been kept in the dark, but he had always known. Raiz was no son of Kron.

"What really happened to Mother?" he asked quietly.

Kron froze, his mouth open with half of a drumstick hovering in the air before it. "I told you. She died from sickness when you were a boy. Let us not speak of this."

"But why did I not get to say goodbye to her? I may have been young, but I remember well enough. It was as though she just vanished. And you never speak of her. Did you even love her? Did you even care?"

"Enough!" Kron said. "You do not speak to me that way. Your mother was dearer to me than light is to Zur. I will not have you question me on this."

Dazen recoiled as if he had been kicked in the gut. "Then you should know what Raiz means to Isha," he said, his voice soft.

Kron rose from the table, wiped his hands, and walked over to Dazen. He placed a stubby hand onto his shoulder. "This is not easy for me, son. I do not wish this fate upon Raiz. But think logically. He is not your brother, not anymore. It was he who killed the Eagle in Lesken. It was he who drove you towards the Eagle in Speakers Hollow. It is he who the King-Radiant wants. You must think about our country. What will happen if you get the blame for the Eagle's death? You have seen what happened to Lesken, what happened to Hirane. This is what must be done if we wish to escape the same fate."

Dazen swallowed a heavy lump. The allure of Kron's words were becoming too strong for him to refuse. Isha was home, she was safe. And yet Trost stood on the brink of ruin, at the mercy of the King-Radiant's wrath. All he had to do was keep quiet and allow his father to hand Raiz over and all would be forgiven.

Would it really though?

The question buzzed in his mind like a fly he was unable to swat.

Raiz had brought this on himself. He had been reckless. It was through his actions that Lesken was no more. It was through his efforts that an entire nation now battled for their lives.

Dazen walked over to the window, banging a closed fist on the ledge. How could he think like this? It had not been long since *he* was the reckless one. Driven by impulse as he dove headfirst into a nest of the capital's own, slaughtering all in his path, all in the name of saving his sister. Did Raiz not do the same? Were his deeds not driven by the same desire, the same passion? Why then did he deserve to die and Dazen to live?

He shook his head. His gaze drifted out into the ring of stone holding his people together. Lords, nobles, workers, farmers, soldiers, and friends. They were all his responsibility. Thus was the burden of a king. He looked towards his father, not with respect, but pity. How did one sacrifice so much for the sanctity of his kingdom and still remain a figure of power?

And then he remembered. All of those years struck by illness. Kron's burden had been heavy. He never showed it in his general demeanour, of course, but his body had spoken for him. The weight of his crown had been heavy. The crown that one day was to be his.

To be King was a great responsibility. He was responsible not just his family, but an entire country full of families. His decisions impacted not only himself, but all of them. That is what Raiz did not understand. His vision was clouded by one singular emotion.

But Dazen could not deny he shared his brother's feelings, shared in his hatred. Why should one person dictate the state of an entire continent?

The pressure behind his temples worsened. He turned from the ledge and made for the door.

"Where are you going, boy?" Kron said.

"To the dungeon, I must speak with Raiz."

"You will do no such thing! We make for Lumindal in three days, I will not risk his escape."

Dazen looked at his father then, determination showing in the form of his Shine, his hands bright with Light. "Have a guard accompany me if you wish, but I will see him before we leave."

For a moment he thought Kron would be unmoving, but his father dropped his shoulders and nodded before returning to his meal as if Dazen had never even asked.

Chapter 30
Raiz

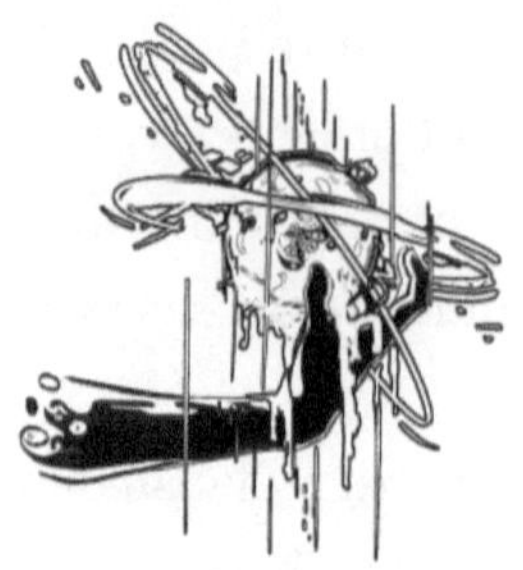

Darkness enveloped him. Twisted shadows formed and re-formed beyond rusted iron bars as flickers of light shone out of sight. A smokey haze seeped through the cracked stone walls, which were damp with vapour and scabbed with mildew.

Raiz wiggled his hands, pulling them apart as if sheer force were enough to break the shackle. It was no use. Kron had specially crafted the shackles out of peridium. *Clever, Father.*

As it turned out, peridium did more than just reflect white-light, it rendered those connected to it practically useless. He reached deep within his well of Shine. Where usually he had access, this time he came up empty. He could still feel it there, sitting idle beneath his skin, but it was as though an impenetrable wall was blocking his way. His body felt weak and vulnerable. His stomach rumbled from hunger, his muscles were slack and weighed down. The peridium itself had a lightness to it, but the effect on his body was equivalent to being sat on by an elephant.

Is this how Isha felt? All of those years locked away with

nothing but her thoughts to keep her company. How had she survived? He had spent the shy side of a month as a captive, where she had spent years. She was stronger than him, that much was certain.

He burned with a newfound hatred for his father. Even after returning his daughter to his arms, still he was ungrateful. He treated him like garbage to be thrown out and disposed of. What had he expected, to be welcomed back with cuddles and kisses? He was angry at himself for walking into this situation. He should never have trusted Kron, nor Dazen.

He sat in quiet contemplation. What purpose did he serve? He had spent his whole life training to become strong enough to free his sister. Now that he had done it, what was left for him?

He still hated the King-Radiant, hated all of them. He wished them dead. But what if saving his sister was all he was meant to accomplish with his life?

His thoughts turned to Hector. The boy had lost everything. His home, his family, his city. And yet still he yearned for justice. Still, he burned with the desire to overcome his fear. How could Raiz protect people like Hector if he was to die? He had been fighting for more than just his sister. He had been fighting to protect everybody. To ensure no more children were to be taken from their homes; to take down the corrupt hierarchy, destroy the weapon responsible for so much death. He could bring a new order to the world, but people like Kron held him back.

He couldn't make change within the blackness of this cell. He hungered for the light once more.

He wondered at Veil. She had warned him against returning to Illidor, and he had not listened. Would she forget about him? Find someone new?

No.

Raiz knew exactly what she would do. There was one thing Veil desired above all else. She would take down the Last Light. Nothing would stop her in her course to bring down the weapon that shattered her family.

A stir came from outside his cell, the shadows dancing in renewed light. Raiz fumbled to sit up straight, combing dust off his clothes. He blew a loose knot of matted hair away from his eyes.

The cell door creaked open, shining welcome torchlight into the dark cell. A shaded figure stepped inside, flanked by another two, close behind.

"Welcome Brother, to my humble abode!" Raiz said, noticing Dazen's pristine uniform. His robes draped over his shoulder, the lengthy symbol of a white sword stretching down a trail of blue silk. "I would see to you personally, but I am afraid I am rather tied up at the moment," he said, holding his shackles aloft.

"I see you have not lost your childish whims during your imprisonment," Dazen said, walking into full view.

"Well, when my dearest elder brother has not come to visit me in a month, what can one do but jest? I was beginning to think you in league with Father. Have you come to free me from these chains?" He lifted his arms up higher.

Dazen's arms locked tight against his chest. His lips pursed, his face a stern and intimidating mask. "You know by now that is not possible Raiz, Father will have none of it."

"Then why have you come? To poke fun? To say you're sorry? To admit you're a coward?"

"That is enough!"

Raiz curled his lip, matching Dazen's glare with his own. "You deny then, that you're a coward? What proof do you offer to the contrary? I see nothing but a lost pup following Father like a fish follows bait."

"You will shut your mouth," Dazen snapped. "You are a criminal. You have placed our entire country at risk."

"You mean 'we' are criminals. Or have you forgotten already your role in that bastard's death? It wasn't me alone who charged the inn. Shall we then call our sister a criminal? Shall we turn her in as well? You made your choice to fight against him that day. And now you turn your back. You're a coward through and through."

Dazen's face grew red-hot, lips pulled so tight Raiz could practically see his teeth through them. "If you had any sense, you would accept your fate. I am not pleased to say it, but Father has a point. Your life will see to the safety and longevity of Trost. I came here to ask you if that sacrifice was one you were willing to make, but it is plain to me now that it is not."

"You know nothing of sacrifice! You see nothing beyond your high walls and fertile lands. You know nothing of the world beyond. Does Father tell you? Of the children?"

Dazen raised a brow.

"He collects them, you know, children born with the Shine. And if they aren't killed, they're put in his service, ripped away from their families for a life of bloodshed and beatings. I've seen it. It's what I was preventing in Lesken, before it was destroyed. Ask yourself, Dazen, is their sacrifice worth your livelihood?"

Dazen moved to speak, but Raiz cut ahead of him.

"And that's not all. People all around suffer. If you think you feel the worst of it, huddled up here in Illidor, you're mistaken. The poor grow poorer, and the rich only get richer. The people of Hirane saw it, they were the only people with enough balls to act."

"And look what became of them!" Dazen said.

"Because they were alone!" Raiz roared. "Nobody came to their defence. Because everybody else were cowards! They all think it. You think it. But the ability to think and the will to act are worlds apart."

Raiz could plainly see conflict on his brother's face, painted in deep lines above his brow. Dazen paced the width of the cell, fingers clenching and unclenching. "We leave for Lumindal in three days. I trust you shall think on the words I have said."

Without another glance, Dazen rushed out of the cell, slamming the door behind him.

"And you mine, Brother," Raiz said, if only in a whisper.

Chapter 31
Isha

The palace below was abuzz with energy. Shapes scuttled about in the distance, moving as if their lives depended on it. Isha cupped a loose stone in her hand and threw it off the high tower, half hoping it would somehow land on her father's head and end this madness.

The stone dropped to the ground, its impact almost as useless as she had been over the past weeks. It wasn't as if she hadn't tried. She had tried everything short of murder to free Raiz from his imprisonment. But what could she do? She wasn't a warrior, wasn't a thief. He was too heavily guarded, and guilting Father wasn't working.

She watched on as more of Illidor's war-band gathered. Blue-white dots of the prestigious White-Swords congregated in tight clusters. They were separated into ranks, which stretched the length of the courtyard. It seemed Kron had rounded up a small army to take with him to Lumindal. He was taking no chances.

She had run out of options. He would not be moved, would not be convinced. This was her last chance to free her brother before he left.

Pushing herself through the window, she made for the hatch. Puk gave her a quizzical look that said more than words ever could.

"Come with me, we have another Glaive to rescue."

The two crept down the spiral staircase, taking care to place each foot lighter than the last. They slowed as they neared the bottom. Isha sighed. Four White-Swords stood guard, their backs turned. The passage through was too narrow for them to sneak past.

With stealth no longer an option, she walked with straight-backed confidence towards them, meaning to walk through them, rather than around.

"Whoa there lassy, hold on," said a tall man with short red hair and a pockmarked face. He turned to face her, placing a careful hand on her shoulder.

"Excuse me, I wish to see my father," she lied.

"I am sorry, my lady, but I cannot allow you to go any further," said the redhead. "King's orders."

"Are you aware that I am the King's daughter? His word is my word. Now, if you do not mind, I will be on my—"

She stopped as the man widened his stance. "I know who you are, and you have my deepest sympathies for the ordeal you have been through. But my orders were explicit. I am not to let you pass until the King and his men are well on their way towards Lumindal."

"You mean Father won't even come to say goodbye?" Isha said, before moving to pass anyway. She hoped to squeeze through the two of them but four hands pushed her back to where she had come.

The redhead crossed his arms and braced his legs. Puk unsheathed his sword, wrapping his free arm around her and pressing her back.

The four guards reacted immediately, swords drawn and pointed towards Puk.

"Tell your man to back away now, Princess. I am not to lay a hand on you, but my orders did not include him."

She bared her teeth into a snarl, but beckoned Puk to lower his sword. "You will live to regret this." She hissed at the red-haired guard. She knew her threat to be empty, but he didn't have to know that.

She made her way back up the winding staircase. Now she truly was imprisoned once more. Only Father would be callous enough to try something like this.

She climbed through the hatch, flexed her arm, and swung it in a wild arc. It smashed into a set of dusty clay pots, breaking them to pieces. She motioned for Puk to approach her. "I don't want to be alone, not anymore. Will you lie with me?"

Puk's thick eyebrows twisted, his body wavering as though he were stuck on a fence and his momentum would take him either way.

"I — I'm sorry Puk. I didn't mean to upset you. You may do as you please, of course."

Puk took a step forward, cupping her hand in his own. He kissed it gently on the knuckle before opening his arms as Isha relaxed into his embrace. He unclipped his sword from his belt and motioned for the makeshift bed.

Isha laid down, exhaustion guiding her movements. She felt a familiar warmth as Puk's toned arms wrapped around her. His rough hands pressed to hers, a comfort she never knew she needed. It reminded her of their escape from Lumindal, of the nights and days spent cooped up in a closet of blackness. To her surprise, she found it to be a fond memory rather than a sour one. With everyone else in her life dismissing her as if she were irrelevant — a simple damsel to be rescued — it was nice to have someone care for her the way Puk seemed to.

"Puk?" she whispered. "You won't leave me, will you?"

Puk's hand left hers, and for a moment her heart sank at the thought of him leaving her as well. But his hand moved up her thigh and rested at her ribs. Firmly but lovingly, he pressed two fingers into the curve of her ribcage.

One poke.

Isha woke to quiet. Unravelling from Puk's grip, she wiped sleep from her eyes with a finger, blinking rapidly as her vision returned. Quietly, so as to not disturb Puk from his deserved rest, she crept to the window she and Raiz had been so fond of as children. The courtyard below was empty save for a few skeleton guards patrolling its width. Father and his army were gone, Raiz was out of her reach, and she had done nothing, could do nothing.

"You should really lock that window, never know who might sneak in."

Isha jumped, her entire body jerking at the sound of another feminine voice. At first, she thought it was Maitreya, but the voice was more modulated, more controlled than Maitreya's. She reached for Puk's sword and turned to face the would-be thief. Puk woke with a start, stepping in front of her and raising his fists.

Isha pushed him back, watching with a keen eye as the invader stepped out from the shadows of the attic.

"I know you," Isha said. "You are Raiz's friend."

"Veil, yes. I suppose I am your brother's friend."

She removed a black hood to reveal her face. Pale white skin surrounded a set of engaging blue eyes set deep within their sockets. She was pretty by men's standards, though there was a darkness to her, a sense of dread, as if her aura were tainted with some form of forbidden magic.

"What do you want? How did you get in here?" She looked from the window back to Veil. "Surely you didn't climb?"

A thumping sounded from above, followed by a thin trail of dust filtering down from the ceiling as a series of footsteps reverberated through the wood.

A sly smile creased Veils full lips. "I see you're a prisoner once more. It's a shame to see Raiz's entire life's work undone so."

"I am not a prisoner!" Isha snapped, taking another look around the room. "Though it seems I cannot leave." She rolled her eyes, crossing her arms. "What do you mean, my brother's life's work?"

Veil's eyes narrowed. "How much do you know of the past eight years?"

"Raiz said little on our journey home. I was hoping for the opportunity to ask him more, but things took a rather different tone than I expected."

"By different tone, you mean your father draping him in chains and offering him up as a trophy to the King-Radiant?"

"I played no part in that! Nor will I."

"Hence, being locked in a tower."

Isha grunted, turning her head away.

"Do you have any idea what he sacrificed for you?" Veil continued. "He gave more than his life. He pushed himself every day to become a man strong enough to see you safely behind these walls once more. He willed himself through trials unimaginable, just so he could see your face again."

Isha's jaw slackened, her arms slumped to the side as she gulped down the sadness in her throat.

"I can't deny that eight years spent as a prisoner in the

capital would have been a tough life," Veil said. "But Raiz fared no better. Every day he urged Celik to storm the capital, to make an attempt at your rescue. He was just past his fourteenth year when I caught him at the foot of Lumindal." Veil paused to laugh. "He'd dressed himself as a bard's apprentice. Was going to bloody sing his way through the gates! All in the name of seeing you free."

Isha nearly choked on her laughter. "I assume he did not?"

"I stopped him. A lucky thing. He hated me for a full year after that."

Isha breathed a deep lungful of air. "I thank you for that. I thank you for looking out for him when I could not. My brother is strong, but he is also reckless. He needs someone to look out for him, to guide him. I am glad he had you."

"Reckless is an understatement."

The two shared another deserved laugh.

"Why is it you have come?" Isha asked.

"I bring opportunity."

Isha raised her right brow.

"Do you wish to see him again?"

"I do."

"Then you're in luck, for I'm in need of someone who knows the capital."

Isha paced the attic, wood creaking with every step. "What of that man? Celik was it? What of his spies? What need have you of a former slave? I will be no use to you in battle."

"Celik's gone. He left us. I don't know where he went, possibly to look for Aroha. But I have no intention of waiting for him to return. By that time, it's likely Raiz will be dead. My plan remains the same. I will take down the Last Light. You said yourself you'd been inside the tower. You know how it works, where to get in."

"I do."

"Then come with me! And together we can stop that which should never have been built."

"And what of Raiz? Does your plan include his rescue?"

"If all goes according to plan, Raiz will bathe in the warmth of the Light once again."

"Am I just supposed to take you at your word? I know you are close with my brother, but I do not even know you. This could be a trick."

Veil crossed her arms. "I guess we're both going to have to trust each other."

Isha turned to Puk, hoping for advice but of course receiving none. "The matter is moot," Isha said. "There is no way down from this tower. Guards flank every exit."

Veil pressed her lips together before placing two fingers into her mouth and whistling a loud tune. The thumping from before returned, inching closer towards the windowsill.

Isha ran over to the ledge, poking her head out to see a muzzle-like face glaring back at her. Thick scales trailed down the length of a long neck.

"Spike!" Isha said, almost screaming the words.

Spike licked her cheek, the scales on his belly changing colour to match the woodwork.

"So, what do you say?" Veil said.

"Raiz will kill us both, but I am with you."

Just then a rumble sounded from down below, and the wooden hatch began to shift. Veil returned to the shadows, and Isha stepped forwards, ready to distract any who would enter. She let out a breath when she saw Maitreya climbing into the room, bringing with her an assortment of fresh fruits.

She must have noticed something amiss, for she wavered. "Isha, what's wrong? Are you okay?" she inquired.

Isha sighed. She couldn't lie to her. Obeyun had made her promise to keep her safe, and now she had to leave. But she couldn't bring her to Lumindal. She couldn't place her in that situation again. She would be safe here. "Maitreya, I have to go. I am so sorry, but I must go to Raiz."

Maitreya gave her a confused look. Veil stepped from the shadows then, and Spike's head poked through the window. Understanding washed over Maitreya's expression. "It's okay Isha," she said. "You should go. You've done more than enough for me already. Go, find him." Maitreya gave a warm smile, and Isha hoped it was not the last she would see of it.

"I have something for you," Isha said, moving to rustle through her pack. She withdrew a small stone. It was black as coal and fit neatly into her palm. "A Koshaki Stone," she said. "I think you should have it."

Maitreya's face lit with glee. She reached to touch it, the stone glowing a deep blue before inching away slightly.

"I don't know what connection you have to them just yet," Isha said, "but I sense these have something to do with what you are. When I return, I want to explore this with you more, but in the meantime, I want you to have it."

Maitreya took it, the stone seeming to settle. "Thank you Ish, and good luck."

Chapter 32
Dazen

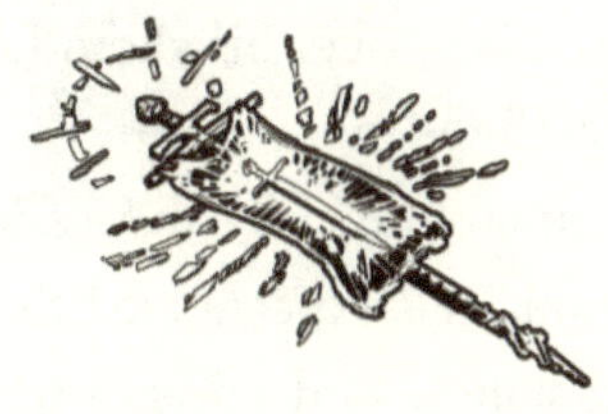

A jagged flash of blinding white light rained down from thick dark clouds ahead. A grumble of thunder followed, reverberating across the hilly landscape of the Golden Forest. A light shower of rain so soft it almost felt like snow patted him on the shoulder as he traversed through the dense wood on a familiar pathway. His shoulders felt heavy, and for a moment he was back atop the Fifty Spears, Rayner Levic's dead body draped over his own as he ran from that cursed city. He shook his head, forcing the thought from his mind, but his solution was a temporary one. What if it was his father he carried over his shoulder next?

"Something on your mind, boy?" Kron asked. He rode atop Gruff — Brock's sire — a black stallion larger than any Dazen had seen. Its nostrils flared, sending clouds of water vapour spiralling into the cool winds. Kron himself was a vision of his former self, no sign of his illness visible. His face was no longer pale, and he had gained more weight, his body thick with muscle and brawn. Dazen swore his hair even looked darker, more its original deep brown, in contrast to the greying white he had grown used to over the past few years.

"I just worry, is all," Dazen said. "I fear we are walking into a trap."

"We swore an oath. All kings of Zapour must answer the King-Radiant's call. There is no choice in the matter."

"Is that why you have brought half of our fighting men with you?" Dazen said, looking over his shoulder at the long line of men trodding through the mud.

Kron huffed, maintaining his calm facade as he continued to lead Gruff up the trail. "It is expected to bring a war-band when travelling such a distance. And I do not trust the Saelmeres to keep their own space."

"Will it not be seen as a threat?"

"There is no threat to Lumindal. Not while the Last Light stands. None would dare take the risk. Not after Hirane. You must understand, Dazen, there is no choice."

Dazen brushed a hand through Brock's mane. "You hate him, do you not? The King-Radiant."

Kron fixed him with a steely glare. "It matters not what I think. I will do what is right for Trost."

"Why do you hate him? What has he done to you?"

Kron pulled on the reins. "It is not your concern. My grievance is my own. And it will not affect my judgement."

"And you think handing him Raiz will absolve us from any blame? All crimes forgiven."

"I know it will. Raiz is lawless. He is a thorn who has forever pained my side. You must put this behind you and look to the future. It is the only way forward."

"How can you say that! What if it was me in his place? What if it was me the King-Radiant wanted? Would you trade me in to die at his hands?"

Kron pulled Gruff to a stop, causing the entire army to halt in their tracks. "Do not burden yourself with such a line of thought! You will be King one day. Only then will you come to know the weight of such decisions. I have made mine, and it will not change. I have tired of this conversation. I suggest you use the time remaining on this trek to gain some perspective."

Kron continued forwards, leaving Dazen and Brock standing in the mud.

Dazen shook his head, wiping away a droplet of rainwater that had made its way into his eyelash. He unsaddled himself from Brock, handing him to his First Sword, Gale. "Gale," he said.

"Yes, my lord?"

"Are we friends?"

Gale stiffened, his mouth working up and down as he fumbled for words. "Y-yes, of course my lord. Why do you ask?"

Dazen stared at him with a vacant expression before looking at his feet. "You are my First Sword. I trust you more than any. But I fear our relationship is born of duty. I fear that in my thirst to prove myself to Father I may have become him. I have neglected those around me. Can I trust you to speak plainly to me? Even if you do not agree with my conclusions?"

"Yes, my lord. Of co—"

"And no more calling me 'my lord'. That title has its place. But not with you. From now on, you shall address me as Dazen."

Gale seemed to relax.

"Now be honest with me, Gale. Do you think I will be a good king?"

Gale took a step back, staring at Dazen as if he were a book. "We have grown up together, you and I. I know you better than you might think. And from where I stand you will make a fine king. It is true that at times you suffer from the burdens any first-born son of a king must face. You can be blunt, and have a tendency to carry the weight of the world on your shoulders. But there is a strength within you, one that far exceeds that of your father. One that he will never possess."

Dazen stood still, his hands dropping to his sides. "I do not know what to say."

"Maybe that you will not tell your father what I just said?" Gale said.

"Hah! Not likely. Besides, you are my First Sword, not his." Dazen put his arm around Gale's neck. "Please, do not forget what I have said. I am in need of a friend. I fear I am losing too many."

"I will be here."

"Now forgive me, but there is someone I must see to."

Dazen filtered back into the crowd of soldiers to where a carriage painted entirely black moved at a leisurely pace pulled by four horses. It was situated dead centre of the moving company and flanked by dozens of Illidor's elite. Its windows were heavily barred and draped with black cloth from the inside. Even with the overcast weather Kron was taking no chances. Not a single ray of sunshine would see the inside of Raiz's moving prison.

Dazen rounded the wagon's rear, signalling for the two guards to let him pass. They looked at each other hesitantly, but one threatening look saw them step aside. "We will be waiting right here," one said. It was clear by his tone that he did not trust Dazen. But he handed over the key nevertheless.

Dazen nodded, twisting the key inside the hole and stepping into the pitch of darkness beyond.

The smell of sweat and body odour overwhelmed him. He pegged his nose shut. Raiz was there, huddled in the corner, knees cradling his head with his arms clasped over his shins.

"What do you want? I could smell you from outside, you reek of cowardice."

"I did not know cowardice had a smell," Dazen said, closing the door behind him.

Raiz grunted. "If you would be on your way, I wish to spend my final moments in peace."

"I suppose peace is something you have had very little of over the years, no?"

Another grunt. "What of it?"

"I wish to know, why did you not come to me?"

Raiz lifted his head. Dark circles of fatigue ringed his eyes. Even in the blackness, his scar stood out, a jagged line jutting from his skin like a ridge on either side of his eye. "Come to you?"

"When we were little, before you left. Why did you not come to me for help? Were we not close then?"

Raiz turned his head away. "You were always Father's favourite."

"We could have made a plan. We could have rescued her together."

"You wouldn't have helped me. Father held you tight under his thumb. He still does. I did what I needed to do. I did what you couldn't do. I ran. I ran to find someone worthy, someone with courage enough to fight back."

"And this Celik is what you say? How well do you even know him?"

"What does it matter?"

"Of course it matters!"

"I know he has a backbone! I know he was once a warrior! And I know unlike you he was willing to fight."

"Do not speak to me in such a way!"

"Does the truth offend you?"

Dazen went quiet. He leaned against the carriage door, letting his weight drop as he slid into a sitting position. "Did you know I raised an army for her?" he said.

This time Raiz went quiet, untangling himself from a web of his own limbs as he looked upon Dazen.

"I was as old as you are now," Dazen continued. "Not three years after she was taken, I found people of similar mind to myself. Good people willing to stand up for their country. Together we marched on the capital, we marched on Lumindal with the intent of seeing our sister free of her chains. Every man there was willing to sacrifice their life for the sake of their princess, for the sake of Trost."

Raiz crossed his legs. "Then why do you yet breathe?"

"Because of Father. He caught wind of my movements and intercepted me before I could make it past where we stand now."

"So, you fought him?"

"Very nearly. I had half of the White-Swords of Illidor ready to die for me."

"Then why did our sister spend another five years of her youth under lock and key?"

"Because I did not wish to slaughter my own countrymen! That is what it would have taken. Including Father."

Raiz clenched his hands, weighed down only by the metal shackles around his wrists. "Maybe that would have been for the best," Raiz said.

"You cannot talk about killing a king so casually! There are conse—"

"Consequences, yes yes, I know. But there are also consequences of inaction! And that's what you don't see."

Dazen chewed on his bottom lip. "You know, I have tried so

hard to hate you. Zur knows I wanted to. You are everything Father says and more."

"Your point?" Raiz said.

"In many ways, you are the person I wish to be. The person I strive to one day become. You are brash, yet strong. Arrogant but also fiercely loyal. And it would seem you have some interesting friends. The dark-haired woman, the one you are close to. Veil, is it? She found me, sought me out."

"Veil's here?" Raiz said, perking up.

"She is," he whispered.

"Count yourself lucky you still have breath in your lungs," Raiz said. "What business does she have with you?"

"You mean besides your freedom and my head on a pike?"

Raiz cracked a knuckle and shrugged.

"She has a plan. A good one," Dazen said. "One that poses little risk to Trost if she should fail."

Raiz's eyes darted upwards.

"At first I thought her insane. But the more I listened, the more I understood. She will stop at nothing to bring that tower down."

"So, what are you saying?" Raiz said. "You wish to aid her?"

"No. That task is up to her. But she is not like you. She is not associated with Trost. If she is to succeed, then it is not something which will disappoint me."

"Speak plainly! What is it you want? Why have you come to see me?"

Dazen sifted through his pockets, working his hands until he found the cool piece of metal he was looking for. "You know Father only made one key for the shackles binding you. Originally, he kept the key on his person at all times. He sought to have it destroyed, smelted to a pile of liquid and so to see you stripped of your Shine for good. To this day he believes it so. Fortunately for us both, I had it recovered."

"I didn't pit you as one to gloat," Raiz said.

"If I cannot take pride in the achievement, then I fear common sense will override my decision making, and what I am about to do will be for nothing."

"And what is it you are about to do?"

Dazen pulled the lump of metal from beneath his robe, twirling it in his fingers. It was ordinary, nothing but a few jagged dents in carved metal. But its significance was far from ordinary. "I hold in my hand this key."

Raiz remained expressionless, likely expecting it to be a trick of some kind. "You would give this to me freely?" he said.

"Freely, no. It comes with a cost. Or more a promise."

Raiz scoffed. "Of course. Nothing but riddles with you."

"Would you care to hear what I have to say, or not?"

"Speak your terms."

"I am putting my trust in you, Raiz. I will give you the key, but would ask you not to use it."

Raiz gasped. "You've gone mad. You lie to me and allow Father to imprison me, and now you want me to trust you?"

"You don't have to trust me. But trust your friend. This was her plan."

Raiz laughed. "You mean for me to hand myself over willingly?"

"That is not my wish, no. But think on it. If Veil succeeds, and the Last Light is no longer a threat, then they are vulnerable. If she should fail—"

"She won't fail," Raiz interrupted.

"Right. But if by some chance she were captured, then Trost is absolved of blame."

Raiz scoffed. "Trust you to think this way. So, what is it you ask of me?"

"All I ask is that you wait. I am sure there will be a commotion once the tower is destroyed. Use that moment to make your escape."

Raiz failed at hiding a smirk. "I will wait, you have my word."

Dazen rose. "I am counting on you," he said, handing him the key. "Keep it hidden, keep it safe. When the time comes, you will know. Rest now. You will need it in the days to come."

Chapter 33
Isha

North was the last direction Isha thought she would go, not again. Years she spent trying to free herself from Lumindal's iron grip, and now she ventured back there, free of mind and free of chain. Maybe she had turned mad, or maybe she just didn't care anymore. One thing was certain, she would not sit idle while others risked their lives to better the world. True, she was no fighter, but there were other ways than steel to make a wound.

She stopped to catch her breath. After Spike had taken them down from the Moon-spire, the trio had met with Draz and made hard for the travelling war-band her father now led through the Golden Forest. She nuzzled Spike beneath his chin, smiling to herself as the pricket's throat vibrated with pleasure. She still couldn't comprehend how big he had grown. She paced the grass, rubbing a hand across his length. Spike's hide was tough, the interconnected scales were shaped like teardrops. They were a natural moss-green but could be changed to adapt to any environment. She had definitely not expected this on the day she had given him to Raiz.

"Where did you get him from?" came a voice to the side.

Isha spun, watching Veil approach. "What?"

"Spike. Raiz said you gave him as a gift. Where did you get him from?"

"There was a healer in Illidor. Eve was her name. She breeds them, gives them as pets to those with unstable Shine. But none I have ever known have come even close to growing as big as Spike."

"He's a marvel isn't he," Veil said, running a hand over Spike's snout. "It's because of Raiz's Shine. That he's this big I mean."

"Because of his Shine?"

"Raiz is special. His Shine is stronger than others. Much stronger. Different too. I don't think he knows it yet, but I can tell. The more Spike feeds, the more he grows."

Isha stared at Spike, rounding his belly and feeling at a stray set of scales protruding from his side. "What is this? His scales do not line up here, like something is growing."

Veil moved over to feel at the place she had indicated. "Could be anything, who knows with Spike. He's full of surprises."

Spike growled at the touch, as if he were sensitive in that particular area.

"He misses Raiz," Veil said.

"We all do. Can you not feed him your Shine?"

Veil averted her gaze as if the question had offended her. "That's not possible."

"Why not?"

"Because I'm not like other Light users."

"I am sorry. I did not mean to offend."

Veil dismissed her apology with a wave of her hand. "Forget it."

"Well, what is our plan then? Where do we go from here?"

"We move up to the high ground over there," she said, pointing towards a hilly outcropping. "The ground there is too rocky for such a large number to venture and makes for a good vantage point. My guess 'is they'll camp at the foot of the hill for the night."

"Then what?"

"Once we're in position, we wait."

Zur's light began to fade, the last rays of sunshine peeked through the densely packed tree-line as the four of them and Spike stood watch over her father's campsite. Veil bent to a crouch beside her, leaving Draz and Puk at the rear.

"Do you see that carriage there?" Veil whispered. "The one painted black?"

Isha narrowed her vision, scanning the area until she found it. More than half a dozen guards flanked it, standing motionless as statues but vigilant as a pack of wolves. "They starve him of sunlight."

"Your father is thorough, I'll give him that."

"Veil," Isha said, her mind elsewhere. "What is Raiz like?"

She turned to her with blue eyes the colour of a sunburned sky. "What do you mean? He's your brother."

"Yes, but it is you who have been with him the longest, not me. I wish to know if he is still the same innocent boy I have always loved."

"We both know he's no longer innocent. But he's not tainted. He never kills without reason, without proper cause. As for what he's like, childish comes to mind."

The two shared a laugh together, glad to agree on something.

"But he's also passionate, and caring," Veil continued. "He'll do anything for the people he loves, even if it leads to his death. He's more than the sword people make him out to be. Above all he desires peace. Unfortunately, in this world, the only road to peace is through bloodshed."

Isha stared at the black carriage, thinking about the boy within. Is this how he had felt all those years, stuck on the outside with no way to reach her?

"You love him, Isha said.

Veil froze, her hands shaking, eyes refusing to look her way.

"Do not worry, I will not tell him, I promise." She placed a reassuring hand on Veil's own. It felt warm. She kept it there a while longer, her hand vibrating as whatever power lurking beneath her skin swirled in her palm like waves crashing into a shoreline. Eventually she recoiled. "You are not normal, are you."

Veil snatched her arm backward, holding it close to her chest.

"Your Shine," Isha said. "Forgive me if I am wrong. I cannot use it myself. But it feels different."

"Unstable?"

Isha nodded.

"I was on the outskirts of Hirane when the Shine-bomb came. Yet for some reason I survived. Ever since, my Shine has been unstable. If I use it, I cannot control how much I expend. If I ever become too worked up, I suggest you stay well clear of me. And I mean *well* clear."

"Why? What will happen?"

Veil said nothing. A long silence followed, not an awkward silence, to her surprise, she found herself comfortable around the slender assassin who held her brother's heart.

"There!" Veil said, pointing into the distance.

"What is it? I cannot see anything."

"Are you prepared?"

"Prepared for what?"

Veil leaned back. "To see your brother."

Veil ran forward, manoeuvring through masses of raised stone with ease before making her way into the brush overlooking the campsite. Isha followed awkwardly behind, nearly tripping over a few pointed stones. She swiped at a stray branch, Veil's shadow crawling deeper into the shimmering forest of yellow and red leaves.

Isha came to a halt before a clearing and crouched low. She watched as Veil's lithe form met another. She couldn't see the features in the darkness, but it looked male. Raiz?

She crept closer. It couldn't be Raiz; too tall, too muscly. "Dazen?" she whispered.

Saying his name may as well have been a threat, for the man stepped out from the shadows, his usually pale face growing red hot. "Isha! What are you doing here?"

It definitely was Dazen. He tried to whisper, but it came out as more of a hiss.

Isha looked between them but found no words.

Dazen turned to Veil. "This was not part of our deal! I knew I could not trust you. Return her to Illidor at once."

Isha stepped out into the clearing to confront her elder brother. "She will do no such thing!"

"This is too dangerous for you. Do you know where we are headed?" Dazen said.

"I do. And while my heart yet beats, I will use what breath I have left to do as I wish."

"But we make for the heart of Lumindal," Dazen said. "The very place you were held captive. Call me a fool if you think I will allow you to go back there."

"Then I say you are a fool. I have my own mind. I make my

own choices."

Dazen interlocked his hands behind his head and paced back and forth.

"What are you even doing here?" Isha said. "I thought you and Father to be of the same mind?"

Dazen continued to pace the length of the clearing. "It would seem the constant scolding from my two younger siblings has cleared my mind of poison."

Isha inclined her head. "So, you are here to help?"

Dazen turned to Veil and shook his head before shifting back to Isha. "I am. But your involvement changes things. I cannot let you do it Isha, I am sorry."

Veil grabbed his wrist and twisted him around to face her. "You have to. She's the only one who's been inside. She knows the Last Light. Without her I'll be blind."

Dazen shook his arm free of her grip. "Find another way. Isha has been through enough. I will not place her in more peril. If you are caught, all of Trost will pay the price."

"Then you best make sure we're not," Veil said. "We're going with or without your help."

Dazen hesitated, scratching at his head. "I still do not like this Isha. I will not have you returned to me only to have you taken again so soon."

"I understand," Isha said. "But this is something I must do. If I am to have my life back it should be mine to choose what to do with it."

Dazen's hand still wavered, but he nodded.

Isha rushed to his side, wrapping her arms around his thick frame. "I am sorry. For what I said the other day. I did not mean it. I know you just want to keep everyone safe."

"You could die, Ish, you realise that?"

"I know. But I cannot live knowing there was something I

could have done. Even if my contribution is little, my mind is made."

Dazen combed a hand through her hair, pulling her closer to his chest. "Then I will do my part. I will see you through the gates."

Interludes
Echo

Echo closed his eyes. He spread his arms out wide and leaned over the battlements of the castle, letting the wind decide which way he should drift. He needed a sign, something to take his mind away from the present, to reassure him he was on the right path.

He took a steadying breath. His burdens still followed him. His misgivings were still painstakingly obvious. He had made no progress towards becoming the person he wanted to be. Dazen set him on the right path that day atop the balcony in Illidor. And what had he done since?

Nothing.

He opened his eyes, staring idly out into the crystalline blue shimmer of the Twin-Lakes of Nanta. Waves lapped the rocky shoreline where the two lakes met. A treeless landscape surrounded its width as hundreds of refugees from Lesken made their way towards the sun-worn docks on the lakes edge like bees to honey.

His gaze drifted from the brightness of the lakes down towards the open field. 'The Field of a Thousand Swords' they called it. The sight was true to its name. Echo leaned closer. Usually, this view brought him peace. It gave him time to pay his respects and remember the deeds of past soldiers of Zuton, but today he only felt despair. Thousands of tiny swords buried hilt-deep into the soil littered the landscape. All men who had died fighting for their kingdom. And what had he done? He was a prince; he was responsible for every citizen in his country. And he sat there, cowering in the corner as his father was struck down and killed before his very eyes.

A strong wind buffeted the parapet, pushing him closer to the edge. His arms wobbled like a bird attempting to fly for the first time. He grabbed hold of the stone railing, bending his knees to support his footing. His breaths came sharp, the thrill of nearly dying giving him a new lease on life.

He thought about his troubles. The future prosperity between Zuton and Trost was all but dissolved, Kron having scrapped the whole idea of marriage with the arrival of his lost daughter and the capture of his youngest son. His brother Petros was to be coronated any day now, leaving him as the useless third-born son and at his mercy. Refugees continued to flood into Nanta from the surrounding villages of Lesken, where his own people feared for their safety. And now the King-Radiant had called for a Council of Kings, leaving the entire realm of Zapour in a state of uneasiness.

He thought about his goals. More than anything he wanted vengeance. To destroy the one responsible for murdering his father. Blood for blood. He wanted to matter; he was sick of being ignored, sick of everyone treating him like he didn't exist. To do both, he needed power. But power was a fickle concept. To make a difference, he needed a significant social standing, along with the physical prowess to back it up. Unfortunately, he had neither. A prince he was, but his title was merely a token of his birth and nothing else.

He grit his teeth. Why had Zur not blessed him with His Light? Why had he been born weak? He was on the eve of his seventeenth summer and still the Light eluded him.

He placed a heavy foot on the parapet, widening his arms and arching his head towards the sun's blinding shine. And then he screamed.

He didn't scream anything in particular, he just needed to get it out. It felt good, frustration flowing out of him as he sucked in a lungful of air and screamed again. The sound of his voice echoed though castle, bouncing off walls and turning the heads of those down below.

His voice grew horse, his call turning into a dry croak as the last of his breath left his chest. He jerked in agony, causing him to stagger.

And then it hit him.

His body surged with an unfamiliar sensation. His muscles tensed as they struggled to contain whatever was threatening to overwhelm him.

His head felt light, his stomach churned, and he resisted the urge to throw up. His hands grew hot, extremely hot. He shook them vigorously, but the heat would not go away.

He scratched at his forearm, nails biting hard into his skin as if he could dig the pain out. Eventually he could take no more. He arched his head into the sky, stretching out his arms and watching as a beam of pure white energy burst forth from both hands. It burned a hole the size of two fists in the stone, continuing out into the blue lake beyond.

He grasped his right arm with his left, staring as his fingertips drew lines of a grey, smoke-like substance. The pain was as intense as any he had known, his arm burning with a thousand aches. But physical pain was only temporary. He had asked Zur for power, and Zur had responded.

He sprinted down the winding staircase, heedless of the watching crowd who had likely witnessed the birth of his powers. He had only one destination in mind. He wanted to show his brothers what he could do. He wanted to see the expression on their miserable faces when he burned with a power they had long since ridiculed him for lacking.

His hand still burned, but a wide grin stretched nearly ear to ear as he neared his brother's chamber. It didn't matter that he was being crowned soon, didn't matter if Petros could end his life with a snap of his fingers. He would have this small victory. He would prove himself useful to the Levic family once and for all.

He whirled past a number of faceless figures, their presence insignificant in the face of his discovery. His legs grew heavy as he neared his brother's chamber. A rather large group of people congregated outside. Barons and baronesses, lords and ladies, and nobles of the court were gathering still. Echo stepped over their pointed shoes, brushed against their tightly fit hose-stockings, and clawed his way through lengthy head-dresses as he squeezed through the crowd. All were taller than him, so he couldn't see what was beyond. They each seemed to inch away from him as he passed, hands covering mouths as they reacted to what he was sure was his newfound link with Zur. They knew what he could do. No longer would people overlook who he was.

He spotted Sumaya in amongst the crowd, her long hair tangled and matted, sticking to her tear-stained cheeks.

"Echo!" she called. "Do not go in there, please. I beg of you." She reached for his shirt, catching it in a tight grip.

"Sumaya, you will never guess what just happened to me, I—"

And then he saw it, out of the corner of his eye. A touch of crimson.

His face went slack as he continued to push past the crowd, ignoring Sumaya's plea and searching for the source of the commotion.

His stomach sunk like a ship caught in a storm. He doubled

over and retched, a mixture of some form of liquid and dry food pouring from his mouth out onto the wooden floorboards, seeping into the cracks.

Both Petros and Huet lay prone on the floor before him, twin pools of blood flowing from their open skin and mixing together, oozing outward in a slow-moving wave of death.

Echo wiped away the drool on his mouth, but his eyes wouldn't part from the scene.

A long silver sword rested against Petros' now slack hands; its point still embedded deep into Huet's heart. A dagger clung to the floor above Huet's dead hand, stained a deep red up to the hilt. Petros' neck was painted in blood, a deep gash beginning to crust at its centre.

Though it was clear both were dead, Echo moved to his brother's side, weeping as he took in the carnage. He placed a sweaty hand on Huet's cold forehead.

And then he saw it, twinkling like a sunrise against a pitch of darkness. The golden crown of Nanta, etched with a wolf's teeth and shining with a dozen jewels. It rested between both Petros and Huet's free hands, as if even with their last breath their fingers inched to take hold of it. Red fingerprints stained its rim, from fingers now lifeless.

Echo took hold of the crown, lifting it away from his brothers' reach. Hiding his face from the staring crowd, tears still running down his cheeks, he pulled it close and didn't let go.

Obeyun

The air was thick with animal musk. Insects congregated into large masses, whirring all around him. Obeyun swatted the air with a sweaty palm, lifting his cloak higher above his head. The sound of rain clattering through the canopy was calming. In his struggle, Obeyun miss-stepped, his boot landing in a muddy pool of murky water.

He sighed, following the trail of water towards a large lagoon fed by a small waterfall against a rocky outcropping. It had been too long since he had returned to Wisha, but he was finally home. He looked up, watching the gently swaying palm fronds catching bright snatches of sun and sky. He climbed his way to the top of the waterfall, his fingers damp after hugging the moss-covered wall of stone.

The Great City of Zhanbu was as he remembered it. Hundreds of small cities and villages, all interconnected. They wove into one through a series of dug-up passageways and roads.

He continued through the jungle, every step bringing him closer towards its centre. When the insects dispersed, he stripped down to his bare skin, tying his cloak to his waist. Where once he would have hidden who he was, today he would shine bright. He knew his skin would bring trouble, but he had not returned to his homeland to become the man he used to be, he had come to be the man he knew he could be.

As he drew deeper into Zhanbu, people began to notice. Everywhere he went, ice-cold stares glared at him through their thatched houses. Forms of deep ebony became more and more numerous, and he knew even more followed in his wake.

He tensed his muscles, walking with a confident gait before a hand grasped firmly around his own. It twisted, pulling him away from prying eyes and into a small wooden hut.

Obeyun span, ready to face his assailant head-on. He balled his fists overhead, issuing a low growl and preparing to strike.

His hand fell slack as a female figure gaped back at him, two dark pools of black staring through him. She placed two hands upon either of his shoulders and opened her mouth as if she wanted to speak, but couldn't find the words.

Obeyun eyed her suspiciously, taking a step back. She had long, dark hair plaited to her hips, pieces of feather and ribbon tied neatly into her headdress. Black freckles spotted her smooth skin, forming into a star-like pattern around her right cheekbone.

"Aia?" Obeyun said.

The girl puckered her lips, swatting away a tear as she nodded and wrapped her arms around him and held on tight. "Obeyun, you are alive! I thought... we all thought... it does not matter. You have returned to us!" she spoke, in perfect Wishan. It had been so long since he had heard his native language. A warm sensation fluttered in his stomach at the sound.

"Sister, I am glad to see you are well."

Aia took a step back, her face bunching into a ball before she struck out with her hand, punching him hard on the shoulder. "Where have you been! Do you know the trouble you caused! It is not safe here. You are not safe."

Obeyun recoiled, finding his sister to have grown in more than just stature since the last time he saw her. It was tough to imagine his little sister had grown so tall. The last time he saw her she was but a few arm-spans high. But now that she was standing before him, there was no mistake, his little sister was all grown up.

"I have come to challenge Ajani for the Wooden Crown," Obeyun said.

Aia stared at him with an open mouth. "Are you crazy? Ajani will kill you. You do not know what has become of Wisha since you left us. There is no kindness left in our brother's soul. The clans of Zhanbu are on the brink of war. Children are forced to burden themselves with the spear. It is not safe for you here. Ajani kills anyone who would threaten his reign. His lust for power has only grown stronger."

"That is why I must fight him on the bridge."

"Have you lost your mind? I only just got you back, I will not let you sacrifice your life for nothing. Ajani has grown strong, too strong."

"Aia please, take me to him. I must see this through. I have run away from my destiny for too long."

Aia rubbed two hands over her face. "You will not be swayed on this?"

"I will not."

She paused, staring at her feet before rising to face him. "Then I will take you to him."

The streets became long and broad the further they ventured into the Great City of Zhanbu. They ran as far as the eye could see in each direction. People continued to gawk, dressed in varying garments of cotton, raffia, silk, and wool. Some donned lavish capes and belts made from beads, feathers, shells, animal skins, and even bones. They parted in his wake, forming into a circle around him and Aia. His skin was a give-away, no white-skin besides the oppressive might of the Golden Talon regime ever ventured this deep into Zhanbu and lived.

Even with half of his skin a deep ebony, his brother had never accepted him, had poisoned minds against him and forced him to either run away or fight. He had run away back then. But he was a different man now. He was a man with courage.

They approached the Hall of Songs, a sea of black at their heels. An exterior wall of red clay stretched high in a circular fashion in the centre of the street. The walls were decorated with horizontal ridge designs and clay carvings portraying animals, warriors, and other symbols of power. Long banners of red and gold draped from the ceiling, the dark pattern of a jaguar stitched into its centre.

Within moments, the ominous thump of spears on soil replaced the quiet murmurs of the crowd. It grew louder as warriors from all around pushed past, continuing to thump the butt of their pointed spears on the ground as they chanted a synchronised, deep war-cry. Obeyun spun in a circle, watching as children as young as ten lined the high-ridged buildings surrounding the Hall of Songs, all with a weapon in their hands.

The men circling Obeyun and Aia drew closer, white-painted symbols of war covering their near-naked bodies. All at once, the chanting came to a halt, replaced by a deathly silence. Hundreds of knowing eyes fixed on Obeyun but he refused to back down.

A scuttle of footsteps sounded from within the hall, and a moment later Ajani made his presence known. His brother walked forth from the clay wall and into the circle. He wore the wooden crown atop his bald head. His muscles were more defined than Obeyun remembered, his face marked with hard lines and scars to match. Several figures flanked him, the most notable, Obeyun knew as Rudi. The giant from the Isidoku clan's nearly eight-foot frame towered over Ajani's side, black markings of tattoos running up his arm and spreading into his chest.

An elderly woman made her way around his brother's other flank. She walked with hunched shoulders, holding a wooden cane in one hand that shook as her line of sight settled onto Obeyun. Silver streaks lined her dark hair as she moved her free hand towards her mouth. Liani — Obeyun's mother.

Nostalgia overwhelmed Obeyun, the sight of his mother causing his attention and focus to falter. More figures stepped forwards. Some he recognised, others he didn't. His childhood friend, Zandre, appeared with the checkered white symbol of the Kanguri Clan clearly marked on his forehead. Senzo of Clan Igibio was next. The elderly man scowled at him through wrinkled brows. Leaders from clans all around Wisha had gathered. Clan Hatsu had a new leader, a youthful looking man too young to have been of any note to Obeyun when he had last been in Wisha. A hardy looking man bore the symbol of Clan Songuri on his barrel like breast, standing with arms crossed, feet bare in the dirt.

"You are not welcome here, Brother," Ajani said, raising his chin to the sky as if he were Zala — the spirit of the forest — himself. "I am the Warchief of Zhanbu, Head of Clan Oromo, Keeper of the Wooden Crown, and King of Wisha. You are nothing. A white-skin exiled from our country. Why have you returned?"

Obeyun squared his shoulders. "I have come to reclaim the Wooden Crown. My name is Obeyun, first son of Obuku. The crown is mine by right of birth."

Ajani took a step forward, snarling through gritted teeth. "You have no claim! You are a stranger to Wisha, and you bear the white skin of their kind as proof!"

"The colour of my skin does not define me." Obeyun turned then to face the crowd. He stood tall, taller than Ajani. But years in captivity had made his muscles lax. His ribs were showing beneath his chest and his shoulders were the angular shape of bone pressing tight into skin. "There is a wider world beyond the confines of Wisha," he shouted. He pointed a thin finger towards his brother. "This man is no leader. He will continue to turn clan against clan. He will continue to hide us in the shadow of the forest. The world outside is changing, and we must change with it, or we will be left burying the corpses of our children."

"Who are you to say what we are," Ajani said. "You have not been here. You do not belong here."

"I invoke my right of challenge!" Obeyun called. A series of gasps echoed through the street at his claim, the entire audience once again reverting to a buzz of quiet conversation.

"I will say it again," Ajani said. "You have no claim to the crown. You are no longer of Wisha."

Aia stepped in-front of Obeyun. "He has every right! He is Father's first-born son, none can deny it!"

Ajani's face dropped. "Sister, you would side with this…thing, over your own brother?"

"Obeyun is my brother!" she said. "And he is also yours. Can you not see what you are doing to our country? Your rule is bleeding us dry! The clans bicker like children over a stick of bread, and for what?"

"If you wish to place blame, then it let it rest upon the white-skins! They take everything from us. The threat from the sky is real. And you would have us side with them?" Ajani said.

Obeyun placed a reassuring hand on his sister's own. "I more than any know the toll they take on our lands. But it does not have to be so! There is a way."

"It is fitting you would come here so soon after the King-Radiant's call to council," Ajani said. "You are nothing but his dog! Come here to do his bidding. Well, I will not be fooled, we will not be fooled!"

Obeyun grimaced, he could feel the crowd begin to turn against him, cries of protest sounding from all corners.

"Kill him Ajani."

"He is not one of us."

"He will bring the Light down on us!"

Obeyun scowled. This is what Ajani had done so many years ago. This is what made him run. But he stood firm. He needed to see this through. "I say again. Let us settle this. I invoke my right of challenge. If you believe yourself more worthy of the crown, then fight me for it on the bridge!"

Ajani laughed. "You wish to win the crown through use of a spear? Look at you. You are skinnier than Aia."

Sounds of mockery arose all around him, men and women alike laughing at their Warchief's chide.

Obeyun walked towards his brother then, Rudi stepping between the two, thrusting the shaft of his giant spear against Obeyun's breast.

Before Rudi could react, Obeyun clasped the side of the spear, wrenching it from his grip before twirling it around his head in a show of skill. Rudi was late to move, but he stepped forward in an aggressive stance. Obeyun brought the butt of the spear down in a sweeping motion, catching Rudi behind his kneecaps and sending him falling to the ground. Obeyun spun again, twirling the spear behind his back before pressing its tip into his brother's neck. A prisoner he may have been, but he had not forgotten his youth. The lessons with a spear were drilled into his bones, the very essence of what he was. "I did not take you for a coward, brother."

PART 4

Chapter 34
Dazen

Dazen stood at the front of half an army, foot-sore and travel-weary. The once luscious glade was now a beaten down pile of mud and squashed vegetation. The glistening white stone of the outer battlements of Lumindal broke the horizon, standing ominously in the distance. He thought back on his foolish attempt at a rescue all those years ago. How stupid he had been. Kron had been right to stop him.

But today was different. He didn't know why, but he had a feeling. This meet was almost certainly a trap. They were likely walking to their deaths. Dazen had met the King-Radiant, witnessed his 'mercy' first-hand. There would be no peace between the nations of Zapour, only death. Why then was Kron so confident? King Rayner had been confident, and Dazen had carried him out of these very gates slugged over his shoulder. Would he do the same with Father?

No.

He wouldn't let that happen. He could see clearly now, could see what his brother had seen all along. But was he willing to pay the price? There were too many variables to have peace of mind, but he would prepare for anything. And now Isha was involved. His sweet, loving sister. He wanted to keep her out of this, to keep her safe. But she was right. Raiz was right. All this time he had wanted to shield Trost from Lumindal's dark shadow, but there was no hiding. Trost was part of the shadow.

"They will not let such a number through the gates," Dazen said, standing shoulder to shoulder with his father.

"Of course not," Kron said. "We take only a score; the rest will remain here and wait."

"Wait for what?"

Kron looked at him. "Expect nothing, but prepare for everything. Gather your finest, the time is near."

Dazen nodded before departing to fetch his men. So, Kron was not as delusional as he first thought. He had planned for the potential bloodbath they may be walking into.

Dazen made for Gale. His First Sword was the best soldier he had, his loyalty unmatched. "Gale! Is everything prepared?"

Gale stiffened, voice crackling with hesitation. "As ready as can be my lo — uh, Dazen. But if I may protest, I would council you to re-think this ruse. It is... a shallow one. Not to mention going against your father."

"You may protest. I always encourage you to speak your mind. But this is the only way. I trust only you with this information. No other."

"Of course," Gale said, "your word is mine to keep. I have done the best I can." Gale stepped to the side, holding out his hand to present four soldiers of Illidor dressed head to toe in blue plate. Painted gold at the edges, the plate was polished to a shining gleam with the traditional White-Sword crested on their breast. The four of them stood with mock confidence. The two on the left looked immaculate, plate fitted to near perfection, helmets covering their features from would be onlookers. They had to be be Puk and Draz. Dazen still didn't know them very well, but he had travelled with them on the road back to Illidor. Both were more than capable. "What is that?" Dazen said, pointing to the heavy sack strapped to the side of one of them.

"His helmet," Gale said.

"But he is wearing one."

Gale shrugged. "He would not part with it. Was all I could do to get him to take it off."

Dazen opened his mouth, ready to question him, but thought better of it. He fixed his attention on the two females to his right, settling his gaze on Isha. Gale had done well. The plate fit her perfectly. For a moment he nearly mistook her for a true soldier of Illidor. "How are you doing in there, Ish?"

Isha shifted. "Well, I can smell my own sweat, but it's nothing I cannot handle."

Dazen issued a low groan. "I still don't agree with you being here. It is foolish and stupid."

"Did I inherit the valour as well as the brains in the family?" Isha jested. "We will be fine. Veil won't let anything happen to me."

Dazen exhaled. He would have to trust her. "Remind me again of your plan," he said.

Isha stepped forwards. "Once we are in, the four of us will make for the Forty-Sixth Spear. There we will search for the Eagle named Salador. I overheard him and Averardus talking about black powder. He stashes it within his Spear. Salador is also a descendant of Gavienus — the head architect behind the Last Light. There is a way inside from his quarters, I am sure. Throw some powder down the throat of the Last Light, kaboom."

Dazen shared a concerned look with Gale. "And this...powder, you are sure of its effects?"

The man named Draz stepped forwards. "Draz is sure. Those golden bastards used it more than once on the Cratans during the war. Makes for a deadly explosion."

"I hope you are right," Dazen said. "For all of our sakes. What of your pet? You cannot take it with you." He pointed towards the pricket, which was hiding behind a nearby tree.

Veil moved to pet it. "Spike has his own way of infiltration, don't worry about him. He's a highly intelligent creature, and he's drawn to Raiz. Linked even. He can change his scales to match any environment."

Dazen shrugged, taking another look at the oversized lizard licking at its shoulder-blade. "Stay in the centre of my guard. Gale, keep these two close. Let us hope Father is too preoccupied with his own problems to notice."

Together, Dazen and his 'soldiers' marched by Kron's side up to the city gates, leaving their war band in the brush to the south. He took a look over his shoulder. Wheels clicked as the black carriage containing his brother was pulled up the dirt road by a pack of horses, flanked by another six of his father's men.

His stomach sank like an anchor in a deep sea. He stared up at the high walls. Layer upon layer of stone loomed over him, threatening to swallow him at any moment.

Kron seemed unfazed. His creased eyebrows were focused on the gate with inhuman intensity. Dazen forced his eyes forward, the instinct urging him to check on his sister nearly overwhelming him. He distracted himself by counting the number of men on the battlements. He made it to fourteen before the gates began to creak open. A familiar official walked through the opening. Dazen recalled that Yvain was his name.

The scene was identical, armed soldiers parting to either side, their black plate shining in the sunlight as they began to surround them, working all the way around the carriage.

Kron remained unmoving, not even flinching as Yvain stepped out into the open ground. He kept walking until he was but a few breaths away from Dazen, one eyebrow raised nearly as high as the wall of stone itself.

"I am surprised to see you here again, Dazen Glaive. I mean, ahem," he paused to clear his throat, "after the unfortunate events of our last encounter."

Dazen said nothing, all of his will power working towards not giving away his ruse.

Eventually Yvain moved on, sighing at Dazen's lack of response. He then fixed his attention towards Kron. "Now here is a sight I thought I would never see again. Kron Glaive in the flesh. Oh, this will be interesting. Very interesting indeed." The herald shook with excitement, his arms shivering up to his shoulders. "There has not been this much drama since... since..."

"You will hold your tongue, Yvain," Kron bellowed.

Dazen's face paled, thinking his father soon to be dead on the spot. But to his surprise, the official just cackled a shrill laugh. "Most entertaining indeed. I see you are fully armoured, why is this? Were you not invited to this meet by the King-Radiant himself? Do you perhaps hold some grievance against His Radiance?"

Dazen froze, his muscles refusing to respond. Yvain was mocking his father, he was sure, but his reproach went over Dazen's head. He was clearly missing something. Even so, such talk threatened his scheme. He took a quick glance towards Isha.

"I will dress as I please, as will those who accompany me," Kron said. "I am a king, and you will treat me as such. Or have you forgotten what I am capable of?" Kron's body radiated power, light plumes of steam flowing into the air in every direction.

The man named Yvain cowed, cursing under his breath as he retreated a step to the safety of his guard. "I see the stories of you were miss-told. I was informed you were frail and sickly. I am glad to see they were mistaken," he muttered contemptuously. "You may dress as you please, but there are to be no weapons inside the capital. Fight me on this if you wish, but you are a long way from Illidor. I suggest you do as commanded."

Kron's demeanour calmed, his shoulders relaxing. He unsheathed his longsword and handed the hefty weapon to Yvain with a mocking smile.

Yvain moved to take it, but thought the better, motioning for his guards to collect their weapons. Dazen again unsheathed his long and short steels, taking note of the man who took them as his comrades, too, unburned themselves of sharp objects.

Yvain inclined his head, arching his back. "What is in there?" he inquired, pointing towards the carriage.

"A gift for the King," Kron said.

"King-Radiant," Yvain corrected. "And I will have to take a look before he receives anything from you."

"As you please," Kron said, stepping aside.

The Herald took slow and steady steps, looking to his guard as he made an awkward show of stepping up to the rear of the carriage.

"Be careful. He bites," Kron said.

Dazen tucked his chin to his left breast, ashamed of his

father for making light of the situation. Raiz deserved better than this.

Yvain hesitated further, moving his hand to and from the handle before grunting and calling for his guard to come and do it.

Kron huffed in laughter, arms crossed as he waited patiently on the dry soil.

His guard obeyed, opening the carriage door and stepping into the dark room beyond, Yvain close by his heels.

It took no more than a few long breaths for the Herald to retreat, scuttling down the step as quickly as his short legs would take him. His eyes were wide with shock as he ran a hand over his forehead, wiping away tiny droplets of sweat. "That is...? Surely that is not who I think it is?" He looked towards Kron.

"It is."

"Why, I am afraid I did not give you enough credit, your boldness is unrivalled. An entertaining meet indeed. Very, very entertaining. My men will take him to the Fiftieth Spear immediately," Yvain said.

"No!" Kron barked. "The boy is my prisoner and is mine to give. He is shackled in peridium cuffs, check if you must. You have my word he is incapable of harming anyone in his current state."

"Surely you do not expect me to—"

"My word," Kron repeated, his intensity back at full scale.

Yvain stumbled. "I will accompany you myself then. With my guards, of course. I trust that is acceptable?"

Kron nodded.

"Then follow me, you should know you are the last to arrive in the city."

Their talking done, the company moved through the iron

gates. Dazen watched as they closed behind him. There was no turning back now, no time for indecision.

He chuckled to himself. During all the commotion about Raiz, no one had even bothered to question his guard.

The streets were as he remembered; white cobblestone in between neatly made white houses that seemed to stretch for miles. Hundreds, if not thousands, of Shine-globes lined the curb, dazzling brightly even in the light of day.

The group followed Yvain down the path, taking a slightly different route than the last time he had come here. People of all ages and sizes stared at them from their windows. Children pointed and whispered as they passed. A bright patch of light caught his eye. As if by instinct he broke from his father's side and rushed over to a luminescent tree, overhanging a double-storied home.

He reached out with his arm, feeling the warmth of Light bubbling below the surface of the wooden tree. "This is a Shimmer Tree," he whispered to himself.

He turned, almost bumping into his father.

"Father, this... this is a Shimmer Tree."

"Come Dazen. People are looking."

"But Father. Only Mother was able to make these."

"Come!" Kron said. "People are starting to watch. We must be on our way."

Kron jerked on his arm, forcing him to return to his side behind Yvain, who had been watching with more than a curious eye.

Dazen tensed, taking another look over his shoulder. Shimmer Trees were a work of art. Instead of imparting your Shine into an inanimate object, watching as they eventually burned out just as a candle would —much like what Dazen himself did with his steels — the trees burned eternally. Dazen still hadn't figured out how she'd done it — nobody had. Heat and wood should not be able to co-exist, but she had done it. She had managed to impart her Shine upon a living thing. And now it seemed another had replicated her invention.

A sadness seeped out of his bones; one he had carried with him for a long time. He quickly pressed it down, manoeuvring it to the back of his mind.

His sister and her companions followed at his heels, walking in a tight formation well-guarded by Gale. Once far enough into the city, Yvain ushered them into a large tavern at the foot of a mound. The shadow of the Fifty Spears and the Last Light darkened the ground all around. Even on his second visit, the tower still sent a shiver of terror running down his spine.

A sense of impending doom loomed over his head like a thundercloud ready to clap, his mind overflowing with second thoughts.

Distraction came in the form of a Saelmere. It had been years since royalty from Trost and Craw had crossed paths. Even still, he would not forget the face of a Saelmere.

Kron approached the central table where they had situated themselves, seemingly keen to take the initiative and confront them.

"Gelvard," Kron said, standing tall and letting his bulk do more of the talking.

The man named Gelvard turned, his round belly jiggling with fat. The ageing Saelmere looked as though he had spent too many years with a goblet in hand, his days on the battlefield long behind him. "I thought I smelled a Glaive. You have balls, approaching me after what you have done."

"Whatever quarrel you have, I assure you it is not with me, old friend."

Gelvard's dark eyes narrowed. "What game do you play? You know well what your son did to my boy. Not to mention the offence committed on my very soil!"

Kron remained expressionless, his face an unreadable mask. "Whatever crimes Raiz has committed were not on my behalf. The boy has long since declared his independence from Trost."

Gelvard hissed through gritted teeth.

It was Ancel however, who spoke up. "Where is he!?"

Ancel Saelmere leaned forward from beneath his father's shadow, his right arm clutched to his chest by a sling.

Kron craned his neck towards Ancel. "He is to be judged before the King-Radiant."

"Give him to me, his life is mine to take!"

Kron looked back towards Gelvard. "Your son barks like an untrained dog. Raiz is mine to do with what I will."

Gelvard rose to his feet, his blubber bouncing with the effort. "You have no right to speak to him so! Especially given the exploits of your own stock recently. There is rumour floating around that Raiz was not the only Glaive to set foot in Speakers Hollow that night." Gelvard looked Dazen in the eyes then, his sinister stare filled with intent. "The King-Radiant will hear of this, and there will be justice. Mark my words."

Much like a wall would, Kron gave them nothing. No hint at his thought process, no retaliation. "Always a pleasure, Gelvard. As you were," he said, walking off to a distant corner of the tavern.

Ancel grabbed Dazen by the arm as he went to follow. "I hear your sister has a new home. Best be careful where you leave her these days." He released his grip, a sly smile stretching the width of his face.

Dazen looked to his guard, finding only Gale and one other trailing his step. For the faintest of moments, he thought

Ancel's threat had proven true already, but a light nod from Gale told him otherwise. His sister had gone, but not by Ancel's hand. They had their own business to attend to.

Chapter 35
Isha

Her heart beat like a drum as the four of them stripped. This was the most excitement she had felt in years. She had been too shaken by fear during her escape to truly embellish the experience. Now was different. The thrill of a successful infiltration made her limbs tingle. She centred herself, taking a deep breath. She needed to focus. People were relying on her. Her brother was relying on her.

She lifted the heavy metal from her torso and stretched her limbs, feeling light again. She watched as Veil unclipped the last of her armour. Veil too took a whiff of her own scent before making an unpleasant face. Isha covered her mouth to stifle a laugh.

"Wouldn't happen to be any baths around here, would there?" Veil said.

"We have more pressing matters than our cleanliness right now, do you not think?" Isha said.

Veil shrugged.

Isha shook her head. Her heart was pounding a thousand

beats a minute, and all Veil could think about was having a bath? This must be what true experience looked like.

She waited patiently as Draz returned from his solo venture. He had stripped himself of plate, though the helm had been replaced by his own — which she had come to learn had a name. He wore Gallant with pride. The black-coated great-helm was more than a piece of amour, it was part of him, an extension of his own flesh. Raiz sure had some strange friends.

"What did you find?" Veil whispered.

Draz whipped out two short swords, a bow, and a quiver of arrows and tossed them to the ground. Veil took one, held it up in front of her to measure its sheen before nodding. "Not bad. Well done, Draz."

Puk picked up the second blade, wrapping his hand around the hilt as he stared at the black streak of the Last Light. It had to be hard for him, fighting against men he used to train with. She placed a reassuring hand on his shoulder. It wasn't much, but it would have to do.

Veil touched her on the shoulder. "You're up kid, lead the way."

Isha's gaze drifted towards the Fifty Spears. She felt her chest tighten as she saw the Forty-Fourth standing taller than most. Her prison. But Averardus was dead. She looked to her hands, picturing blood trickling down her wrists as she lunged again and again with her knife, cutting her former master to pieces and watching as he lay dying. She blinked, and the blood was gone. Her hands were clean, her mind clear.

The conversation between Averardus and Salador was as fresh in her mind as the day she had heard it. They had been so confident in their security that they didn't bother to think on the ramifications of their gloating. Every conversation, every detail they shared in her presence came to her in a flood. None had cared to hide it, why would they? No slave had ever escaped Lumindal.

She remembered distinct memories of Averardus talking about Salador, about his ancestral history and his link with Gaveinus — the architect behind the Last Light. There had to be a way into the tower through him.

"Follow me," she said.

With renewed determination, Isha ushered the small company through the winding streets of Lumindal's Middle Sector. The place was a maze. All of those years memorising every footstep; every corner, every landmark, would now be her saviour. She had gathered the knowledge for her eventual escape. She never would have thought to be using it for infiltration. "This way," she whispered, walking with casual grace past three Blackwings on patrol.

She came to a sudden stop. Veil crashed into her back.

"Ow!" Veil said, stumbling to the side. "Is something wrong? Are you lost?"

"No, it..."

Isha stared out into the empty space. This was where the people from Lesken had been executed, where the *children* had been executed. The streets were clear now, as if nothing had happened. She shied away, as if hiding would rid her mind of the memories.

"What is it?" Veil said.

"Nothing. We go this way."

The four intruders pressed on, coming to a rest in a narrow alley near the gates barring the Forty-Sixth Spear. "It's useless," Veil said. "Between your eyes and tin-head here we stand out like the moon on a cloudless night. And that building's too heavily guarded."

Isha sighed. "Any suggestions?"

Veil's eyes flicked back to where they had come, hovering over the three Blackwings standing vigilant on the corner.

"Oh no, you're not getting me into another suit of armour, no chance," Isha said.

Veil twisted her lips into a broad smile. "Who said anything about me and you?" She turned towards Draz and Puk. "What do you say?"

Of course, Puk was unable to speak for himself, but he seemed content.

"Like we have a choice once your mind is made," Draz said.

"And don't you forget it," Veil said. "Which one do you want?"

Draz hesitated, peeking through his visor at the selected targets. "One on the left looks like Draz's size."

"Huh!" Veil said. "Not likely."

Draz cracked his knuckles, ignoring her chide.

"Try not to make a mess this time," Veil said. "We need at least two suits intact."

"What do I do?" Isha said.

"Fancy being the bait?" Veil suggested.

"Bait? What do you — you can't be serious?"

Veil blinked pleadingly at her. "Take Puk with you, make a show of it," Veil said. "Draw them in however you will. I'll be on the roof just there," she pointed towards a tiled roof overhanging the alley and then offered the sword to Isha. "Take this, I hope you won't need it, but Raiz will kill me himself if anything should happen to you."

Isha grasped the hilt of the short blade, wincing as the vision of blood trickling down its side again rushed her mind. Is this what she had become? A killer, just like them?

She shook herself free of the vision, content with her choices. She was whoever she wanted to be. Averardus' life was hers to take. She refused to regret being the instrument of his death.

With Puk by her side, she tucked herself down the back of an overlapping alley. The streets in this part of the city were narrow, the spaces between houses even more so. She walked halfway up, still shrouded in shadow.

She felt strong with Puk near, and not just because of the physical protection he provided, either. She felt comfortable, as if their fates were intertwined. She wanted to know more about him, to learn his hand signals. But there would be no tomorrow if they didn't make it through today. So, she screamed.

She screamed as loud as she could. "Heeeelp. Pleeeease. Heeelp."

She tugged on Puk's uniform, pretending to try to break free of his non-existent grasp. Puk looked at her in a muddle of confusion. He stepped back, trying to remove himself from the situation before finally clueing in to her ploy. He put on a show of some of the worst acting she had seen in a long time. His back was stiff as a nail, his hands weak, and his hold on her more a pet than a use of force.

She played it up, though, bucking and pulling, all the while screaming for help. She took a glance over her shoulder to see the three patrolmen running in her direction. The wings of an eagle were stretched across their breasts. Gilded with gold, they shone bright in the darkness of the alley.

The three moved to surround her, walking with cautious steps, swords drawn and at the ready. They didn't even find time to witness Puk's abysmal acting as Veil's arrows shot through the air, whirling past her head and into the inch of unarmored skin between neck and shoulder.

Two dropped to the ground with a clink, leaving the third standing with his shoulders tucked to his neck, sword raised high.

With an echoing war cry, Draz leapt from the rooftop, landing on top of the poor soldier and piercing his sword nearly to the hilt through his shoulder in a downward strike, shattering the armour and the man inside.

Within a few blinks, the deed was done; another three lives sent to their graves. The old Isha may have felt guilty for her part in it, but her new self felt only pity. She mourned their lives spent in servitude to corruption. In a way, they had been set free. No longer would anyone hold power over them or bind them to a will that was not their own.

Puk hovered in front of her as though there was still protecting to be done. She took another look at the deceased. What if they could have reformed, the way Puk had? Given the chance, would they have turned? Or were their souls already tainted black?

She turned her head, dismissing her thoughts as mere fantasy. If there was good to be done, it was in toppling the Last Light. That was the real threat.

"You just couldn't help yourself, could you Draz," Veil sighed. She ran a hand down the crack in the armour of the man Draz had felled, which was split in two halves, parting one wing from the eagle's body on the breast.

Draz shrugged. "Can never be too careful with these bastards. Draz doesn't pull punches."

Veil exhaled. "Lucky for you, I don't miss," she said. "Now start stripping these two, we don't know how long we have. The council meets tonight. And wipe off that blood. Can't have you walking around this city in a suit tarnished with red blotches."

Draz and Puk got to work stripping the dead of their armour.

"So, what exactly is your plan?" Isha said.

Veil hunched over the bodies before craning her neck towards her. "You're not going to like it."

"Try me."

Veil scratched at her head. "On the way here, when you mentioned your plan and this 'Salador' fellow. You said he wanted you, yes?"

"Yes, he is an animal. But what does that have to do with... oh no. You cannot be serious." And then she saw it. Only two suits of armour, four of them. "You mean for us to hand ourselves in?"

"I'll be by your side. Draz and Puk will be with you all the way. They'll protect you."

"No. No, no, no. No way am I giving myself to that man. I have been there before. I have seen this man. He is vile. His heart is blacker than a starless night. He has always wanted me. If he gets his hands on me..."

"It's okay Isha. It was stupid of me to ask. We'll find another way. Probably for the best. If Raiz found out..."

Isha shrank inside herself. Veil's words were barely even audible underneath her shroud of anxiety and doubt. Her breathing doubled, hands shaking. She had spent her entire life trying to escape this place, and for what? So she could lead a lavish life back in Illidor? Pampered, praised, and likely married off to some distant noble or prince? But the thought of being taken again, by a man worse than Averardus, plagued her mind. The risk was high, perhaps too high.

She turned, her mind split with a pain worse than any headache. She remembered being inside the tower, watching as children risked their lives feeding Light into its belly. She remembered the overwhelming heat when the bolt of Light shot from its tip. What about those on the receiving end? A whole city dead, and for what?

That is what she fought to destroy, the evil that needed ending. What was her life in comparison to hundreds of thousands?

"I will do it," she said, turning back to face Veil. "What do you need me to do?"

Veil stared at her as though she had just slain a mighty beast, her eyes wide in admiration. "I'll be with you the entire way. We just need to walk."

Chapter 36
Isha

"This helmet stinks of Blackwing shit," Draz said, standing next to Puk in another suit of armour that was not his own. Dark splotches of smudged blood still stained the black metal. Isha rubbed a loose piece of cloth in circles over Puk's stolen left pauldron.

"Just suck it up a little longer," Veil said. "We need you for this."

The four of them rounded the bend leading towards the steps at the foot of the Forty-Sixth Spear. Again Draz carried his peridium helm in a sack tied to his waist. "You better know what you're doing," he said.

"Just stick to the script and we'll be fine," Veil said.

Draz grumbled through the hard metal. "Lead the way then."

Together they marched, Isha's legs heavy with fatigue as they neared the gate. Her hands were bound behind her back. To the outside world, Puk was holding her captive, but to her, his hand pressed to hers was reassuring.

A jet-black tower spiralled high into the sky above them.

Isha strained her neck as the four of them peered into the clouds. A layer of breen coated the towers tip. It looked like a waxed candle, only the design was more purposeful and intricate.

A dozen or so Blackwings moved to block their path. "Halt! Who goes there? State your business," said a freckled man with a fraction of his left ear missing.

Draz stepped forward. "Osh is the name. And this here is Sten. We were with Averardus' guard. Now that he is no more, we wish to fill our purses with a new master."

The man with half an ear circled him. "Lord Salador is not taking recruits at the moment. Move along." He flicked his hand in a shooing gesture.

Draz remained unmoving. "We bring gifts for the lord of the Forty-Sixth Spear." He pushed Isha and Veil forward.

"Do not make me repeat mys—"

"Gifts that will surely be well received."

Isha looked up, playing the part of a defeated woman. She blinked her violet eyes at the freckled man. He stumbled backward. Another man caught sight of her and moved to whisper in the ear of the first.

"Ahem," said the freckled man, clearing his throat. "Right this way, sir."

Isha withheld a smile, pleased to see their plan working. Even so, she stayed close to Puk, her heart drumming in her chest.

Together they followed a pair of Blackwings up a spiral of stone steps, fifty shadows bathing them in darkness as they crept higher.

"Stay here," the guard said, leaving the four of them to stare at his back as he strode through the double doors of the massive structure.

"Is this it?" Draz whispered through the metal.

"Yes," Isha said, hugging her chest with her chin.

"Should we make a break for it?" Draz said.

"No!" Veil spat, coughing to cover up the noise of her speech.

The remaining Blackwing turned his head towards her and held for a moment. Isha's whole body tensed, but he soon lost interest and his gaze drifted elsewhere.

"We need Salador alive. We wait until we're inside," Veil continued.

Before anyone could acknowledge her comment, the doors swung wide, smashing against the stone as more figures emerged from its depths.

A tall man walked with an awkward stride towards them. He ran a hand through slick black hair, his blood red robe dragging behind. "By the Light, it cannot be," he said.

Salador forced his way through the protection of his guard and pressed his body close to Isha's. She let him cradle her head with bony fingers as he stared into her eyes with devious intent. "What stroke of luck brought you to me?" Salador said. "No, not luck. Fate. Do you not see girl? You are where you are meant to be. With me. Averardus never deserved you. He never cherished you as I will. You are home." He turned to Draz and Puk. "Where did you find her?"

Draz stepped forward and placed a fist to his breastplate. "We recovered her from Illidor. With our master gone from this world, we seek a new home. We bring her to you as a gift in the hopes you might bring us fortune."

Isha again covered up a grin. He was a better actor than Puk, that was for sure.

Salador studied Draz and Puk like a predator sizing up prey. He then relaxed, opening his arms in a welcoming gesture. "And fortune you shall have sir!" he exclaimed. "You cannot comprehend the value of what you have brought me this day."

Draz nodded. "We wish only to serve."

A wicked smile creased the side of the Eagle's lip. He exhaled a heavy sigh before curling his palm across Isha's shoulder. She shrank into herself, slumping in an attempt to seem weak and helpless, even though inside she burned with fire.

"And what of this one?" Salador asked, pointing towards Veil. "Is she someone as well?"

"Found her with the Glaive girl. She must be her servant or something," Draz said.

"Very well. You may take her as part of your reward. Do with her what you will." He looked Veil up and down. "Not much meat to her, but she is pretty enough."

Isha resisted the urge to lash out then and there. But if the last eight years had taught her anything, it was patience.

"Come," Salador said. "Let me introduce you to your new home, dear. It might not be as quaint or decorated as your old one, but I assure you my position is rising by the day. I will soon be the wealthiest man in all of Zapour if my vision proves true."

He turned once more towards Draz. "What is your name, brave knight?"

"Osh, m'lord. The name is Osh. This here is Sten. We were of Averardus's house guard."

"Very well, I shall have someone see to your reward. Follow me."

The door slammed behind her with a thud. Salador led them down a long hallway devoid of colour. It seemed he was more a man of practicality than splendour.

Metal boots clicked against the smooth tiling, echoing down the hall as Salador ushered them through another series of low-hanging walkways. Blackwings were posted at each turn. The closest one barely batted an eyelid as she stared at him on the way past. Their discipline was unmatched. He made her think of Argon. She had never liked him, not really. Not the way she liked Puk. But he could have turned her in, could have stopped her plan for escape at the final hurdle. And yet he didn't. He had deserved better than his fate. She should have protected him, like he had protected her. Were there more like him? More like Puk? If given the choice, would these soldiers truly side with men such as Salador and Averardus?

She set her mind towards the task at hand. Eventually, they entered through a wide archway leading to a vast open space. Symmetrical staircases wound their way around the room to meet in the middle, leading to a second hall beyond.

Isha's jaw slackened as Salador led them to where a dozen women dressed in flimsy, low-cut silken dresses lounged leisurely atop soft velvet furniture and cushions. An array of five half-naked men accompanied them, indulging in the presence of their beauty.

She watched with open eyes as a woman with fair skin and long, braided hair pawed at one of the men's necks with claw-like nails. She left a trail of kisses running down his chest as he arched his back in pleasure.

A similar scene was unfolding on the couch behind them, only the slender girl in nothing but her britches shivered, her arms draped across her chest in the form of a cross as a man with wrinkles matching the shrivelled leather of the cuffs on his wrist forced himself on her.

Isha felt the harsh up-heave of her own insides threatening to rise from her throat.

Salador opened his arms in a wide gesture, basking in the glory of his own company. "Have you ever seen such raw sexual chemistry and emotion, young Osh? I assure you I treat my own well. All of this and more will soon be yours. You made the right decision bringing the girl to me. I admire a man who understands their own worth, and the worth of those above them."

Draz did nothing, didn't even move.

"Oh, I have never been so excited!" Salador said, pressing his hands together as his whole body shook. "And just in time too, Lunet is holding a gala this very night! Oh, I cannot wait to see her face as I parade you around as my property in front of everyone. Averardus be damned, but you are beautiful," he said, again cradling Isha's chin in his fingers. "You have a keen eye, Osh, I trust you know well the value she holds for me."

"Aye," Draz said. "Draz knows her value more than most. Though Draz is afraid no jewel in the world is enough to save your head from a meeting with his fist."

Salador blinked repeatedly, his face as blank as an empty page. "What did you say?"

Quick as a dart, Veil spun, cutting her bonds on Puk's waist dagger before grabbing it by the hilt and throwing it into the neck of the closest Blackwing.

The man dropped to his knees, and then to his inevitable rest, face-first on the tiled floor, a pool of red his only friend.

Salador wobbled on his back foot, stumbling over his legs as he called out. "Guards!" It came out as more of a croak, with no real breath behind it.

The four remaining Blackwings in the room came at them from all angles, desperate to protect their master. But Puk and Draz were prepared. Puk moved first, running at the closest man before he had the chance to group up with the others. His sword streamed behind his body like a flag in the wind. He thrust it forward, cracking it like a whip as it cut through armour and sunk deep into flesh. Puk hadn't even broken stride before he was onto his next victim. If he felt any remorse for killing his own, his actions certainly didn't show it.

Draz was next to initiate, opting instead to point his sword and wait as two drew in close.

Isha looked around at the carnage unfolding, wondering how she could be helpful. She swore to Zur then that if she was to make it out of this alive, she would have Dazen teach her to fight. She was sick of feeling helpless.

She watched as the near naked women screamed in horror, covering their flesh with whatever material they could find, too frozen with fear to run for their lives.

Salador made it back to his feet and was making for the spiral staircase. Without thinking, Isha rushed towards him, sweeping her leg in a low arc and tripping him as he ran. His legs buckled and he sprawled into the railing. He recovered quickly though, grasping for a table knife and waving it at her like he would a torch in the dark.

Her first instinct was to run, to flee the scene before he caused her any more harm. But she was better than that now. She had promised herself she would no longer be the flesh, but the knife.

Sidestepping his pathetic attempt at a slash, Isha grabbed hold of his arm, pushed herself close to his body, and bit him on the neck.

She clenched her jaws with dog-like ferocity, holy blood flowing into her mouth. Only there was nothing holy about this man. He bled red, just as Averardus had.

Salador cried out in pain and fury, bucking hard before a blinding flash of white-light caused her to release her hold.

Her vision was a blur of red and black shapes, and she stumbled backward, rubbing her eyes with frantic hands.

"You whore!" Salador shouted. "If you thought life with Averardus was hard, you have no idea what you are in for! I will make you beg for mercy by the time I am done with you! There will be — ughh." A bone-shattering crunch sounded where his voice had been.

Isha blinked away the light, the muddle of shapes forming into solids once more. Draz stood before her, clenching and unclenching his fist in triumph. Salador's unconscious form lay in a crumpled heap at the foot of the staircase.

Draz leaned over the fallen body. "Draz warned you, no jewel in the world is enough to stop your head from a meeting with my fist."

"**W**akey wakey, princess."

Veil crouched over Salador's body, one leg planted on either side. She pinched his cheeks, grinning widely as he mumbled his way back to consciousness.

"Wha — ahh. Get off me, wench! I will have you flayed for this, mark my — gahhh!"

Veil's knee sunk between his legs with a sickening thump. The immobilised Eagle wriggled and writhed in his bonds, gasping for air that would not come.

"Let's start this again, shall we?" Veil said. "Now, if you value the jewels between your legs half as much as you value the ones you collect, you'll tell us what we need to know."

"Who are you? What do you want from me?" Salador pleaded. "I have gold! Lots and lots of gold. Take it. I will give it to you. Just leave this holy place."

Veil leaned in close, her heart beating so hard Isha could hear it thumping. "This place is no more holy than my arsehole.

We didn't come here for trinkets."

"Wh-what then? What is it you want?"

"Justice," Veil said.

The fallen Eagle gulped lost words down his throat before taking a deep breath. "The only justice you will find here is a swift strike from the executioner's blade. Or would you prefer a noose? I will enjoy watching your pretty neck snap."

Veil huffed a derisive laugh. "Aww, he called me pretty." She then placed a heeled boot on his neck and began carving a line of red up his thigh.

Isha turned away from the scene. She had no fondness for torture, having seen enough of it in her time with Averardus. Her back might be clean of scars, but it pained her still that poor Obeyun's was not. She forced herself to turn back and bear witness, however, for she was stronger than the woman she used to be, and though Veil's tactics may be an injustice, they were a necessary one.

Salador's mouth bubbled, spittle frothing at his lip as he cried out in pain. Veil's hand touched his nethers. "Careful now. Don't get too excited, or I might have more skin to cut," she said.

"What do you want of me?" Salador spat. "Speak, speak! For the love of..."

Isha made her move then. "We seek the stash of black powder you keep beneath your home. I know you have it."

"I have no such powder. We Eagles are banned from such explosive material. I would not."

"Oh spare me," Isha said. "I know you have it. I heard you and Averardus bargaining over a price, do not think me a fool!"

Veil pressed the knife closer to what she was sure he valued most.

"Okay, okay! I will talk, I will talk! It is as you say. I keep it in the cellar beneath the base of the building. Take it! Take it and leave. The damn stuff is more trouble than it is worth anyway."

"Take us there, now," Veil said, pulling him to his feet.

Puk stood guard over the cluster of frightened women and degraded men, who were still without clothes.

"They are not to leave this room," Veil said. "If any attempt to escape, point them towards the corpse of the last man to try."

Puk edged towards Isha, an expectant look on his face.

"It is okay, Puk, do as she says for now. I will be back in a moment," Isha said.

"Move those skinny legs!" Veil said, urging the broken Eagle toward the exit. "And no more Light tricks. I see one flash and I kill you on the spot."

Draz threw something across the room. An object landed at her feet, the heavy metal clinking on the tiling. "Put this around his neck," Draz said. "Peridium collar, he has dozens of them lying around. Seems pretty women aren't his only fetish."

Isha picked up the collar and snapped it shut around Salador's neck, who winced at the sudden burden.

Salador led them down a series of dark corridors and stone stairwells. Stripped to his undergarments with a sword at his throat, it was hard to believe the power this man had once held at his fingertips.

"You know you will not get away with this," he said. "Even if you are to kill me, the King-Radiant will hunt you down. You have signed your own death sentence, and for what? To steal some explosives?"

Veil prodded his back with a light touch of the pointy end of her stolen sword. "Move! And do not try to delay us, or do you need a reminder of what I can do?"

"I am moving, I am moving! Just calm down. It is just down

this hall."

Veil rolled her eyes, pushing him closer.

They came to the end of a dimly lit hallway, the faint flicker of a distant Shine-globe highlighting a thick wooden door with a metal frame. Veil pushed on it, but it did not budge. "Open it," she said.

Salador bit into his lip and reached into his pocket. With a trembling hand he pulled out a set of keys before trying unsuccessfully to place the right one into the hole.

"Take any longer and you might get your wish as we die from boredom!" Veil said.

Isha looked at Veil, wondering just who it was her brother had fallen for. Only now did she see who she was to him. Two of Zur's children lost in the same space, searching for meaning. Searching for something, or someone, to make sense of their lives. They were meant for each other. If their world was broken, why not fill the hole with another broken piece?

She saw her love for him, driven by the same desire as Raiz, to right a wrong, no matter the cost. She would not rest until her goal was met, same as Raiz.

The lock clicked, and the door creaked steadily open. Veil pushed Salador aside, Draz following close behind as they entered the darkness.

"Light, I need light," Veil said.

Isha scrambled down the hallway to where the Shine-globe rested on its perch. The spherical ball of light was near blinding when looking directly into its core. She arched her back and flexed her fingers before plucking it from its resting place. Despite Averardus' extravagant collection, she had never touched a Shine-globe with Light inside of it. She was expecting it to be hot and burn her skin, but it was quite cool. The wax-like breen casing made of dead Shine acted as a kind of barrier against the intense heat within.

She cradled it in her arm and rushed back, holding it aloft. The room lit up. Bundles of goods lined the length of the damp room, covered in fine cloth and neatly organised into rows according to make and material. Veil peaked underneath the closest, recoiling as a glint reflected from the light of the globe. Tens, perhaps hundreds of gold bars shone in a tightly packed stack.

"You are indeed a wealthy man, Lord Salador," Veil said with a mocking laugh.

Salador grumbled an inaudible retort, refusing to meet her eyeline.

"Must have taken you a while to acquire so much wealth. Makes one wonder where you got it all from?" Veil said. "Some foreign liege maybe, paid in tribute, grovelling on hands and knees. Or did you perhaps pry it from those most in need? Those with nothing to their name but the clothes on their backs. Those who spend their entire lives working simply to keep their family afloat, only to have their last coin ripped from their dirty palms to sit idle in the basement of some snob who thinks himself a god.

"No. You don't seem the type to get your hands dirty. I bet you had some lackey do it for you. I bet you've never lifted a finger in your entire life, save maybe to pleasure yourself. Had the entire world handed to you on a platter, stuffing your face while the rest of us suffer. I'm surprised your belly doesn't swell further."

Salador brushed the dirt from his bare legs, sucking in his stomach and standing straighter. "I will not have my good name sullied by the likes of you. Murderer. Thief. Whore. You should learn your place in life. I am a holy relic, a divinity. All know it, and all fear it. You are less than the dirt beneath my fingernails."

Veil kicked him hard behind the knees, causing him to drop to his stomach.

"The balls on this one," Veil said, resting her sword on his skin as he shuddered beneath its weight. "You know what, I actually understand it. Playing god that is."

She drew another line of red up his back, slicing through hair and flesh as the Eagle cried out in agony.

"I see how real the temptation is. To hold absolute power. To hold the life of another at your mercy. But make no mistake, you only play at being a god. Do not think your so-called divinity holds any shred of truth. You bleed red just as I do."

Salador crawled away from Veil's grip, his weak arms only taking him so far. "You think you are better? You are the one wielding the sword."

"Oh, I'm well aware of what I am. I'm a monster, I'm what you'll have nightmares about when daylight fades and darkness descends. I'll do the work needed so those who lack the strength to fight may find it once more. I'll be the dirt beneath the fingernail, and that dirt will be your end."

Salador let his head rest on the ground.

"Now, where is the powder?"

He lifted a bloodstained finger towards the corner of the room.

Isha followed his finger and pulled back a long bolt of cloth, revealing several barrels. There were eight in total. She dug her hand into the closest one, felt the smooth texture run through her fingers like dust. The substance was black, like coal, only finer, sticking to her hands like soot. She brushed them together, watching as the powder puffed into a cloud before floating back into the barrel.

"Is this it?" she asked, turning to Draz.

Draz came bounding over, removing his glove before feeling the powder for himself. "Aye, this be the stuff. A whole lot of it too."

"Enough to topple a tower?" Veil asked.

Draz shrugged. "Only one way to find out."

Isha tried to lift the barrel, pulling with all her might. Her knuckles went white, and she recoiled, fearing a splinter. The barrel would not budge. "How in Zapour are we going to get eight of these up a tower so tall?"

The three of them looked at each other, expressions blank.

Draz held his hands on his hips. "We will need a labour force," he said. "Draz has an idea, but it's risky."

Chapter 37
Dazen

Dazen's composure was fleeting. His arms and legs had turned to mud, weak and useless. He hid his limbs under a thick oaken table in the centre of the throne room. A red-velvet curtain was draped across the length of the room, cutting them off from the outside and leaving only the large dais.

He forced himself to express confidence, broadening his shoulders and keeping his head high. He was a prince, and would not be easily intimidated. He didn't feel very powerful, though, more like a clueless child leaning on his father for support.

The curtain made the room look small. Whitewashed walls covered in tapestries lined either side. Red banners bearing Lumindal's coat of arms — two eagles next to a crown of gold — hung from the ceiling in lavish fashion.

The silence was deafening. Kron and Dazen sat idle on one side, Gelvard and Ancel Saelmere on the other. Dazen rapped a finger on his knee. So, this was the famous Council of Kings. All the kings and princes from each respective kingdom of

Zapour were expected to attend. So far, only the representatives from Trost and Craw were present.

If Evanon Lightfire himself did intend on making an appearance, he was yet to make his presence known. The true purpose of the council was still not clear. The message had been vague, but Dazen figured he had a fair idea.

At least twenty Knights of the Golden Talon circled the room, each heavily armoured in suits of shining gold. Red plumes arched from the helms and trailed down their backs. Sharpened halberds pointed to the ceiling, ready to be used to deadly effect the moment anyone stepped out of order. He studied them, wondering how many could wield Zur's Light.

He risked a glance over his shoulder towards the ornate double-door at the room's rear. Raiz was somewhere back there, under heavy guard and watched closely by Yvain. What if they discovered the key?

He heard a stir from outside; footsteps shuffling and muffled voices. The door shifted open. In walked a tall man with slouched shoulders. He almost had to duck under the door frame, so large was his stature. A silver crown lay atop his head, the horns of a bull carved into the shiny metal. Dazen had never seen him before, but he had heard tale. He was Hanns Balsto of Kogon. His son — Prince Valter Balsto — trailed behind him. While nearly equalling his father in height, he still had not enough years to his name to have developed his father's bulk and muscle. Valter stood tall and proud, lifting his face high as if he were the brightest and finest in the room.

"Cousin Hanns! Welcome, welcome," Gelvard said, opening his arms wide as if this was his own city.

The pair couldn't have looked more opposite. Gelvard was short and fat, whereas Hanns was tall and lean. Dazen leaned towards Kron and whispered. "These two are cousins?"

Kron huffed an amused sigh. "Distant cousins."

Hanns bowed low. "Gelvard, I trust there is good reason me and my countrymen braved the early winds of winter to travel here."

Gelvard rose. "If you wish to place blame, dear cousin, I suggest you turn your head across the table."

Dazen felt four sets of eyes turn to shoot daggers into his side. Gelvard's bulging stomach bounced as he thrust an accusatory finger their way.

"You will stay your tongue, Gelvard," Kron barked. "Trost has been ever loyal to the Crown. If you wish to place blame, look to your own borders. Or was Averardus himself not slain on your very soil?"

Gelvard's eyes grew wide, his lips pressed together so tight that Dazen thought he might swallow his tongue. "You dare mock me!" he said, saliva frothing at his mouth, little droplets of spit cascading down his chin. "We both know who was responsible for his death, and he sits in this very room!"

Dazen slumped back into his chair, saying nothing.

"And you have proof of this?" Kron said.

Gelvard went a shade of red, his knuckles tensing as he reached for a sword that was not there. "All the proof I need will be in your pathetic castle. Or did you fail to recover Averardus' little pet whore when you intruded upon my lands?"

Dazen watched as Ancel smirked, his features shaded behind his father's bulk. To his surprise, Kron remained calm, clasping his hands together as Hanns and Valter took their seats across from him.

Gelvard huffed a dismissive sigh before returning to his seat with a loud thud. He continued to study his long-time adversary as if his motive was not quite clear. "Tell me, Glaive," he said with out-of-character calmness. "Why is it your dedication to the King-Radiant runs so thick? What he did to you would have broken even the best of men. Why then do you support him, after what he has taken?"

Kron remained quiet, sparing a quick glance towards Dazen before regaining his composure.

Dazen narrowed his eyes, not quite following the conversation. What had Evanon done to him?

Gelvard apparently caught his confusion, his face lighting up like a Shine-globe in full dark. "The boy does not know!" He leaned back into his chair, resting his arm on the rest as he licked his lips clean. "Oh Kron, I knew you to be harsh, but this. Shielding the boy from the fate of his own mother." He shook his head with mocking slowness.

Dazen placed two hands on the table, looking his father up and down as if demanding answers.

The veins in Kron's forearms bulged, his entire body tense as he stared down Gelvard as if had just, well, killed his wife. "You will stay your tongue!"

"What is he saying? What happened to Mother?" Dazen pressed.

Kron ignored him, instead deciding to glare swords, more than daggers, into the very soul of the King of Craw.

Gelvard plucked an apple from the decorated bowl of fruit on the table and took a large bite. He chewed with his mouth open, leaning into the comfort of his chair. "Well, you see child. A long time ago--"

"You will shut your mouth!" Kron shouted. The chair behind him flung backwards as he rose. He planted two fists on the table. Half a dozen knights lowered their halberds and stepped towards him, ready to impale him with one stray step.

Thick tendrils of translucent white-light circled Kron,

wrapping around his arm like a veil. The tip of a metal halberd hovered over his throat, ready to draw red. Kron remained unmoving, the stubborn Glaive within refusing to back down, his vision focused on the taken-aback King of Craw.

"Father," Dazen pleaded. "Now is not the time."

Like a switch, Kron relaxed, the Light dissipating, his intensity vanishing as he thumped back into his chair. The semi-circle of pointed swords and halberds retreated in unison, the knights taking two steps back as if nothing had happened.

Dazen wiped a droplet of sweat from his brow, blowing cool air between pursed lips as he too tried to relax. A question still burned in his mind. Kron was hiding something from him, something about Mother.

He vowed to himself he would find out what, but now was not the time. Any minute, Raiz could be put to death. His focus needed to be on his brother.

With the crisis abated, the room grew still once more. It wasn't until another round of shuffling boots came from outside the door that everyone craned their heads in anticipation.

Excluding the dead Kingdom of Hirane, three of the five remaining kings of Zapour waited impatiently for the fourth and fifth.

Again the door swung open. In walked another handful of black and gold-plated knights, parting and forming a straight-backed line as the fourth King entered through the archway.

Dazen found his breath lost in his throat. He tried to catch it, but it came out as a kind of muffled gasp. In walked a man clad in a loose-fitting tan robe threaded with gold. It covered most of his body, but his hands and face were showing clear as day. Split down the middle as if painted, one side showed skin as black as charcoal, the other white as alabaster. It shone like a lantern as the man walked into the room with an air of authority. A wooden crown of simple make circled his forehead, shining brighter than any metal.

Dazen's jaw dropped. "Obeyun?"

Kron looked from the Wishan King back towards Dazen in puzzlement, eyes narrowed with suspicion.

What was Obeyun doing here? And apparently, he was King? Dazen wrestled within himself, trying to remember some clue or piece of information that would help him decipher this puzzle, but he came up short. He knew this man only as one of his sister's friends, rescued along with Isha when he and Raiz charged the inn back in Speakers Hollow. The man had seemed nice enough. He had his respect for taking care of his sister all of these years...but a king? He shook his head. The question remained, whose side would he turn to when the inevitable happened?

Wisha had always been a private country. Isolated deep in the forest, they preferred their own company, refusing to trade or even breathe in the same presence as outsiders. But make no mistake, they were part of Zapour, bound by the same laws as Trost, forced to bend to their knee at the King-Radiant's call. And call he had.

Dazen almost missed the small figure trailing at Obeyun's feet. An elderly woman, dark in colour, walked in with a staff too tall for her body. The sharp click-clack of the wooden stick pounded against the marble floor, echoing through the room as she scuttled up to her seat beside who Dazen could only assume was her son. Knots of grey matted hair swayed at her breast as she clasped two hands together and smiled to no one in particular.

Obeyun remained quiet. He did spare Dazen a subtle wink when he caught him gawking for longer than he should.

With Obeyun's entrance no longer a surprise, the room stilled once more. Dazen could practically taste the distrust in the air as Hanns and Gelvard snickered to each other, teaming up in their already forged alliance and leaving both those born of Wisha and of Trost to ponder in silence.

The door had barely closed when another shuffle sounded. The scene was identical, guards parting, tension rising as the four kings awaited the fifth.

Dazen rubbed at his chin, wondering which twin had taken the Zutonian crown. He expected it to be Petros; he was the oldest, and though they both shared but a nut-full of sense between them, he was the smarter of the two. He could not discount, however, the hunger in Huet's eyes. The deep pit of jealousy lurking beneath those deep hazel irises. Who had emerged the victor? Perhaps they shared the crown?

His vision steadied towards the door, forearms tight as he braced himself for whatever the twins had in store. It was likely they had not taken Kron's abolishment of the marriage proposal well. He arched his neck in an attempt to see beyond the blackness of the guards. He saw the crown, a golden spark dazzling with jewels. A wolf's teeth, sharp as the point of his steels, were etched to its rim. Dazen remembered it well, he had carried it with King Rayner from this very hall. His gaze drifted lower as the man wearing it stepped into full view. It was not Petros, nor was it Huet.

"Echo!" Dazen said, rising on two feet.

The once Levic prince welcomed his call with a warm smile as he nodded politely. There was a strange calmness about him Dazen had not seen before. An aura of power surrounded him, one which had nothing to do with the crown. Even his face looked different. He still had the same boyish features, his body not yet grown to its full potential, but his jaw was cut with a line of evenly groomed stubble over his chin. His hair was combed back into neat streaks of brown, the golden crown resting as if made to form around his head. Dazen knew it to be mainly a facade, a brave face to hide his misgivings. But to his credit, the boy wore his newfound title with dignity.

Gelvard, however, thought otherwise. His belly swelled and his throat vibrated as a cruel bellow of deep laughter left his lips. "Bahh! What is this nonsense?" he said in between bouts of laughter. "I did not come here to treat with children and animals!"

If Obeyun and Echo were bothered by his comment, they did not show it.

"Is this the best Zuton has to offer?" Gelvard continued. "A pup barely fit to lift a sword? It is no wonder your country is in such a state. Surely there is someone who… well, what do we have here?"

Dazen paused before following Gelvard's line of sight towards the girl behind Echo. Lady Sumaya walked in graceful strides. The woman he was to marry, the woman he dreamed of at night when Zur's Light faded.

Her skin was deeper than honey, her hair set free and flowing in curls nearly to her waist. She moved to stand beside her brother. Her features were knotted in determination fit for a warrior, but her rose coloured silken dress fluttered outward onto the marble floor in an image fit for a princess.

Gelvard swiped at a droplet of drool on his lip. "Perhaps I spoke out of turn, young Prince. Should you perhaps find your country out of favour after this meet, my own son here will make for a fitting husband to your dazzling sister there."

Dazen looked to Ancel, the sling holding his arm gone. He too goggled in not-so-subtle admiration, his eyes wide with want and lust.

Dazen burned with what he could only describe as jealousy and disgust. He would die before seeing Sumaya with that man. But this battle was not his to fight, and he knew it.

"My apologies, respected King of Craw," Echo said. "But my sister's mind is hers to choose her own suitor. I assure you our political stability is quite strong, as are our fighting forces." He said those last words slowly, leaning forward as he spoke.

In one sentence the new King of Zuton had shown respect, mocked, and threatened them. And all the while, Echo held his calm demeanour.

Where had this *man* come from? And where were his elder brothers?

His comment seemed to have quieted Gelvard, for he crossed his arms and leant back into his chair, muttering nonsense to himself.

Echo took his place next to Dazen, Sumaya a seat further. Dazen didn't know where to look. His father was about to sentence his brother to death, so looking at him only deepened his desire to speak his piece. The Saelmeres and Balstos sat across from him, their pig-headed and egotistic glances making him want to puke. And to his right sat the woman he was falling for, who had been all but cast aside the moment Kron decided it should be so.

He decided to settle his gaze on Echo. "I see you have done well for yourself in my absence," Dazen said.

Echo leaned his way. "It seems I may have taken that first step you spoke so fondly of."

A brazen smile creased his lips. "It would appear so. Might I ask how you came by that piece of gold cresting your head?"

"Perhaps another day. Today we have some business to attend, do we not?"

Sumaya turned her head to listen in on the conversation, her eyeline meeting his. He retreated with an awkward yelp. She placed four fingers to her mouth as Dazen's cheeks turned the same colour as her dress.

His moment of infatuation became overshadowed as Hanns slammed an open hand onto the table, sending an assortment of crockery bouncing away from it. He pointed a thin and gangly arm at Echo. "You dare come in here with no shame? You are the reason we are here! If your city could do as they were told, none of us would be dragged into this mess. I should be sitting on my ass in the comfort of my own home right now riding out the winter. Instead, your father's foolishness has me riding the cold winds all the way to this shit-hole."

Echo stared right at him, refusing to back down — a trick he learned from Dazen, no doubt. "My apologies, King of Kogon, for not being more mindful of your ass. But it would seem there are more pressing concerns. Or have you perhaps forgotten your little pact with the highlanders up in Crata?"

Hanns' face was a picture of fury. "You insolent weasel! You lie!"

"I do not wish to quarrel with you. I simply wish to remind you that perhaps your country and mine share more similarities than you might think."

"I will have your head on a pike if you speak but a word to—
"

His voice cut short as again the knights drew their swords and pointed towards Hanns' long neck.

"Oh dear," came a familiar voice. "Is this what has become of my council when left to their own devices?"

Every head in the room turned. Hanns' lips quivered as he bowed his head low. "Lord Radiant, my deepest apologies. I did not know you had arrived."

The knights withdrew their swords from his throat, leaving

Hanns to fall onto the table, gasping for breath.

King-Radiant Evanon Lightfire walked into the room, hands clasped behind his back. Thick black hair trailed down his neck, resting atop a fur coat which cradled his shoulders. A groomed black beard covered a strong jawline. Sharp emerald eyes roamed the room with a sense of pity. He inhaled a deep breath through his nose before releasing it in an exaggerated exhale, wisps of water vapour curling from his mouth like smoke.

"Do you see that?" he asked.

The room grew deathly still, all eyes fixed on Evanon. Dazen clenched and unclenched his fists beneath the table. He wanted this man dead.

"My very breath is all but frozen. And it is not because winter is upon us," Evanon said.

His words hung in the air like a rain-cloud ready to weep.

"It is because Zur - the lifeblood of Zapour, our beloved star, our god and saviour, the foundation of our joined nations - fades. The heat of his warming light leaves us by the day, and do you know why?"

Nobody dared answer.

"He fades because somebody out there is murdering my Eagles," Evanon continued, his voice shaking with anger as he walked towards the empty chair. Only now did Dazen notice the form of the Queen Mother shadowing his steps, her sunken eyes darting to and from each respective king.

"For centuries this regime has survived," Evanon said. "For centuries Zapour has prospered underneath the veil of protection offered by their divinity! I too am but a tool wielded by Zur's own hand. Their Light is one with his own, and yet their flesh remains mortal. When one bleeds, so do we all! When one's Light fades before another can be named, our star weakens."

The air vibrated as if his words themselves carried a weight, but Dazen knew it to be a trick of Light and heat. Kron had used the very same tactic to intimidate Yvain at the gates.

"I will not sit idle while the world around curls into shadow. You are all kings and princes in name, but do not make the mistake of thinking yourselves above them. I allow you all to self-govern. I allow you all to have your own arms, to breed your own magic, to breathe the same air as us!"

Evanon paused, giving his words time to sink.

"Gallion is my ancestor. He forged this realm under the watchful eye of Zur's Light. He and his Eagles banished the Skae to the forgotten realms. And I am his blood. We are what keeps the sun shining in the sky. We are the pillars holding the shadows at bay. I would not see his image tarnished. I will not see all that he has created, mocked and spat on. All I ask is that you obey. And you repay me by allowing the very essence that bathes light upon your lands to perish at the hands of a rebel. An outlaw who never should have been born!"

The intensity around the room vanished as Evanon took his seat upon the final chair, twitching his head as if cracking a kink in his neck.

"F-forgive me, my lord," Gelvard said. "We all feel their loss very deeply. But if you wish to place blame and to seek vengeance, then I suggest you look towards Trost and the Glaive family. They are responsible for—"

"I am aware of their role in past events, Saelmere," Evanon interrupted. "I assure you, if there is disloyalty to be found, it will be dealt with accordingly. But I speak of a deeper strain of disloyalty among all of you that, if not handled this day, will continue to fester. I speak of rebels playing hero in Lesken. I speak of outlaws allowed to roam your lands free of check. I speak of secret pacts with the remnants of a fallen kingdom."

Evanon eyed each one of them. He turned to his mother, who showed an emotionless face before turning back to the council. "If you think you can hide your disloyalty from me, I assure you, you cannot. When I took over from my father as King-Radiant I sought to fix his mistakes. Never again will I allow what happened in Hirane to occur. If my laws are harsh, it is because you made them so!"

Evanon's chest rose and fell like the tide. He let his arm rest on his chair. "Let us begin with the matter at hand." He turned towards Kron, his emerald glare unwavering.

Kron stared back, his pupils shaking as they shrank.

"Where is he," Evanon said. "I know you have him. Bring him to me."

Kron's nostrils flared, his head lowered to peer at the King-Radiant's waist. He rose, unable to look him in the eye, as if under the fear of turning to stone.

In all his life, Dazen had never seen his father so flustered. Usually, it was *he* doing the intimidating, but looking upon him now, Kron may as well have been a child sentenced to his room for having misbehaved.

What had happened between these two in the past?

Kron gave a half-bow before heading for the door, his teeth clenched, mouth curling into a defiant snarl as he showed his back towards a man even more powerful than himself. Kron wanted him dead just as much as Dazen, maybe even more. That much was clear.

Why then did he obey like a dog on command? What did Evanon hold over him to make the great Kron Glaive shiver like a slave?

Evanon's speech lingered like a bad odour. What if he was right? What if their Light was linked to Zur's own? He could not deny the drop in the weather, the early winter. He felt his

Light fading in strength by the day.

Was their plan to bring down a centuries-old regime wrong? Perhaps it was he that was destined to bring evil upon the lands of Zapour.

No.

He would not accept that. Zur would not abandon this world to be lost under the oppressive thumb of such vile and evil creatures. He refused to believe in their supposed divinity. They were a lie, a ruse put in place to protect those in power. He saw clearly now what his brother had always seen. The King-Radiant was as fake as the puppets he commanded, a shadow of what Gallion Lightfire and his original Eagles stood for. But why then did Zur's Light fade?

The trail of unanswered questions continued to pile, forcing Dazen's mind off the matter at hand. The four remaining kings awaited Kron's return with impatience, Evanon's knuckles growing whiter the longer he took.

Yvain's rounded head entered through the door. He approached Evanon with quick steps, hands shaking with terror, but his mouth twitching with excitement. He whispered something into his ear before shuffling back as more figures emerged.

A dark sack, black as tar, covered the man's face, his teenage muscles pulled taut as he tensed against the constriction of the peridium cuffs at his wrists. Kron stood towering behind him. He pushed Raiz in the back as if he had never known him.

With a deft hand, Kron pulled the sack free, revealing Raiz's youthful yet refined face. His hair had grown long, falling down the side of his cheeks in locks of deep brown. The scar covering his eye stood out, peering into the room full of royals like it had a mind of its own.

Echo joined Dazen on the edge of his seat, their mouths

agape. Ancel looked as though he wanted to leap across the table and strangle him. He held his arm close to his chest as if experiencing the bone breaking all over again. Obeyun too leaned forward, his dark eyes squinting as he looked from Raiz to Dazen.

Dazen then made an active effort to stare at a wall. It was all he could do to keep himself in check.

"What madness is this?" Gelvard cried. "Traitor!"

Evanon waved his hands, and two bulky knights brushed a willing Kron aside to stand behind Raiz, holding him in a vice-like grip.

Then, much to Dazen's surprise, Kron bent to his knee. "Your Radiance, I have apprehended the outlaw responsible for the deaths in your order." From the outside he appeared calm and collected, but there was pain in his voice. "It is true, this man was once of Trost. But he has not been a part of my kingdom for nearly a decade. He was branded outlaw long before he committed such heinous crimes. I give him to you willingly, as a gift, to reassure you Trost stands united with Lumindal, and holds our oath." Kron returned to his seat.

Nobody spoke, but Dazen knew they were all thinking the same thing: It takes a cruel man to give up his own son.

Dazen watched as Evanon circled the room, his eyes never leaving Raiz's and Raiz's never leaving his. The two were locked in a mental battle worthy enough to be written in song.

Dazen held his breath, praying Raiz had the composure to hold his rage a little longer. He looked to the ceiling, hoping Veil and Isha were close to their goal.

Evanon ran a hand over the rough skin healed over the gash on Raiz's eye. It lingered there for what seemed an eternity as the two exchanged an awkward moment, before Evanon's hand recoiled as if struck by some unseen spark. Evanon's bottom lip trembled in a rare show of vulnerability. "So much potential," he said, taking a backward step, "wasted."

He continued to stare as if it were just he and Raiz in the room. "You do not even know what you are, do you boy?" he said. "What do you have to say for yourself? I wish to hear from the boy with guile enough to risk the safety of Zapour."

Raiz clenched his jaw and straightened his posture. "Your system is a lie, as are you," he said.

The whole room gasped as if he had struck him. Evanon remained calm, despite the insult.

"Your pets are no more divine than my father is brave," Raiz continued. "They are a farce, a shield put in place to protect your power so you may continue to rule without opposition. But you already know that."

If Evanon was bothered by the remark, he did not show it. "So young," he said. "So naive. Your mind has been poisoned, child. Tell me, who has infected you with these ideas? Who set you to the task of murdering my Eagles?" He laced the last few words with quiet fury, his eyes flickering to Kron.

Raiz laughed. "My father has not the courage to see the truth for what it is."

Evanon inclined his head. "I will get the answer from you, one way or another." He turned his attention to Kron. "I must admit, I did not expect to see you here today. Part of me believed you might have abandoned our agreement, abandoned *her*. And yet here you stand, giving up your own boy for her. I wonder what she will think of you, of what you have become."

Dazen watched through skeptical eyes as Kron lowered his head in shame.

"You have failed me, Kron," Evanon continued. "Your negligence led us to this. You could not even care for a single child."

"He is not my son," Kron said. "He never was. A fact you know too well."

Dazen felt a near overwhelming heat press against him as Evanon's rage boiled. "I think you are in need of a lesson, Glaive! I think we are all in need of a lesson." He raised his arms wide, smiling as he stepped back and glared down the length of the table.

"Yvain!" He called. "Bring me my wife."

Chapter 38
Isha

"**W**hat happened here?" snapped Veil, staring dumb-faced at the two dead bodies at Puk's feet.

Puk — obviously unable to answer — shrugged.

"They tried to escape," came a voice, "and he killed them. Good riddance too, filthy pigs."

Isha turned to see one of the half-naked women on her feet. She remembered her, the one with the crossed arms and shameful look on her face. She had fashioned herself a cloak and had the all too familiar look of vengeance in her eye.

Veil turned to Draz, who dragged a near-naked Salador by the neck and flung him onto the marble floor before the assortment of women. "What's the plan?" she asked.

Draz looked to Salador. "Where is the entrance to the Last Light?"

Salador crawled backwards towards nowhere in particular -- just away from Veil. "What nonsense is this? I gave you what you wanted, now leave this place."

Veil leaned down low, placing two hands on her knees. "But

we're just getting started. Tell us what we need to know, and maybe we'll leave your balls attached to your body when we're done."

"The tower? Can you not see it? Step outside, I'm sure you will find it plain as day."

"Do not think us fools! We know who your ancestors were. We know Gavienus built the Last Light. And we also know you have a secret entrance hidden somewhere within the Forty-Sixth Spear. Now talk."

Salador looked around with panicked gestures, asking for help that would not come. His line of sight settled on Isha, eyes narrowed with suspicion. "Do not trust her," he said. "She is a liar, the very best of them. Do you not know what she is? She is a Mystic. A witch. Why do you think Averardus held her in such high regard? She will turn on you once she gets what she wants."

If Veil believed any of the rubbish Salador was spitting, she did not show it. "You amuse me. The things a rat will say when trapped. You just all but confirmed our suspicion true."

"I — I do not know what you are talking about, I know of no such tunnel."

"Tunnel? Who said anything about a tunnel?" Veil said.

Salador's breathing doubled. "What use do you have for it? What could you possibly want with barrels full of black powder and...?"

He trailed off, as if everything clicked.

"You cannot be serious!" he continued. "That is a suicide. The King-Radiant will not have it!"

"And just what do you think the King-Radiant would do if he found out one of his pets keeps a large quantity of explosive powder oh so close to perhaps the greatest piece he holds in this game of power? I have half a mind to march straight to his quarters right now and inform him of your disobedience," Veil said.

Salador paled, his mouth twitching.

"Now tell us what we need to know, and maybe I'll spare your life."

"P-promise me."

"Come again?" Veil asked.

"Promise you will spare me, if I tell you."

Veil scoffed. "Very well, I promise I won't kill you afterwards."

"And my — uh — privates stay attached to my body."

"Hah! Your balls may stay attached to your body. But only because that is one sight I hope I never have to see."

Salador issued a low groan. "Very well," he said grudgingly. "I will show you the way."

Veil took a step back and nodded. She nudged Draz. "You're up."

"Huh?" Draz said.

"I said, you're up. Your plan... remember? The one you spoke of?"

"Oh, yes. Yes, of course. Ahem."

"I swear sometimes I think there's nothing under there Draz," Veil said, pointing towards Gallant.

Draz bowed his head low before righting himself.

"Draz has a proposition," he said, opening his arms in a welcoming gesture before the assortment of exotic women seated on the furniture before him.

Isha creased her brow.

"On the promise of freedom, will you help us?"

Veil palmed herself in the head. "This was your plan?"

Draz shrugged.

The women before them looked at each other, confused

expressions painted on their faces.

Isha felt for them. They were beautiful, no two the same, each distinctly different from the others. A Wishan woman with smooth black hair and dark skin sunk deeper into the furniture, using a pillow to cover her nakedness. Another with a petite figure and clear alabaster skin cowered in the corner, arms crossed over her breasts as she looked towards the others for support.

"Why should we help you?" said one of the women. Her chestnut hair was tied into a neat bun at the top of her head. She had a muscled frame and a strong jaw that accentuated her delicate face, which was caked with a thick layer of make-up. If Isha were to guess, she was a woman born of Kogon. Unlike the others, she had refused to cover up, her breasts on display. She moved with slow and controlled movements, as if it were all a play, and this her main scene. "I have a life here. A roof over my head. Food to fill my belly. What reason do I have to trust a group of thugs who have all but signed their death sentence by coming here?"

Isha could see their commitment wavering, all of them. She didn't know what Draz had planned, or how they could help, but she remembered what it was like to be as they were. Maybe not in the same way, but they were prisoners, just as she had been. "I was a prisoner here for eight years!" she said. "Locked in the Forty-Fourth Spear for the entertainment of men such as these," she gestured towards Salador. "Every day I dreamt of being home once again, of the fresh air. Of leaving this forsaken city! I had no voice, no family, no choice. But now I have all three. And Zur may strike me down, but I will spend every moment making sure these animals pay for what they did to me, for what they continue to do. Maybe you do not know what a life outside of here looks like, and I cannot blame you for that.

But know that there is so much more to this world!"

Veil stood open mouthed, her pale face staring at her as if she had just caught the sun in her hand. Draz was similarly silent, taking a step backward as if to let her have the show.

"I will help, if you will have me," came a voice. It was the girl who had come to Puk's defence, her doubt and anxiety replaced with a high head and a keen eye.

"As will I," came another, this time from the Wishan woman.

One-by-one the women opted to help, leaving Isha with a proud grin on her face.

Finally, it came to the woman from Kogon, who crossed her arms and tilted her head to the ceiling. "Fine, I will do what I can. But I do not see what use we will be."

Isha nodded and turned to Draz. "What, uhh, what exactly do you need them for again?"

Draz huffed a proud sigh. "Follow me."

Together the ladies formerly of the Forty-Sixth Spear worked with Draz, Isha, Veil, and Puk as they hauled barrels full of dangerous explosives up and down the winding corridors of the structure's inner sanctum. Threatened at knife point by Veil, Salador led them down a dark tunnel, hidden behind a series of other dark tunnels. Only the constant glow of a Shine-globe gave them any sense of direction in the dense under-dark.

"This is it," Salador said. "Take this north all the way to the base of the tower."

"Would you be so kind as to show us the way yourself?" Veil said, poking him with a light prod of her sword.

"Like I have a choice."

"That's a good Eagle. This better not lead us into an ambush."

"Of course it leads to an ambush. The Last Light is the most heavily guarded structure in Zapour! You are walking to your death!"

Veil sent another slice of encouragement prickling into his skin. "Lucky we have you to bypass such security and send us straight into its core."

"It will never work," he said, staring at the open wound on his hip as if he had never seen his own blood before.

"Just move," Veil said.

Isha worked in sync with the women she had coerced into aiding their endeavour.

It was tedious work rolling a barrel. Sometimes it would roll like a wheel down a hill, others it would falter and stutter, catching a stray rock or falling in some pit or crevice. Not to mention that at any moment the barrels could ignite and blow them all up. Draz had reassured them, however, saying the powder was only explosive when in contact with Shine. Since Veil and Salador were the only ones among them to use that particular gift, it made sense that they travelled at the front. Even so, Veil's tale about her unsteady and unpredictable Shine was troubling. Isha could already see the cracks starting to open. Through Veil's mirage of violent confidence, Isha could see the frail girl within, ready to snap.

She doubled her efforts, pushing the barrel almost by herself and watching the defiant lady she had come to know as Freya, standing with hands on her hips in the dust.

A shooting pain exploded through her shoulders. They felt as if one more step would cause them to drop off, but she kept going.

An eerie silence filled the tunnel as the fear of what they were about to do set in, the gloomy darkness beyond not helping. The rough clank of wood on stone was the only audible sound as each second seemed to stretch an hour.

"We, are, here," Salador said, hands on his knees and puffing as though this was the most physical exercise he'd had in years -- perhaps his life.

A shabby looking wooden door carved into the side of a particularly slimy wall of stone stood in their way.

"Now what?" Veil asked.

Salador unlocked and pushed on the door, which was just wide enough to fit a barrel through. Draz stepped in and waved the Shine-globe, checking both left and right.

"Now we climb," Draz said.

"Climb? Up there?" Freya said, waving her arms in a ridiculous 'you've got to be kidding me,' gesture. "The Last Light is as tall as the sky itself. There is no way I'm going up there, I'm done. Good luck to you."

Isha looked around at the ladies, covered in soot and shivering in the damp, murky under-dark. They leaned over the barrels, exhausted. They had done enough. "Let them go, this is not their battle," she said. "It is ours."

She took one of the swords Puk had acquired from a dead guard and moved for Freya. "Take this. I hope you will not need it. Have Salador show you the way out of this city. If he moves to escape, kill him."

Veil stepped forwards. "You can't be serious. This man is vile. This man is..."

"You promised to let him live, did you not?"

"Yes, but we aren't finished. You can't set him free, not here."

"Then what would you have me do?" Isha said. "They cannot come with us. It is too dangerous."

"Then let them leave," Veil said. "But the Eagle stays."

Isha moved to protest, but one look from Veil told her not to question her. Instead, she turned to Freya. "I am sorry. I wish I could have done more. This tunnel leads into the Middle Sector. From there, I suggest you find a way out of the city. You do not want to be in Lumindal this night."

Freya nodded, turning towards the other women. "Let's go. I know a place we'll be safe," she said. "We're dead if we stay."

Huddled together, they departed, the soft patter of their footfalls fading into the blackness.

Beside her, Veil sighed. "I hope you know what you're doing, Isha."

Salador shuffled his feet.

"Move," Veil said, shoving him in the back.

Together they stepped through the rounded door and into the base of the Last Light.

"Anyone up for a little stealth mission?" Draz said.

"Read my mind," Veil replied. "As long as I get to lead."

"Aye, Draz can live with that. Leave the barrels here, they're close enough. We need a clear path to the top." He looked to Isha, handing her a small hatchet. "The time comes to fight, don't hesitate."

"I will not," Isha said, surprised at the confidence in her voice. She lifted the unfamiliar weight of the hatchet, brushing a finger against the sharp metal. She recoiled, accidentally drawing a thin sliver of blood. Reassured that it was indeed sharp, she sucked her finger dry, tucked the hatchet away and motioned for Veil to take the lead.

The inside was not much different than the tunnel, though the musty tang of ages-old metal began to overwhelm the rest of her senses.

Isha followed Draz and Veil through a dark corridor, taking care to step lightly. She watched as Veil moved with practiced precision, her boots barely touching the ground before returning to the air.

The sound of laughter filled the tomb-like corridor. Veil pressed a finger to her mouth before creeping closer. She looked to Salador. "One word and Draz here will slit your throat."

Her sword drawn, she stalked the two shadowy figures at the end of the corridor. It was almost too dark to see, but before Isha could even see the outline, the laughter ceased, replaced by a soft gurgle and then a thud. Veil returned moments later, her sword glinting with a crimson wetness. She motioned them forwards and Draz began dragging the bodies away by their legs. Isha caught a glimpse of a face, with eyes open wide as the sea, but a stare as blank as an unspoiled canvas. Strangely, she felt no pity, nor did she feel satisfaction. She felt only emptiness, as vacant as the dead man's stare.

Once the bodies were safely tucked away, they continued forward. They reached the spiral staircase Isha had walked during her short venture here. She remembered catching a shivering child as their foot slipped on the climb, whispering words of hope in their ear. Words she had known to be false.

"What do we do now?" Veil asked. "We can't move the barrels up the staircase, it's too high."

"We don't need to make it the whole way up," Draz said. "Just high enough to dump the powder."

"Oh, sounds easy then," Veil said. "Dump a couple pounds of explosives into the belly of a burning inferno and get out before it's too late. Great. Perfect. Can't wait."

None of them spoke for some time after that. The words *'you knew what you were getting yourself into'* were left unspoken.

"There is another way up," Isha said.

She watched as everyone stared at her expectantly.

"All the Spears of Lumindal are fitted with elevator mechanisms."

"Hah!" Veil said. "Only Eagles would figure out a way to have to walk less." She nudged Salador, who merely huffed his derision.

"Draz has heard of these. Large pulley systems. Draz's clan worked with them back in Crata. Look for an opening on the wall," Draz said.

"We'll get lost before we find it," Veil said. "Are you sure one is here?"

Isha shrugged, turning to Salador.

The dishevelled Eagle balked, preferring to stare at his feet.

Veil grabbed his shirt, which she had since returned to him. "Where is it! Show us to the elevator."

Salador turned his head.

"You know what I am capable--"

"Shhh," came a cry from behind. It was Draz. "Quiet," he said, pressing his metal head against what looked like hard stone. He rapped a hand on the surface. "Hah! It is hollow."

Draz raised a fist and struck the stone hard. His arm fell through. The wall broke like paper as he ripped it apart.

"Your elevator," Draz said, surely smirking behind Gallant.

Isha took a peek. It looked nothing more than an empty room, though the wooden base hovered over the ground like it was floating, a fist sized gap of air on each side.

"Care to explain?" Veil said.

"See these ropes?" Draz said. "They're connected to a series of wheels up top and down below. All you have to do is pull." He pulled on the extended line of rope dangling from the ceiling. "And the plank moves up."

Isha watched the wood rise.

"It's like water from a well," Draz continued. "Only on a larger scale."

"Large enough to lift a few barrels?" Veil said.

Draz huffed a cocky sigh. "How do you think they built this place so high?"

"I always pictured a very tall ladder," Veil said, causing Puk to snigger in what was his version of a laugh.

"Something catch your tongue?" Veil said, before she too shared a laugh at her own stupidity. "Come to think of it, a giant ladder never sounded very plausible."

"Leave the engineering to Draz, will you," Draz said.

"As you say, master Greysword," Veil said.

Isha watched with curiosity as Draz's demeanour changed at the mention of the Greysword name; his hands gripping tighter, his feet shifting. She chose to ignore it, figuring there were more important matters at stake right now.

Their trip back to the door went by surprisingly quick, it seemed they had nearly done a full lap of the structure. She wondered how the girls were doing. Were they nearly out of the city yet?

The four of them casually rolled exploding barrels of doom across the eerie under-dark of the Last Light. Once all the barrels were safely at the foot of the contraption, Isha relaxed, issuing a sigh of relief as she wound her shoulder around in its socket. "What now?" she said.

"Load them up, maybe two at a time, and pull," Draz said.

"We need someone to go up with them, yes?" Veil said.

"Aye, we do. Any volunteers?"

"I will do it," Isha said, more from wanting to be involved than any act of courage."

"Very noble of you," Veil said. "But I'll go. I'm the lightest, and we don't know what's waiting for us up there. Besides, Raiz will kill me if I let anything to happen to you." Veil hopped onto the platform. "Don't worry, if anyone's up there, I promise to make it quick." She twirled her knife around her knuckles.

Puk and Draz took hold of the rope. Isha took the rear, making an effort to at least contribute as the two brutes' muscles bulged with the pressure. "Tug twice if you want us to stop, three times when you want to come back down," Draz said.

They pulled, Veil and the barrels of black powder vanishing out of sight.

After what seemed like an eternity, the rope moved twice. They ceased their efforts, Draz tying the rope in a knot around a knob.

As they waited, Isha rapped her hands against her thigh. What if she was dead, their plan over, dozens of men just waiting for them to rise? Perhaps even now they scrambled down the staircase, manoeuvring into an ambush. What of Raiz? How would he cope with the loss of the woman he loved?

She rapped faster, so fast that Puk had to intervene, catching her wrist on the way down and holding it tight. She smiled at him in return, once again comforted by his silent presence.

Just as her worries had all but washed away, she felt the rope in her other hand tug three times. "Finally," she said. "Draz, it's Veil, she is alive."

"Of course she is," replied the metal-head. "Takes more than little men playing with swords to kill her."

Together they let the rope slowly slip beneath their fingers. It felt lighter this time. The platform returned into eyeshot, the sturdy plank of wood coming closer and closer until she could almost touch it.

What returned was not Veil, or rather it was Veil, but with one significant difference: she was painted red. Tiny droplets of blood spattered her face. Her clothes were soaked through with blood, and her hair was covered with the stuff, colouring her short, brown locks a dark shade of red. Even her lips were red, as if she had literally bitten into skin.

"W-what happened up there?" Draz said, his tone serious.

Veil shrugged. "I killed them."

"Them? How many were up there? How did you—"

"Are you going to help me load up these next two barrels, or do I have to do everything myself?"

The group mechanically loaded another two full barrels onto the platform, Isha inadvertently keeping her distance from the blood-soaked assassin.

"Isha," Veil called. "You're with me this time, I could use the company."

Isha pressed her lips together as if to mouth the word 'but', then quickly thought the better of it.

"I assume the two of you can handle a heavier load," Veil said, turning towards Draz and Puk.

Draz bent into a row, shaking his head in resignation as he prepared to pull.

Isha stepped onto the platform, Veil and the powder by her side. She watched as the contraption worked its magic and they climbed higher.

Veil sat crossed-legged, controlling her breath as if she were not covered in blood.

Isha impatiently waited for the platform to come to a stop.

"I'm not like Raiz," Veil said, breaking the silence.

"Excuse me?"

"Your brother. I'm not like him. I'm not good for him."

"What do you mean? Of course you are. I see the way you two look at each other."

"I thought that were so," Veil continued. "I thought he was good for me, that he could help me. That we could be together. But we can't."

"What do you mean?"

Veil paused again, and Isha could see the struggle within. "There's no cure, for my condition I mean."

"You don't know that."

"Yes, I do. I think I've always known. Me and Raiz, we've tried everything. Peridium doesn't stop me like it does others. My Shine, I can't drain it, can't control it. Every day I struggle to hold it back. One of these days it's going to kill me, kill someone I love."

"You cannot think like that!" Isha pleaded.

Veil took her by the wrist. "I'm a killer Isha! Nothing more. I was a fool to think life could offer me anything better. I don't deserve someone like Raiz. He's always fought for something, fought for you. Everything he has ever done has been to make sure that you return home safely. He's always had a reason to kill."

"Right," Isha said, not quite understanding.

"That's not me. I have only one singular reason to fight."

"And what is that?"

"Revenge. I have no sister to rescue, no family to go home to. Mine were taken from me. Taken by the very bastards we mean to end today. I have no higher purpose, nothing to believe in. I'm a killer through and through. A bomb ready to explode, like these barrels beside me. I've accepted it, and I need Raiz to as well."

"That is just not true. What are you saying?"

"I need you to tell him I'm sorry. I need you to tell him I want him to be happy, to find someone else if he needs to."

"He loves you. You know he loves you."

"I know he does, that's why I need to end this before he realises what I am."

"He will not—"

"Just promise me! Promise me you'll help him have a life, a

real life. After all of this is done. Promise me you'll care for him like he cares for you."

"Of course I will, but—"

Veil tugged twice on the rope and the platform stopped still. The pair walked out into another corridor and Isha nearly choked on her own bile as the pungent smell of death flooded her nose.

Body upon body littered the ground, almost piled on top of each other. Blood oozed from open wounds as dead hands clutched empty air beside them. There had to be half a dozen, no, nearly a dozen bodies, all fully armoured, armed with deadly sharpened metal that now rested peacefully at the feet of their corpses.

"Promise me," Veil reiterated, casually unloading the barrel from the platform and joining it with the others.

Isha was too stricken with fear to respond. She stepped awkwardly over a severed arm. Her jaw dropped at the sight of teeth marks running down the side of another man's neck where a small chunk of skin was missing.

I promise.

The next two trips went by with minimal conversation. When asked what had happened, Isha could only shake her head. Draz seemed to understand, not pressing the matter. "So, are we ready to do this?" he said.

Isha nodded, overcoming her uneasiness.

Veil placed a bloody hand on Draz's chest. "There's a problem. All the barrels are safe up there, but I don't have the strength to load them onto the supporting platform by myself."

"Aye, Draz can help you there. Though one of us will need to stay to guard the pulley. And him," he gestured towards Salador before turning to Puk. "Lad, are you able?"

Puk's eyes went wide, looking towards Isha and shaking his

head.

"Do not worry, Puk," she reassured him. "I will be safe with them. It is only for a moment, I promise."

Puk nodded in slow motion, tightening the grip around his blade.

Draz moved for the slouched Eagle sitting defeated in the darkness. He cut into a length of rope and used it to tie him to a nook in the wall. "Take us up," he said once they were all on the platform.

Slowly, Puk's face faded into nothing as Isha rose to an uncertain fate.

"This is it then," Draz said, staring into the belly of an inferno.

They were a little more than half-way up the length of the Last Light, judging by the depth of the frothing liquid bubbling like a volcano below. Once the elevator had stopped and they had manoeuvred the barrels past Veil's carnage, they had made their way towards the searing heat that was the centre of the structure.

Isha ran a hand down the grey-black peridium that encompassed the entirety of the Last Light's inner sanctum. It ran like a tube from top to bottom and made Draz's helmet seem an insignificant piece of junk in comparison.

The interior was even more interesting. They peered into a wide hatch large enough to fit several people through. The silvery glow of burnt-out Shine moulded into the peridium like honeycomb in a beehive.

"How is this even possible?" Veil said, issuing a low gasp.

Draz cleared his throat. "Once expended, Shine turns into breen. When Light is emitted from a body, it can no longer take liquid form. It solidifies and can be moulded, but after the heat dies away it becomes practically useless, at least on the offensive."

"Then why use it here?" Veil said.

Draz ran a finger over the breen coating. "Breen can be used as a buffer against active Shine. It traps it, stops it from solidifying. Think of this tower as one giant Shine-globe."

"This is insane," Isha said.

Draz grunted. "Insecurity breeds insanity."

"It's barbaric," Veil said, as if she had not just slaughtered a dozen Blackwings in cold blood.

"It's a weapon," Draz said. "And a bloody big one at that."

"How do you know so much?" Isha said.

Draz bowed his head and placed a hand on the peridium wall. "Draz used to be a mercenary of Clan Greysword. It was often our job to hunt down wielders of the white-light."

"This can't stand tall any longer," Veil interrupted. "Too long has Zapour been held hostage. Too many people have died under its destructive breath." Her hand began to shake, and she quickly hid it behind her back.

Isha placed a reassuring hand on her shoulder. "So, how does this work?" She turned towards the loaded barrels.

"Well," Draz said, "you see, where peridium reflects Shine, this baby ignites it." He thumped the top of the barrel. "They are opposites in a sense."

"So, what you are saying then," Isha ventured, "is that we now stand half-way up the side of what is basically an active volcano ready to pop?"

Draz placed his hands on his hips. "Well, when you put it like that, yes."

"Great. Perfect," Isha said.

"It's not a perfect plan, Draz admits."

"Not a perfect plan? This is lunacy."

"Go," Veil said, her demeanour changing.

Isha stared at her as though the word 'go' was not yet in her vocabulary.

"I can do this myself," Veil continued.

"What are you talking about?" Draz said.

"You too, Draz. Take Isha and go. Help me line up the barrels and then leave."

"Draz will not leave you—"

"I said go! I'm dead soon anyway, and you all know it!

"Veil, don't talk like that," Draz said. "Raiz will find a cure."

"Don't make me send you down that hole in pieces Draz!"

Isha wanted to protest, to stand her ground and refuse to leave her side. But she was right. There was no point in three people dying where only one was needed. But Isha had come to like the violent assassin, enough perhaps to call her a friend.

Veil must have planned for this. She must have known this to be her fate before coming here. That is why she wanted Raiz to move on. She knew this day would be her last.

Isha clasped Veil's hand in her own, the two sharing a look of mutual respect before her fingers slipped free.

Draz came next, head bowed low.

"Fancy removing that helmet for me?" Veil said. "I absolutely cannot leave this world without seeing that ugly mug of yours at least one time, if only so I can hold it against Raiz."

"Huh! Tell you what. You survive this and maybe, just maybe, Draz will let you see the beauty behind the metal," Draz said.

Veil scoffed. "You don't have to live in fear, Draz. I know what happened to your father. But don't let his death define you. You're meant for greater things."

Isha watched as Draz shied away.

The two returned to the platform, pulling three times on the rope before slowly descending the elevator shaft, the sight of Veil's mischievous grin and the sound of her cracking knuckles vanishing quicker than she could blink.

They were perhaps half-way down the shaft when she felt it jolt. The platform shook. Her feet were swept from beneath her as she fumbled over Draz in a tangle of limbs.

"What was that?" Isha cried, her voice cracked. "Was it Veil?"

"No, she'll wait for us. There must be a problem down below."

"With Puk?" Isha said, scrambling to her feet.

"Aye."

"Maybe he is just having trouble hauling us down. It cannot be easy pulling this much weight by yourself."

"No no, it's not that. This system is rigged with so many ropes a child could pull it."

Draz went to speak on, but before he could finish his sentence the platform dropped in a sudden whoosh of motion. Isha's heart sunk as she was thrown off her feet.

The floor descended faster than she could think. She let out a shrill scream, holding onto Draz like a king would his crown.

The platform continued to stop and start, the ropes bending and shaking in the air. The constant uncertainty was overwhelming, the thought of smashing into the ground at such a speed biting at her composure. With another jolt, the two were pulled downward. Her body thrashed against the wooden platform as she slid to the side. Her legs dangled off the edge, the gap widening on one side as her feet swung like a pendulum.

Draz recovered, snatching her forearm and pulling her back to the relative safety of the platform.

The mechanism started and stopped, falling for one moment

and then steady the next. Isha and Draz held on to each other like long lost lovers, their fates out of their own hands. All hope rested on Puk. She didn't know what was worse, the threat of the dawning and inevitable explosion from up above, or the gruesome and heart-shattering fate that awaited them down below.

After another three or four rough stops -- which she was sure would cause bruising later -- the lift finally made it to the ground. Isha and Draz poured out onto the smooth tiling like a returning soldier would his bed.

Puk's shadow loomed over them, causing the pair to push through their dizziness. She moved to embrace him, but her foot caught on something. She looked down to find a human leg strewn across the opening of the hidden elevator. She regained her senses and backed up. She hoisted the hatchet Draz had given her, ready to defend herself. Two bodies lay lifeless at her feet. Blackwings.

She heard the heavy sound of panting and turned to see Puk. He stood over the rope, his left hand tightly wound around it. His right hand was shaking, holding his stomach, which she now realised was covered in blood.

Isha rushed to his side, wrapping her arms around the back of his neck. He winced, his throat gurgling as he bent over to ease his pain.

"Oh Puk, what have you done to yourself?" she said.

"He's managed to hold off two Blackwings is what he's done. All with one arm too, by the looks of it. It's a bloody miracle we made it down at all is what it is. Where did you find this one?"

Isha was too distraught to answer, already ripping a piece of cloth from her outfit and putting pressure on Puk's wound. "We have to get out of here!" she said. "Help me carry him."

"What about him?" Draz said, looking to Salador, who was still tied to the wall.

Isha looked him over, turned, and moved to aid Puk. "Leave him."

"What! No! You cannot leave me. I will die. Take me with you," Salador pleaded.

Isha ignored him, her and Draz placing an arm beneath Puk's armpit and scuttling towards the door they had come through earlier.

After an exhausting stretch of walking, Salador's pleas for help faded. Puk shrugged free of her and Draz's grip, holding his wound with one hand and curling his fist around his sword with the other, saying with actions rather than words that he could now move on his own.

Isha ran to where she was sure the opening was only to find it bolted shut.

She prised at the hinges, working her dirt-filled fingernails beneath the cold metal to no avail. "Locked."

"It can't be," Draz said. "It was open a moment ago." He spat on the floor. "Damn Blackwings must have found it."

The sound of multiple footsteps echoed through the cylinder-like chamber. They grew louder until the faint outlining of metal plate became visible in the distant light.

The three of them huddled together in the darkness. Puk's free arm was drawn around her waist, pulling her behind him even as he bled through his linen arming coat.

Draz growled as several Blackwings inched closer from either side, surrounding the trio and trapping them in a corner. "Come on then you dogs! Have at it! Who wants to die first!"

The crazed mercenary jumped in front of Isha and Puk, arms spread out in a wide arc with a sword in one hand, axe in the other. "Who be brave enough to take Draz on, come and--"

His voice trailed off as a Blackwing thrust forward with his right arm, only to lose it a second later as Draz's axe slashed down with all the might he could muster. "That one's for my father. Now, who's next?"

The soldiers hesitated, but rallied together, the armless soldier wailing a desperate cry as he cowed to the back of the group. They came at him with full force and Isha felt Puk lash out, blocking a strike meant for Draz's head.

"Gahh, bastard!" Draz cried as one hacked at his shoulder, drawing blood.

Even in the face of defeat, Draz refused to give up, throwing his body into the fray recklessly, knocking two to the ground in the process. He head-butted another, metal ringing against metal, with Gallant coming out the better.

A hulking figure appeared from within their ranks, capped with a helmet of black steel, and holding a long silver broadsword with two hands.

Draz tripped over one of his own victims, dropping his weapons in the process. He backed away, his ass dragging along the ground as he awaited his inevitable death.

Isha refused to look, squeezing her eyes shut. She didn't want Draz to die. It was her fault. She was useless, she may as well be armed with a spoon for all the help she had been. She held onto Puk's waist, finding at least some comfort as they waited for death.

Only death didn't come. She opened her eyes. The heavy-set figure from before was still standing, cutting and chopping with the ferocity of a wild boar. Only it was not Draz's limbs on the chopping block.

Crimson blood splattered against black metal as the giant longsword was used to deadly effect against the Blackwings.

Isha stood, hand covering her mouth. Puk and Draz were

not ones to squander an opportunity, taking up arms to fight alongside the crazed Blackwing intent upon killing his own men.

With him on their side, the battle was over quickly, Draz embedding his axe deep into a man's torso in one last scream of bloodlust.

Isha clutched her chest, hoping she didn't look as hopeless as she felt while Draz and Puk circled the mysterious newcomer.

"Who are you?" Draz said, re-firming his grip on his axe.

The newcomer thrust his longsword into a nearby corpse before letting it clatter to the ground. With a slow hand, he moved to his helmet, unclipping the straps before removing it entirely.

"By Zur's stinking breath it can't be," Draz said.

"Aroha!" Isha cried.

"Missed me?" Aroha said, running a hand through her long braids.

Isha didn't know her brother's burly companion very well, but she had forgotten just how pretty she was. Even in the current circumstances she felt a pang of jealousy creep through, wondering how someone could have both the strength of an ox and a face to make even the wealthiest of princes weep with lust.

"What in Zapour are you doing here?" Draz said.

"I'll explain later. What's the plan? Where's Raiz? Where's Veil?"

"Well, you see, about that..."

As touching as the sight of a familiar face was, the reunion was cut short when a sound equivalent to a thousand drums beating at once rang through the chamber, sending a shockwave that shoved man, woman, and stone flying into the wall.

470

Chapter 39
Raiz

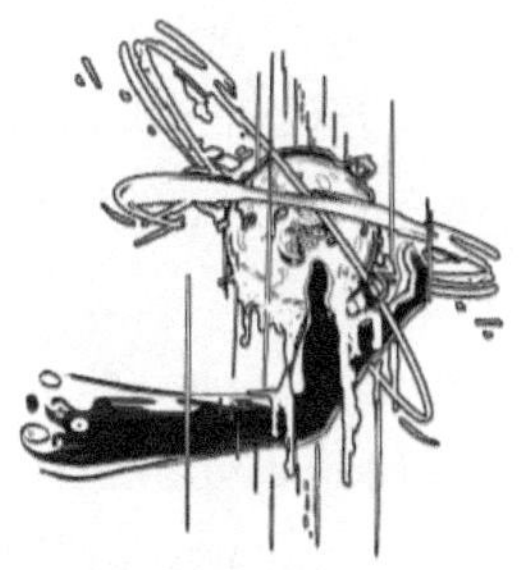

Kron Glaive, King of Trost, master of the white-light, and Raiz's father, had been reduced to a babbling puddle of tears.

Raiz wanted to kill him. He deserved death after the way he had treated him, after abandoning his own daughter to a life of slavery, and now all but sentencing his own son to death. But watching him now, he felt only pity.

What could make the great Kron Glaive weep so? What foulness did the King-Radiant hide behind that curtain of red?

The whole room held their breath. He met Dazen's gaze and found the same blank and confused expression as his own. He took the opportunity to wiggle the key down his sleeve. It felt cool against his skin, his own saliva sticking to it as it made its way toward his hand. He had smuggled it in beneath his tongue, spitting it into his shirt when Yvain turned his head.

He surveyed the room, finding what he was looking for. A thin sliver of light shone between two drapes. If he could get himself free, it should be enough to fuel his Shine. He still held onto a well of it, but the peridium cuffs made it nearly impossible to access. It felt as though his life-force, the very air he breathed, had been cut off.

The curtain moved, the trimmed velvet at the bottom tugged to the side in one swift motion. The King's Herald led a figure into the room. Raiz couldn't see the form clearly, but a flimsy yellow dress flowed out from behind the Herald's flanks. The spindly looking man stepped away, revealing a woman so beautiful Raiz could hardly breathe.

Her hair streamed down her sides in long braids of brown so dark it was almost black. Her skin was a light shade of honey, dark enough to hide an imperfection, but pale enough that it was clear it had not touched Zur's warmth in a long time. She was tall, but not an intimidating kind of tall. Her features looked light and fragile, as if she were made of glass and might break if dropped.

Raiz scrunched his face into a ball, wondering why this woman had been brought here. Wondering why that hard exterior his father was known for holding had been liquified.

Kron's face dropped further upon seeing this mysterious woman. He reached out with one hand as if grasping at a ghost.

Raiz knew then who this woman was. He knew his whole life had been a lie. His stomach sunk as his suspicions were confirmed. The woman opened her eyes, her lashes like a butterfly spreading its wings, splashing waves of violet.

Mother!

Nearly every royal in the room gasped, stricken with a dread so foreboding it stretched like the silence before a battle.

Evanon rose from his throne with all the guile of a man in his prime who knew he could not be defeated. "My kings, princes, and princesses of Zapour. I believe in all my years, I have not introduced to you my wife, my queen. Celia Lightfire."

He extended his arm, opening his palm as if expecting a cheer from an audience.

Raiz's head throbbed, his mind buzzing with a thousand thoughts. He watched as Kron's thick, muscly arms began to tremble and shake. His lips were pressed tight, tears running down his cheeks before mixing in with his beard.

If grief and sorrow could be painted, they would be a portrait of Kron's face right now. His features slowly gave way to an untamed rage barely held in check by some long-learned sense of self-control.

Raiz could see clearly now, Evanon was baiting him. He wanted Kron to react, he wanted him to explode. To reach across the room and try to throttle him. That would be the excuse needed to end him, to end Trost. Not that he needed much excuse.

It was all beginning to make sense. Kron's inaction when Isha was taken. His reluctance to fight back, to resist against the King-Radiant. He did it all for the love of his wife, for Raiz's mother. Raiz knew it in his bones; Kron loved this woman more than Cova loved the night. It did not excuse what he had done, did not make up for a lifetime of neglect and abandonment, but at least Raiz had a reason for his father's actions now. A cause. And a solution.

Celia looked a vision of distress. Her voice was lost beneath her hand as she bent to her knees. She looked at Raiz and her eyes swelled. She exhaled, tilting her head in a look only a mother could give to her son.

"Why are you doing this?" she said, turning back to Evanon. "Why am I here? And what have you done to our son?"

Raiz's neck snapped to the side, his pulse heightening to a crescendo at hearing those last two syllables.

'Our' son.

The world around him began to spin, the room a muddle of lines and shapes. The puzzle that had been his life, each piece once scattered and lost, was slowly beginning to fit together once more. If he believed before that his life had been a lie, that feeling now hit him again tenfold.

He could hear their voices, close as they were, but they sounded like faint echoes in the distance to him now. His fingers tingled with a numbness.

He began to rally, to draw himself back to his broken reality. He studied the King-Radiant then. He had the same angular jaw as himself, the same chiseled facial structure, the same emerald eyes set deep within their sockets.

It was true then. Kron was not the father he had always thought him to be, not to Raiz anyway. He had always wondered why he and Dazen looked so different, and now he knew. Dazen's blood still ran through his veins, it was true, but only half.

This was his mother, a woman he, Dazen, and Isha had long thought dead. Yet another lie told by the King of Trost. Though he supposed to Kron, her fate was as much a death sentence as any.

But who was she to Raiz now? Did she love him still? Why hadn't she been there for him, why was she here?

"Let him go!" Celia said.

It took Raiz an extra moment to realise she was talking about him. She rushed over to his side, pulling at his shackles.

"What is this, Evanon?" she cried. "This is our son. You cannot treat him this way!"

Evanon walked closer, his hands clasped behind his back he spoke with an unnerving calmness. "A son you stole from me. A son you took as a babe and sent scurrying across the plains of Zapour to be raised by your former lover. A fact I have not forgotten."

"You were never fit to be a father, you never will be," Celia snapped.

If the King-Radiant was wounded by the comment, he did not show it. He simply stood straighter and inhaled a deep breath through his nose. "A man should be aware of his capabilities, both strong and weak. Alas, fatherhood was not for me. And so, I allowed your little stunt to go unchecked. But make no mistake, I knew. I knew, and I understood where your true loyalty lied. But you are mine. Forever and always I will love you. I remake that vow right here before the ears of all the kings of Zapour. You. Are. Mine."

Kron rose to his feet then, flexing his muscles in an attempt to regain some semblance of his former self. "You may hold her body captive, but you will never hold her heart, you tyrant."

Raiz, like everyone else in the room, looked on with wide eyes. He didn't think his father had it in him. It was true, Kron had physical strength equivalent to that of a bull, but his emotional spectrum had always been lacking in depth.

"Is that so?" Evanon said. "You amuse me, Glaive. That is probably the reason I have kept you alive this long. You think yourself my equal? That you are more worthy of her love? Tell me then, how is it Raiz came to be shackled so? Because," he paused to scratch his head, "I am certain it was not by my hand."

Celia stopped trying to twist the metal cuffing Raiz's hand, turning to face her former love.

Kron went to speak, but released only a low gargle.

"What does he mean?" Celia asked. "What have you done?"

Again, Kron could only gargle and mutter in response. "Y-you do not know the burden of..."

"The burden!? Do not speak to me about burden. I have

spent half of my life in this place so that my son may live. So that our children could live. What have you done to my son?"

"The boy's fate was his own doing," Kron rambled. "It was his choice to run from me all of those years ago."

"Years?" Celia bent down to a knee, clutching her chest as if her heart were tearing in half. "I entrusted him to you. For you to raise, away from this place. How long has he been on his own?"

Kron looked away, unable to stare his love in the eye.

"And now you bring him back to this place? Beaten and chained?"

"I did it for you!" Kron said. "Everything I do is for you, to keep you safe. To keep our kingdom safe."

"Oh Kron, you are truly lost. Do you really believe it would be my wish to see my life put ahead of my own child?"

"I — I could not bear to lose you again."

"You lost me the moment you placed my child in danger!"

Evanon snickered in the background, clearly amused by the spectacle he had created.

Raiz grit his teeth. Evanon was clearly trying to embarrass him. To showcase his hold over the five remaining kingdoms. What better way than to make Kron grovel?

Evanon had won, the whole room knew it. He had put on a performance, with the entire upper royalty of Zapour as the audience. He wanted this done publicly, he wanted them all to watch as he broke the toughest man in the room. Who would dare challenge him after such a display?

Raiz looked around the table. The Saelmeres looked on with guilty pleasure. The Balstos were of similar mind, if a little more empathetic.

Raiz only just now registered the mix of familiar faces in the room. Zur's beard, what was Obeyun doing here? And with a crown, too.

Echo was the most surprising, however, the young man he had entrusted to care for Hector. Where were the two idiot twins? How did a mere boy become the king of all of Zuton? Raiz looked towards the boy's fist. Was that... Light in his hands?

Evanon raised his arm in the air before planting a heavy fist on the table, causing every eye in the room to look his way. He let their gaze linger, building the tension even higher. "Overseers of Zapour, I have brought you all here for more than just appraisal. There is a threat to our lands. A man calling himself the Sun Prince has usurped the throne in Yagos and has declared his intentions towards us to be violent. We must settle our differences and re-unite as one under me."

Raiz watched a mixture of emotions flood the room. Zapour had never been an empire. Ever since Gallion Lightfire defeated the Skae and formed the Six Kingdoms, each had always held a separate ruler. Of course, all were sworn by oath to the King-Radiant and his Eagles, but no King-Radiant in history had declared himself Emperor. It seemed with the Last Light active once again, Evanon's boldness had no bounds.

Kron grumbled again. "You pathetic little swine. This is a ruse. There is no threat from Yagos. That continent has been dormant for years. We will no longer be bullied by you! You are not fit to be King-Radiant. You never were. Nor was your father! You are a stain on your ancestors' name."

Time seemed to stop as the whole room stood and stared at Kron. Raiz found himself to be one of those staring. Where was the coward who had abandoned his only daughter upon the fear of this man's wrath? It seemed seeing Celia again had broken him. There was nothing left but to stand and fight.

Evanon recovered from his shock. "Ah, the famous Glaive

temper. It would seem your new Emperor no longer has need of your leadership."

"I'll gut you where you stand," Kron said.

"Guards, apprehend this man on the charge of threatening the King-Radiant."

Raiz felt Kron's rage as if it were his own. For once the two of them were in agreement. This man — his father — needed a sword through his heart.

Kron put up a fight, stray fists swinging in the air as four Knights of the Golden Talon surrounded him.

"Do not do this Evanon!" Celia continued to plead for her former lover. "If you love me, you will spare him!"

Dazen rushed to his feet, fists balled before his head in a brave display of defiance. "If you kill him, you will have to kill me too."

Raiz cursed under his breath. Things were getting way out of hand. There was no sign of Veil having destroyed the Last Light yet. Raiz didn't much care for Kron, but he couldn't sit idle while his half-brother was murdered as well. He had to act.

"Lay down your fists, young Glaive," Evanon said, taking a step towards him. "It is a noble act to want to defend the honour of one's father. But his reign is finished. I have no quarrel with you, do not make one."

"I will die before a single drop of his blood spills," Dazen said, glancing at Raiz and nodding.

"Then so be it," Evanon growled, motioning for his guards to pursue.

Raiz shook his hand, clutching the key and twirling it around his fingers.

A knight thrust at Dazen with the point of his halberd, but Dazen was no slouch in combat. Even unarmed, he sidestepped, grabbing hold of the wooden shaft and pulling it free of its holder, elbowing him right where his temple would be behind the hunk of shining metal. He twirled it around his body in a glorious show of skill before striking at the baffled guard with the intent to kill.

Evanon stood tall, cackling with laughter as if this were all just sport to him. In a sudden whirl of movement, the door to the great hall smashed open and in came a swirl of black and gold. The Knights of the Golden Talon surrounded the two helpless Glaives in a ring of death. A thin pocket of air separated Kron and Dazen from at least a dozen waiting instruments of murder. They stood back-to-back, Dazen's lone halberd their only defence.

The situation was helpless, but Raiz had no choice. He had to act. He twisted his fingers, placing the key into its home and hearing a welcomed click.

Free of his bonds, he moved for the sliver of light. His head bent back as a familiar tingle ran through his entire body. He opened the drapes as the warmth of Zur's fading breath rushed over him, mixing in with his stored Shine like oil to fire.

Reinvigorated, he moved to help his brother. Before he could unleash the fury buried not so deep beneath his skin, however, a blinding light flashed. Raiz covered his eyes with his elbow, shielding himself from whatever threat lurked within.

Slowly, he opened his eyes. Knights looked around in clueless horror. Celia had stopped weeping to stare as Evanon dropped to his knees, clutching at his shoulder.

Echo Levic stood behind him, his outstretched arm shaking as if he had just been drawn from the deepest depths of Abyss. His fingers burned with what to Raiz was a familiar heat. They pointed to where Evanon had been.

"That was for my father," the boy turned king said.

Raiz cursed him then, for not being a better shot.

Evanon rose to his feet, left hand still clutching at the small hole in his right shoulder. His earlier canter had been all but erased. He glowed a deep red hue, the room around him a victim of his radiant heat. If Echo's Light had been blinding, staring at the King-Radiant in his current state was like looking directly into the sun and hoping for mercy.

Evanon turned and ran to Echo, who now stood frozen with fear, his earlier confidence shattered. He reached for his throat, grabbing him and hoisting him above his head. Echo scrambled to break free, clawing at his grip to no avail. Raiz could see the life draining from his frail body like a match losing its flame.

Raiz felt a rush like none before threatening to overwhelm him. His restraints no longer holding him back, he called for his foe. "Father! Turn and face me! You will pay for your sins."

The King-Radiant's neck twisted in a sinister, serpent-like manner. His dead eyes looked to Raiz, the red now akin to a flame of Light around his chiseled muscles. With little effort, he flung a helpless Echo into the wall, the lad landing with a sickening crunch; alive or dead, Raiz didn't know.

Evanon turned towards Raiz, death in his stare. "Why must you all continue to defy me? Why must all challenge my reign? Do you not see? We are gods among men. Tools, yes, but gods none the less. To kill us is to doom this world to a fate far worse than any I could oversee. I brought you all here to show you the truth, to re-shape the monarchy of Zapour so that all would believe one destiny. But I see now my vision is not possible. So, I will create a new vision. I will bring down the monarchy, each and every one of you. And I will start anew. All shall fall so that we may thrive!"

The knights surrounding Kron and Dazen widened their stance, some peeling off to surround the entire table of nobles, stepping inch by inch closer to their new targets.

Gelvard's amused grin faded quicker than a platter of cooked chicken placed before his nose as he and Ancel went on the defensive. "Lord Radiance? What is this? We have ever served you faithfully!"

"Kill them all!" Evanon shouted.

The room erupted in a fit of chaos. Kron reacted first, unleashing a torrent of molten Light upon the three closest knights, burning through their weapons and armour like melted cheese. They screamed in a cry worse than agony, but were only replaced by three more, who Raiz noticed had donned rounded shields.

Kron repeated the same barrage of Light, shooting it from his palm with increased vigour, recapturing his youth. This time though, the beams of Light ricocheted against the shining metal shields, changing trajectory and burning three holes in the ceiling.

Evanon acted next, the red aura surrounding him expanding and gaining in weight. He looked set to unleash a massive wave of Shine, wiping out the entire room in one fell swoop — Knights of the Golden Talon included. He hesitated however, sparing a glance at his wife — Raiz's mother.

Raiz wasted no time sprinting towards him, tendrils of white-red Shine frothing at his fingertips like lightning crackling in the sky.

He tackled his father in a spear-like embrace, his head lowered as their two auras combined into one.

Raiz screamed, the heat coming from his father's body too intense to maintain a grip though. He lurched free from his grasp, holding his weaponised hand above his father's head, ready to bring the full might of his Shine thrashing down on his skull.

And then came a bang.

It echoed loud across the room, thundering like an earthquake and snatching the legs from anyone standing, sending them crashing to the floor.

Evanon was first to recover, having already been planted square on his arse before the explosion. He turned towards the source of the commotion and bolted towards the wall, one dead arm dangling loosely at his side. He thrust his good arm forward, sending forth a massive bolt of Shine. It burned a man-size hole through the wall like it was butter.

Sparing only a quick glance behind, Evanon stepped through it, leaving the massacre that was the throne-room to play out without his hand.

Chapter 40
Raiz

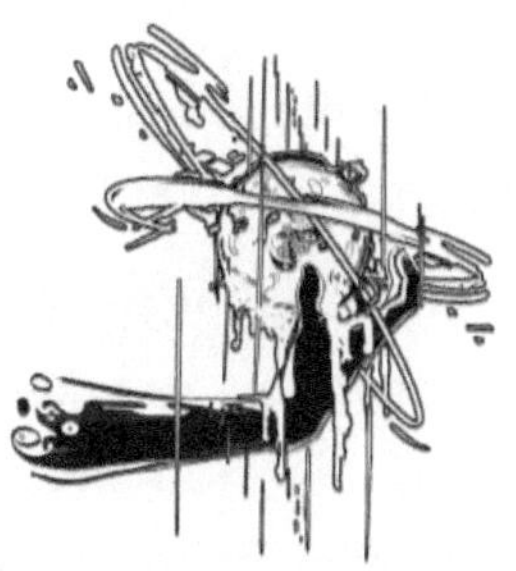

Raiz didn't know what to think, his mind caught in a tangle of lies and truths. He watched his father — his real father — disappear into a cloud of dust, leaving the mess of his own creation behind him.

Raiz didn't really know much about his newfound father, the King-Radiant. He knew only what Celik had told him. Evanon was responsible for every injustice in his life. It was his disciple who had taken his sister from him. It was his family who ended the False Kings War, who murdered Veil's parents and caused her affliction. It was his own father who had been the one to order — perhaps even perpetrate — the Shine-bombing of Lesken.

Celik was right, Evanon needed to be killed, and Raiz had his blood running through his veins. Was this why his Shine was different to others, ever tinged with red? Why his Shine was morphing into something too powerful to comprehend? All because he had been marked with the blood of a King-Radiant.

Did that in turn make him evil? Was he destined to a fate

beyond his consideration the moment he was born into this broken world?

No.

He refused to believe in a fixed destiny. He was in charge of his actions, he alone, no matter the blood he carried. It didn't matter before when he believed Kron to be his father, why should it matter now?

He took three steps towards the hole, ready to chase him down and end his reign. For some reason, each step felt heavier than the last. It wasn't because he was tired. He burned with more energy than ever. He stumbled, almost tripping over himself and wondering what in Zapour was causing his legs to falter.

And then he heard it, the sound of his sobbing mother. The desperate roar of his elder brother — his real brother, despite only sharing half his blood. There was no mysterious weight bonding his legs to the ground, only the realization that he was no longer alone in this world. He had somebody else to fight for, a family to love. Justice could wait a moment longer.

He turned, planting his feet firmly on the marble and feeling the weight drop away. The knights had regained their footing and were engaged with Zapour's royalty. Rays of white-light were bursting from fingertips with no regard for personal safety. Raiz saw Ancel Saelmere place two hands behind his back in an all too familiar motion before unleashing a barrage of Light, burning through three knights who had so thoughtfully lined up in front of him.

Gelvard and Hanns had managed to salvage a halberd and a short sword respectively, poking and prodding at any who dared come close while protecting a hard-pressed Valter. Obeyun stood guard over his own mother, disarming and throwing roundhouse kicks at any who came within reach as though he had trained for this moment his entire life.

Raiz searched for his mother. He found her huddled in the corner, hands over her head and shaking with fear. He moved to help, but the knights were not after her. She was in no immediate danger.

He turned and saw Kron throw another barrage of radiant Light recklessly into the rounded peridium shields, sending shimmers of violent sparks ricocheting into the surrounding walls.

The ceiling creaked and groaned as small pieces of rubble began to give way and drop to the floor, one particularly large chunk crushing an unlucky knight as he made to cut at the throat of a fortunate Obeyun.

Ancel became more and more enraged, surrounding himself with a thin veil of Light similar to what Raiz had once used against him. Only Ancel had turned defence into offence, wrapping the veil into an overly large gauntlet and using it to punch through armour. An agile knight moved to intercept the crazed prince, tackling him into the curtain of red, Ancel's hand inadvertently setting it alight and sending plumes of smoke drifting over the battlefield that had become of the throne-room.

Raiz found Dazen then, swinging his Light-fuelled halberd around in a wide arc, fending off perhaps six or seven Talon knights in the process. Sumaya fought by his side, lunging with all the grit and vigour she could muster. The pair, back-to-back, covered each other's flank as though they had been married their entire life

Echo lay crumpled against the wall behind them, looking dead to the world, blood oozing down his cheek, his golden crown broken, the pieces shattered all around him.

Raiz leapt into action, clenching his weaponless hands and

charging into the fray. He had never much fancied himself an adept swordsman, the metal felt awkward and unnatural in his hands. He preferred the element of surprise and the look of sheer horror upon his opponents' faces when he brandished a spear-length glaive born of pure Shine. He did as he had imagined, waving it threateningly and cutting visible lines of red and white through the air. Today was no different it seemed. A scared knight tripped over his own feet and fell backward before his Light as Raiz cut him in two.

He wasted no time, moving towards Dazen and making quick work of the four remaining knights. It took no more effort than an extended wave of his hand, cutting through their armour like ribbon. He barely even felt the blade as it sliced through both skin and bone.

Dazen looked at him as though he were Zur himself.

"What?" Raiz said.

"Y-you are glowing," a dazed Dazen said, mouth open and one arm draped over Sumaya.

Raiz looked down and noticed his body had taken on a white-red hue, the red in his Shine now more prominent than ever. "I don't, I—"

His fumbling speech was cut short as a sword swept through the air, cutting at where his head would have been if he had not ducked.

Raiz responded by shearing the man's hand clean off, leaving him staring at the stump which Raiz's glaive had so kindly cauterised.

"Evanon left," he managed to say, turning back towards his brother. "Do you think that quake was Veil?"

"It had to be, they must have done it. They must have brought down the Last Light."

"We need to find them, now."

Dazen nodded. "First we need to save them," he motioned towards the still struggling royals.

"We owe them nothing, let them die," Raiz said, only realising after the words left his mouth how callous that sounded.

"I like them even less than you do, but we need them if we are to take this city. Are you with me?" Dazen said.

Raiz took one last look behind before issuing a half-nod.

Together Raiz and Dazen muscled their way through chunks of rubble and dead bodies. Kron was the first in line, the big brute showing no signs of his true age as he hacked at a peridium shield with relentless vigour.

Raiz and Dazen almost didn't know how to intervene. The King of Trost's wild and chaotic swings were so unpredictable even Kron himself probably didn't know where they were headed next.

Eventually, one of his adversaries strayed too far from his reach, leaving him vulnerable as Dazen crept up and poked him through with his Shine-infused halberd. Raiz watched with curiosity as Dazen stopped to loot his kill, only to emerge moments later with his famous long and short steels firm in his grip. He flashed a brazen smile towards Raiz before lighting his sword like a spark of flint to a pyre.

As one they picked off another knight, melting through his armour with ease. The two of them ducked to the ground as a beam of Light brushed past them, singeing the hair on Raiz's head in the process.

He patted his head free of the miniature fire and brandished a circular peridium shield he had taken from a dead knight, taking care to avoid the metal. Grasping the wooden handle, he angled it before his head as another bolt of Light came sizzling towards him. Like sunlight on a mirror, it bounced off with a metallic ring and shot straight back in the direction it had come, running through the poor soldier where his heart had been. Raiz was beginning to understand why Draz was so attached to his helmet.

He whisked around, ready to continue the fight. He lifted his glaive into the air and moved to bring it down on the next unlucky soul.

He stopped short, however, when he came face-to-face with Kron. The enraged King lifted his sword in the air with gnashed teeth. Raiz thought he was going to swing, to end him now for all the trouble he had caused him.

But he, too, stopped short. They stood staring at each other even as the cries of war echoed through the chamber, neither backing down for fear the other would take the opportunity. It wasn't until Dazen stepped in that they lowered their weapons.

"Enough!" Dazen shouted. "Sort out your quarrel another time, we have a common enemy who needs our attention."

Kron huffed a dismissive sigh before turning his efforts towards the room around him. Gelvard and Hanns were hard pressed, fending off a trio of knights, but other than that, the screams began to fade. Obeyun stood triumphant, an array of dead bodies, and what Raiz could only assume were brains, spattered haphazardly before his feet.

Kron moved first, running over and stabbing an unaware guard in the back as Gelvard and Hanns finished off the last two knights in the room.

Everyone paused to catch their breath, heavy panting the only audible sound above the creaking of the walls.

Sumaya rushed to Echo's side, checking for a pulse and holding him in a tight embrace when she found one. Kron moved for Celia, who brushed him off with a shrug. Ancel had recovered from his fall and was limping back to his father's side. But it was Hanns who wept the hardest, bending to his knees as he leaned over the dead body of his son, Valter. The lanky eldest son to the Balsto family lay dead atop a pile of black and gold armour. His leg was cut open to the bone, a pool of red dripping to the floor. That was nothing, however, compared to the gaping hole in his chest where he had been struck by a blast of Shine.

"My son!" cried Hanns. "What have you done to my son!"

The remaining royalty gathered around the fallen prince, half-wanting to pay their respects and half not knowing what to say.

Gelvard turned to Raiz. "This is your doing! You brought the King-Radiant's wrath upon us! You and your wretched family."

Raiz puffed out his chest. He felt his aura growing, as if it had a physical weight to it now. He remembered Dazen calling it 'the Flare' but he hadn't had time to question him properly on the subject. Gelvard seemed to sense it too, taking a backward step as if Raiz were pushing against him with some unforseen barrier. "You are all blind," Raiz said, taking advantage of the situation. "Blame me if you will, I will bear the burden. But do not delude yourselves. Zapour was a model of insecurity long before Evanon. Zapour is broken. You have seen it for yourselves. Maybe the Eagles were great once, but no longer. They are a fabrication, an illusion put in place to preserve their power."

Hanns stood up from the carcass of his son, tears streaming down his cheeks. "Why should we believe you, Glaive? Or should I say Lightfire? The King-Radiant's blood runs through your veins. Who then should I take vengeance upon for my son's death? The heir to my kingdom! Evanon will pay for this,

I swear it. But these hands yearn for blood now, so why should I not take his son from him as he did mine?" He extended his claw-like hands in front of his body, bloodshot eyes shaking with bloodlust.

Raiz pivoted and snarled, his Shine-glaive still glowing red-hot.

"Enough!" came a voice from the side.

The room turned to see Obeyun standing atop the wooden table where only a handful of minutes ago everyone had leisurely been seated.

"You are all fools! The lot of you," Obeyun said, projecting his voice.

"And who are you?" Gelvard said. "I have never heard of any half-skinned king."

"My name is Obeyun. Head of Clan Omoru. Warchief of Zhanbu. And Northern King of Wisha."

"Never heard of you. You should head back to the mountains where the dirt-skins belong," Gelvard responded.

"If mocking me helps to sate your ego, then do so knowing you mock the entire nation of Wisha," Obeyun said." My words carry the weight of my nation, you would do well to heed them. For too long have we hidden in our mountains and forests, pretending we are not a part of the land you walk upon. Too long has my country suffered in the face of men like you. No longer.

"I have suffered through the brunt of Lumindal's regime for the past eleven years. Held captive and put on a pedestal as people both insulted and admired me. No longer! If you think insults will put me in my place, then you must try harder, for my skin is much thicker than your own, no matter its colour."

Raiz relaxed his posture, content to let this mysterious man his sister had called a friend speak his piece.

"I do not speak up this moment to incite a war," Obeyun continued. "I speak in the hope of creating peace. Peace between the five remaining nations of Zapour."

"We already have a peace," Gelvard interrupted.

"Is this," Obeyun waved an open hand towards the carnage of the throne-room, smoke still floating through the air as the last of the curtain turned to ash, "what you call peace?

"The King-Radiant has made his choice, and he has chosen to abandon his oath. We can either stand together, united as one, or we can stand opposed, fighting individual battles, and be picked off one-by-one. Make your choice."

A long minute of ashamed silence followed as almost every powerful figure in Zapour paused to consider their options.

To everyone's surprise — Raiz more than others — Kron was the first to respond, taking measured steps towards Gelvard and holding an outstretched hand in a sign of peace.

Gelvard looked his dishevelled rival up and down, walking in a semi-circle as if to test his motive. He turned then towards his son, Ancel, limping at his side. His arm looked as though it had been re-broken, crushed beneath the weight of the knight's bulk. He held it tight, cradling it in his other hand. Gelvard turned to his cousin Hanns, who was still weeping over the body of his dead son. Finally, he met Kron's hand with his own, the two clasping in an audible clap.

"What is this, some play on a stage?" Hanns interjected. "My son is dead!"

Sumaya spoke next, appearing beside Dazen and standing tall. "Let us rebuild the alliance that should have been. My men will follow me, but you must treat Echo. He will die without medical attention."

Obeyun nodded, and the elder lady he had come in with moved to Echo's side. "Leave him with me," she said. "I will treat the boy."

"So, what is your grand plan, eh?" Gelvard said, looking at Obeyun.

"I travelled here with over one thousand Bakai," Obeyun said. "The Bakai are Wisha's greatest warriors. And they are prepared to die for me."

Dazen pushed past his father. "We have three-thousand strong camped in the glade by the hill. Two-hundred wield the Light."

Gelvard balled his fist. "Why so many, Glaive? Expecting trouble?"

"Trouble seems to follow wherever Saelmeres lurk," Dazen bit back.

"You little weasel, I will—"

"Enough!" Obeyun bellowed. "Gelvard, how many do you number? We cannot take the city without you."

Gelvard took a step back. "I have five-thousand by the lake. Three-hundred with the Light."

"Not expecting any trouble there," Dazen scoffed.

Gelvard shrugged.

"I have a handful of my own," Sumaya said. "Two-thousand or so. They will follow me."

"It is not enough!" Hanns interrupted. "The walls of Lumindal are too high and thick. There will be no taking it."

"We need a combined assault," Dazen interjected. "If we can co-ordinate our armies with men on the inside to open the gates, we stand a chance."

"The Saelmere banner will not fight side-by-side with a Glaive!"

Kron grunted in agreement.

"My White-Swords will go with Obeyun and Sumaya and their men to the southern gate," Dazen said. "You and Hanns take the northern. Once there send a rider to your men and we will attack from each flank." He paused, staring Gelvard directly in the eye. "If even one of my men so much as catches a glancing arrow from yours, I will personally cut your throat."

Gelvard smirked, huffing a loud belly laugh as his fat jiggled. "To peace!" he said, holding an imaginary cup in the air.

"And what of the King-Radiant?" Hanns said. "I will not trust anyone but myself to end him."

"He will head to the Last Light, I will follow him," Raiz said.

"You? I am to pin my hopes on a mere boy?"

Raiz tensed, extending his aura until it covered him almost completely in red and white Light. "I can handle my own."

Hanns shrunk, offering no retort.

"Then it is settled. The city falls," Dazen said, sheathing his steels as if he were placing a new-born babe back into its crib. "But what of the Eagles? What of the prophecy? What if they truly are linked to Zur himself? We cannot kill them."

"That is a lie," Raiz said. "How can you not see, Brother?"

"Not all of us are willing to risk the fate of the world on a hunch. I am more than skeptical, but centuries worth of religious order cannot be so simply discarded as myth."

"The boy makes a point," Gelvard said. "I heard talk of a gathering on the Forty-Second Spear. I would say they will be held up there for the siege. We can decide what to do with them after we take the city."

Dazen and the gathered royals nodded.

The newly formed alliance broke off into two.

"Raiz, a word," Dazen whispered, gesturing him forward.

Raiz obliged. "What is it? You know my stance on those creatures will not falter."

"This is not about them. This is about something else."

"Then speak, and make it quick, I have a king to kill."

Dazen went quiet, bowing his head low. "There is something you must know, before you leave."

Raiz shook his head and flailed his hands, urging him to spit it out already.

"Veil is not up there on her own," he finally said.

"Yes, I know, Draz is with her."

"No, that is not what I meant. Isha is with her."

Raiz felt the radiant heat within him return three-fold. "What is she doing here!?"

"I could not... I tried... she would not take no for an answer."

"Not good enough! This is no place for her! What was she thinking? What were you thinking?"

"This was her own choice! She was coming here with or without my permission. You know how she gets."

"But she could die!"

"I know Raiz! But she has Veil and Draz watching over her, as well as the mute."

Raiz paced, pulling at his hair. "I will find her, and I will bring her home safe."

He moved to leave, wanting to waste no more time on senseless talk, when Dazen grabbed his arm.

"Raiz," he said. "When all of this is said and done, things will be different. I promise it! I will make everything right again."

Raiz released himself from his brother's grip, sparing one last glance at his mother's violet eyes as they flickered with uncertainty before he vanished into the hole his father had made. He had so many questions for her, so much to still find out. He only hoped he had time enough left.

Chapter 41
Raiz

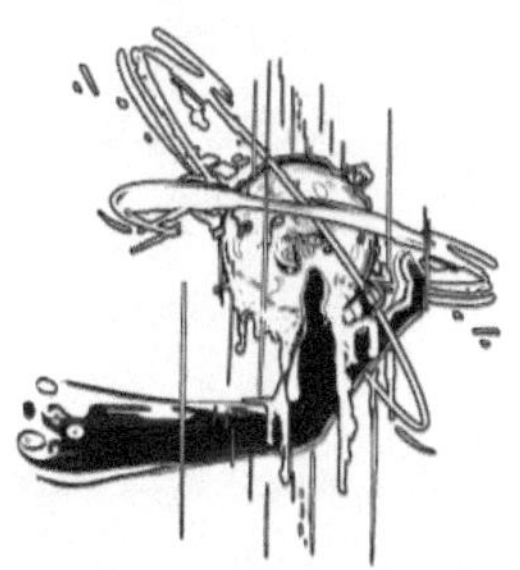

The ground felt light beneath him. Raiz could feel a new sensation compelling him forward, a familiar yet distant power growing inside of him. His heart thumped in his chest. His Shine was changing, morphing into something else entirely.

Zur's heat beat down on his body as the god of light began his decent from the lonely sky, feeding him the last of his strength. His fingertips tingled with seemingly unlimited power, the red hue now more prominent than ever.

He pressed forward with unnatural speed, fuelled by a power he did not yet understand, he made for the black streak staining the skyline.

It was still standing, an aggressive blackness staring down at him from its immeasurable height. Did that mean Veil had failed?

His question was answered as he drew closer. A large crack lined the side of the enormous structure. It ran down its length like a lightning bolt, splitting the hard iron down the middle. A slow-moving hand of liquified white-light oozed from the jagged splinter. It ran down the side of the tower like magma from a volcano.

Raiz cursed, doubling his speed before coming to a stop at the foot of the tower. Dozens of Blackwings flailed around the base, their clueless expressions searching for direction.

He paused, looking for a way through, but finding none. He didn't have time to think up a plan. Any sense of rational thought was thrown out the window as the urgency of his situation took hold. He pressed forward, taking advantage of the disorganised line of soldiers still trying to process the breach.

He re-formed his Shine-glaive and caught the first two unawares, not even stopping to watch as they dropped to the ground behind him. The four in front of him did not attack, they barely even raised their swords in defence, covering their face with their hands as if Raiz was the sun itself.

He didn't make it far before another contingent rounded the bend to cut him off. He was trapped between two fronts. He held his glaive high, ready to smite any who dared come close. But he was wasting too much time. His friends needed him.

The Blackwings closed in, stepping foot by slow foot in one moving wave of black. Raiz snarled a defiant growl, but their increased numbers seemed to give them a renewed confidence.

Raiz bit into one who stepped too close, slicing his neck with his glaive. But the dead Blackwing was only replaced with another. He swung a wide arc, forcing the circling line back a step. One lashed out at him, the metal tip of a halberd drawing a shallow line of blood up his shoulder.

Raiz recoiled, regretting his decision to forgo a stealthy entry. He saw a glimmer of movement blur behind the line of black. It was subtle, but it was there. Raiz breathed in through his nose, sniffing the air before brandishing another sinister smile.

Before the Blackwings could react, a nearly transparent tail whipped into them, sweeping half of the line off their feet. Raiz pounced, silencing the fallen with his glaive as Spike's hide returned to its natural moss green.

"I knew you would find me, boy," Raiz said, nuzzling the pricket under its chin. Spike let out a comforting yelp before leaping upon his next victim, biting into his plate with a sickening crunch and thrashing the hapless soldier up and down.

Raiz held his hand out, dripping some of his new-glowing Shine into Spike's maw and watching with pleasure as he licked it clean.

With the guards dispatched, the two made their way to the tower's entrance. They ran through a shadow filled corridor before any more decided to chase.

Led by the light of his own glow, he continued forward. He came to another pool of light and heard a crunch as Spike bit into the glass casing of a Shine-globe, guzzling the Light down in one gulp.

Raiz laughed and went to scold the pricket when a murmur sounded in the distant blackness. Thinking it to be more Blackwings, he charged, not content to let any man stop him from achieving his goal. He growled a war-cry, all sense of secrecy already lost through the radiance emanating from his moving body.

A large knight stood between himself and his destination. He raised his glaive ready for yet another culling, but the figure was unmoving. Either through a puzzling feat of bravery, an unmatched sense of duty, or by the sheer force of fear before death, the knight held its ground, planting two massive feet in a brace against his attack.

"Raiz, is that you?" the figure in black said.

Raiz's guard dropped at the mention of his name, his Shine-glaive vanishing as if it were mist. He knew that voice. "Aroha?"

There was no mistaking her brutish femininity. Her bright hazel eyes were tinted a shade of red, though Raiz noticed the red was only a reflection of his own glow. She huffed a pleased sigh through tight-pressed lips.

"It is you," she said. "I had a feeling you would find your way here sooner or later."

Raiz looked to her chest and clenched his fists as the golden crest of an eagle's outspread wings stared back at him.

"Raiz!" came a voice from the darkness. Isha rushed him, wrapping her arms around his neck. "Ow!" she yelped, recoiling. "You're... so hot."

"Isha!" Raiz responded. He wanted to accept her embrace, to show her his love, but he looked down at his still-glowing hands. He shook them violently, as if that would somehow turn them off. "What are you doing here? You should be back in Illidor, it is not safe."

"Spare me, little brother. I of all people know what life here is like. I came because I can help."

"If you know what this place is like, then you should never have come! You cannot even wield Shine."

"I do not need a lecture from my little brother about what I can and cannot do. I am more than capable of handling myself."

Raiz grit his teeth, knowing too well an argument with his sister was like punching into a stone wall.

"Is that Raiz Draz hears? 'Bout time you showed up."

A ragged looking Draz limped over, clutching his right leg with one hand. A jagged crack similar to the one lining the length of the Last Light ran down the side of Gallant. It was a miracle it was still intact.

"You're harder to put in the ground than my sister is likely to listen to sense," Raiz said.

"Aye, Draz may not be touched by the Light, but there's iron in his bones, be sure. Will take more than a knock to the head to bring Draz down," he muffled.

Raiz noticed a fifth body present in the chamber. Puk hissed a cry of pain that sounded like a gargle. He was laid down and leaned against the wall, one hand clutching at a wound to his abdomen.

"What is wrong with him?" Raiz asked.

"He was hurt defending us," Isha said, moving back towards Puk in an effort to console her suffering friend. "I need to get him out of here or he will die!"

"I can get them out," Aroha said, cradling Draz in her arms.

"Draz could use a softer pillow," Draz said, resting his head against Aroha's armour. Aroha tightened her embrace, causing Draz to wheeze.

"Be happy you still have your teeth," she said.

"My brother is leading his troops in a charge through the western gate. Meet up with them if you can and see Puk gets aid."

"I will see them safe," Aroha said, stamping her foot before turning to leave.

"Wait!" Raiz called. "I have already been betrayed once. I must know, your armour. Are you one of them again? Or is this just a guise?"

"Be at ease, Raiz," Aroha said. "It is a guise. My brother had trusted friends here. I got into contact with them, and they slipped me into the castle. Once I heard word of your capture I waited here for my opportunity."

Raiz stared through skeptical eyes. "So, you have not abandoned us?"

"Abandoned? No. I just needed time to process what happened, to think."

"Do you still blame me for what happened to your brother?"

Her jaw clenched tight. "No, I do not. And I think I know who is to blame."

"Who?"

"I think it was Celik."

Raiz gasped. "You have proof?"

Aroha shook her head. "Just a hunch, be careful of him."

Raiz nodded and turned to Isha. "There is something else you must know."

"What is it?"Isha said.

"It is our mother."

"Our mother? Our mother is dead, long ago."

Raiz shook his head. "She is alive. I do not have time to explain, nor do I fully understand myself. But she is alive, be sure. The King-Radiant calls her wife. If my instinct proves correct, I think he has held her against Kron for years. That is why he never came for you."

Isha stood frozen. Raiz could practically see her mind working to put all the puzzle pieces in place.

"It cannot be true," she said. "Mother is alive?"

"Yes." He wanted to tell her more, to tell her the whole truth. That Kron was not his father, that he was the true heir to the Light Throne, but the words never left his lips. Some words were better left unsaid, at least for the time being.

"Raiz," came a call from behind, which he knew to be Draz. "It's Veil. You must go to her."

"Where is she?" he cried, snapping his neck around.

Draz pointed his index finger towards the ceiling. "She's up there, alive or dead Draz doesn't know, but that blast, it—"

He trailed off.

"She is alive, believe it. Some people are even harder to kill than you," Raiz said.

"But the tower," Draz said. "It still stands. We have failed. All our effort has been for nothing. If the tower still functions, we will have nothing left."

"You did not fail. The Last Light has a fracture. It is split down the middle and oozing Light. One more push and it will be finished."

"Then go!" Draz said. "Go to her, end this madness once and for all."

Raiz shared one more lasting look at his friends and family, savouring their faces while they yet drew breath, then he left.

His legs felt like wings as he raced up the black steps. Spike ran by his side, his four stubby legs matching his pace. The tower was several times larger than the Moon-spire. Finding Veil was like looking for a particular sword in the graveyard of a battlefield.

"Veil!" he shouted repeatedly, until his voice grew hoarse and his lungs could carry no more breath. Every level he was met with the same empty response, the distant groan of a wounded building inside a bottomless pit of blackness.

He cursed to himself. The structure might collapse at any moment. He rounded another bend, creeping through another corridor of darkness.

Nothing.

Maybe he had passed her? Maybe she was somewhere below, buried beneath a pile of rubble and Raiz had missed her? He dismissed the thought. He would know if she was close. He would just know.

His nose twitched, and he smelt the rusty tang of blood. He followed it, rounding a corner leading to a trail of corpses. He pegged two fingers over his nostrils, the stench overwhelming his senses. He sifted through the dead, praying that Veil was not among them.

This was definitely her work. No other could slice up their prey with such delicate and precise cuts.

"Veil!" he shouted. "Are you here?"

Spike's long neck perked up, then the pricket bowed low and crawled nose-first into a dark corner. Raiz followed, knowing Spike had likely caught her scent.

"R-Raiz? Is that you?" came a croak from the inky-blackness.

"Veil! You are alive! What happened here?" he said, rushing to her side and removing a chunk of metal covering her legs.

"Why are you here?" she asked.

"I came to help."

"Get out," Veil shouted.

"What?"

"This is not your fight anymore. It never was. You have your sister back. You should go, go and live a life with your family. This tower is my burden to carry, my right to destroy. It took everything from me. I have nothing left. But you, you have a life waiting for you. You can start anew."

"You can have that too, Veil. If you will just—"

"No, this is my end. We both knew it was coming. Please Raiz, let my death have meaning."

"No, I won't have it. I won't leave you. If you want to kill yourself, then you'll have to take me with you."

"Raiz, don't be such a hero! You don't have to save everyone! Some people are just meant to die. At least let me go at my own design, let me have my vengeance."

"Vengeance? Vengeance is not worth your life! You may not think your life has meaning, but to me it does. I don't want you to go. Stop your act of self-pity and let us see this through together."

Raiz felt a shudder creep down his spine. "If there is anyone who should be wallowing in self-pity, it should be me. You want to hear something? You know Kron? He's not even my real father. You want to know who my real father is? Evanon. The King-Radiant is my bloody father. And he very nearly just killed everyone at the council. Oh, and my mother's alive, there's that."

Veil's expression went blank, and for a moment she may have just forgotten what she was about to do.

Before Veil could respond, a surge of energy swept the room. The tower shook with some unknown force of immense power. The very air itself began to rise. Raiz felt at the peridium wall holding in the mass of Shine, his strength fading the longer his touch lingered. The Shine was surging upwards like a stream flowing against the slope.

"It's him," Raiz said. "He's at the top."

Spike removed a piece of rubble from the wall. White-light rose from within like a slow-moving river. Spike opened his mouth, filling his gullet with the oozy white substance.

Veil's hands were shaking, her chest glowing with infused Light. "Raiz, it's coming. I can feel it. There's still a chance for you. You must leave me."

Not knowing what else to do, knowing no other way to calm her down, Raiz wrapped his arms around her and pressed her tight. "No," he said.

She did not recoil, did not pull away from his overbearing aura. Instead, she collapsed into his arms as if she had nothing more to give. She melted into his chest, her warmth burning hotter than his Shine ever could.

"Let us finish this. Together," he said, kissing her lightly on the top of her blood-stained head.

She nodded, taking his hand and hopping to her feet.

Together they climbed. Raiz draped one arm beneath Veil's as they dragged themselves to the top. Veil's ankle was sprained, perhaps broken. But Raiz would gladly carry her burden, for she had forever carried his.

The walls grew narrow, and Spike's bulk was too great to continue. They came across a large, open window. Raiz whistled, motioning for the pricket to climb outside and meet them at the top. The intelligent creature understood, clawing at the opening before making himself scarce. Raiz wanted to climb with him, but Veil was too injured, leaning on him for support.

The tower continued to surge, as if charging up with power. Raiz had seen this before, or at least the aftermath. He couldn't let it happen again.

"We're nearly at the to—" Raiz said, before another quake swept his legs and sent him crashing into the wall. It was pure luck that he managed to shield Veil from the brunt of the fall. "We must hurry!"

Raiz felt at Veil's pulse. It was racing, but the wildness had calmed somewhat.

"I see it!" Veil said as they approached the end of the staircase. A large dome-like structure encompassed them. A wall of cylindrical peridium shot through its centre, puncturing the roof like an arrow through its target. Raiz found another set of steps pointing at a steeper angle. He took her hand and ran.

Chapter 42
Dazen

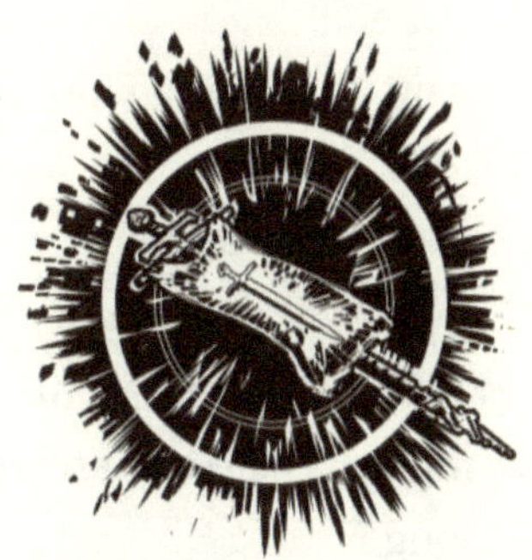

Lumindal was in chaos. With the King-Radiant's disappearance and his entire personal guard wiped out, there was no leadership, no organisation. Dazen took advantage, leading Sumaya and Obeyun down the Fiftieth Spear. They carried Echo's unconscious form under their arms. Obeyun's mother had done what she could, bandaging his head to stem the bleeding, but he was not safe here, none of them were.

Kron followed behind, though he seemed too traumatised to lead, constantly checking on Celia. Dazen looked at his mother, a million questions buzzing in his mind, questions that would have to wait.

Together they made it to the base of the Spear, where he met with Gale and the rest of his guard.

"My lor — Dazen," Gale said. "You are covered in blood. What happened up there? The Last Light, it is falling."

"The King-Radiant has gone mad, he tried to kill us all. Come, we must move quickly. We need to reach the southern gate and prepare for an assault on Lumindal."

Gale's eyes widened, though he nodded and moved to organise the rest of the guard into a protective ring.

Dazen watched as Gelvard and Hanns departed in the opposite direction. He had to trust they would hold to their promise, he had no choice.

"Obeyun," Dazen said, moving in close so that he was only a breath away from the Wishan. "My sister counted you a friend. I trust I can call you the same?"

Obeyun nodded. "Isha is like a sister to me. I would be glad to call you a brother. My Bakai will see us through the gates, though I suggest we make haste. They are disoriented for now, but that will not last long."

Dazen pointed over Obeyun's shoulder. "There is a stable just beyond this wall, once we have the horses, we make a charge through the city."

As Obeyun began ordering his men, Dazen turned to Sumaya. Her face was wrought with worry and confusion. She had cut her dress at the knee, allowing her to move without worry of tripping. She gripped a short sword tightly in one hand, its tip still wet with blood.

"Sumaya," he said. "I know this is not the time, nor the place, but I wanted to say I am sorry. I have not acted like a man deserving of your hand. I will do better. I will be better."

Sumaya remained impassive, though Dazen thought he saw a slight hint of surprise in her expression, a faint flicker in her emerald gaze. "We are all a victim of our circumstances," she said. "It is what we choose to do about them that defines us. You have done nothing to suggest you are anything but the man my brother thinks you to be. Though my concern right now is only for Echo. Help me see him to safety, to clean this mess, then we can talk about the future."

Dazen's mouth edged into a smile, but he nodded,

motioning for Gale to begin the charge.

They were met with little resistance at the stables. A couple of Blackwings stood guard, but Obeyun's Bakai ripped them apart like animals. A giant of a man, larger than any Dazen had seen, thrust his spear into the nearest soldier, impaling him through the stomach before lifting him over his head and slamming him to the ground with the force of ten men.

Dazen continued forward, glad they were on his side. He found Brock still saddled and leapt onto the war-horse, cutting him free and watching as others did the same. The man who had impaled the Blackwing left, returning shortly after atop a stallion black as a thundercloud and larger even than Brock.

Dazen spurred Brock into motion, the others following his lead. Fortunately, the city of Lumindal was like a cone, its streets sloping slightly downward when moving away from its centre.

Their momentum carried them through the streets. Ignoring frightened citizens and alarmed soldiers, they bullied a straight-lined path toward the southern gate. Dazen spared a glance over his shoulder. The Last Light was bent, leaning to one side. Liquid Shine ran down its surface, the sheer amount of it forcing its way out burning through iron as it dripped onto the Spears below.

People were out in force, their eyes drawn to the commotion. Dazen took advantage, riding past patrols who had not yet become aware of the situation. As far as anyone knew, he had been invited here, and was welcome.

He pulled Brock to a canter as they neared the southern gate, holding up a fist so his company would do the same. "Let me handle this," Dazen said, turning to Obeyun and Sumaya. "We need control of the gate. If they will not let me pass, we take it by force."

The others obliged, leaving Dazen to trot up to the gate by himself. Giant wooden doors studded with iron were closed shut. Guards lined the gate's base and the high walls above. All were staring at the Last Light. Some were scrambling, trying to find out more information, others just stood and watched. One saw his approach and moved to intercept.

"Hold!" the Blackwing shouted. "State your business."

A couple more turned to Dazen now, their attention shifting toward him and his company.

"I am Dazen Glaive, Prince of Trost," he said. There was no point lying, they didn't know he was the enemy yet.

"I know who you are," the Blackwing retorted. "I said state your business. The King-Radiant has ordered no one in or out of this city until the conclusion of his meet."

"But it is concluded," Dazen said, dismounting and walking up to the guard. "The meet is over."

"What happened?" the guard asked. "Are we under attack?"

Dazen hesitated, sensing an opportunity. "Yes, the Last Light has been infiltrated, the Fifty Spears under siege. I am on orders from the King-Radiant to return with fresh troops to rout the deceivers."

Now it was the Blackwing's turn to hesitate. He looked over Dazen's shoulder, the crippled tower lending weight to his story. Other men had formed up behind the guard now, whispering in the ear of the first as they conversed. "Marsh!" the guard called to a nearby soldier. "Send a rider, go and find out what the blast is happening up there!" He turned back to Dazen. "Do you have a signed writ?

Dazen's fingers inched closer to his steels. "There was no time, the King-Radiant is wounded."

"What!" the guard said, eyes wide with shock. He quickly righted himself, however. "I am sorry, but no man is to pass by these gates without a writ from the King's court. If you want to pass, you will have to send a rider to fetch one, siege or no."

Dazen scowled. "Have you not seen what is happening! There is no time. I will send a rider, and he will return with two papers. One to let us pass, the other for your head to be put on a spike!"

The guard clenched his teeth and took a backward step. The moment stretched as the Blackwing contemplated his next action. "Very well," he said. "Open the gates!"

Dazen resisted a smile as the gates creaked open. He motioned for the others to follow, walking Brock beneath the giant curtain wall of stone. He was about to step outside the gate when a bolt of Light whistled past his ear, flying harmlessly through the crack in the gate and into the lake beyond.

Dazen span, cursing under his breath as a line of black and gold emerged from the city. More bolts of Shine battered them, one catching a White-Sword in the chest. He fell, dead.

"Get to cover!" Dazen yelled, pulling Brock behind a stone wall. Others followed, Sumaya and Obeyun hiding behind a thin column of stone as a horse cried out in pain before drawing its last breath.

"Traitors!" a voice called over the commotion. "Do not let them through the gate!"

Dazen rested his head against the wall. He took in a series of deep breaths. The gate began to shut. He could make it through, see himself to safety. But the others were too far away, they would never make it. He thought of Sumaya, thought of his mother. She was huddled in the corner, Kron's bulk shielding her from harm.

"Gale!" he shouted, even though he was right beside him.

"What should we do?" Gale said.

"I will stay here and hold the gate. I need you to get word to our men. Take Brock, he will not let you down."

Gale mounted and was about to rush through the gate when a boulder as large as a man fell from a hole in the ceiling, crushing a Bakai at the foot of the gate. The doors slammed shut, their escape cut off.

Dazen cursed, slamming a fist into the stone wall. He grabbed his pained wrist, an idea forming in his mind. "Father!" he called across the battlefield that had become of the stone pillars either side of the gate.

Kron responded, the two locking eyes. His father was the only person he knew strong enough to withstand a Golden Talon barrage. "I am going to force my way out!" Dazen screamed. "I need cover while the others escape!"

Kron rose to the occasion, walking out among a field of dead men and horses. He weaved his hands, a sheet of Shine manifesting from the tips of his fingers. A bolt of white-light hit against it, Kron's own Shine coming out the stronger.

Kron continued to stretch the defensive wall of Light until it covered a portion of the passageway. Others joined him, Dazen's White-Swords and Sumaya's men of Nanta both stepping in and pouring their own Shine into the wall. Kron looked back at Dazen. "Hurry!" he shouted.

Dazen didn't hesitate. He stepped out into the open. He rarely used his Shine in this manner, for the threat of burnout was constant in his mind. But this was not the time to hold back. He drew his hands behind his back, gathering his Light in his palms. With a thrust, he let it go, the searing heat blasting a horse-sized hole in the middle of the gate.

He motioned for Gale. Obeyun and Sumaya caught wind of his plan, mounting and following Gale through the hole. Sumaya spared a glance at him before she left, and Dazen hoped with all his heart he had not seen the last of her. Another rider followed, carrying the unconscious form of Echo with him.

Dazen turned, joining the others in their effort to keep a defensive wall of Shine. His mother hid behind a stone pillar, hands covering her ears as she huddled in the corner.

The regiment of enemy soldiers were drawing closer. With their attempts at a ranged assault failing, they sought to turn it into a melee. Dazen watched as Kron held firm, his determination renewed.

A light in the distance caught his attention. He inclined his head, watching through the transparent wall of Shine as something gathered at the top of the Last Light. He felt the presence of immense power, the heat equivalent to a second sun dotting the sky. His heart sank. If that dropped on them, it was all over. All of his efforts would be for nothing. He re-focused, trusting in Raiz to handle whatever was happening atop the tower.

A knight rounded the shield of Light, attempting to cut them down from behind. Dazen withdrew, drawing his steels. Their swords clashed, the knight coming at him with aggressive slashes. Dazen waited for him to overstep, whirling past his defence and cutting him at the nape of his neck. But they numbered too few, and the enemy forces rushed them in a wave. Dazen watched, helpless, as the Knights of the Golden Talon overwhelmed the other side of the Shine-wall, cutting down two White-Swords.

His mother cried out as a knight grabbed her by the wrist, Dazen unable to come to her aide. The world seemed to still as Kron screamed. His cry was deep, and the wall of Shine dissipated as another power took hold of the battlefield. A white aura emanated from his father. All around him were struck by an invisible force, sweeping friends and foe to the ground.

Dazen was forced to shield his eyes as Kron's Flare hit him. The latent power of those closest with Zur was strong, overwhelmingly so. He tried to right himself. Kron seemed to begin to focus his assault, targeting the assailants. Dazen took advantage, cutting those struck by Kron's Flare down even as they lay crawling on the ground. He moved without mercy, without hesitation. He had chosen his side, and he intended to see them to victory.

Chapter 43
Raiz

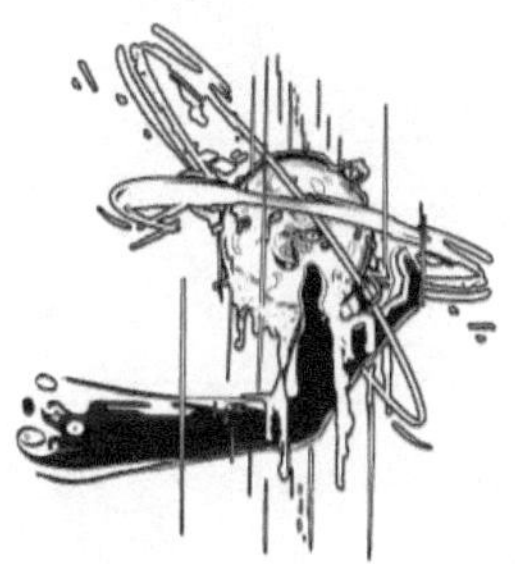

Raiz covered his eyes at the sudden burst of light. A set of eight peridium coils rose from the tower, arching into the sky in a symmetrical pattern so that each met in the centre. Poised within the coils was a mass of Light so intense it was almost like a second sun. Plumes of fluorescent Light poured upwards in an upside-down waterfall as white-light was drained from the pit and added to the bulk of Shine gathering above, reflecting bright against the smooth surface beneath Raiz's feet.

The air was so thin he had to gasp several times before righting himself and finding a steady rhythm. Veil was of a similar mind, clutching his hand as though every second was a fight to hold onto her power.

Raiz peered across the surface, searching for any sign of his father. He spotted a silhouette-like shadow on the opposite side, only it seemed like more. He rubbed at his eye, opening them again to confirm there were indeed two figures. And they were — fighting?

Raiz pushed closer, using the shadow of a peridium coil to

mask his approach, Veil not far behind. A simmering rage boiled within him. He had to end the suffering, bring down the ladder of power. If that meant he had to kill his father, so be it.

It seemed someone had gotten to him first. Was there someone with more reason, more anger towards him than even Raiz?

He edged closer, listening as their argument echoed above the raging winds and searing heat.

"You should never have been named King! You are a disgrace! You will send this world into oblivion."

That voice sounded familiar.

It couldn't be.

Zur dipped further below the horizon, allowing Raiz to see the picture more clearly beneath the ball of white-light above.

Celik stood before Evanon. Raiz's mentor, the man who found him when he had been most in need. The man who had given him purpose, given him the means to achieve his goal.

His two arms still dangled to his sides, long sleeves covering useless limbs as he stared the King-Radiant down. Both Celik and his father were too enveloped in their own quarrel to notice his approach.

"I am who I am today because of you, Father," Evanon said.

Raiz stopped. Did he just say, *Father*?

"You believed me weak and useless. You cast me aside as a mere inconvenience to be disposed of," Evanon continued. "Well, look at me now, Father!"

There was that word again.

"Look at what I have accomplished!" Evanon gestured towards the mass of Shine gathered above. "I know what you thought of me. I know how people snickered behind your back. The great Urion Lightfire — King Radiant of all of Zapour — born with a son unable to wield the Light. I know how you hated me for it, how mother was barren and could bear you no more children. But you were wrong. I can wield the Light. The red Light of Gallion flows through me. Your hatred of me drove me to this."

"You are a fool, Evanon," Celik said. "I was right to hate you. The Eagles have manipulated you, they pulled you into their game. They are not divinities. Their blood is not sacred. You must know it to be a lie. We are the true heirs. Our blood alone holds the key to unlocking the true potential of the Last Light. And you would waste it. The Skae will return. Zapour must be prepared."

"Is that why you covet my son and send him against me? You think him more worthy than me? I should have burnt you whole! The Eagles are mine to control. They do what I say. This whole continent does what I say!"

"Raiz is nothing like you. He is strong. And he is more powerful. You were foolish to let him go."

Raiz's feet felt as though they were stuck to the ground. He peeked from behind a peridium coil, Veil's hand squeezing his tight as the two of them listened to the confrontation.

"How could I raise him?" Evanon said. "Me of all people, a father? Unlike you, I know who I am. I could not subject my child to the same torment I endured from you. He was better off living in Illidor."

Celik went to speak, but Evanon cut him off. "I have heard enough! Your words are poison. Let us finish what should have been ended long ago!"

A bolt of Shine whistled through the air from the tip of Evanon's finger. For a moment Raiz thought Celik dead, but with a burst of Light Celik jumped through the air, landing a perfect backflip before leaping from side to side as Evanon continued his barrage.

Shine gathered at the ball of Celik's shoeless feet. Raiz knew Celik had once been able to manipulate Light, but had always assumed him incapable anymore. He had been mistaken.

Celik propelled himself forward, using his Shine to boost through the air. A red streak trailed in his wake. Before Raiz could muster the sense to enter the fray, the two engaged in close-combat, Celik twisting and turning, using his feet like twin spears trying to penetrate Evanon's defence.

Evanon blocked and parried, deflecting Celik's Shine-infused kicks with two dagger-like claws of his own making. Evanon's shoulder was still injured, giving Celik the advantage.

Raiz was content on watching the fight play out, but Veil prodded him in the side. "We have to do something about that," she said, pointing towards the gathering Shine.

Raiz looked about. "What can we do?"

Veil leaned over the cylindrical hole in the centre of the platform. "Look here, the Light has stopped gathering. I think Evanon is controlling it. I think his will is driving the Shine towards the coils. It only stopped once Celik engaged him."

"So, we must kill him then," Raiz said, circling back to his original desire.

"There is another option," Veil said.

"Veil no. Don't even think about it."

"I can feel it coming Raiz, there will be nothing I can do."

"Just hold on for me, please. Promise me, promise me you will hold it."

Veil nodded, but Raiz was taking no chances. He sprinted towards his father and grandfather, charging and screaming with little subtlety as he shot arrows of pure red Light in their direction.

The two stepped to the side, each addressing their new

adversary with piqued interest.

The three of them stood in a triangle, eyes darting back and forth.

"This is quite the reunion," Celik said. "Three generations."

Raiz looked at his long-time mentor. "It seems I am gaining family members by the score today, however unwanted. So, it is true then?"

Celik nodded.

"Then you finding me as a boy, that was no coincidence?"

"Afraid not, no."

"Was anything you told me true?"

Celik gave him a blank look.

Evanon's harsh laughter interrupted their interaction. He turned towards him now. "What lies has he told you?"

"I have told him no lie when it comes to you," Celik said. "Only the truth of what you are."

"Of what I am? You made me what I am! If I have been harsh in my methods, be assured I learned from the best."

Raiz conjured a ball of Shine in his good hand. "Celik has always been good to me. His lessons may have been harsh, but they were necessary for me to achieve my goals."

"Ah yes, your sister," Evanon said. "How unfortunate. Her capture was rather callous of dear Averardus. Perhaps his death was indeed his own doing."

"You dare absolve yourself of guilt!" Raiz shouted. "You abducted my mother! You stole her from Kron and locked her away!"

Evanon's calm demeanour changed, his red aura glowing even deeper than Raiz's own. "I did no such thing! Celia loved me. She came to me willingly. Why do you think Kron never told you about her? Because he is a liar, just like my father."

"You have gone too far, Evanon," Celik said.

"Strange how you draw the line here, but beating your own son because he cannot conjure the Light is not beneath you," Evanon said.

Celik went quiet, telling Raiz all the truth he needed to know.

Evanon turned back to Raiz. "Perhaps I was wrong about you. I am more than I once was. We can be more. You have a king's radiance. Our Light is born of Gallion. Only ours glows red with Zur's hidden power. Come and join me. I will forgive your crimes against my Eagles, if you but come to me. With the two of us as one, nothing will be able to stand against us."

"Do not listen to him, Raiz!" Celik snapped. "You cannot forget everything he has done."

"Shut your mouth!" Evanon cried. "Do you not see what this man has done to you? He has manipulated your entire life. Just ask him. He does not care for you, he never has. Everything he taught you was to drive you against me."

Raiz turned to Celik. "So, when you told me they took your son from you, this is what you meant?"

Celik nodded.

"Is it true? Did you seek me out, craft me into a weapon just to use me for vengeance?"

"This is common knowledge, Raiz!" Celik spat. "Even you are not naïve enough to think I had any other agenda."

"Show me your Shine."

"Why?"

"Just do it!"

"Raiz, do not listen to him. Can you not see him for who he is?" Celik pleaded.

"Just. Show. Me. Your. Shine."

Celik shook his head, but obeyed. His legs lit with bright energy, though the colour was not white.

It was red.

"You are the one who killed Argon!" Raiz hissed. "You killed Aroha's brother! Not me!"

Celik twisted his head as he scoffed. "What matter is it who killed him. He is the man who gave you that scar, he deserved to die."

"His life was not yours to take. He knew who you were, didn't he? He recognised your former identity, so you killed him."

"I did what I needed to do."

"Did you know my mother was alive?" Raiz said.

Celik huffed another dismissive sigh.

"Answer the question, Celik!"

"Of course I knew."

"And yet you kept it from me."

"Of course I kept it from you! I struggled enough trying to stop you from prematurely attempting to rescue your damn sister. Add a deranged mother into the mix and you would never have learnt the skills that were necessary!"

Raiz's anger swelled. Had anyone ever told him the truth?

Veil brushed past him, a fire in her eye. "You are Urion Lightfire," she said. "You lied to me! You took me in upon the promise of vengeance. You said you would help me find a cure, you said you would help me punish those responsible. When really it was you! You were the one responsible."

Crack. Veil's balled fist connected with Celik's cheek.

Crack.

Crack.

The old man gasped and wheezed as Veil unleashed the full fury of her wrath upon his bearded face.

Raiz and Evanon could only watch as Celik drifted further and further into a state of unconsciousness.

"Veil, stop!" Raiz pleaded, but only because she was pushing herself too hard.

Raiz pulled her away, wrapping his arms around her stomach as she continued to claw at the air. She turned, weeping into his arms as Raiz tried desperately to sooth her into a calming state.

He looked up to a surprised but pleased Evanon.

"I am glad you got the chance to see him for who he truly was, son," he said, offering his hand to him. "Join me, and we can rule together. Join me, and you can do whatever you like. Your sister can live her life free of burden. I will even spare that snake of a Glaive and his son if you wish, though their reign is over. I offer you the chance my father never gave to me. I see your strength. It is a gift, a treasure greater than any metal. What do you say?"

Raiz, still clutching a grieving Veil, looked into his father's eyes. He could see the power lurking beneath, the immeasurable wealth of pure radiant energy and the sincerity of his request. There was no lie in his voice, his tone did not waver. This man meant what he said, Raiz could be a king. He could be in a position to make the changes this world so desperately needed.

But at what cost? Above all this man was a tyrant. He may not be responsible for how Zapour was today, but he did not genuinely seek to change it. He sought only to please himself, and that is why Raiz had to kill him.

"I will never join you," he said. "Your soul is lost, tainted. I do not blame you for who you have become, but who you have become must not be allowed to rule."

Evanon paced the iron platform, rubbing at his chin as if he had expected this outcome but was still disappointed by it. "I see, and you are unmoving in this?"

"I am."

"Then you, too, shall die."

In one swift hand movement Evanon thrust a ball of red Light towards the pair of them. Raiz had time to react, but a wounded Veil crouched beside him. He couldn't see them both away in time, and he wouldn't leave her. Instead, he braced himself, setting his feet and crossing his arms. He shied away from the Light, expecting it to consume him any moment.

But the heat did not come. He opened his eyes to see Spike kneeling before him, his mouth open wide as he took in Evanon's Light.

Raiz and Veil moved in sync, hands full with Light ready to unleash upon the King-Radiant, but were pushed back as some unsurmountable force charged through them.

Evanon screamed, his aura expanding rapidly, as he had been ready to do in the throne-room. Wisps of red Light emanated from his body, flailing in the air around him and cutting into Raiz's skin like a thousand whips, buffeting him and sending them flying towards the tower's edge.

Spike leapt forwards through the rush of wind but was rebuffed with a wave of Evanon's hand. The pricket let out a pained yelp as he was sent sprawling into the bubbling pit of molten white-light below.

"Spike!" Raiz screamed as he scrambled for a bearing.

Raiz clawed at the air in an attempt to grab hold of something, anything to stop him from plummeting to his death. He pushed against the lightning-like wind, fighting against the thousand cuts which now openly bled over his entire body. His clothes were in tatters, ripped and torn all over.

He saw Veil falter to his left, swept off her legs she slid to the edge, clinging on to the side for her life.

Raiz ran to her. He held out his hand and caught her wrist as she fell. But his momentum was too great, the force of the wind too strong. The two of them toppled over, Raiz managing to just barely hold on to both the edge and Veil's wrist.

For a moment that stretched for an eternity the two hung, facing certain death. Raiz's fingers burned with the desire to let go. The muscles in his arm screamed at him to release them from this burden.

The miniature Light-storm above seemed to recede, for Raiz no longer felt its overwhelming presence. It was replaced by the steady rhythm of approaching footsteps.

"You should never have gone against me," came a voice. "I gave you the chance to live, now you must face the consequences."

Raiz grit his teeth, "Veil, I'm going to use my Shine."

She looked up at him, her blue eyes dazzling bright in the light of the sunset. "What do you mean?"

Evanon stalked closer, his voice becoming louder. "I see your friends down there," he said. "Look for yourself."

Raiz risked a glance down below, and true enough, squinting through the breeze, he could see hundreds — perhaps thousands of tiny black dots moving down the slope and towards the giant walled city of Lumindal. His mind instantly thought of Dazen, of Isha. Were they among them?

An insurmountable wave of panic shot through Raiz as he urged his body to find the strength to lift them both to safety. All he could do was hold on to the edge as Evanon drew even closer.

Evanon raised his hands and tensed his muscles as the massive ball of pure white-light grew even larger above him.

"Watch. Watch as I prove once and for all who has the power here!"

"Veil," Raiz shouted above the noise and heat. "Did you see how Celik used his Shine?"

"What does that have to do with anything?" she said.

"I'm going to gather my Shine at the balls of my feet. I need you to hold on tight."

"But what of—"

"Just do it, please."

She nodded.

Raiz closed his eyes, concentrating as he soaked up what remained of Zur's heat before it faded below the horizon. He channeled a massive surge through his bloodstream so that instead of gathering at his hands, it did so in his feet.

"On my mark," he said, waiting a moment longer for Veil's grip to tighten.

"Feast upon my Light! And perish beneath it!" Evanon screamed, his gathered Shine reaching its climax.

"Now!"

He felt a pulse shoot through his legs as the burst of Light propelled them both upwards. Raiz managed to clip the side of his father's head with his own as his momentum carried him well beyond. The two came down in a nosedive, Raiz ducking and rolling before almost falling into the pit of bubbling white-light down below.

He saw Spike making his way back to the surface, white liquid coating his skin. But he was alive.

Evanon turned to face him, blood spilling out from a cut over his eye, heightening his rage. "You will not win boy! No one will hinder my reign!"

Raiz nearly tripped over Celik's unconscious body as he ducked a bolt of Shine meant for his head. He sent one of his own in return, feeling the familiar tingle through his fingers as he reached his limit. Much more and his fingers would turn grey, as useless as his grandfather's arms.

The two danced across the platform, shooting and dodging and blocking each other's blasts with their own.

Evanon reached behind with his hands, drawing in a massive amount of power. As if by instinct, Raiz did the same, gathering every scrap of Light he had and pouring it into the palms of his hands. He felt the air begin to move. It swirled around them, wanting to flee the heat but also unable to stay away.

As if in sync, both father and son unleashed the full fury of their power at one another. The two streaks of red clashed, shaking the very world around them. Sparks of Light melted together as the two continuous beams met, breen gathering on the floor below them.

Hands outstretched, Raiz cried out in both pain and anger. His hands began to burn, and he could literally feel the life draining from his fingers. But he refused to stop, pushing more and more Light through them and watching as it pulsed towards Evanon, who was leaning on his back foot.

But just as Raiz did not yield, neither did his father. No matter Raiz's strength, no matter his morals, his father had more experience, and was gaining the upper hand.

In a surreal moment, Raiz looked to Veil. His vision was blurred, and his mind felt as if he were floating, but there was no mistaking her. She looked at him and spoke an inaudible string of words.

What had she said?

And then she was gone.

Raiz's Shine seemed to push through the barrier, flying uselessly into the cloudless sky beyond. Raiz looked about, searching for any sign of Veil or his father.

And then he saw them.

Veil glowed white-hot, just has she had that day back in Lesken and in times before. Raiz knew what was about to happen, he knew and could do nothing to stop it. Veil was on the floor, tied in a tangle of limbs with Evanon. She clung to him like Draz to his helmet. No matter how much he hit her, she refused to let go, refused to back down.

Raiz rushed to her aid, he would do anything to stop her from what she was about to do. If he could just—

The pair of them rolled until they were at the edge of the pit. Raiz reached out with one hand as if he could summon her to him with some yet-undiscovered power. With one last pull, Veil flung both herself and Evanon into the pit.

Raiz moved to scream but there was no air left in his lungs.

The explosion that came then broke his heart. His body was thrown into the air as the shockwave swept through him. A torrent of intense energy shot through the air, snapping the tower in two.

The force of the blast sent Raiz flying through the air, unable to do anything more as he fell from the tower's height, his hand still reaching for Veil's as he fell to his death.

Chapter 44
Raiz

The life that could have been flashed before his eyes. His mind was lost amidst a dream so real, yet so far removed from reality. Images of the bustling streets of Illidor swam into focus. Raiz was napping, soaking in the distant sun's glare as his sister stood over him, waving a blurry hand before his face. She mumbled a few words, but Raiz was too deep in his trance, disconnected from the world he had created.

Two violet eyes blinked at him. She was younger here, her skin soft and unblemished by hardship. Dazen was here too, snickering at him as if he had just done something incredibly stupid. He too was as he was back then, a boy on the verge of becoming a man.

Kron walked up to Dazen, clapping him on the shoulder and sharing a laugh that was more than likely at Raiz's expense. Raiz awoke fully in his dream, eyes darting, attempting to understand the jest before slumping into himself upon the realisation that he had been at its centre.

Then his mother came. Celia Glaive stood before him and

Kron in all her beauty, long hair whistling in the wind as she thrust a hand upon either hip and scowled at both Kron and Dazen.

Raiz grinned cheekily behind his mother, watching as the two of them scrambled an incoherent apology his way.

This couldn't be real — this wasn't real — was it?

And then Raiz awoke, his consciousness moving away from the dream that could have been and back to reality. Tears stung his eyes, whether from the raging winds cutting at him from this height, or from the empty hole in his heart, he couldn't tell.

He floated towards the ground more than fell, his mind struggling to comprehend the hundreds of emotions rushing through it at once.

He had heard accounts from survivors of great battles talking about seeing their entire life before their eyes the moment they thought themselves about to die. Raiz could see now that it was not true. The life he had lived did not come. Instead, what came to him was more. Greater even than he could have hoped. It was the life he wanted to have lived. The life he never had the chance to see. The life that was taken from him.

What would have become of him if Isha had not been taken? If his mother had remained in Illidor? Why did he not deserve a peaceful life?

None of it mattered now, for Veil was surely dead, and he was about to die.

His stomach felt as though it had left his body. Wind circled his limbs, careening its way through the open wounds caused by Evanon's Light-storm. He tumbled, his body twisting and turning as he fought to regain his composure.

He could see his death, the ground like one giant canvas. The Fifty Spears loomed like a giant pit below, white-coated spikes ready to impale him at any moment. It wasn't until he reached the halfway point of his descent that he realised he didn't want to die. He struggled, kicking and flailing as if he could sprout wings and fly.

He reached for that last scrap of Shine still lurking beneath his skin. He waited until he could see the colour blue painted on the glass window of one of the Spears before he unleashed it. He focused on the soles of his feet and the palms of his hands, spreading the Light between them and releasing it in one burst.

It did not have the effect he intended. Instead of floating seamlessly to the ground, he was thrust upwards. His momentum halted and he was flung in the opposite direction as if he were on a string. He twisted and turned, trying to right himself, but gravity pushed him back down, except this time there was no string to catch him. He was still too high, his momentum too strong.

A blurry shape formed in the corner of his vision, followed by a gush of wind as the leathery beast that was his companion swooped from the sky, catching him in his thick, taloned claws. Slimy, bat-like wings had sprouted from Spike's side, spreading wide as he glided through the air. Raiz caught his breath, hanging on to Spike's leg with all his strength. But Spike's wings were still weak, born too quick for him to master, and Raiz was heavy.

The two began to fall towards one of the Spears below. Together, they crashed through a paned window. Shards of glass splintered and fell along with them.

Raiz hit the ground hard. His vision blurred and his body arched in torment before he faded into the realm of unconsciousness.

Raiz awoke. Was he dead? He couldn't be, he felt pain. And pain was for the living.

He sat up, clutching his chest as he drew in a few deep and welcoming breaths. His ears rang with a dull whine that would not go away, no matter how hard he shook his head. He looked upwards, beyond the broken glass and into the blackening sky above.

The Last Light was shattered, the blast had broken it in two. A silvery cloud dotted the sky. Plumes of white smoke and grey haze coloured the landscape. The bottom half was a splinter. White, lava-like liquid oozed from its top, making its way down its length with increasing haste.

Raiz spread two hands over his face and rubbed at his eyes. No one could comprehend his loss, no one would know her sacrifice. How could he have let her do it? He should have stopped her, should have stopped him.

He wasn't strong enough to protect her, wasn't strong enough to protect anyone. Everything he touched turned to dust. He was the unwanted child. Maybe this was just who he was, a tainted soul destined for a shallow grave.

He wished then that he had died in the fall, to join Veil in the afterlife. Perhaps there he would find his peace.

He looked around, regaining some small measure of his senses. Spike was next to him, unconscious but breathing, his chest slowly rising and falling. He only now noticed the dozens of faces staring down at him.

Their faces were blurry, like a painting that had not yet been given finer details. He rubbed at his eyes again, willing them to come into focus. Slowly their features revealed themselves. They seemed hesitant, edging steadily away from him.

His first instinct was to defend himself, balling his fists and trying to summon Light that was not there. The faces reacted, jumping back in one line that almost sent them all tumbling over each other.

He looked at his broken body. Small shards of glass had cut into his skin where the Light-storm had not, and he was bleeding from dozens of lacerations of varying sizes.

He rose to his feet. The men were dressed in fancy, bone-white robes embroidered with gold patterns formed into the shape of a broad-winged eagle at its centre. The women donned long gowns covered by luxurious tunics, which in turn were decorated with fine lace and rich gemstones. Their faces were pale. They covered their mouths as though looking at a stain on their carpet.

Raiz knew immediately who they were. Where he was.

He rounded his head in a full circle. There were dozens of them. Raiz broadened his vision. Slaves lined the outskirts of the room, chained to the walls like cattle.

Knights of the Golden Talon were present also, though most were busy on the opposite side, bracing against a large double door.

A consistent thump echoed around the chamber, repeating every fifteen seconds or so.

Thump, it sounded again.

Thump.

Thump.

More knights rushed to the door, throwing their bodies against the wood. A couple turned, driven toward Raiz by the cry of a frightened Eagle.

Raiz studied the slaves, watching them scratch at the shackles binding them. He searched their faces, looking for any flicker of emotion that might lend him strength. But he could not make them out, he saw only his sister. Isha's face was everywhere, bright eyes staring at him as if through a hundred mirrors.

He looked to the Eagles. This was all their fault. Why should they be allowed to live while innocent and caring people such as his sister suffered beneath their feet? What gave them the right to dictate? They were nothing, they were the stain on their own carpet. It was their fault so many people suffered. If not for them, Veil might still be alive.

Raiz's mind drifted into a bottomless pit of grief, as if a metaphorical switch had been flicked and the lever broken off.

A knight swung at him, called to service by the cry of his master. Raiz dodged, swinging to the side as if his body were on a pendulum. He rocked backward and struck with his hidden blade, felling the knight.

An Eagle let out a shrill scream as she stumbled over another, falling to the ground before him. Raiz felt no sympathy for the fallen Eagle, only pain. He took the dead knight's sword and ran it through her, watching as she drew her last breath.

His glow had receded, but he still felt its strength. Even unable to draw from his Shine, he felt its unnatural power coursing through his veins.

A knight moved for Spike, going in for the kill before the beast woke.

Raiz reacted, dancing through the mass of gathered bodies, cutting and slicing with his stolen weapon. Red was the only colour that made any sense to him now. It surrounded him, painted him, was him. He was Gallion incarnate, delivering Zur's justice, the radiance of a king coursing through him.

His movements were a blur, but with each turn, each step, he remained standing, and they did not.

He heard the distant sound of more thumping.

Thump.

Thump.

It continued, playing in the back of his mind like some endless tune.

Raiz continued his assault, moving with inhuman speed as he swept the entire hall, leaving dead Eagles behind. None could flee. They were like bugs trapped in a box ready to be squished.

The thumping stopped, replaced by a loud crash and the sound of a thousand cries of war.

The Eagles were all dead, but Raiz kept swinging. He looked around and, blinded by his grief, saw only his sister, staring back at him with her thousand faces.

"Raiz," came a voice from the wall.

His eyes darted, searching for the voice.

"Raiz it's me, it's Isha."

Raiz refused to believe it, thinking it some trick, some illusion concocted by his enemies to undermine him. But the voice, it sounded just like her.

He shook his head clear, only now recognising the carnage he had created. He looked at his blood-stained hands, then back to his sister. "What have I done?" he said.

Another figure appeared from the line of soldiers. "Isha stop! Raiz is not himself, he could harm you."

Was that…Dazen?

Isha ignored him, continuing forward. She took his bloodied hand in her own.

"She's gone," Raiz said. "Veil is gone."

He dropped his stolen sword and collapsed into her arms, hoping her embrace would comfort the hole in his heart.

"It's okay, I am here. You can rest," she said as his mind drifted to the safety of unconsciousness once again, content that no more harm could come to him, or to anyone he loved.

Epilogue
Isha

Slowly the distant cries of the war-ravaged city began to fade. Lumindal had fallen. The King-Radiant was dead, his Eagles slaughtered. And yet the world had not ended. Zur still rose from his bed to blanket the city in light. And Isha had her brother back. She lay by her brother's side, on the bed of a repossessed home, refusing to leave as he slept. She could see him struggling, eyes flickering beneath their lids as his body twitched and squirmed. She cradled him tighter, stroking his arm to show him she was there, even if he was asleep. It seemed to sooth him somewhat, his prone body settling into the nook beneath her shoulder.

Spike lounged at the foot of the bed, the overgrown pricket resting his snout on Raiz's foot. Spike had grown a full half-metre in less than a day. And that was not all. Two leathery wings sprouted from his shoulder-blades. Still slimy from their sudden growth, the thin, eerie looking bones spread out wide, ending in a curved yet blunted tip as the pricket tucked them away over his back.

Sumaya and Echo lay on a bed parallel to Isha and Raiz,

with Puk on another. They were alive, though Echo had not yet woken.

Dazen walked in, along with the unusual company of Obeyun and Aroha. "How do they fare?" he asked.

Isha and Sumaya looked up. "Raiz is fine," Isha said, before Sumaya could answer. "He is cut up pretty badly and has burns to his hands and legs. The doctor says he will pull through, but he has not woken yet."

"He will be glad to have you by his side, I am sure. What of Echo?" he inquired, turning to Sumaya.

Sumaya looked to the nurse who had been tending to the wounded.

"He will be fine," the nurse said. "He suffered a heavy blow to the head and won't be holding a sword for some time yet, but with lots of bed rest and a little love he will suffer no long-term damage."

"He was very brave," Dazen said. "In the throne-room. Very stupid," he added. "But brave, nonetheless. He may have saved all of our lives."

Sumaya curled her lip. "Seems he has been drawing inspiration from the wrong sorts if you ask me," she teased, narrowing her vision towards Dazen.

Dazen smiled. "Echo has come far in the recent months. I predict he will become a worthy king in the time to come."

Isha coughed, diverting his attention. "How fairs our situation?" she asked.

Dazen cleared his throat before standing up straight. "We have taken the capital. Once the Last Light fell, Lumindal offered little resistance. Gelvard and Hanns continue to pursue those still fighting, but the battle is won."

"What a relief!" Isha said. "But, well, what do we do now?"

"Now, we rebuild," Dazen said. "The Five Kingdoms of

Zapour are united again, in more than just paper. Now, we try our best to hold on to these alliances and build a world to be proud of."

Isha nodded, turning her attention to Obeyun. "Obe!" she called, eyes bright with energy.

He stepped from Dazen's shadow. He looked... different. He still had the same charismatic boldness, the same discolouration that through his choice or not, made him who he was. But there was a certain air about him. Isha had only ever known him as a slave, forced to wear whatever Averardus deemed appropriate. Now he stood proud. His face was painted with an array of symbols she had never seen before. He wore an elaborate brown robe which stretched the entire length of his legs. A plain wooden crown sat comfortably on his bald head.

Isha smiled at him. "I knew you would do it. You were always meant for great things."

Obeyun leaned over her and Raiz, his presence filling her with a warmth she hadn't even realised she had been missing. "I owe it all to you, Isha. It was you who gave me the strength to become the man I was born to be. Without you beside me all of those years, I am certain my will would have been broken. The whole of Wisha owes you their thanks."

Isha didn't say anything. Instead, she took his offered hand and kissed it, a single tear running down the length of her cheek.

"It is us who owe you our thanks," Dazen said, interrupting their moment. "If you had not spoken as you did, this fight would not be over. There must be something we can offer you?"

Obeyun turned to face Dazen, clasping his hands in his own. "You do not owe me anything. I did what I thought was right. Though, when it is appropriate I wish to open up my country to the world. For too long we have lived in isolation. I want to show my people that there is a world beyond Wisha, and to perhaps show the world what Wisha has to offer."

"It would be my honour to visit your country," Dazen said. "I will make sure the people of Trost welcome yours as if they were their own kin."

"I welcome the day with open arms."

Aroha stepped forwards, brushing past Obeyun and Dazen to kneel down on the bed beside Raiz and Isha. "I should never have left him. I should have stayed. Maybe this wouldn't have happened, maybe I could have prevented it. I should have trusted him."

Isha took Aroha's giant, calloused hand and moved it towards Raiz's. "You did all you could. Raiz now has his own battle to fight."

The clinking of boots rattled behind them all as another figure approached. "Well shit, Raiz sure made a mess in there! Guess that proves the whole 'the worlds gonna end if the Eagles die' debate."

Every conscious body in the room turned to face the newcomer. A pattern of raised brows and puzzled expressions stared at the pale-faced man. He had thick black hair drenched with sweat that fell to his shoulders. Bright brown eyes were brought to life by his exuberant energy and self-confidence. A patchy beard covered his rounded jawline, which suited him well. Isha thought the man quite handsome, not that she knew who he was.

It seemed her confusion was warranted, as neither did anyone else.

"Can we help you?" Dazen said, standing between him and Raiz.

The stranger looked from face to face, scowling. "One

moment." He rushed out of the room, leaving everyone wearing the same perplexed expressions as when he had come in.

He returned shortly after, donning a familiar metal helmet. As if the room were audience and his entrance the cue, they all spoke. "Ohhhhh."

"D — Draz?" Aroha said, her mouth open as wide as the length of her hand. "Is that you?"

"The one and only."

"But, Gallant? You can take it off?"

"Of course Draz can take it off. The damn thing's not bolted down."

"I'm sorry, I'm just surprised. Why now? Why show us your face after all this time?"

The metal man turned towards Raiz, then to the ceiling. "I promised a dear friend I wouldn't hide anymore."

Isha lowered her head, pained by Veil's loss just as Draz was.

Aroha moved to Draz and punched him in the arm. "Show me again. I want to see you."

Draz recoiled. "Come take it if you want another look."

Aroha gave a wide grin and began wrestling with Draz for another peek beneath the helmet.

"Ahem, if you two don't mind taking this elsewhere," Sumaya said. "This is a place of rest."

Aroha and Draz straightened. "Of course," they said, Draz elbowing Aroha in the ribs.

Isha felt Raiz stir beneath her grip. His body wriggled and shook, then his eyes began to flutter. He leapt upwards, gasping for air with quick and frantic breaths. "Where am I? Where are they? Veil!" he cried.

"Shhh. It's okay, you're safe," Isha said, making sure she was the first person he saw. She positioned herself in front of him, blocking out any distractions until his breathing became steady. "We have taken Lumindal, we have won. You don't need to worry anymore."

"Veil, where is Veil?"

Isha breathed a deep sigh. Even she could not find the words to comfort her grieving brother.

Raiz's memories seemed to flood back in a wave. He slumped into his bed, head landing softly on the pillow as his eyes swelled and grew red. "I failed her," he said.

"You didn't fail anyone, Raiz. Veil made her choice. She made it long before her death. She saved us."

"It hurts."

Isha kissed him gently on the forehead. There was nothing she could say right now to cheer him up. He just needed time to grieve.

Aroha and Draz moved to his side, followed by Dazen.

"We are here for you, Brother. Forever this time, I promise," Dazen said.

Raiz cried into Isha's shoulder for a while longer, before Aroha decided to lighten the mood. "I got to see Draz's face."

Isha elbowed her in the ribs. "Not now, please."

Aroha shrugged. "Just trying to—"

"I was to be the first to see that ugly mug," Raiz said, wiping his cheek clean.

Draz flinched back. "The world is not yet ready for such beauty twice."

"Show me," Raiz insisted.

Draz shrugged.

Raiz lurched forward, pushing Isha aside as he leapt for Gallant. His fingers brushed its edge before he doubled over in pain, clutching at his stomach as a bandage came loose.

Isha held him in place with a firm hand. "Never have I met a bigger pair of idiots than the two of you. If you don't lay back and rest so help me I—"

"Aroha," Raiz said, taking on a more serious tone. "I am sorry, for your brother. It was not me who killed him, but I should have shown you more respect."

Aroha waved the comment away. "I forgive you Raiz. I never should have doubted you."

"It was Celik."

Aroha nodded.

"You should also know he is the former King-Radiant of Zapour. My grandfather."

"I knew there was something off about that man!" Dazen shouted.

"I should have known," Aroha said. "I should have seen it."

"You could not have known," Raiz said. "He was presumed dead.

"How could this be?" Aroha said. "What reason could he have?"

Raiz sat up, fighting against the pain. "He wanted vengeance on his son. He wanted to use me in his plot against Evanon. I don't know what happened between the two of them, but it must not have ended well. I think Argon must have recognised him in the field that day, or at least Celik thought he did. Everything he put us through was to hit back at the son he wished he never had."

Aroha took a moment to digest this new information. "Does he live?"

Raiz shrugged. "I cannot say for sure. Everything happened so fast."

"And Evanon?"

"Dead, Veil saw to that."

Aroha bowed her head. "Raiz," she said after a time. "I'm glad I met you."

The three Glaive siblings were together once more. As one they watched the sun rise in the east, Isha staring as her two brothers drew strength from Zur's warmth.

"Isha," Raiz said. "I'm sorry. Sorry that you had to see me like that."

"Like what? What do you mean?" she said.

"Everyone pretends like they don't remember it, like they didn't see it. But I remember. I know what I did. I killed them, every last one of them."

Isha gulped a lump down her throat. "You did what you had to do."

"No," Raiz said. "I did it because I wanted to, because they deserved to die. Am I…evil?"

Isha turned her head. "Evil comes in many forms. There are some who might call you so, yes. But there are many who might call you hero, too. The lines are always blurred when it comes to right and wrong."

Raiz's brow knotted as he thought. "And what do you think?" he pried.

"I think that you are my brother, and I will love you no matter what."

Raiz sighed. "And what of you, Dazen?"

"I have no love for the Eagles after what they put Isha through. There are some who would have wanted to see them on trial for their crimes, but what is done is done."

Raiz went to respond, when a Saelmere banner impeded their view. Gelvard walked past them, followed by his son Ancel and two of his guard, who held a female prisoner between them.

Dazen moved to intercept. "That is the Queen-mother. Where are you taking her?"

The prisoner lifted her head. Lady Sephare stared straight through her. Her once neat and combed hair was now a matted mess.

Gelvard put his hands on his hips. "Sephare has commited several unforgivable crimes against my country. I am taking her to Craw to see trial. Do not challenge me on this, Glaive."

Raiz stepped in front of his brother. "Let me ask her one question first," he said. "Please."

Gelvard's eyes narrowed, and Ancel looked as though he were about to start a fight. Gelvard held out an arm to stop him. "One question, make it quick."

"It was you, wasn't it," Raiz said to Sephare. "You were the one sending messages to Celik — to Urion —" he corrected.

Sephare issued a sinister smile. "Yes, I was helping Urion reclaim his throne. Evanon was my child, but he was never fit to rule. He did not understand the true purpose of a King-Radiant."

"And what is the true purpose?" Raiz said. "I need to know, what am I?"

"You will find out soon, my child. The Skae are coming, be sure. And without the Last Light, I am afraid Zapour has little hope."

"The Skae? They are myth. The Last Light was a weapon, it needed to be destroyed," Raiz said.

"A myth the Skae are not," Sephare said. "And a weapon, yes. But the Last Light was not built to defend Zapour against the corruption of humanity. It was built for something much greater."

Gelvard yanked on her chain. "Enough of your poisonous words, witch." He turned to go.

"Gelvard, wait!" Dazen called.

"What is it, Glaive? My patience runs thin."

"Where do we now stand, are we friends or foes?"

Gelvard took a moment to consider. "If you stay out of my way, Craw will stay out of yours. But do not try to put a king back on that throne. Craw will bow to a King-Radiant no more."

Dazen nodded. "When events begin to calm, I hope you will be open to something more," he said, watching as Gelvard huffed and turned to walk away.

Isha mulled Sephare's words over in her mind, trying to understand her meaning. Before she could, Kron made his way over, her mother close behind.

Kron's huge shoulders spread out wide, blocking the rising sun as he drew closer. There was a sombreness to his face, his features dropping low as he approached. "What did he want?" he said.

"Nothing of note," Dazen responded.

Kron nodded, then turned to Raiz. "I am sorry," he said, drawing in a deep breath. "I do not deserve your forgiveness. Nor yours, my daughter. But I pray that one day you will find it in your hearts to forgive my sins. I have been lost for many years, a shadow of my former self, too caught up in my own rage and grief to see the truth for what it was. I have wronged you. I have wronged all of you. I see that now."

Raiz looked taken aback, staring as though he had seen a ghost. He didn't respond, only nodded and stepped to the side. Something as precious as forgiveness didn't happen overnight, it would take time for Raiz to come around, if he ever would.

"Dazen," Kron said, turning to his eldest son. "I have something for you."

Dazen furrowed his brow. "What do you mean, Father?"

With a slow hand, Kron reached for the crown atop his head.

"This is for you," he said, handing Dazen the crown. "I am no longer deserving of such a right. You have shown more courage and leadership than I ever could. You are more than ready to take the mantle, King of Trost."

Dazen took a backward step, eyes wide and mouth agape. "Father, you cannot, I am not worthy."

Kron huffed. "You are certainly worthy. Besides, I think retirement will suit me well. I have much to atone for," he looked at Celia, who stood emotionless at his side. "I will let the four of you become acquainted with one another. Be at peace."

And then he left as if he were never there, leaving Dazen staring dumbly at a chunk of gold he had no idea what to do with.

The three siblings watched in awkward silence as their mother stood before them in all of her beauty. Her cheeks blushed a light shade of red as she looked to the ground in shy embarrassment. Her yellow dress flowed wildly in the wind as she patted it down with frantic hands. "Ugh, they made me wear this dress. I always hated the colour yellow," she said. She looked up at them and Isha felt an overwhelming warmth as the two pairs of violet eyes met. "I am sorry my children, I have so much to tell you."

DID YOU ENJOY A KING'S RADIANCE?

It's done. Now I can relax, right? I poured my heart and soul into this novel and am so happy with the result and to be in a position where I can share it with the world.

From the bottom of my heart, thank you for dedicating your time to A King's Radiance. This is but the start of my writing journey, this is my passion. I will keep writing, and I will get better.

An honest review is the most powerful tool I have when garnering attention for my books and allowing me to continue to write. If you enjoyed A King's Radiance it would mean the world to me if you could take just a few moments out of your day to leave a short review on Amazon.

It makes a huge difference.

Until next time, may Zur's light guide you, and Spike protect you 😉

Follow me to stay up to date with new books, competitions, fantasy content and just daily life. You can find me on
Instagram: @luke_schulz_author
Or twitter: @L_R_Schulz

Acknowledgements

There are so many people I need to thank who have helped me along the way. Firstly, to my beta team for helping to deflate my growing ego and for forcing me to re-think and re-structure certain sections.

To my editor Luke Marty who practically convinced me to choose him to edit this book after he did such a great job beta reading it. Luke's enthusiasm and attention to detail was just the spark I needed.

To Lena for creating the map of Zapour after I gave her my blob of a draft. She is amazing and her work speaks for itself. To Roxana for the proofread. To Tom at Fictive Designs for the chapter header designs and Vanda for the title page art. An extra thanks to Sien or 'Brushseven' for his fabulous front cover artwork, he was great to work with and such a talented artist.

To my family for **their** growing support for my writing. To Nik for putting up with my constant ramblings and incessant questioning. And lastly to the amazing community on Instagram who continue to inspire me through their fantastic reviews and support for authors in general.

Thank you to all,

Luke Schulz

About the author

Luke was born in 1992 in Melbourne, Australia. He discovered a passion for fantasy at a young age which developed into a love for the imaginary and a desire to write. Despite an early passion for storytelling, Luke obtained a teaching degree before beginning a career as a primary school teacher.

When he is not reading and writing, Luke enjoys spending time with his Golden Retriever named Gem, gaming, and surfing.

A King's Radiance is Luke's debut novel, though he is always coming up with ideas for his next project, as well as working towards a sequel.